Jest Right

Jest Right

A XANTH NOVEL

Piers Anthony

OPEN ROAD

INTEGRATED MEDIA

NEW YORK

Cover design and illustration by Amanda Shaffer

ISBN: 978-1-5040-5996-1

Published in 2020 by Open Road Integrated Media, Inc.
180 Maiden Lane
New York, NY 10038
www.openroadmedia.com

Jest Right

Chapter 1

CURSE

Jess saw that someone was already at the rest stop: a young man standing by the pond, about to remove his clothing so he could wash. That
wouldn't do; he might be seriously embarrassed to be discovered naked
by a young woman.

"Yoo-hoo!" she called, to alert him to her arrival.

He heard her and turned. "Hello," he said. "I'm Magnus. What's up?"
He had a nice voice.

Now she got a better look at him: he was tall and handsome, with clas-
sic facial features, dark brown hair, blue eyes, and muscles in his arms.
Exactly the kind she'd love to have take hold of her for naughty attention.
She was attracted to him already. But of course it would never happen.

"My name is Jess. I am traveling to see the Good Magician, and this is
the last stop before his castle. I'd love to share it with you overnight."

He laughed. "No, really, who are you and what are you up to?"

And there it was: her curse, right on schedule. She would have to try to
explain. "I'm serious. But I am cursed to have nobody take me seriously.
So even though you think I'm joking, please, please try to accept what I
say at face value."

"I'll say this for you, whatever your name is: you can make even straight
lines come across as funny. It's a rare talent, but it's time to turn it off if we
are to get along. Please answer my questions."

"I'm trying to!" she flared. "It's the bleeping curse!"

"Yeah, sure."

Jess had had a long day walking along the enchanted paths. She was
tired and more than ready to rest. It would have been so much better if she
could have remained alone. But as it was, she was frustrated to distraction.

"Bleep, bleep, bleep!" she swore. Then she collapsed in tears. It was not at all the kind of scene she wanted to make, especially before a handsome man, but she was overwhelmed.

Then she felt his hands on her shoulders. He was gazing into her watery face. "You're crying," he said, surprised.

Worse and worse. "Just leave me alone!"

"I think I'm beginning to understand. You really are cursed."

"I really am," she agreed, miserably. "Now let me suffer in peace."

He put his arms around her and brought her close. "I'm sorry."

What was this? He couldn't be taking her seriously. But she was beyond common sense. She put her face to his shoulder and cried into his shirt. It might be the illusion of comfort, but it was better than nothing.

"Let me explain," he said as he held her. "I'm a showman. I put together entertainments. My talent is verisimilitude, the semblance of truth: that is, making it seem real. I've seen many acts, and I pride myself on being able to know reality regardless. But your curse caught me by surprise. It didn't let me take you seriously. Even when you tried to explain. But I'm not stupid. My feeling says you're joking, but my common sense tells me you're cursed. I apologize for misunderstanding. I will try not to do that again."

Her tears faded. "You believe me," she breathed.

"I believe you," he agreed. "Understand, my emotion thinks this is one big joke. But I do have a mind, and now I recognize and am trying to counter your curse."

"You're taking me seriously."

"On the intellectual level. But that's fragile."

"I had better get away from you before you burst out laughing."

"Yes," he said seriously. "There are limits to my intellectual control, and your curse is pushing them."

She disengaged and stepped away from him. "Thank you for that much."

He gazed at her with compassion. "It's easier when you're apart from me. I was almost choking on suppressed laughter."

"I know exactly how it is."

"I was about to wash up, before it gets dark."

"I'd like to too." Jess looked at the pond. "Is it safe? No water monsters?"

"What, you think there'll be a kraken weed monster in there? This is part of the protected area."

"That's right," she said, remembering. "And a kraken would be addicted to krack, and not all that dangerous."

"That's a folk story. They're plenty dangerous."

She sighed. "I had thought it was humor."

"Oh. I was trying too hard to counter your curse. But maybe we can use it. If I took you seriously, emotionally, I'd be mortified to have you see me naked, since you're not my girlfriend. But as it is, maybe not."

"Maybe not," she echoed, intrigued.

Magnus stripped off his clothing, hanging it on a convenient deposi-tree, the kind that never filled up, and stood naked. He was a glorious figure of a man! Then he strode into the water, and soon was neck deep. "It worked!" he called. "My body thought it was all in fun, so didn't react."

Now Jess was curious how far this could go. She had never seen a man without clothing before, and had no fear at all. In fact she wished she could be naked with him. Wished she could somehow get serious with him. It was a kind of personal challenge.

Well . . .

"Do you mind?" she called. Then without waiting for his answer she stripped away her own clothing, hung it on the deposi-tree and stood on the bank as nude as a nymph. She knew her figure wasn't bad; the problem was that nobody took it seriously, either.

He laughed. "It's a game! Good thing I didn't see your panties."

She hadn't thought of that. The glimpse of a girl's panties could freak out just about any man. "Should I put them back on?"

He laughed again. "This is fun! I can enjoy your human form without frustrating you, since we both know this is only a game. But no, don't put anything back on; come on in and swim, if you care to. The water's fine."

She needed no further invitation. She waded in, and soon was happily swimming. "I've never done this with a man before." But it was hardly the beginning of what she would like to do with a man.

"I'm a fair judge of people," Magnus said. "I have to be, to assemble my show. There's something different about you, and I don't mean your body or your curse. The way you look around, the way you disport yourself. Something about you appeals to me."

"Most men don't like smart women."

"That's it! You practically radiate intelligence."

"I try to conceal it. My curse is bad enough without that."

"I'm sure it is. But I am attracted to smart women."

"Are you teasing me?"

"No. I'm serious. I'm attracted to that aspect in you. Unfortunately—"

"I know."

"I think I can guess why you're coming to see the Good Magician," he said as she swam closer. "To abate your curse."

"You got it. And you?"

"Far more mundane. I need to find a good assistant for my show." Then he paused. "And suddenly I have an idea."

"Why do I suspect it's not to kiss and stroke a bare woman in the water?"

He laughed again. He laughed often and well, and surely not just when her curse prompted it. "No offense, but I can't take that idea seriously at the moment."

"No offense," she agreed sadly. The curse was firmly in place.

"It's that we just might be able to solve each other's problems, and not need to see the Good Magician at all."

"Oh?" She was surprised.

"I need an assistant to warm up the audience. To make the people laugh. To divert them when I'm changing sets. You could do that."

"I could," she agreed guardedly.

"Also to do the incidental things I tend not to keep up with, like tracking the tent pegs."

"Tent pegs?"

"I have to put up a big tent for the show. It's traditional. I'm not very good at it, and that messes up the show. Women are better at that sort of thing."

"I could track tent pegs," she agreed. "But it's not what I want in life."

He gazed at her across the water between them. They were both standing in the shallower section now, with only their heads above the surface. "What do you want in your life, apart from abolition of the curse?"

"A good man."

He laughed, then choked it off. "And. You. Are. Serious," he said word by word, fighting his automatic dismissal of it.

"Yes. I'd give him anything he wanted."

"If you abolished the curse, you could probably get a good man. You are not bad looking, and that's what counts, for a man."

"Yes."

"Would I be the kind of man you want?"

There was no point in trying to avoid the issue. She was finding herself seriously attracted to him. "Yes."

"I was afraid of that." He raised his hands in the water in a gesture of surrender. "I mean no offense. It's that with your curse—"

"Exactly."

"But the thing is, I need you as you are. To make folk laugh. Which means—"

"You can't be my man."

"Not the way you want," he agreed. "I'm sorry, Jess. I think we might make a fine show together, but not as a romantic couple."

"That's right," she agreed sadly.

He pondered further. "Actually, we might even make a couple, if only—"

"It weren't for my curse. You can have me one way or the other. Not both."

"And you want both."

"Yes. But I will settle for one."

"I don't want you to have to do that."

Jess laughed without a trace of humor. "You have an alternative?"

"I may. But I doubt you'd like it."

"Let me have it."

"We might fake it. Pretend to be lovers. I could hug you as a joke. Kiss you as an act. Maybe even—"

"I'll take it."

He did a double-take. "What?"

"I am so desperate that I'd rather have a fake romance than none at all. Especially with you. To be hugged and kissed by you, to be told sweet nothings by you, even knowing they are pretense. But I have to warn you . . ." She trailed off, unwilling to say it.

But he understood. "You might fall in love with me. Not pretense."

"I'm already on the verge. You are the first man to take me seriously even to this extent, to understand me. To treat me as a person rather than a clown."

"You're not a clown!"

"Yes I am. A figure everyone laughs at. You too, of course. But behind your laughter you do care. You could fake everything with me, making me at least look like a girlfriend, at least to others."

"That would be utter cruelty. I wouldn't do it. I'm not a sadist."

"I'll take it," she repeated. "I'm that desperate."

"Bleep, Jess—"

"The traditional story is boy and girl meeting at the outset, suffering adventures together, and marrying happily at the end. This is a variant. If you want it, take it."

"But you know that all I really want is a competent assistant. That nothing beyond that is real. That I am only using you."

"Use me. Please."

"This is ridiculous!"

"No, it's my curse. Frankly, I'd rather be unhappy with you than away from you, and I think I could fool myself that I'm not really unhappy with you."

He paused, considering. "It seems that my choice is between cruelly using you, or cruelly sending you away. Both are abhorrent to me."

He was fundamentally decent. That made it worse. "I apologize for putting you in this situation. I know it's not fair to you."

"Fair to me! What about you?"

"I can still go to the Good Magician. Maybe he'll have an antidote to the curse."

"And maybe he won't. Then where will you be?"

"With you or without you."

He considered again. "Let me try the fake. Maybe you won't be able to stand it. That would be an answer."

"Welcome to try," she said, hoping he would.

"I am going to pretend I want you for something amorous, and want only to fool you into going along with it. Nothing I say will be the truth. It is all one big joke. If that doesn't revolt you, then maybe it's an option."

Jess smiled, this time sincerely. "Revolt me, Magnus."

He moved toward her in the water. "I want to be with you, you lovely creature." Then he paused. "No, I can't say that, because it implies you are ugly in reality, and that's not true, so I'm not lying. You do look kissable and holdable, especially nude in the water."

"The lie," she said firmly, "is that you *want* to hold and kiss me. How I look is irrelevant." Could he actually do it despite the curse, phrasing it this way? She very much feared he couldn't.

"Yes, I suppose that's right. On with the show." He resumed movement toward her. "I love you, Jess. I want to kiss you and hold you and be naughty with you and summon the stork with you."

He was almost upon her. When would he burst into helpless laughter? "I, too," she said. *She* was in no danger of laughing.

He reached her. He put his arms around her as they stood in the water. He drew her in against him, torso against torso. She yielded gracefully so that their contours fit together with no space between. In fact she flattened against him. He put his face to hers. He kissed her. She kissed him back.

Only one thing was missing. There was no manly passion in him. In this position it was easy to tell.

"Maybe if you feel my bottom," she said.

He moved his hands down and did so. Still nothing. He was making the motions, but his body was not taking her body seriously.

"Or kiss my breasts."

He took a breath, then moved down and did so. Still nothing.

The curse remained.

"I'm sorry," he said, and he wasn't laughing. "You'd think that with a willing woman I'd be more ardent." He was plainly embarrassed.

Still, it was infinitely better than nothing. "Maybe if I try?" she asked hesitantly.

"Try," he agreed.

She stroked his hair, kissed his ear, and then his lips, languorously. She took his hand and stroked her breasts with it. She lifted her legs, spread them, and wrapped them around his hips. It was easy to do in the weightlessness of water.

They might as well have been children climbing on each other.

"Bleep!" he swore, giving it up.

"But the point is not whether you can make it with me," she reminded him. "It is whether I can handle the pretense. I can. I'm not revolted, only saddened."

"That's right," he agreed, brightening slightly. "We can fake it."

"You can fake it," she agreed. "I actually liked it, what there was of it. If you can handle it, so can I."

"You're sure? Because I'd really like to have you join me in my show."

"I will join your show if you will regularly pretend to desire me in the way we just tried. That means, among things, kissing me and letting me kiss you. Spending the nights in bed with me, both of us bare. Letting me try to arouse you. Making others think we are a romantic couple. So that I can live with my curse. Deal?"

"Deal," he agreed, bemused.

"Then let's get on with the evening, as a couple," she said. "I think we are both clean enough now."

Now he laughed, and it was with her, not at her. "We were washing up!"

"And we got distracted, making out in the water. Couples do."

He did not argue the case.

They waded out of the pond, harvested towels from the towel tree, dried each other off, dressed, and harvested pies from the pie bushes for supper.

"What's that?" Magnus was eyeing a tree bearing small brown bottles.

"One of those grows near my home village," Jess said. "It's a boos tree."

"Booze?"

"Not exactly. I can't explain it because you'll think I'm joking. Try a sip."

He picked a bottle, uncorked it, and took a swallow.

"Booo!" a voice yelled.

"See, it's a boos tree."

He nodded. "Now I understand. Like boot rear, only audible."

Then they heard something. "Is that a child crying?" Jess asked.

"It's off the enchanted path. It could be a spook."

Because there were myriad dangers in Xanth. The enchanted paths guaranteed security so that folk could get safely from one place to another, and wise folk did not stray far from them, if at all. Demons and monsters sometimes assumed appealing forms and tried to lure innocent people off the paths, to ravish them, consume them, or worse. Nevertheless, the two of them hurried along the path toward the sound.

"But suppose it's real?" Jess asked.

"I don't mean to insult you, but would a monster take you seriously?"

"I doubt it. Nobody takes me seriously, and a monster is a body."

"Then maybe you could check it with less danger than I could. Ordinarily I wouldn't let a lady risk it, but—"

"I'll do it."

"If it attacks you, I'll fight it." Magnus had swept up a spear at the edge of the camp, evidently left there for just such a purpose.

They came to the place. There behind a bush was the sound, close by. It was definitely a child crying.

Jess forged off the path toward it. She saw a large animal grazing nearby, but recognized it as a gulli-bull, a harmless bovine that was very easy to trick. No threat there.

She rounded the bush and spied an eight-year-old girl. She had hazel eyes and mouse brown hair. "What's the matter?" Jess asked.

The girl looked at her. "Are you a monster in disguise?"

"No! I'm a woman."

"I don't believe you."

Uh-oh. It was the curse. Even a child in trouble couldn't take her seriously.

"Magnus!" Jess called. "It's safe, I think. I think we need you."

Magnus came charging toward them, spear ready.

"I think this child is real, but she won't believe *I'm* real," Jess said. "You know why."

"Ah." Magnus halted, no longer threatening with the spear. He spoke to the child. "I'm Magnus, and I'm a regular man, not a monster. Who are you, child?"

"I'm Myst," the girl replied, evidently believing him. He was easy to believe, because of his talent. "I went off the path to wee-wee, but then got lost. I couldn't find my way back!"

"You shouldn't leave the enchanted path," Magnus said. "It's dangerous."

"Not to me," Myst insisted.

"Monsters love to gulp down children," Magnus said. Jess stayed out of it, as she really couldn't help.

"They do," Myst agreed. "But they can't hurt me."

"I don't understand."

"Touch me."

He reached out cautiously to touch her. His hand passed through her arm. "You're a ghost!"

"No, I just misted. See." Myst dissolved into a small cloud of vapor floating a few feet above the ground. Then it coalesced back into the girl. "It's my talent."

Magnus nodded. "It's a good talent. But if you were in no danger, why were you crying?"

"Because I was lost. I couldn't find the enchanted path. Monsters can't hurt me, but I don't want to be lost forever. I hate being alone."

"Oh. Now I understand." Magnus turned around. "I know where the path is. I'm good with directions. I never get lost. Follow me." He set off for it, and the child followed, with Jess bringing up the rear. Seeing how he handled the child, she was more than ever satisfied that she wanted to be with him, whatever the arrangement. He was neither condemning nor dismissing Myst; he was treating her as a person in her own right. "And here we are," he said with a flourish as they stepped back onto the path. "The rest stop is just up ahead, there." He pointed, and started walking that way.

"Oh goody!" Myst exclaimed, following. "Now I can get there in time."

Magnus looked at her. "You are going to see the Good Magician?"

"No. To join my siblings on Fibot."

Magnus exchanged a questioning look with Jess. "Who or what is Fibot?"

"The Fire Boat. My sisters and one brother are there, helping crew it. I'll help them."

"It's a boat? But there's no big river near here."

"That's okay. It floats on air. It's going to be at the Good Magician's Castle tomorrow, so I need to be there to catch it."

Magnus caught Jess's eye again. It seemed that from this distance he could take her seriously. Then he continued his questioning. "There is a boat that sails in air?"

"I think I have heard of it," Jess said. "Doesn't it have a fiery sail?"

"That's it," Myst said. "Win helps it go, because she always has the wind at her back."

"Win is one of your sisters?" Magnus asked as they arrived at the camp.

"Sure. Sort of. So's Squid."

"That sounds more like a fish," Magnus said.

"Well, 'cause she's a squid. You know, like a octopus."

This was becoming stranger. "Your sister is an octopus?"

"Sort of."

They digested that. "I think we need to get to know each other better," Magnus said. "Suppose we introduce ourselves more completely to you, while we eat supper, and you can tell us all about you and your siblings?"

"Sure," Myst agreed happily.

While they ate fresh pies, they got into it. "Jess and I are a couple," Magnus said. "We just met an hour ago."

"Oh, no," Myst said. "You want to be alone!"

"We don't have to be alone," Jess said.

"Don't lie to me! I don't like it!"

There was the curse again.

Magnus held up a cautioning hand to Jess. "Why do you think we're lying?"

"Cause my folks are the same way. They want to summon the stork, and they don't want me around while they're doing it. It's the Adult Conspiracy, and I hate it. That's why I ran away."

They were learning more about the child. Myst needed support and guidance.

"We won't be summoning the stork," Magnus said, artfully avoiding the serious matter of running away from home.

"But you said you just met, and you're a couple."

So of course they were eager to start stork signaling, generating the three dots of the ellipsis that zipped away at the speed of desire and told storks all they needed to know. Would it were true! "This is complicated to explain," Jess said.

"I'll bet," the child said witheringly, not crediting it. Of course.

Magnus took a breath as he exchanged another glance with Jess. At least he was able to do that seriously, maybe because it was about a different person. "I think we can satisfy you on that score, Myst. We just didn't think you would be interested."

"Why not?" the child demanded. "Because I'm a child?"

The irony was that no matter how much Myst railed against the Conspiracy when young, the moment she became adult she would change sides. It was part of the background magic of Xanth.

"First you need to understand Jess's nature," Magnus said. "Her magic talent is a curse: nobody takes her seriously. That's why you don't believe her when she talks."

"She's got a weird talent? I know about those. My brothers and sisters have them, sorta."

"Sorta?"

"Well, they're not really my siblings. We're in five different families. But we believe in each other."

So the "sorta" referred to the siblings rather than their talents? Or maybe both?

"This promises to be interesting," Magnus said. "But let's finish with Jess first. Can you believe her curse?"

"Oh, sure, now you've told me. Nobody believes her."

"Yes. So we have trouble being a couple, because I can't take her seriously. So we aren't going to try to summon any storks, and we don't need to be alone."

"Oh. Okay." When he said it, the child accepted it.

"But we are a couple. A pretend couple. We want other people to believe we are romantic about each other."

"Why?"

There was a tricky question! "Because I can't have a real boyfriend," Jess said. "So I'm taking a fake one. It's a role."

"Like a game," Myst said, perhaps understanding because this was a clarification of a pretense. "I get it. Like the way we five children are siblings, only we're really not."

"Like that," Magnus agreed. "Sometimes appearances count more than reality."

"They sure do," Myst agreed.

Jess really admired the way Magnus was handling Myst. He was clearly good with children.

"So Jess and I are a couple, but you don't need to worry about us demanding privacy. But if you want to be with us, you have to pretend to take her seriously when she talks to you. It's part of the game."

"The game," Myst agreed. Children understood games. "Sure."

Magnus glanced at Jess. She took the cue and picked up the dialogue. "We are really curious about your siblings," she told Myst. "How is it that you are only sort of brothers and sisters?" Could the pretense of seriousness become a kind of reality?

Myst started to laugh, then stifled it, playing the game. "It's complicated."

"We will try to understand."

The child took a moment to organize her thoughts. "It really started with Astrid Basilisk. She—" She paused, seeing their expressions. Then she laughed. "Now *you're* not taking *me* seriously."

"You do know the nature of a basilisk?" Jess asked gently.

"Sure. You meet her gaze, and you die. But she's a nice person, and we all love her. And she wears a veil."

Jess caught on. "She's in human form?"

"Yes. She can change forms. When she's human she's the prettiest girl you'll ever see, if you look at her. Anyway, she got together with the Demoness Fornax to—" She broke off again. "Look, are you going to take me seriously or not?"

Jess tried, while Magnus smiled in the background. "It's just that capital D Demons are, well, out of this world. I have heard of Fornax. She's the patron spirit of anti-matter. Anything she touches explodes. You can't bring her into a story without some clarification."

"Okay. She's got magic to stop herself from touching anything here. Mostly she stays clear. But when she's home in the Fornax Galaxy she can make it possible for us regular-matter folk to be with her, to touch her. She's nice too, when you get to know her. We call her Aunt Fornax, same as we call Aunt Astrid. We love her, too."

Jess was really coming to appreciate the problem others had with her curse. She really had to try to believe what the child was saying. "So the basilisk and the Demon, both in human form, got together," she said. "What did they do?"

"They decided to rescue some children from the future."

Both Magnus and Jess had to stifle their disbelief. The child was serious.

Then a bulb flashed over Magnus's head. "You're one of the children!" he exclaimed.

"Yes, the littlest," Myst said proudly. "We were on a track fifty years in the future where Xanth was about to be destroyed. They couldn't stop that from happening, but they could get some of us out of it. They rescued five of us, and took us back in time with them, and got us different families here, and that put us on another track so Xanth won't be destroyed."

"You were five children in a family?" Jess asked.

"No. We're from five different families. But we became one family, with Aunt Astrid and Aunt Fornax. Now we're in different families again, adopted, but we'll always be Family to us. We're all from the same world, and nobody else is. Because it's gone, or will be in fifty years."

It was coming clear at last. They were all orphans who had made their own family, unified by their tragedy. "So you are going to join your siblings on the fiery boat," Jess said.

"Yes. Because they'll understand."

"And the boat will be near the Good Magician's Castle tomorrow."

"You got it."

"So tomorrow we'll part company, but tonight we can be our own family."

"Yes. If—"

"No storks! We promise."

"Okay." Myst looked at Jess. "You know, once I got into the game, I could play it. You're a couple the same way I have siblings. We just agree to make it so. Nobody else matters much."

"Yes. We have to keep playing the game. Otherwise—"

"I know. It's like looking into Aunt Astrid's eyes. Not smart to do."

Astrid the Basilisk. "Not smart to do," Jess agreed.

Magnus stepped in. "It's not real, the way others see it, but it can be real to us. Maybe Jess is a little bit like Astrid, in her fashion."

Now Myst looked at him. "Can you kiss her?"

"As part of the game, yes. We're like actors on a stage. It's all make believe, but we try to make it look real."

"I mean, really?"

"I will demonstrate," Magnus said. He stood up. Jess stood up. They came together, and he kissed her. Jess loved it.

"Yuck!" Jess exclaimed. "Mush stuff! It sure looks real." Then she reconsidered. "But Jess doesn't have to fake it, does she? I mean—"

"I can take him seriously," Jess agreed as she separated from Magnus. "My curse affects others, not me."

"Sort of the way I can touch others, but they can't touch me, unless I want it." Myst dissolved into mist, then reformed. "I think . . . I think I am coming to understand you better, Jess. You're nice, at least in the game."

"Thank you." Jess stood there a moment longer, hesitating, as emotion surged. The child really did understand her, in a manner. "May I . . . could you stand it if . . . if I hugged you? Like a daughter? I may never have a daughter of my own."

"I've been hugged before."

"I mean—"

"I know what you mean. It's part of the game. I've been lonely, too. Sure, hug me."

Jess knelt before Myst and put her arms around her. She hugged her, her tears overflowing. Myst started to dissolve into mist, but then firmed again, forcing herself to play the game. Then she hugged Jess back. "You *are* a little like Astrid."

She was being compared to a basilisk. But it was a compliment. "Thank you."

"Now we'd better turn in for the night," Magnus said. "We're a family, a pretend family, but it will do, so we don't need to stand on ceremony. Jess and I will sleep together, holding hands, sometimes kissing, the way couples do. Do you prefer to be near us or apart from us, Myst?"

"Near you. I told you, I don't much like being alone. Getting here was awful."

"We'll see you safely to the fire boat," Jess said. Then she reconsidered. "Only—"

"Only we have to go through the challenges," Magnus said. "I don't think you do, Myst. Will the boat come for you, away from the castle?"

"I don't know. Squid and Win don't know I'm coming."

Squid and Win. The octopus and the girl with the wind at her back.

"Then maybe you should take the challenges with us," Jess said, not expecting to be taken seriously. "Then we can all see the Good Magician."

"Why are you going there?" Myst asked as she settled down beside Jess.

"To see the Good Magician?" Jess asked.

"Yes."

"Well, I need to get rid of my curse, and Magnus needs an assistant for his act."

"No, really: why are you going?"

There was the curse again. "You tell her, Magnus."

"Wait a moment," Magnus said, surprised. "It's not the curse, she's right. We don't need to go."

"But—"

"I have my assistant, and you can live with your curse. We worked it out just before we heard Myst. We no longer have to go."

Jess's mouth dropped open in the darkness. "That's right! I forgot. We can skip the challenges."

"But your show," Myst said. "Won't you have to travel a lot?"

"Yes," Magnus said. "From village to village. There always has to be a new one, because any show quickly gets old with the same audience. It's always fresh for a new audience. Also—" He broke off.

"Also?" she prompted.

"Well, pretty girls tend to throw themselves at me. It's a complication of my talent. They believe in me. But if I stay long, they try to get serious. I can't afford that."

"And I am one of them," Jess said. "Except I'm not—"

"Stop it!" he snapped. "Don't disparage yourself. I'm just saying that those girls are a nuisance."

"Most men would like it," she said.

"Oh, I do, to a degree. But I know better. They would want me to settle down, become a troll farmer or something, but my heart is in traveling with the show."

"Troll farmer?"

"Working on a farm where they grow nasty trolls for export into Mundania. So I need to move on before they get ideas like that."

"Yet you seemed ready enough to try for something more serious with me."

"Confession: I said all I wanted was a competent assistant. I believe you could be that. But I also want a regular girlfriend."

"But you said—"

"One who would travel with me. Be part of the show."

"Oh. Still—"

"To fend off the pretty girls. To advertise that I'm taken."

Oh, again. "And since it would not be real, with me, you'd be without responsibility."

He winced. "If I could take you seriously, I'd be hurt by your implication. I would like it to be real with you, because you're not—"

"A pretty girl?"

"Bleep, Jess! I'm saying you're not superficial. You're the kind of woman I really could respect and love, if only—"

"If only you could take me seriously," she finished. "Now I understand."

He sighed. "I'm not quite sure you do. But I can't even argue with you effectively, because of your curse. I think I need some other way."

Jess decided to change the subject. "How will you get to the new villages?"

"Oops. I hadn't thought of that."

Neither had Jess, before. "We'll just have to do a lot of walking."

"You're not mad at me? You're willing to be with me?"

"Yes. And willing to walk."

"That will mean very limited equipment," Magnus said. "No prepared sets or heavy tents. Bleep."

"And here I was all set to hammer tent pegs."

"Take the boat," Myst said.

They pondered that, and the more they pondered, the better sense it made. "I guess we do have to see the Good Magician," Jess said. "Because we have no relatives aboard that boat. We'll have to ask for it to be arranged."

"That means the challenges," Magnus agree morosely. "And the Service."

Because the Good Magician demanded payment for his Answers: a year's service, or an equivalent mission.

"Are we sure we want to do this?" Jess asked.

Myst began to cry. Jess knew why: if they did not proceed, the child would have to try to navigate the challenges alone, to reach the boat.

"Yes, I think we do," Magnus said.

The crying stopped.

So they were committed after all.

Jess actually felt relieved. She wasn't sure why, but suspected it was because she so much wanted to be part of a family, even a pretend family, and this was a family undertaking. The challenges would be no joke. They would face them together. As a family. At this point it hardly mattered to her whether they succeeded or failed; it was the togetherness she craved.

Magnus took her hand. "Me, too," he murmured.

Myst took her other hand. "Me, too."

Was it really a game?

Chapter 2

CHALLENGES

In the morning Magnus woke first, and had already harvested assorted pies and milkweed pods for their breakfast by the time Jess and Myst stirred.

"Dad's like that, too," Myst confided as they quickly washed up in the pond before eating.

The game was still on. Within that framework, maybe they could talk seriously. "You ran away," Jess said cautiously.

"Not forever. Only so they could be alone. I'll come back when they've finished with the stork."

"Happy couples don't finish with the stork soon."

"Oh, sure. But they slow down after a while."

Was there more to be learned here? Jess was not easy about harboring a runaway child. "So you're not mad at them, really."

"No. I just thought they'd be better off without me, for a while."

"Won't they worry about your absence?"

The child paused. "I didn't think of that. Maybe they won't notice."

Jess was pretty sure they would notice, and be alarmed. "When you get to the boat, promise me you will send word to your folks that you're safe, and where you are."

Myst laughed. "You're just like mom!"

"Thank you."

"She worries about every little thing."

"I'm sure."

They returned to the shelter for breakfast.

"You said you were adopted," Magnus said as they ate.

"Yes, we all were. Merge adopted me. Then she married Hapless."

There were two more names: her parents. "You have a problem with Hapless?" Magnus asked.

"No, I like him. He's great. He's a conductor."

"A what?"

"For music. He conjures instruments, but he can't play any himself. But he can organize others so that they play really well."

"That's an interesting talent. What's your mother's talent?"

"Merge? She's really five women, sisters. But they're happier being together, you know, merged, so usually there's just one of her. Sometimes when she gets mad they separate. It's funny."

"It must be," Magnus agreed.

Then there was a sound. "Oooo-oooo!"

Myst jumped up. "That's Blue! She's calling me!"

"Who?" Jess asked as they ran outside.

"Blue. Mom's blue self. The others are Brown, Black, Red, and Yellow. You can tell by their hair."

Jess exchanged a quick glance with Magnus, no words needed. Glances were easier to take seriously.

"Here!" Myst called.

In little more than a moment, maybe a moment and a quarter, the woman appeared. Sure enough, she wore a blue dress, and her hair was light blue. She also carried a blue urn. She was nymph-like in her beauty.

"Myst!" she exclaimed, rushing up to hug the girl. "You're all right!"

"Sure I'm all right," Myst said.

"We were afraid something had happened to you."

"Nothing happened to me. I just ran away."

"But why?"

"So you could be alone with dad. For the stork."

"You didn't need to go for that! We can do it in our room."

Myst shrugged. "It seemed better."

"Myst," Blue said, exasperated. "We couldn't do anything while we worried about you!"

"You wasted your time alone?"

"Utterly. We've been out and around all night searching for you. That's why we split into components, so we could cover more territory. We couldn't rest until we found you."

Myst began to tear up. "I'm sorry. I thought I was helping."

Then Blue became aware of the others. "Hello," she said awkwardly.

"These are Magnus and Jess," Myst explained. "We made a family for the night."

"An ad hoc family," Magnus clarified. "Like the siblings."

Blue looked at Myst. "They took care of you?"

"Yes. We're going to do the challenges, so we can get to Fibot."

"Fibot?"

"You know. The flying fire boat. My siblings are there."

"Oh, yes," Blue said, remembering. "They joined the crew."

"I want to join the crew, too. I know I can help."

"And you'd like to be with your siblings again," Blue said.

"Yes. While you and dad, you know."

Evidently that point scored. "I suppose you would be safe on Fibot. Dell and Nia are good people. They wouldn't let you get into mischief."

"Not much, anyway," Myst agreed mischievously.

Two more names. Jess hoped she could remember them all.

Blue faced them. "Hello. I am Blue, one fifth of Myst's mother. It's complicated."

"We understand," Magnus and Jess said almost together.

"I suppose it would be good experience for Myst to join her siblings on the fire boat. They have a rather special history."

"So we understand," Magnus said. "They're from the future."

"Astrid Basilisk rescued them," Jess added.

"Yes. Astrid is wonderful. They're all adoptive, but they're very close to each other. We fear that Myst felt a bit left out. If you don't mind seeing her to the boat . . ."

They didn't even need to exchange glances this time. "We don't mind," Magnus said.

"You're letting me do it!" Myst cried, hugging Blue again.

"This time. But don't run away again."

"I promise," Myst said tearfully.

"Then I will merge with the others and let them know." And the woman in blue faded out.

Magnus and Jess stared.

"It's okay," Myst said. "Blue is just part of Merge. She can merge from anywhere. When she does, the others will know everything she knows."

"That's nice," Jess said weakly. She had thought her talent was strange, but it was apparent that there was plenty of other strangeness.

"Now that that's settled," Magnus said briskly, "Let's head off to the Good Magician's Castle." He paused, "Understand, there's no guarantee we'll make it through the challenges. If we don't, we'll try to figure out some other way to connect with the boat. We won't desert you."

"I know," Myst said. "We're an ado . . . aho . . . a family."

"Ad hoc," Magnus said, smiling. "It means for this purpose."

They cleaned up whatever mess they had made, and walked on toward the castle whose turrets were just coming into sight.

The castle itself was impressive, with a number of high turrets. A moat surrounded it, and they could see a formidable moat monster even from a distance. Beyond the moat was an orchard with a number of trails through it.

"That doesn't look too challenging," Jess said. "Except for the moat monster, but we'd cross on the drawbridge."

"I understand the challenges manifest once you get close," Magnus said. "And they are always tuned to the folk who try to get through."

"And there's always a way," Myst said. "If you can find it."

Sure enough, as they came closer, something appeared. It was a glade in the orchard, with a giant book on the ground, from which a dozen huge pages had been torn. There was print on the pages, but from this angle they couldn't make it out.

"I don't know what to make of this," Magnus said. "Are we supposed to put the book back together? That would be a chore, considering the size of those pages. They are like bed sheets!"

Jess bent down to take hold of the edge of a page. She tugged, but it wouldn't budge. "It seems to be anchored."

"Let's see what it says." He leaned over the page to make out the enormous print. "UP."

Myst went to look at another. "DOWN," she announced.

They checked others. Each had a different word printed. LEFT. RIGHT. NEAR. FAR. IN. OUT. FAT. THIN. HAPPY. SAD.

"I am not getting the point," Magnus said, frustrated. "In fact I don't know what use this book would be, even to a giant, if it were in good condition."

"Maybe it's a primer for giants," Jess suggested. "So they can learn one word at a time."

There was a bleat. An angry ram was charging into the glade.

They hastily ran for the sides, ready to climb trees if necessary. "Looks like a battering ram," Magnus said. "They're pretty silly animals."

"But we don't want it to batter *us*," Jess said.

The ram heard their voices and skewed around to orient on them. Then it charged again. They hastily dodged to the sides and hid behind tree trunks.

"Which seems to be exactly what it means to do," Jess said.

"Maybe it won't take me seriously," Jess said. She stepped out in front of the FAR page. "Hey, butthead!" she called. "What's on your mind?"

The ram changed course to charge her. She held her ground, gambling that her curse would take effect. The animal smelled her and veered at the last moment, running onto the page. It had indeed not been able to take her seriously as a target.

"Hey neat talent!" Myst called.

Sometimes it was, if she used it correctly.

The ram halted on the page, looking at it. Then it snorted and leaped off. "What, wrong page?" she teased it.

Another bulb flashed over Magnus's head. He seemed to be good at ideas. "That's a page. He's a ram. Rampage!"

"He needs to get on the right page," Jess agreed.

"I'll do it!" Myst cried. She ran to the page that said RIGHT. "Hey, sheepish! Over here!"

"Don't do that!" Jess called. "It won't avoid you!"

"I know." Myst put her spread hands to her ears and wiggled them at the ram. "Bet you can't get me, wool-for-brains!"

The ram pawed the ground, then charged her.

"Get out of there!" Jess cried, horrified.

But the child remained in place as the animal hurtled at her.

And through her, as she puffed into vapor at the last second. Jess had forgotten Myst's talent.

Now that ram found himself in the RIGHT page. "Bleep!" he bleated.

Then the ram and all the pages faded out, leaving the glade bare.

They had solved the riddle, and passed the first challenge, working cooperatively.

"We make a good team," Magnus said. "Good work, girls."

"Thank you!" Jess and Myst said together, laughing. But it was true: they had worked together to figure it out, and to resolve it. They did make a good team. So far.

"Still, there's an oddity."

Jess raised an eyebrow at him.

"It is my understanding that folk who undertake the challenges are deprived of their personal magic talents while doing so, reducing them to basics. We have been using ours. I have been making sense of things, and Jess made the ram dismiss her as a target, and Myst misted out to avoid the charge. Why are we allowed to use our talents?"

Jess nodded. "We would not have worked nearly so well together without them."

"Maybe the Good Magician wants us to be together as a family," Myst said. "Even if it's a pretend family."

"A pretend family that may last only until we get to the fire boat," Magnus said. "Then you'll be with your siblings."

"Oh, sure. But I had a family in the future. Then one with Merge and Hapless. All of us siblings have families. But we're always siblings, too. I'm happy with you two."

"And we're happy with you," Jess said, experiencing another surge of emotion. "Can you stand it if I hug you again?"

"Sure. It's all part of the game. Hug your worst."

Jess did so, and the child did not burst out laughing. She was a good enough little actress.

"Let me in on that," Magnus said. He put his arms around the two of them.

"Why are you crying?" Myst asked Jess.

"I'm not sad. I'm happy. I love being hugged, even if it's not really serious."

"You're crying because you're happy? I'm trying to believe that, but it's awful hard. Your curse is getting to me."

"Believe it," Magnus said. "She longs to be part of a family, even if it's just a semblance. We have to play the game, to avoid rejecting her, but Jess doesn't. So she can express her true emotion, and that can make an adult cry."

"Weird."

"Adults can be weird," he agreed.

They walked on, alert for the next challenge. But all they found was a pretty fountain, whose water splashed into a pond. Beside it was a plaque: FOUNTAIN OF SMART.

"I don't trust this," Magnus said. "I have heard of fountains that can be quite potent, such as the Fountain of Youth, that makes anyone who touches its water young. They have to be treated carefully."

"Youth elixir," Jess agreed. "A little can be valuable, but too much is mischief."

"I don't want to be younger," Myst said. "I'm eight, and that's young enough."

"This, however, seems to be smart elixir," Magnus said. "How can being smarter hurt a person? There has to be a catch."

"The pond extends across our route," Jess said. "We'll have to wade in it to get through."

"Which suggests that we may not want to wade. Why not?"

"It's clearly a challenge of some sort. We need to understand it before we run disastrously afoul of it. For one thing, we don't know how deep it gets."

"We might get smart feet," Magnus agreed. "Too smart for our heads. And if we tripped and fell in it—"

"We'd have smart asses," she finished. They both laughed, and the child giggled.

"I could mist out and float across it," Myst said.

"Two problems there," Magnus said. "The first is that there's a breeze, and it's blowing the wrong way, surely by no coincidence. The second is that wouldn't get the other two of us across, and we don't want to separate."

Jess liked the way he thought. In fact she liked everything about him, especially his fine understanding of her situation. But this wasn't getting them anywhere rapidly. "I'll go touch it. Maybe it will make me smart enough to figure it out."

"I still don't trust this," Magnus said.

Jess was not deterred. She walked to the fountain and put out a hand to touch the falling water. There was a flash of pain. "Ooo, that smarts!" she exclaimed, shaking her hand.

"Oh, bleep!" Magnus swore. "We missed the obvious. Smarting can mean painful."

"It certainly can." Jess's wet hand was turning red.

"Now we know," Magnus said ruefully.

"I'm sorry," Myst said tearfully.

"It's not your fault, dear," Jess said.

"Maybe I can help."

"Oh, I don't think—"

But the child was already misting into a little cloud as she held on to Jess's fingers. The vapor coalesced around her hand—and cooled and soothed it. Soon the pain was gone.

The cloud floated off, and the little girl re-formed.

"Thank you!" Jess said. "I didn't know you could do that."

Myst shrugged. "It's just part of my talent. It's not much."

"It's enough."

"Sometimes Firenze burns people," she explained. "So I help."

"Who?"

"Fir-EN-zee," she said, pronouncing it carefully. "My oldest brother. When he gets mad, his head gets all fiery. Aunt Astrid adopted him. He's not on the boat."

"That may be just as well," Jess said. The siblings were clearly remarkable children.

Meanwhile Magnus had been looking around. "I found some suits," he announced.

"Women don't wear suits much," Jess said.

"Neither do children," Myst said.

"Well, they vary. Some may be swim suits."

"We don't want to swim!" Jess and Myst said almost together.

"Actually they seem to be general purpose clothes. When I tried on a jacket, it shifted to fit me perfectly, like a second skin. The way some swim suits do, at least on women. They must be here for a reason."

"To trick people into trying to swim in the smart pond?" Jess asked disdainfully. "That's mean."

"I wonder. Maybe they're more like wet-suits."

"Well, of course they would get wet in the pond. But that wouldn't do the swimmers any good."

"I wonder," he repeated. "Maybe I should try it."

"Try swimming? Your whole body would be smarting!"

"Maybe not. Okay, I'll change. You don't have to look if you don't want to, but it's all in the family."

"Men look funny when they change," Myst said. "I've seen them. All knobby and bony. Not smooth like women."

"So let's not look," Jess said diplomatically. The two of them turned away.

"Okay," he said after maybe two and a half moments.

They turned back and looked. Magnus was in a form-fitting blue suit that covered him literally from head to toe. It covered his hands and feet, and also his face, with goggles for his eyes and a round snout for his mouth.

"You look like a blue frog," Myst said, laughing.

"Thank you," he said, his voice tinny. "Now let's see how it works." He strode for the pond.

"But what if it's porous?" Jess asked, alarmed.

"It's not." He waded on into the pool, "It's keeping the water out. I don't feel a thing."

Then he disappeared into the water. His head reappeared in a moment. "Deep spot," he reported, then swam on. Soon he was at the other side, clambering onto the bank.

The suit worked. "Change and come on across," Magnus called.

"I'll use a suit, tow you along, if you'd rather float," Jess said.

"Oh, I like swimming."

"Then let's find suits."

They pawed through the pile of clothing, finding a nice tan suit for Jess and a pretty red one for Myst.

This seemed almost too easy. That made Jess suspicious.

"What are those colored fins?" Myst asked.

Jess looked. "Loan sharks!" she said, horrified. "They'll take an arm and a leg if you let them."

"Do we hafta let them?"

Jess gazed at the circling fins. "No! But that means we can't swim across."

"Bleep!" Magnus called. "Now we're separated."

And that was surely mischief. What to do?

Myst looked at Jess. "I'm taking you seriously, because of the game. But those sharks aren't in the game, are they?"

"What are you suggesting?" But Jess feared she knew.

"That mad ram didn't butt you. Maybe the sharks won't bite you."

And maybe they would. Even a glancing bite that tore the clothing would be devastating.

"I believe in you," Myst said.

Did Jess believe in herself? Her curse had messed her up all her life. Could she depend on it to mess up the sharks? Did she have the nerve to try?

The child was gazing at her expectantly. So was Magnus from across the pond. This was her family. Fake, temporary, but more than she'd ever had since leaving her mother, who had been immune.

"This had better work," she said grimly. "Stay close to me."

"I will."

They forged into the water. Their suits kept them dry. The sharks oriented.

"Come and get us, fish-faces!" Myst called to the sharks.

Jess would have preferred that the child remain silent, but didn't argue the case. She waded in chest deep and stood facing the sharks. She put her arms around Myst. Her heart was pounding. If she got the child bitten to death she'd never forgive herself, even if she herself no longer existed. But what else could she do? "Well? Make your move if you're going to." She was dreadfully afraid that they would.

The sharks converged, each one racing to get the first bite. And veered off at the last moment, crashing into each other in their haste to avoid the woman and the girl. The closer they got, the more force the curse had, making them unable to take the proffered meals seriously.

Well, now. Still fearfully nervous, Jess started swimming, Myst right in beside her. More sharks zoomed in, but sheared off. The curse was an effective shark repellent!

In a few more strokes they reached the far side of the pool, where Magnus anxiously waited. He reached out to help them out of the water, while the sharks angrily flashed their fins. They had made it!

"That was the bravest thing I ever saw," Magnus said. "You just swam right through, daring them to attack!"

"I was scared," Myst said. "Even though I could've fogged out."

"I was terrified!" Jess confessed.

Magnus spread his arms. The two of them got into them and cried all over him.

"I guess we're pretty happy," Myst said, smiling through her tears.

"I guess we are," Jess agreed.

Then they all had to laugh.

"Who's up for some kissing?" Magnus asked.

"Yuck!" the child exclaimed, drawing away.

But Jess took him up on it. "This may be a game to you, but it's real to me."

He kissed her. Then he drew his face back a bit. "I feel the repulsion, but I also feel relief at your success, and admiration for your courage. You are some woman! I don't have to try very hard, right now." He kissed her again, more lingeringly.

Then the curse regrouped, and he had to let her go. But it was heavenly while it lasted.

"Wow!" Myst said.

They looked around. The scene had entirely changed.

The pond and fountain were gone, so was the pile of clothing, along with their own outfits which had been set beside it. Instead they seemed to be in the middle of a big hedge maze. They were surrounded by solid green walls of foliage with several openings. In the center was a glade where a white sheet or page had landed. On it was printed ANSWER.

"Maybe it's one of the pages from the other challenge," Myst said. "It was supposed to be there, but it got lost."

That seemed to be as good a theory as any. "I wonder what the Question is?" Jess said, bemused.

"That could be part of this challenge," Magnus said. "We'd better find our way out before a ram or shark comes looking for us."

"What about our clothes?" Myst asked plaintively. "We don't want to go about in swim suits."

"Easily resolved," Magnus said. "These are general purpose outfits, remember? Just focus on what you'd rather be wearing." As he spoke his own swim suit became a handsome suit similar to what he had before.

"Oho!" Myst's suit became a cute green dress, complete with green slippers. "These are better than what we had before."

Jess followed suit, as it were, and focused on an ordinary day outfit. But what she got was a clown suit. "Oops."

"It's not taking you seriously!" Myst exclaimed, laughing.

"Allow me," Magnus said. He put a hand on the shoulder of her suit, and in three quarters of a moment it became a trim woman's business suit.

"Thank you," Jess said, embarrassed. "My own effort is atrocious."

"As my assistant, you can call yourself Atrocia," he said.

"I will."

They picked a passage at random and followed it through the maze. Their feet left faint tracks in the dust on the ground. It soon came to an intersection as another passage crossed it at right angles. "Which one do we take?" Myst asked.

Magnus shrugged. "Let's go straight ahead. If that doesn't lead anywhere, we can return and try one of the side branches."

That made sense. Jess reflected on how he was a sensible man. She liked that about him. But of course she liked everything about him, so maybe it didn't count for much.

They walked on. Soon the passage emerged from the hedge. Just like that they were through! "As mazes go, this isn't much of a challenge," Jess remarked.

"And this is the third challenge," Magnus said. "We must be missing something."

Beyond the hedge was a wall of doors. Each was closed and featureless except for a number: five, six, seven, and so on. They followed the wall, and discovered that it entirely circled the hedge, the numbers going from one to fifty.

"It seems we have to pick a door to enter," Jess said. "But which one?"

"That is the question," Magnus agreed. Then he paused.

Jess caught the same thought. "In the center of the hedge is says ANSWER. Could that be connected?"

"It surely is connected," he said. "In the challenges, everything counts. We just have to figure out how."

"But it doesn't give an actual answer," Jess said. "Just the printed word ANSWER."

"We're still missing something."

"Maybe it's under the page," Myst said.

"Could be," Magnus agreed. "Let's look."

They returned to the passage they had used. Now they saw that it was actually one of two that diverged at a sharp angle. Was the maze supposed to be solved from the outside? Then why had they found themselves in the center? Jess feared that they were missing more than a little. This whole setup did not seem to make much sense, and that was a troubling sign.

"I'll take this one," Myst said brightly, stepping into the one they had not taken before. "You take the other. That way you'll be alone so you can act mushy without bothering me."

Magnus and Jess laughed together. "We'll do that," he agreed.

"You don't have to," Jess said as the child disappeared down the slanting passage.

"We're posing as a family, and it's working pretty well," he said. "I also find it a private challenge to get around your curse. I can see you're a good woman, deserving of such attention."

"But I don't want to be a burden on you."

"That's part of your goodness. So unless you really don't want it . . ."

"I want it," she breathed.

"Then here's a nice kiss and a naughty pinch, so as not to disappoint the child." He did one to her mouth and the other to her bottom. She loved both. If only they could be real!

"I know what you're thinking. I wish I could do them for real, too, instead of faking it. I know I'd really like doing them, if that curse didn't straight-arm me."

Just so.

They moved down the passage. They came to the cross passage.

"Boo!" Myst cried, jumping out.

"Oh!" Jess exclaimed, putting her hand to her heart as if terminally startled.

"Ah, you're faking it," the girl said. "I know you're not serious."

And even if she had been serious, it would have seemed otherwise.

"So they do connect," Magnus said.

"Sure," Myst said happily. "It made a sharp turn and came right here."

"As long as we're here, let's see where the other passage goes," Jess said.

They followed the other passage, but it soon dead-ended, going nowhere. "There's something about this," Magnus said. "I can't quite place it."

They returned to the intersection, and continued on into the center. There was the page. They lifted it up, but all that it said was QUESTION; there was nothing on the ground beneath. "Another dead end," Magnus said, disgusted. "We're getting nowhere fast."

"The page can be oriented either way," Jess said. "It seems that ANSWER is the way it's supposed to be, for what that's worth."

"That is the message," Magnus agreed. "Too bad we're not smart enough to understand it."

"The prior two challenges were more physical than mental," Jess said. "This one seems to be more mental."

They took the next passage to their right as they faced out of the center. This was curvaceous rather than straight, and had no intersections. It emerged outside, but also continued back into the hedge, where it finally dead ended.

There were no other passages. They had traveled them all, what little there was of them.

"There's something odd about the shapes," Jess said.

"They're numbers!" Myst exclaimed.

"That's what nagged me," Magnus said. The straight lines, the angles, the intersection—the number four!"

"And the curvy one, two," Jess said. "But what do they mean?"

"Now it is coming together. The word ANSWER is in the center, as if designating the maze itself. And the maze spells out the number forty-two."

"But what does that mean?"

"I'm still working on that."

"But don't we already have the Question?" Myst asked. "Like which door to use?"

Magnus and Jess stared at each other, mutually chagrined. "We had the Question," Magnus said.

"And forgot it," Jess said.

"We'll try Door Forty-Two," Magnus said. "But I don't think we're quite there yet. *Why* is that the right door?"

"I have no idea."

"And we'd better figure it out, so we know we're not wrong. This challenge is so devious I don't trust it not to pull a fast one."

"Fifty doors," Jess said. "Why isn't number forty-one the right one? Or number forty-three? what's special about number forty-two?"

"My folks were talking once," Myst said. "They said that the adventures of Xanth are numbered by the Muse of History. When Aunt Astrid and Aunt Fornax fetched us from the future, that was number thirty-nine. when the Goddess Isis made the Orb, that was number forty. when Hapless met Merge, and they got married so they could make a family for me, that was number forty-one. And—"

Both Magnus and Jess were following intently. "And?" Magnus asked.

"Maybe it's not relevant," Myst said, made nervous by their attitude.

"It's relevant," Jess said. "What is Story number forty-two?"

"That's Fibot. When my siblings went to help crew it. And—" She broke off, realizing what she was saying. "And that's where we want to go! Fibot!"

"So that must be the right door," Magnus said. "Now at last it's making some sense."

"Pretty crazy sense," Jess said.

"Xanth sense," Myst said.

"Xanth sense," Magnus agreed. "Lets go open that door."

"But will it put us in that story, instead of our own?" Jess asked worriedly.

Magnus considered. "More likely it's just a signal that we've figured it out, and the fire boat can come. This is all a challenge, remember, not reality."

"A game," Jess agreed. "Like our little family here."

"Yes. Let's go."

They hurried back out of the maze and to Door Forty-Two. Then Magnus paused. "And would number forty-three be our own story? Maybe—"

"We're already in our own story," Jess said. "Where we figure out how to find Fibot. Let's not overthink it." She was concerned that they might throw away what they had gained.

"Okay," he agreed. He put his hand to the knob and turned it.

The door pushed open. There stood a woman a middling age. "Congratulations, folks," she said. "I am Wira, Magician Humfrey's daughter-in-law. I will take you to the Designated Wife of the Month, Rose of Roogna."

Jess remembered that Wira pretty much ran the castle, because she was always there while the wives switched out every month. They followed her through the halls and galleys to a garden.

A garden?

A garden. A woman, also of middling age, was watering a bed of white roses. She was in green jeans with a white apron and brown cogs, and her hair was tied up in a loose bun.

"Mother Rose," Wira said. "The querents are here."

The what's?

"Those who come to query the Good Magician," Magnus murmured, sensing her confusion. "To ask him a Question, and get his Answer."

Oh.

"What's a—" Myst started.

Jess nudged her. "Us."

"Oh."

The woman straightened up to look at them. "Oh, I forgot! I'm not dressed for company."

"I'm sure they prefer informality," Wira said diplomatically. "They are Magnus, Jess, and Myst, an ad hoc family. They just navigated the challenges." Then, to the three: "This is Rose of Roogna, Magician Humfrey's Designated Wife of the Month."

"What kind of wife?" Myst asked, confused.

Wira smiled. "When the Good Magician went to Hell to rescue his wife, he wound up with more than he had bargained on: all his former five and a half wives, who had faded out over the centuries. It's the kind of bargain one finds in Hell. Since by Xanthly custom a man is supposed to have only one wife at a time, they take turns. Rose was originally his third wife. This happens to be her month."

"Thank you for that clarification, dear," Rose said graciously as she brushed dirt off her apron. "But of course they're not interested in such mundane details."

"I am," Myst said. "I know about funny families. You must be pretty old."

Both Magnus and Jess opened their mouths to caution the child, but were already too late.

But Rose laughed. "Oh, it's good to encounter a child again! Yes, I am old, dear. Four hundred and fourteen years, to be specific. But we all use youth elixir to keep us at our preferred ages, so I am at present about forty-five." She glanced at the others. "Wira will take you to the sitting room for refreshments, while I finish watering my roses and get cleaned up and changed for company. I apologize for forgetting."

"Please, no apologies," Magnus said. "We did not mean to intrude."

But as they turned to go with Wira, they discovered she was gone. She must have had other business to attend to, not realizing that they would be moving on.

"Oh, dear," Rose said. "I am confusing things again."

"That is quite all right," Magnus said. "We will be happy to help you water the roses." He glanced at Jess and Myst, who nodded.

"Your manner," Rose said. "I feel your magic."

"My talent is verisimilitude. That is—"

Rose put up her hand. "I know the word. You make things come together so they are believable. That's a fine talent."

"Thank you."

Rose looked at Myst. "I feel yours too, dear. You remind me of a lovely summer cloud."

"Thank you," Myst said, taken aback. A cloud, of course, was vapor. Mist.

Rose gave them watering cans, and they toured the beds of roses. "Do be careful not touch touch any," Rose warned. "Their thorns can be cruel."

They were of five basic colors. "I may have heard vaguely of your roses," Magnus said. "Aren't they magic?"

"Yes. They signal true emotions. The red ones are for Love, the white ones for Indifference, the yellow ones for Friendship, the pink ones for Romance, and the black ones for Death. Folk come to take them to prove their true feelings, such as for Love. The roses always know."

"I wonder," Magnus said.

"Yes?"

He murmured something Jess didn't hear. But Rose nodded. "Perhaps it can be arranged."

"Thank you."

Jess, watering a red bed, accidentally touched a stem. No thorn scratched her.

"You are in love," Rose said.

"Much good may it do me," Jess said a bit sourly.

Rose looked more closely at Jess. "And you are an odd one. I can't quite fathom your magic. Somehow it repels me. That is, pushes me away."

"It's my curse. Nobody takes me seriously." Jess glanced at her companions. "They are pretending I am his girlfriend and her mother. That way we can act like a temporary family without them bursting out laughing."

"And you . . . you wish it could be true."

Jess felt herself blushing. "Yes. But it can never be."

"I am not sure of that. I have been cultivating experimental new varieties of roses. Let me lend you one."

Had she gone totally irrelevant? "But—"

"This one." Rose indicated a large brown rose. "I think you can pick it."

Rather than argue with the nice woman, Jess reached out and picked the rose on its stem. There were thorns, but they did not prick her. She stepped back to stand between the man and the girl, holding the rose. It smelled faintly of, well, acceptance.

"What happened?" Myst asked, surprised.

"What, indeed?" Magnus echoed, similarly surprised.

"It's just a pretty rose," Jess said.

Rose of Roogna smiled.

"Maybe we should demonstrate," Magnus said.

"Yes," Myst said.

"Demonstrate what?" Jess asked.

Then Myst stepped in and hugged her. Magus reached around them both, drew Jess into him, and kissed her. She was so surprised that she was caught off balance with her mouth partway open. Yet there was something different about the contact. Something divine.

Then she caught on. "You're not faking it!"

"Your curse is gone," Magus said.

"But—"

"The rose!" Myst said.

"The rose," Rose agreed. "I have cultured this variety to suppress magic in the one who holds it. I have not had much use for it, until now."

"I'm not cursed," Jess breathed, amazed.

"Your magic remains," Rose said. "It merely is nullified by the rose, at least for a day or so while it remains fresh. That will allow Humfrey to take you seriously, as he needs to. As it happens he is indisposed today, and in any event the firesail boat won't arrive here until tomorrow morning, so you will need to wait. I hope you don't mind."

"Give them a room," Myst said. "Give me another. I can be alone for one night."

"There is no need, dear. You can stay with me tonight. In fact you can help me finish watering the roses."

"Yes! I love the roses!"

"But—" Jess started.

Wira reappeared. "The room is ready," she reported. "This way, please."

Magnus took Jess firmly by the elbow and brought her along with him as he followed Wira. Completely confused, Jess went along.

Soon they were alone together in the room. There was food for a meal on the table, a kind of magic called Room Service.

"You're beautiful," he said, gazing at her.

"I'm plain."

"No. It's the curse that makes folk see you as plain. Now I see you as you are. I'm glad I knew that I wanted you before I saw that. It means I'm not being unduly influenced by your appearance."

"I find that hard to believe."

"Then believe this." He led her to a person-high mirror.

She looked. There was this exquisitely attractive couple. The man was Magnus, handsome as ever. The woman was as lovely as he was handsome, matching him perfectly.

Or did she? "It's a magic mirror!" she said. "Showing me as I wish I were."

"No. It shows you as you really are. The curse affects even you, in this respect, making you see yourself as others see you. So you think you're plain. You're not. The rose shows the truth."

"I'm not," she breathed, amazed.

"Jess, I knew intellectually you were the woman for me from the first! That's why I worked so hard to get around the curse. It prevented me from saying how much I respected you. Now, while I can, I want to do everything with you that I couldn't do before, especially the physical part. Rose of Roogna understood. Myst knew; that's why she agreed to leave us alone for a night, the way she's leaving her folks alone. Just keep holding on to the rose."

This had to be a dream! A wild indulgence with no reality outside her imagination. But she loved it. She let it continue. Her suit became a vaporous negligee.

"Unless I have been misreading you," he said. "Is this not something you want as much as I do?"

"Do what you want with me," she said. Her heart was pounding. What harm could there be in a dream? "Please!"

Magnus did not delay. First he kissed her mouth. Then he took off her negligee and kissed more of her. He was doing it! "More," she breathed, afraid he would not.

"Oh, yes." Then he loved her on the bed. She moaned continuously in rapture. She was transported. But always, she clung to the rose. Even in sleep, she knew it was the secret to this experience.

They slept embraced, and woke, and made love again. "But you said pretty girls throw themselves at you," she said as they rested between efforts. "I'm not pretty."

"There you go again. You're not ugly! You're ordinary with the curse, and that's fine with me. The girls I have met are shallow creatures," he said seriously. "All they want is the notoriety of being stars briefly on stage. They see me as just a means to that end. I prefer a girl of a different kind."

"I'm different," she agreed. "Because of my curse."

"You are different regardless of your curse. You have emotional substance. You are the one I want to be with." He paused, thinking. "Jess, ask the Good Magician to cure you. Or to give you a whole garden of brown roses. I want to take you seriously for the rest of my life."

This was getting too serious for a dream. "I wouldn't be much good as your assistant without the curse. You know that."

"If I must choose between having you as my assistant, or having you as my wife, I want the wife."

That utterly thrilled her. But something in her would not yield. "I would love to marry you, Magnus. But it's something I think I should earn myself, not as a gift of a rose. I must keep the curse." She could hardly

believe she was saying that, even in the dream, but there it was. She had
never been one for easy answers.

"Somehow I knew you would say that. I respect you for it. There has
to be another way."

"Another way," she agreed sadly. Why did doing the right thing feel so
bad?

"But we still have tonight," he said. "Let's make the most of it."

"The most," she agreed, relieved that he was not arguing the case further,
because she was not at all sure she could hold out much longer if he did.

They dissolved into another storm of rapture.

Jess woke beside him in the morning. She was wonderfully worn out,
and she was sure he was, too. What a night it had been!

Had it really happened? Or had it all been a dream sponsored by the
rose? She still clutched the rose, but now it was starting to wilt. Its power
had been expended. Her curse had returned.

She saw that the food on the table had all been eaten. They must have
taken some breaks along the way.

Magnus woke. He reached for her, and paused. "Bleep!"

"The rose has faded," she said.

"Maybe I can fake it."

She laughed unhappily. "No. Let's not mess up the memories."

"Right," he agreed. "You were great, Jess."

"Thank you."

"There has to be a way."

"I hope so."

They got up, cleaned up, dressed, and were ready when Wira came to
fetch them for breakfast.

They joined Rose and Myst. "How was your night?" Rose inquired
politely.

"It was a dream," Jess said.

"Some dream!" Myst said.

Magnus just smiled.

Then it was time to see the Good Magician. "He was bottling some
vapor from a forget whorl," Rose said. "His hand slipped, and some of the
vapor touched him. He quickly cleaned it off, but it did affect his memory.
He is not quite himself today."

"As long as he can help us get to Fibot," Magnus said.

"Oh, that is not the problem. The boat will dock here within the hour."

"Then what?" Myst asked.

"As you know, he requires a year's service, or the equivalent, for an Answer to a Question," Rose explained. "He has a mission in mind for the three of you. But he can't remember what it is."

They looked at her. "Is there any hint?" Magnus asked.

"Yes. It involves Fibot. Also the participation of one nightmare and one day-mare. And perhaps one or two future princesses."

They continued looking at her.

Rose shrugged. "That is all I know, because it is all he knows."

"But how can we perform a mission if we don't know what it is?" Magnus asked.

Rose smiled somewhat wistfully. "Consider it a challenge."

The three of them exchanged a rather wavering glance.

"One irony is that it's not the worst of our problems," Rose said. "The next querents working their way through the challenges are twins. One has the talent of banishing things to the Void. The other can recover things from the Void. Both talents are extremely dangerous, as they know, and Humfrey needs to devise a way to nullify them. But with his memory messed up, that will be a challenge in itself."

"We appreciate the challenge of it," Jess said. It seemed that even the Magician of Information had problems.

Wira showed them up a winding staircase to the Good Magician's cramped little office upstairs. It was mostly filled by a giant book spread open on a table. Jess knew about this: it was the Book of Answers. The Magician needed to provide the Answers to querent's Questions.

"The querents are here," Wira said, and faded back.

"Thank you, dear," the Good Magician answered. He was gnomishly small, and looked about a century old. Jess was surprised, because why would he be that age when he had youth elixir to youthen him?

"State your Question," Humfrey said grumpily.

"We wish to obtain transport aboard Fibot from village to village for our show," Magnus said.

The gnomish eyes squinted at him. "Not to obtain the perfect assistant?"

"I have already found her."

Humfrey looked at Myst. "Not to be reunited with your siblings?"

"That, too," Myst said. "But I want to help the show first."

Finally the Good Magician looked at Jess. "Not to be rid of your curse?"

For half an instant she was tempted to change her mind. Without the curse she could be beautiful! Then she bore down, banishing it. "I want to help the show, too."

"So be it. Here are three boarding passes. The craft will be at your service as long as you need it, between its other missions."

They accepted the passes. "Uh, about these versatile clothes," Jess said.

"Keep them," Humfrey said impatiently. "You'll need them on your mission. Whatever it is."

Then Wira was ushering them out of the study and down the stairs. "I think you surprised him," she murmured. "That doesn't happen often."

"Maybe he forgot our revised mission," Magnus said.

Chapter 3

FIBOT

An hour later they stood in the forest glade marked forty-two and watched the boat come in. It was an impressive spectacle. It was an ordinary small craft, except for two things: it was sailing through the air, and its lone sail was made of fire. That was the fire sail, unlike that on any other boat.

A child sat at the stern, a nine-year-old girl with her hair blowing forward so that it formed a kind of bonnet around her face. "Win!" Myst screamed gladly.

Startled, Win looked, and the boat veered before she reoriented. "Myst!" she cried.

The craft landed neatly on the ground, its square sail flickering and expiring. Win jumped out as Myst ran toward it. The two collided beside the hull, gladly hugging each other. Win was a little taller than Myst, but they were of similar size.

Another girl appeared on the boat. She jumped down to join the other two. She was one size bigger, age ten.

"Those would be her sisters," Magnus murmured.

Myst hugged her also, then turned to face Magnus and Jess. "This is Squid. She's our Mock Octopus."

"Hello," Squid said shyly.

"I don't mean to insult you," Magnus said. "But you look exactly like a girl."

"Thank you, sir." She giggled. She was young, but she was clearly impressed by him. Jess realized that his magnetic handsomeness affected girls as well as women.

"These are my pretend family, while I'm away from my real one," Myst said. "Magnus and Jess. They're in love, but can't show it."

Squid looked at them. "Why not?"

"It's complicated. Sort of like you being a girl. Show them your tentacles."

"Okay." Squid shifted, becoming bulbous with tentacles every which way. It was an amazing transformation.

"Thank you," Magnus said politely. "Our problem is that Jess is cursed: nobody takes her seriously. I would like to, but usually I can't. So she can love me, but I can't love her back, at least not openly. Maybe you can take her seriously, being inhuman."

"Hello, Squid," Jess said. "You are impressive."

"You're joking," Squid said, reforming back into the girl.

"She isn't joking," Myst said. "But you can't accept that, because of her curse."

Squid nodded. "The way some folk can't accept me as a girl, because I'm a squid. Now I understand."

Maybe that would do.

Two adults appeared on the boat, a young man and a lovely young woman. Where had they come from? The craft was hardly big enough to hold more than four people.

"Dell! Nia!" Win called. "These are them!"

The two stepped down from the boat, the man helping the woman though she did not look in need of it. He was nondescript, with light brown hair and eyes, and forgettable face and body. She, in contrast, was a stunningly lovely creature, from her glossy dark brown hair and scintillating gray eyes all the way down to her dainty feet. How had an indifferent man like him won such a beauty? There was surely an interesting story there.

The two approached the three of them, for now Myst was shyly wedged between Magnus and Jess. Jess remembered that while the child knew her siblings, she did not know the others on the boat.

"The way she walks," Magnus murmured, perhaps unaware that he spoke aloud. Jess understood; the woman radiated nuanced sex appeal from every moving curve. It was surprising that one so young seemed so practiced in her manner.

The two halted before them, framed by the two girls. "Hello," the man said.

"Hello," Magnus replied. "I am Magnus, and this is my assistant Jess, and Myst. We are a, well, a make-believe family. The Good Magician granted us the use of Fibot for our traveling. We hope that is all right with you."

"It's fine," the man said. "We got the call, and came over immediately. I am Lydell, Dell for short, and this is my wife Grania, Nia for short. We make a make-believe family with the children, too."

"We are sure we'll get along," Nia said. Her voice was dulcet. "The Good Magician always has good reason for what he does, even if it is not immediately apparent to others." She laughed, and Jess nudged Magnus to prevent him from freaking out. That bosom in motion was a threat to male sanity. "We discovered that ourselves. We never suspected we'd become a couple."

Jess laughed, too. "This time it's not apparent to the Good Magician either, because he forgot what our mission is."

"You're joking, of course," Nia said with a sophisticated hint of disapproval.

"No," Myst said. "It's true. He forgot. So we have to find out what it is."

"Jess is cursed," Magnus said. "Nobody takes her seriously. That's why you thought she was joking."

Nia eyed him in a manner that threatened to blow him away. Jess realized that she, too, was responsive to his masculine appeal. "Yet evidently *you* take her seriously."

"I'm faking it. I have learned to accept what she says despite not believing it."

Dell and Nia exchanged a significant glance.

"It's true!" Myst said. "I do, too."

"And we know our sister," Win said. "She's not a liar."

"Then perhaps Myst should translate for Jess, when there's a question," Nia said.

"Sure," Myst agreed, not picking up on the irony. "We're a family."

"Let's get aboard and introduce the others," Dell said.

"How many does that little boat hold?" Jess asked, determined not to be shut up at the outset.

"She means—" Myst started.

"Peace, child," Nia said. "Nobody believes about Fibot, either, until they have seen it." She smiled. "Just as they don't believe about me."

Squid and Win laughed together, though Jess couldn't see what was funny. She was watching Nia, though there was something odd about her manner.

"Fibot is larger than it looks," Dell said. "This way."

They walked to the boat. Then Dell helped Nia climb aboard, and Magnus helped Jess. The two girls smiled as Myst puffed into a cloud and drifted up to the deck before reforming.

"Did you forget to tell us something about your sibling?" Nia asked Win.

"Oh, that's right," Win said. "It's her talent. She can turn misty, and back again. The way the wind is my talent, and—"

"I believe I have the picture," Nia said. Jess was privately satisfied to see the woman caught by surprise.

Dell led the way to the center of the craft, where there was a hatch that led down. Nia climbed down into it, though obviously it couldn't go far; the ground was right below the boat.

Yet in less than a moment Nia disappeared below. Jess peered after her. There was a hole that went well below ground level, with handholds all around it.

Then she remembered: Fibot was larger than it looked. It was one of those magic things that were larger on the inside than on the outside. That explained a lot.

"You're next," Dell said. "We were surprised, too, when we first boarded Fibot. There's a lot more to it than the fire sail."

Myst clambered down. Then Jess went, carefully. Then Magnus. Dell and the two girls remained topside.

Below it was relatively enormous. This was clearly the interior of a ship, not a boat. "I will show you to your cabin," Nia said. "Once you're settled, I will introduce you to the others."

"Thank you," Jess said somewhat faintly.

"She means it," Myst said.

"So it seems." Nia led them down a short hall, her graceful body swaying with a natural allure that caused Magnus to shade his eyes with his hand. "This suite should do," she said, opening a door. "If it is unsatisfactory, we'll find another."

The suite was palatial, with a family room, bedroom, child's room, bathroom, and phenomenal closet space. In fact the whole external Fibot could just about have fitted inside it. Jess had not encountered magic of this nature before, and was horribly impressed.

Magnus looked at her, lifting an eyebrow. "It will do!" Jess said.

"Excellent," Nia said. "I will prepare a meal while you get settled. Do you have any preference?"

Jess looked appealingly at Magnus. He took over without hesitation. "We will be happy to have the house special, thank you," he said. "We will be out shortly."

Nia nodded and gracefully exited, closing the door softly behind her.

Now at last Jess could relax. "You said pretty girls threw themselves at you, but this is beyond the pale."

He laughed. "A pretty girl is one thing. Nia is another. I've never seen a woman like her. She wasn't even trying, yet she was close to blowing me away."

"I noticed."

"Remember, she's married. She doesn't want me, anyway. Don't go getting jealous on me."

"I'm not jealous!" Jess exclaimed.

Both Magnus and Myst laughed. "Good thing we don't believe you, anyway," Myst said.

Jess realized she was making a foolish scene. "I'm sorry. I never had a man take me seriously before, even for one night, and I'm not used to handling it."

"Remember, I have a mind as well as an eye," Magnus said. "I look at women, but I know you are the one I want."

"Kiss her," Myst said wisely. "She needs it."

Magnus took Jess into his arms. "I am faking it because that's the only way I can do it. But behind the fakery, it's real. I hope you understand."

Jess was suddenly very glad they had had the prior night together with the rose. That had clarified his real interest. "I do."

He kissed her. She loved it.

Myst applauded. "Notice I didn't even say 'yuck.'"

"Thank you."

"There's something funny about Nia," Myst said. "Maybe she's magical."

"She could be a nymph in human guise," Magnus said. "It doesn't matter as long as Dell is satisfied."

"What man wouldn't be satisfied with a nymph?" Jess asked. "They have perfect bodies and are effectively brainless."

He smiled. "I wouldn't. I encounter too many of those at my shows. But I agree, most men would."

They used the facilities to wash and primp and handle natural functions. They then went out to brace Nia again.

She had a lovely meal set out on a kitchen table. Her taste was perfect.

Jess could no longer contain her curiosity. "How do you do it?"

"This craft has everything including kitchen sync, so as to synchronize dishes. That makes it easy."

"I mean you seem so competent for one so young."

Nia smiled. "Just as Fibot is larger than it looks from outside, I am older than I look. Outside I am twenty-one. Inside I am sixty-one."

"Sixty-one!" Jess exclaimed.

"I had an encounter with the Fountain of Youth, and lost two thirds of my age. As it happened, Dell liked that, so we get along. I have a fair amount of experience, and make sure to give him what he wants, even if he does not always know what he wants."

"He thinks you're twenty-one?" Magnus asked.

"He knows my age, mentally, and prefers it, but is satisfied with my younger body. We were friends before it happened; he first knew me as the grandmother. We understand each other."

"I appreciate that," Jess said.

"She means it," Myst said.

"Yes, I believe I am coming to understand how to relate to you," Nia said. "You are not what you seem, in attitude, just as I am not what I seem in appearance. We should get along."

Jess rather thought they would, now.

"Any other questions?" Nia asked graciously.

Jess looked around. "There's even art on the walls. It looks like sheer quality. How did you get that?"

"It's not original," Nia said. "We gave a lift to a traveler with the talent of the spitting image. Where he spat, there was a perfect copy of an original painting."

Jess remained amazed. "Everything here is so bright and colorful. Not grubby the way a boat can be."

"We gave a lift to another traveler, Polly Ester. Her magic was to make everything colorful."

"You certainly managed well."

"And I think you are not being facetious."

"I am not," Jess agreed.

"Now you must meet the others," Nia said as they finished the meal and she cleaned off the places. She snapped her fingers.

A boy appeared. He was about twelve, ordinary, but there was something about him. "This is Santo," Nia said. "Santo, these are Magnus, Jess, and—"

"Santo!" Myst cried, leaping into the boy's embrace.

"Oops, I forgot," Nia said good naturedly. "Of course you know each other. You're siblings!"

"We sure are," Myst agreed happily.

"You're from the future, too," Magnus said.

"Yes."

"However," Nia continued, "There are two other things you should know about him."

"Let me tell them!" Myst said. "One, he's a Magician, or almost. He makes holes. Big holes. You'll see."

"You will see," Nia agreed. "We couldn't travel properly without Santo."

Jess decided to keep quiet, though she didn't see what was so special about making holes.

"And he's gay," Myst said.

Neither Jess nor Magnus knew what to say about that, so they were silent. They could get more details from Myst later, if they needed to. Obviously it made no difference to Myst.

Santo lifted a hand in parting, and departed.

Nia snapped her fingers again. This time a girl responded. This was a ten-year-old girl with orange hair and eyes. "This is Ula," Nia said. "Whose talent is being useful in unexpected ways. She is not a sibling, but has bonded with the others and they accept her as one of them. Ula, these are—"

"Magnus and Jess," Ula said. "Win and Squid told me." She glanced at Jess. "Neat talent."

"Thank you," Jess said, bemused.

Ula looked at Magnus, and went silent. She, too, clearly felt his aura.

"And our animal complement," Nia said, snapping her fingers twice.

A little robot dog walked in, with a screen for a face, and a small black bird perched on its shoulder. "Tata Dogfish," Nia said. "Our chief source of critical information. He's a robot."

Jess looked at the dogfish. He was male, metallic, with fish-like scales, and a fish tail, but also stubby legs, or maybe descending fins. Taken as a whole, a remarkably strange creature, whether alive or dead.

"I understand it was raining cats and dogs, and he came down in the storm," Nia said. "Later he came to join the crew of the boat, as he can be of better service here."

The fish tail wagged affirmatively.

"And the Peeve, our chief source of irritation."

The bird flew up onto her shoulder. "Thank you, harridan," it said in Nia's voice. Then it turned to Magnus, while Nia kept her mouth clearly closed. "We know of you, circus man," Nia's voice continued. "Tata knows everything, when he looks it up in his database."

"Close enough," Magnus agreed.

The bird turned its beak toward Jess. "As for you, you lovely creature—" It broke off, then tried again. "You are a marvel of discretion."

Now Nia laughed. "What's the matter, birdbrain? Cat got your tongue?"

"It's not coming out right," the peeve complained.

"And do you know why? Because nobody takes her seriously. Not even you. You can't seriously insult her." Nia faced Jess. "The peeve's talent is the insult. It seems you're messing it up." She was clearly enjoying this.

The bird made an effort and tried again. "You really are blessed, because—"

"Let me say it for you, peeve," Nia said. "BLEEP!!"

"Thank you, crone."

"Why don't you go join her? I'm sure she'd love your company."

The bird spread its wings and flew across to Jess, landing on her right shoulder. "You are looking gorgeous today, Nia," it said in Jess's voice.

Even Jess had to join in the laughter.

"Would you believe," Nia said, "the peeve actually went to Hell for a while, but got kicked out because it overstayed its welcome?"

"I am beginning to," Jess agreed.

"You see, peeve, her curse nullifies yours," Nia said. "You can't insult anyone while you are with Jess."

"That's lovely," Magnus murmured.

The bird turned angrily to face him. "What's it to you, handsome?"

"Thank you."

"Maybe the peeve should stay with Jess," Myst said brightly. "People would really like them together."

The bird started to spread its wings, then folded them again. "Maybe so, beautiful."

"And now the introductions have been completed," Nia said grandly. "Let's go topside."

They didn't ask why; the woman seemed to have something in mind.

They mounted the ladder and stood on the upper deck beside Dell. Magnus and Jess gasped.

The boat was no longer ground-bound. It was floating several hundred feet high in the air. The Good Magician's Castle was visible immediately below.

"But we never felt it take off," Magnus said.

"You don't, from inside," Dell said. "It's deceptively comfortable."

"Where to?" Win called from the stern.

"That we still have to decide," Nia said. "What did the Good Magician tell you, Magnus?"

"We will need the participation of a night mare, a day mare, and one or two future princesses," Magnus answered promptly. He evidently had a good memory.

"One of whom may know what your mission is," Nia said with insight that was not, after all, beyond her years.

"What say, Tata?" Dell asked the dogfish.

The creature's screen flickered. THE MARES.

"And where will we find these unspecified mares?" he asked. The man was evidently used to working with the dogfish robot.

The dogfish trotted over to join Win. She nodded. Then her hair blew out before her face as she turned the tiller. The square fire sail, quiescent before, brightened as the wind caught it. The Good Magician's Castle drifted back behind as they sailed across the landscape. They were on their way.

"How far?" Dell asked.

"About two hours," Win called.

"Then we have some time to kill," Nia said. "Let's go below and get to know each other better."

Jess would have liked to stay topside and admire the passing scenery. But she realized that there was bound to be plenty of time for that, as they pursued their mystery mission, and the passengers and crew did need to get better acquainted. They might be working together for some time.

Then the craft rocked violently. "Blip!" Win swore. "We just ran afoul of an invisible air foil that fought my wind. I have it under control now."

"That's good," Dell said.

The boat rocked worse than before. "Curses!" Win swore. "Foiled again!"

Jess couldn't help smiling.

They descended to the interior and took seats in a broad circle in the main chamber. Only Win and Tata remained above, guiding and propelling the boat.

"Now that we are on the way to perhaps discovering your mission," Nia said to Magnus, "Perhaps you can clarify for us what it is you do." It no longer seemed odd to Jess to have a twenty-one-year-old lovely woman running things.

Jess discovered that she was quite curious about that herself. She knew he put on a show, and she would assist him, but the details had never come forward.

"By all means," he agreed. "I put on a show, a kind of structured free-form play that involves the audience and provides the spectators a unique experience. I have been quite successful in my local village, but now want to expand my range." He smiled. "I crave success; that is my reward."

"Most of us do," Nia agreed. "I craved romantic success, and now am achieving it, thanks to the youthening I encountered." She glanced at Dell, who smiled tolerantly; he was obviously well satisfied with their relationship. It occurred to Jess that an experienced old woman with the body of a nymph could make any man happy, if she wanted to. "However, your outline lacks detail."

Translation: clear as mud, so far.

"I think a demonstration is in order," Magnus said. "We have here a sample audience of three adults, four children, and a bird." For the peeve remained perched on Jess's shoulder, possibly snoozing.

"An audience of eight," Nia agreed.

Magnus stood in the center of the ring of chairs. His suit became a flashy showman's outfit. "I will tell a story, of a kind, speaking the lines for the volunteer actors in the play. No one needs to memorize anything; just follow my lead. Now who would like to be in the play?"

"Me!" all four children exclaimed, jumping up.

"And me," the peeve said in Jess's voice. "I'm sure you will impress us all."

Magnus smiled again. He had a winning smile, which was probably why he used it so much. Jess found herself wanting to please him, and knew the others were similarly moved. It was part of his talent. "But you, peeve, will be insulting folk right and left the moment you leave Jess's shoulder and stop getting balked. We can't have that; we're trying to make a good impression. So I lay one stricture on you: you will merely perch on a chair and remain silent. I assure you, you will be the center of attention throughout."

The bird huffed up as if to make a scathing refusal, but was balked by the curse. "Of course," it said meekly.

Dell and Nia laughed. "I like this play already," Dell said.

The bird shot him a clean look.

Magnus eyed the children. "Santo, you will be the lead man, the leader of the band."

The boy nodded.

"Ula, you will be the protagonist. That is, the main character."

"Me?" she asked, surprised and startled. "But I'm nothing."

"Exactly. The secret truth is that most of us are nothing inside, but some of us pretend we are something. You are in excellent company."

Ula shrugged. "I hope I don't mess it up."

"You won't. I'm sure you'll make a fine actress."

He turned to Myst. "You will be Santo's little sister, sometimes resenting but always supporting him."

"That isn't even acting!" Myst exclaimed, laughing.

He turned finally to Squid. "And you will be a beautiful nymph, out to catch a foolish boy and eat him."

"Easy," Squid agreed. "I hope he tastes good."

"Peeve, perch on this tree branch," Magnus said, taking a chair and setting it in the center of the circle. The peeve obediently flew across to perch on the back of the chair. To Jess, it almost looked like the branch of a tree.

"Now for the story. Ula has always admired birds, and would like to have one as a pet. She feels that would give her life meaning. One day as she is out walking with her sister Myst, she spies the perfect bird. It is sitting on a branch, perfectly still. It is absolutely lovely."

Ula looked at the peeve and clapped her hands in delight. She was getting into the role.

"This is my pet," Ula exclaims. "I will take it home with me so everyone can admire it."

"But it's not moving," Myst protests. "I think it's dead."

Myst made a disparaging gesture toward the bird. She, too, was getting into the part.

And so was Jess. The room now seemed more like a glade in a forest. She saw Dell and Nia similarly intrigued. Magnus's magic of verisimilitude was taking hold of them all.

"No, it's merely asleep," Ula insisted. Actually Magnus was speaking for her, but now the words seemed to be coming from her mouth.

"I don't know," Myst said doubtfully.

"I will take it home," Ula said. She took firm hold of the branch and managed to break it off, as it was a dead stick, anyway. It came away in her hands, with the bird still perched on it.

They walked home. "See what I found!" Ula said, proudly holding up the branch with the bird. "Isn't it beautiful?"

Now it was Santo's turn. "That's a stuffed bird!"

"No no! It's alive! I just need to win its respect. You'll see."

"You're crazy! It's either stuffed or dead, in which case it will stink up the whole house."

"No," Ula said. But her resolve was being tested, and she was near to tears. Nobody believed in her pet bird.

There was a motion from the other side of the scene. A lovely nymph had just stepped out from behind a tree. "Come to mee, you handsome booy!" she called to Santo. "I will give you such a nice piece of caandy!"

Intrigued, Santo went to her. But as soon as he got there, the nymph turned into an octopus and flung her tentacles around him. "Now I will bite off your head!" she cried hungrily.

Santo struggled, but the tentacles bound him tightly and he couldn't get free.

Ula saw what was happening. What could she do? All she had on her was a vial of youth elixir she had found on one of her walks in the forest. She had no use for it, of course, already being younger than she liked. All of them were.

Then she thought of something. She put down the branch with the bird, uncorked the vial, and ran to where the octopus was just opening its mouth wide to bite off Santo's head. She flung the liquid at the creature. Some of it splashed into its mouth.

The octopus's expression went weird. Several of its tentacle quivered. Then it youthened into a spider and slunk away. Santo was free.

"You saved me!" Santo exclaimed. "When I was cruelly teasing you!"

"Well, I had to help if I could," Ula said, returning to pick up the branch with the stiff bird.

She paused, staring. For the bird was moving. Its head turned to look at her, and its wings fluffed. "It's coming alive!" Myst said, amazed.

"You won its respect," Santo said. "And mine."

Then the bird jumped to Ula's shoulder. It had become her pet.

"Oh, phooey!" Squid's voice came from a distance. "Now I'll never get to bite his head off!"

The play was done. The adult audience applauded. Jess was impressed. She had gotten so wrapped up in the story that she really cared about Ula's success.

She was even more impressed with Magnus's talent. It was truly a good one.

But that brought up another matter. "Why do you need an assistant?" she asked. "You're doing fine on your own."

"Because in a village things are more complicated," he said. "I need to focus on the play, or the effect dissipates. I lose track of details. Someone has to keep it organized. And between acts I need to catch my breath, drink some water, and organize my mind for the next one. That's where a supplementary act is perfect."

"Supplementary? I don't know how to act, and no one would take me seriously if I did."

"Ah, but you're wrong, Jess. You can be a great actress, when you make your talent work for you instead of against you."

"I don't understand."

"Bear with us a moment," Magnus said to the others. "We'll have another act coming up soon."

They were glad to talk among themselves, adults and children alike, because of the experience they had just had.

"I really feared I'd get my head bitten off," Santo said.

"I really felt like a decent bird," the peeve said.

Meanwhile Magnus took Jess aside. "Here is what you do," he said. "You will become Atrocia, making fun of your curse."

"Fun? It's not fun!"

"In the show. Pretense. The way you do with me."

Oh. With his attention right on her, she almost believed. That talent of his was in full force. He might not be taking her seriously, but she was responding seriously to him. As she had that night at the Good Magician's Castle.

"You'll need a prop." He went briefly to Nia, who exited and returned with a bag. He gave it to Jess.

Then Magnus joined the audience, and Jess was on stage with her bag. Could this possibly work? All she could do was try.

"I am Atrocia. Nobody takes me seriously," she said truthfully enough. Then she went into her little story that Magnus had made for her, just as he had made the story for the children. "I told my boyfriend that I loved him and wanted to marry him, and he laughed his head off." She paused, then reached into the bag. "And here it is." She drew out a manikin head with an open mouth, as if laughing.

And the audience, adults and children, burst into laughter. She was a success!

She realized that while Magnus' talent had set the scene, with the audience ready to respond, her own talent, the curse, had augmented it. She was truly unbelievable, and this joke played right into it. She could after all be an actress. A comedienne.

"And that's it," Magnus said. "The details will differ from village to village, as the people differ, but that's the essence. We'll make them laugh and cry."

"You certainly will," Nia agreed. "Now we understand."

"Atrocia," Dell said. "That certainly fits the role."

The audience broke up. "I'm going to take a nap," Magnus said. Jess saw, now that he was unguarded, how tired he was; putting on his act evidently was a strain on him. She wanted to go hold him and comfort him, but knew it would have the opposite effect. Better to let him be.

"I'm going to play with my siblings," Myst said. She was clearly thrilled to be back with them. "We're going to learn the Alphabet. You know: A-corns, B-corns, C-corns, all the way up to Uni-corns."

Jess suppressed a smile. That was certainly one way to do it.

"I will check on progress topside," Dell said. "We should be getting close."

"I'm with you," the peeve said, flying to perch on the man's shoulder.

"That leaves me," Nia said. "Do you want to talk? I believe I can take you seriously enough now, if I don't get too close to you."

"Actually, yes," Jess said, surprised.

Nia nodded. "You had that look about you. Come to the cockpit and we can relax and watch the world go by."

"How did you know I wanted to see that?" Jess asked, surprised again.

"I'm a woman. An old woman. I know the signs."

They went to the cockpit, which turned out to be a comfortable chamber surrounded by glassy walls that showed the outdoors around the craft. The Land of Xanth was slowly passing beneath them, its colored fields and forests and mountains and lakes forming a splendid tapestry.

"I remain amazed by this magic boat," Jess confessed. "I've never even imagined anything quite like this before."

"The three princesses, Melody, Harmony, and Rhythm, made it as teens for their diversion," Nia said. "You know of them? Each is a Sorceress in her own right, and any two together square it, and the three together cube it. When they outgrew it they turned it over to the Good Magician, who assigned Dell and me to run it, to our surprise."

"You seem like ordinary folk," Jess said. "If I may ask, how did you qualify for such, well, power?"

"We *are* ordinary folk, with one oddity: we are compulsively honest and essentially incorruptible. That was what qualified us, though we did not know it at the time. We will never knowingly allow Fibot to be misused."

"How does it feel to be old, with a young body?" Jess asked. "I don't mean to pry, but I'm curious as bleep."

Nia laughed. "It's great. I spent my first life learning through my mistakes, and I made a lot of mistakes. So I knew a lot, too late to do me much good. Until I got youthened. Now I am making sure not to repeat those mistakes. I take the best possible care of Dell, knowing how. It's not just stork summoning."

"Not," Jess agreed morosely. "If only it were!"

"Magnus can't take even that seriously, with you?"

"Even that," Jess agreed. "It frustrates us both."

"I can imagine."

Time to get off that subject. "Do you have a magic talent? Is your physical youth it?"

"I have a minor talent, that the Good Magician enhanced. Do you see those eyes?"

Jess became aware of a floating pair of eyes staring at her. She could have sworn they weren't there before.

"They weren't," Nia said. "That's my talent: spot on the wall. Actually two spots on the wall, which now I can form into eyes that actually work. That is, I can see through them." She laughed. "I can spy on anything I wish, near or far. Don't worry; I won't be spying on you and Magnus in your bedroom. That would not be ethical."

"I wish there was something to see." Jess considered briefly, then decided to say it. "Except last night, when Rose of Roogna gave me a rose that countered my curse for a few hours. That was phenomenal."

"I hadn't known she had that kind of rose."

"It's a new type, it seems."

"At least you had one night to verify his intentions."

"One glorious night," Jess agreed dreamily.

"I have never encountered magic quite like your curse. It must be horrible."

"Often it is," Jess agreed.

"Have you any idea what your mission is?"

"None. I can't figure what a day mare and night mare could have to do with it, or two princesses."

"Two princesses," Nia repeated. "We do have a visiting princess."

"You do? One of the trio who made this boat?"

"No, she the daughter of one, Princess Rhythm. She got married recently, and her ten-year-old daughter Princess Kadence visits from the future."

"How does she do that? As a ghost?"

"No. Her spirit comes and animates Ula as a host. That is one of the unexpected ways Ula proved to be useful, per her talent. We like her; we would keep her around anyway, but this is convenient."

"Animates as a host," Jess repeated. "She pushes out the person whose body it is?"

"No, they share. They're compatible. Ula likes being a princess, at least in a manner, and is glad to let Kadence do what she wants. There's a subtle change when the princess takes over; you can see it if you pay attention."

"I will try to pay attention. But this, too, is remarkable to me. I am having trouble relating to either Ula or the princess. I mean, why either should want to associate with the other. Aren't they of quite different stations?"

"They are," Nia agreed. "But Kadence evidently likes the company of the girls, who accept her as a girl rather than a spook or a princess. I am thinking that Kadence could be one of the princesses you seek. But that still doesn't tell me your mission."

"It's a mystery," Jess agreed.

They lapsed into silence, watching Xanth go by. Jess found it relaxing, partly because of its pleasant novelty, but mostly because of Nia's company. The woman did know how to put a person at ease.

Then the peeve flew in. "We're getting there. Time to go topside."

Nia nodded. "Time to go topside," she agreed. "Our next engagement is upon us. With luck it will clarify your mission."

"With luck," Jess agreed hopefully.

Chapter 4

MARES

Fibot had landed beside a clog tree with a number of ripe clogs. Not far from it stood a sandalwood tree with wooden sandals. That was all.

"I don't understand," Jess said.

The dogfish's screen flickered. Tata, being robotic, was relatively unencumbered by human emotions, and was able to take her seriously. "Tata says this is Mare Imbri's tree," the peeve said from her shoulder.

"Who?"

"Mare Imbrium, the former night mare. She is now a dryad, a nymph of a tree."

"How could a night mare become a tree dryad?" Jess asked, confused. "They're completely different species."

Magnus joined them, shedding a few leftover flakes of sleep. "I know of night mares. They bring bad dreams to folk who deserve them. Without that punishment, bad folk would quickly take over Xanth, fearing no punishment. The mares are spirits, as are the nymphs; in special cases one can assume the role of the other."

"That is what Imbri did," the peeve said. "She liked a faun, and this was how she could be with him. She had lost her original body; it's a long story. Capsule edition: the Horseman, an evil crossbreed, was taking out the kings of Xanth. And she, having become King of Xanth, kicked him in the head and killed him. Then she had to get rid of his magic amulet that gave him too much power, by throwing it into the Void, so that it could never be used again. But in the process she got caught in the Void herself, and lost her body. Fortunately she had obtained a soul, and that survived. She is one of the very few creatures who have survived a fall into the Void, in her fashion. Later she joined a tree, as a nymph spirit, and it provided her with new bodily substance. Now she and the clog tree support each other, and both prosper, and she sees the faun every day, and maybe some nights too . . ." The bird paused for a naughty ellipsis.

The Void. Jess remembered that the next querents for the Good Magician had the talents of sending things to, or fetching things from, the Void. Too bad they hadn't been with the night mare. "So what do we want with her now?" Jess asked, her confusion clinging valiantly to her like a foggy cloak. What a history that mare had had! "Don't we need a night mare who is still practicing the trade?"

Tata's screen flickered, and the peeve translated. "Imbri retains some contacts with her old night mare friends. She may be able to find one who will join us. We can't just go to them directly; the night mares' home base is on the moon, out of our reach."

Oh. Jess felt slightly stupid. That irritated her.

"Well, let's talk to the mare turned dryad," Magnus said briskly.

"Hey, naughty nymph!" the peeve called loudly to the tree, using Jess's voice. "Get your curvy little—" It paused, choking on a word. "Oh, bleep! I can't say it!"

"Yes you can," Magnus said. "Just rephrase it as a polite compliment."

"Bleep!" the bird swore. But there was no help for it. "Please bring your lovely posterior out to talk with us."

A nude nymph appeared in the tree. "You look like the peeve, but you can't be," she said.

"Allow me," Magnus said. "This *is* the peeve, but it is perching on the shoulder of Jess, who is cursed never to be taken seriously. That interferes with the dirty bird's natural mode and it is unable to insult you at the moment, to its considerable frustration. We are on a mission for the Good Magician, and think that you may be able to help us, if you are kind enough to do so."

The nymph looked at him, visibly impressed, as most females were. "You're not bad at expressing yourself. Who are you?"

"I am Magnus, Jess's companion. But she is, I think, the central character of this story. The protagonist."

"Oh, one of those! I was one once. So was my friend Forrest Faun. That's how we met." She turned to Jess. "What do you want from me?"

"The Good Magician said we need a night mare and a day mare for our mission. We hope that you can help us find them."

"No, seriously, what do you want?"

"Please take me literally," Jess said. "Remember my curse."

"This is difficult."

"Perhaps I should speak for her, for now," Magnus said. "We need the participation of a night mare and a day mare. Can you help?"

Imbri sighed. "I am not sure I can. Both the night mares and the day mares are severely distracted now, and don't have time for incidental tasks."

"Distracted?" Jess asked.

"It's complicated."

"Everything is," Jess said ruefully. "But we must do what we can."

Imbri nodded. "Let's get to know each other better, so as to see what we can make of this. Have a seat."

Three branches of the tree slowly descended, shaping themselves into comfortable seats. Magnus sat in one, Jess in another, hoping the tree would take her seriously. Fortunately it did; it was not a child's chair. She settled into it, and Imbri sat in another opposite them, crossing her bare legs. Jess cringed inwardly at the view that was giving Magnus, but knew it was unintentional. Tata lay on the ground, and the peeve perched on Jess's shoulder.

"Now tell me something," Imbri told Jess.

"The Good Magician, or rather his wife Rose, gave me a rose that nullified my curse for a few hours," Jess said.

"Now I am taking you seriously!" Imbri said. "Because my tree does, and it is sending me your essence. I had hoped that would be the case. Trees have remarkable powers, when they care to exert them."

Good enough. "What is distracting the mares?" Jess asked.

"Somehow the Night Stallion switched places with the Day Stallion," Imbri said. "Now the night mares are carrying sweet dreams to bad people, while the day mares bring bad dreams to undeserving people. It's awful!"

A bulb flashed over Jess's head. "Could that be our mission? The Good Magician suffered an accident with a forget whorl and couldn't remember. That could account for our need for the two mares. To show us around their realms, so we could tackle the problem."

"It might," Imbri agreed, surprised. "But as I said—"

"You were a night mare," Magnus said, gazing at her knees and perhaps a bit more. Jess knew he would have freaked out by now, had the nymph been wearing panties.

"I was, and still am in essence," Imbri agreed. "But I am no longer under the dominion of the Stallion, so am not affected."

"Could you do it again?"

Imbri stared at him, amazed. "I suppose I could, for a while. I do sometimes miss the old nights. But I can't go far from my tree, physically, for very long; our connection would weaken and we would both suffer."

"Suppose you had a human host?" he asked.

"My spirit in a living person? That would enable me to travel far, yes. But I would be unable to leave that person when far from my tree, and I doubt a human woman would care to be possessed for so long."

"That's not necessarily the case," the peeve said with Jess's voice. "Ula hosts Princess Kadence often enough, and they get along fine."

"Maybe if there were a host who didn't mind," Imbri said. "But I'm not sure how to find one on short notice."

"I know one," the peeve said, and flew off.

"Maybe if the two of you can meet," Jess said. "And try it for a minute to see if you're compatible. Certainly it would be in a good cause."

"Yes. I must confess that now that the notion has been broached, I am increasingly intrigued by the prospect. I love my tree, and I love Forrest Faun, but sometimes I do miss the rest of Xanth. If I could visit it—" She shook her head. "But I fear that is not realistic."

Win approached them from the boat, the bird perched on her shoulder. "This could be fun!" she exclaimed. Evidently the peeve had told her all about it. "Maybe I could be like Ula!"

"I am no princess," Imbri said. "In fact I'm a mare masquerading as a nymph. Only partly human."

"A mare! I love horses! I used to wish I could be one!" Then Win sobered. "But you know, I'm a child. I'm only nine years old. You're—"

"Several hundred," Imbri said. "But I believe that in such cases, the older participant prevails, at least in outlook. You would be an adult in a young body. That might be awkward."

"Like Nia!" Win exclaimed. "She loves it!"

"Our assorted talents would go with the one in charge at the moment," Imbri said. "Within limits, such as the Adult Conspiracy."

"Oh, phoo!"

Imbri smiled. "There may be compensations. For example, I can assume my natural mare form."

"Yes!"

Magnus, Jess, and Imbri circled a glance. Could this actually work out?

"Why don't you try it now," Magnus said. "To see if you're compatible."

"Yes!" Win exclaimed again.

Imbri uncrossed her legs and stood. Jess nudged Magnus to prevent his freak. "Take my hand," the nymph said to the child.

Win extended her hand to meet Imbri's hand. They stood for a scant moment. Then Imbri dissipated into vapor and disappeared. Only Win remained.

"What happened?" Jess, cried, alarmed.

Tata's screen flickered.

"It's okay," the peeve said. "Watch. Listen."

The child's posture and expression changed. "I am Mare Imbri," she said. "I have taken possession, with the host's acquiescence."

"But Win!" Jess asked. "What about her?"

The posture and expressing changed again. "I'm still here," Win said. "See, I've got my talent." Her hair splayed forward as a gust of wind blew by her. "But I'd rather let her take it. I'm just along for the ride."

"Uh, maybe Dell and Nia should be here," Jess said. "In loco parentis."

"They're our loco parents," Win agreed. "While we're on the boat."

"They're coming," the peeve said. "I told them, too."

"To or too?" Magnus asked.

"Both, you nice fellow," the bird snapped.

Sure enough, the two were approaching, along with Santo, Squid, and Myst. Only Ula was missing, and Jess realized that she must have been designated to guard the boat. They probably took turns at that, when there was need.

"Watch this!" Win said, and faded back into Imbri. Then, as the others stared in unison, she transformed into a horse.

Jess was surprised on more than one account. The mass of the mare seemed much greater than that of the child. But of course this was magic;

size had little to do with it. The horse trotted around, circling the others. Then she halted. She neighed.

"She says someone can have a ride," the peeve translated.

"Meee!" Myst exclaimed.

Dell picked her up under the shoulders and carefully set her on the back of the horse. Then the mare walked slowly in another circle. "Oooo!" Myst cried in rapture.

It did seem to be working out.

The mare halted, the child slid off, and Win reappeared. She and Myst hugged, mutually delighted.

Then Imbri reappeared. It was interesting seeing the subtle shifts in the child's body and manner as the piloting changed. "I can go with you. But I must tell Forrest. He will need to keep an eye on my tree."

The others remained by the tree as the horse reappeared and galloped to the other tree. "It seems we have our night mare," Magnus said. "But the day mare may be more of a challenge."

They watched as the horse reached the sandalwood tree and shifted to nymph form. It occurred to Jess that the wood sandals of one tree matched well enough with the clogs of the other tree; obviously they were compatible.

A faun appeared; even from this distance Jess could see his hooves. That would be Forrest. The two talked for a moment. Then the nymph hugged him tightly. In another moment the filly was back and galloping toward them.

"That's chaste," Magnus remarked. "Fauns and Nymphs normally celebrate much more evocatively."

"These are more responsible ones," Nia said. "They care about their trees."

"Also, there are children present," Squid said wisely.

Suddenly Jess saw the nymph in her mind's eye. She spoke, and a little speech balloon appeared over her head. "He says okay," it printed.

Jess glanced at the others. They looked similarly startled. It seemed they had seen the picture, too.

The dogfish's screen flickered.

"That's how night mares communicate without actually talking," the peeve explained. "They send speech dreamlets."

So it seemed.

The filly arrived and became the girl again. "Forrest understands," Imbri said. "I am with you for these few days."

"We got your dreamlet," Nia said.

"It was cute," Myst said.

"Now we need to find a cooperative day mare," Magnus said. "Do you have any likely prospects?"

"The day mares are in the same bind as the night mares," Imbri said. "But first: do you have a suitable host?"

"Mee!" Myst exclaimed.

Imbri paused, evidently conversing internally with Win. Then she nodded. "You will do."

Myst clapped her hands. "Goody! Will I be able to turn horsey, too?"

"Yes, if you want to."

Suppose Win had given her sibling a bad reference? Jess wondered. No, that would never happen; these children had an extraordinary bond, and their background experience made them more responsible than ordinary children.

"But about the prospect," Magnus prompted Imbri. "You said that both day and night mares are distracted by the exchange of stallions."

"Yes. I know of one day mare who is more independent than most. That's why she got banished to a bad course. She may be ready to separate from it for a while."

"I gather the stallions run the herds," Magnus said, "They don't like independent mares?"

"They don't," Imbri agreed. "Mares are supposed to know their place. They are good for only one thing."

"Children are present," Nia murmured warningly. At the moment she almost looked her age.

"Delivering dreams," Imbri concluded. "Good or bad, as the case may be."

Nia relaxed. "So who is this filly?"

"Mairzy Doats."

That struck Jess as an odd name. But of course she was not conversant with day mare customs.

"And where is she to be found?" Nia asked evenly. Her age and experience were showing.

"You need to understand the system. Night mares' home turf is the surface of the moon. They have seas of the moon named after them, as I do: Mare Imbrium. Day Mares' home turf is more challenging: the gulf course."

"The what?"

"This is where human emotions tend to be most intense. Gulf is a game consisting of using a stick to knock a little ball into a little hole. Men seem to like it better than women. Something about balls and holes. They can get very annoyed when the ball misses the hole."

The girls tittered. Nia shot them a warning glance. They were evidently picking up more nuance than was proper for their age.

"It sounds silly," Magnus said.

"Devotees take it quite seriously. Courses are scattered all across Xanth and Mundania. They even have gulf tournaments."

"To see who can stick the ball in the hole fastest?" Magnus asked.

"And who can swear the worst," Imbri agreed. "Gulf is said to be excellent practice."

"Where does Mairzy Doats hang out?" Nia asked.

"It's on the fringe. It is called Abandon Hope."

"Where geographically?"

"Midway upon the journey of a life, in a dusky wood."

"That does not seem very specific."

"You have to follow the dream path."

"Because the mares deliver dreams," Magnus said. "That does make sense."

"Everything makes sense in its fashion," Imbri agreed.

"Can you lead us there?" Jess asked.

"Yes," Imbri looked around. "But it's a day path, and night is coming. We'll have to wait until morning."

"Then come aboard the boat," Nia said. "It has been a busy day. We can all use the rest."

Imbri looked at the boat. "Is there room? You must be quite crowded already." Then she paused, receiving another internal message. "It seems there is room."

They walked to the boat. Soon Imbri was sharing a bedroom with Squid and Ula. She was quite impressed with the facilities. "This is almost as good as a stable."

"Almost," Nia agreed wryly.

Jess relaxed with Magnus and Myst in their room, before supper. "We do seem to be getting closer to our mission," Jess said. "Assuming it is to restore the stallions to their proper habitats and roles."

"I am wondering who or what could have exchanged the stallions," Magnus said. "They are quite powerful entities in their own right. What could prevent them from simply returning to their home turfs?"

"And why?" Jess asked. "What possible purpose could there be in messing up the dream realms?"

"That perhaps has an answer: bad folk, who get punished by bad dreams, would want to get rid of them, so they could be bad with impunity. They wouldn't care that good folk suffer."

"So a bad person would have the motive," Jess said. "Who is bad enough and strong enough?"

"Maybe Tata would know."

They asked the robot dogfish. His screen flickered, then came up with a short list of names. THE SEA HAG. RAGNA ROC. THE GODDESS ISIS. COM PEWTER ON A BAD DAY. BUT NONE ARE PRESENTLY AVAILABLE.

"I have heard of Isis," Magnus said. "She's not evil, merely ambitious and sexy."

"And I'm sure Com Pewter would not do anything like this," Jess said.

"Which leaves us nowhere," Magnus said. "The Hag and Ragna got banished and locked up."

Nia knocked on their door. "Something has come up."

"Not serious, I hope," Jess said, concerned.

"We are docked on the ground for the nonce. I went out to harvest some fresh pizza pies for dinner—they are best when fresh—and a local villager spied me. Somehow the word has spread that we have a show on board."

"Well, we want news to get around," Magnus said. "It's no secret."

"They would like to see a show tonight."

Magnus looked at Jess. "Why not?"

"It does serve as a kind of cover for your real mission," Nia said. "You can travel to key places in the guise of finding new audiences for your show."

"Exactly," he agreed. "Tell them we'll be there in an hour."

Jess was nervous, but kept her mouth shut. She did want to work with Magnus, and this was the way.

Nia told them. They had a quick dinner of freshly harvested pizza pies, then sailed to the village.

Jess went on deck to clear her head, as the boat sailed over the trees, and was startled. "Wasn't the fire sail square? Now it's round."

"It varies according to its mood," Win explained. She was back at the tiller, in charge so that the wind at her back could drive the ship forward. She was clearly an important member of the crew. Tata was snoozing at her feet, ready to guide her. "When Dell and Nia discovered each other, when she youthened, it turned heart shaped."

Live and learn. The sail was evidently more than just an old flame. Jess returned to her room, hoping Magnus was lonely. Unfortunately he wasn't; he was all business, preparing for the show. "I will ask for volunteers, then brief them behind scenes while you warm them up with your act."

It was a completely ordinary village surrounded by beer-barrel trees, boot rear bushes, assorted pie plants, milkweeds, beefsteak tomato plants and other garden variety vegetation. There was a paved central square with room for the boat to dock.

Nia went out to set the anchor so the boat would not drift, and Jess went with her. But there was no place.

"Hello!" Nia called to the nearest man. "Maybe you can help me."

He came over, as eager to meet her as any man was. "Hello. I'm Sam. What can I do for you?"

Nia smiled. "I'm Nia, co-proprietor of this craft, and this is my friend Jess. I can't find a place to set the anchor. It won't hold on this pavement."

"Ah. I can help. My talent is to locate things that are related, such as a missing shoe. What is related to an anchor?"

"A patch of ground," Nia said.

Sam touched the anchor, then looked around. "There, I think."

Jess didn't see anything, but the man went confidently to a spot a few paces away. He squatted and pried at a tile with his fingers. It was loose, and lifted away to reveal a patch of ground below. Nia smiled brilliantly and bent over to drop the anchor on the patch, where it took instant hold. "Thank you so much," she said.

Sam had almost freaked out when she leaned forward, but he recovered enough to respond. "You're welcome."

Jess could only envy the way Nia used her sex appeal to get help, without making a scene of it. It never would have worked for Jess.

When the villagers assembled, Magnus took over. He was in his element, thrilling the people with his mere presence. "Greetings, all! I am Magnus, Master of Ceremonies, and this is my assistant Atrocia. She's awful." He frowned in a manner that showed he didn't mean it. "Now we have no regular cast of characters; we will draw on you, our esteemed audience. Our story this time will be completely original: Boy meets Girl, Boy loses Girl, Boy recovers Girl." The audience gasped at the sheer novelty of it, already falling under his spell. He was certainly making an impression. "I need a Boy, a Girl, and several supporting players. Do I have any volunteers?"

There was an enthusiastic show of hands. Several were pretty girls who looked set to throw themselves at him the moment it was feasible. He had clearly not been fooling about that. Jess tried to stifle her burgeoning jealously.

Magnus picked a handsome young man, a pretty girl, and three indifferent folk. The girl made a lunge for him, but he deftly avoided her, and she pretended she had merely stumbled. "Now while I brief my cast, Atrocia will appall you with her story." He took the volunteers backstage, leaving Jess to face the audience alone.

She was nervous, but depended on her curse to pull her through. She saw Sam in the audience, and focused for the moment on him. After all, they had met, in a manner. "I am Atrocia," she said boldly. "Nobody takes me seriously."

When she produced the manikin head, the villagers roared with laughter, including Sam. She was a success!

"I was more careful with my next boyfriend," she continued as the humor faded out. "I did not talk to him. I gave him no chance to laugh. I stood close before his face, bent over, and flashed him broadside with my panties." That was of course the way a girl nailed a man: the sight of her panties freaked him out so he couldn't escape.

She paused for a full three quarters of a moment. "You have heard of projectile vomiting? Splat! Soaking my panties! I've washed them several

times, really scrubbed them, and still can't get the stain out." She waited
for the laughter to diminish. "Worse, that stuff burns. My butt is blistered.
I can't sit down. That's why I'm a stand-up comedienne."

By the time the laughter expired, Magnus was back with his briefed
cast, and Jess faded back. She had done her part, diverting the audience
while he prepared. He took them through a marvelous little romance
where Boy finally won through to recover Girl, and the villagers were sati-
ated with fond emotion. Jess hoped the villagers didn't notice the way Girl
sneaked glimpses at Magnus as much as at Boy.

The show was a success. Word would spread quickly. There would be
no lack of villages to visit hereafter.

"You were wonderful!" Magnus told her privately once they were back
in the boat. "You're the perfect assistant. I wish I could—"

Jess looked around. Myst was with her sisters at the moment, and the
two of them were alone in their room. "Why don't you?"

"I'd have to fake it," he said regretfully. "You deserve better than that."

"Then fake it. Please."

He looked at her with understanding. Denied the reality, she would
settle for the fake, as before; it was better than nothing. "I'll close my eyes
and try to pretend you are that Girl in today's Play." He sighed. "Some day,
some way, somehow, this will be real," he promised. "As it was when you
had the rose."

"Some day," she agreed prayerfully.

He embraced her. He kissed her. He took her to the bed. But he was
unable to take it further. The curse prevailed. "Bleep!" he swore.

She really appreciated that bleep.

In the morning they set off for the Abandon Hope Gulf Course. This was,
Imbri explained, on one of the Sometime Islands that appeared occasion-
ally along the coast of Xanth. They were permanent in their own right, but
did not always align with Xanth. The trick was to catch this one during its
alignment. Tata was able to orient on it, and they sailed across and above
the water to it, the fire sail now triangular.

"Now comes the hard part," Imbri said when Win docked the boat and
turned the body over to her. "You will have to play a game of gulf."

"Play a game?" Magnus asked. "Why?"

"Day mares do not appear until summoned by a vacant mind, or a sufficiently aroused one. Only an actual game will put you in the proper frame."

"This smells like nonsense," Magnus grumbled.

"Don't fracture your stable. You are beginning to get there already, emotionally," Imbri said with a certain equine humor. "Stay the course."

So they docked and turned Fibot invisible—that was another trick that surprised Jess—and made a foursome for gulf. Magnus and Jess formed a pair, and Win and Myst formed another. Imbri manifested just long enough to clear it with the proprietors. They got gulf clubs, one for each player, and gulf balls.

Jess tried hers, and the ball flew backward away from the hole. It didn't take her seriously, either. "Now what?" she asked, exasperated.

Magnus considered the matter. "I doubt that balls are very smart," he said. "Try hitting it as far from the hole as possible."

Could that possibly work? Jess faced away from the hole. "I'm going to knock you so far from that hole you'll never find it again," she told the ball. Then she took a vicious swing at it.

The ball snagged on her club and scooted back toward the hole.

"Bleep!" she swore. "Get out of there!" She tapped the ball away from the hole.

It went the wrong way and dropped in. "Bleepety bleep with curse burrs on it!" she swore villainously.

"You're just a poor loser," Magnus said, playing along.

The girls played the hole, not caring about the score. Then the foursome moved on to the second hole.

This one was more of a challenge. It was on a low hanging cloud that drifted back and forth across the region, always in motion. They had to hit the ball up onto the cloud so that it could roll on into the hole.

"Bleep," Magnus said. He was definitely getting into the mood.

It took so many tries that the others lost count before they finally managed to hike their balls up onto the cloud. Jess, in contrast, didn't sweat it. "I'm going to drive you so deep into the ground you'll never see daylight again," she said, and bashed it as hard as she could.

The ball flew up to the cloud and made a hole in one.

"Bleep to the Nth power!" she swore. The surrounding green turned brown. This was almost fun.

The third hole was set within the embrace of a circling sleeping drag-on's tail. It was clear that any miss that struck the dragon would wake it, with fearsome consequences. Exceedingly delicate play was required.

Jess tackled it first. "I'm going to knock you right into the dragon's fiery snout!" Then she set out to do just that, and the ball skittered to the side and landed in the hole. "Peelb!" she swore, so upset it came out backward.

The others rubbed it in by giving her that hole.

The fourth hole was nestled in the middle of a nest of nickelpedes, the bugs that liked to gouge out nickle sized chunks of the flesh of any crea-ture they encountered. But the players were improving, and managed to scoop their balls over the 'pedes and into the hole without arousing them.

The fifth hole was in a nest in an ogre-twisted tree. Strike the trunk too hard and the tree would suddenly untwist and hurl the ball to the moon, making it almost unplayable. Again they stroked carefully and managed to complete their round without that particular mishap.

But the sixth hole was more of a challenge. It was on a turf plate that angled erratically to roll the ball into the nearby lake.

They all tackled it, only to lose their balls as the tilt countered what-ever they tried. Even Jess could not get it, because what she truly did not want was to lose her ball in the drink, and her curse had caught on to that. So all four of them were steaming. They linked hands and swore. "BLEEP-ING BLEEP TO HIGH HADES!!!!" they chanted in bold tilting caps with an exclamation point for each of them. The grass around them scorched and a small fire broke out.

The day mare appeared. "Don't do that!" her speech balloon exclaimed. "It's bad for the environment."

The four humans stood still and silent. This was the contact they had come for. They let the night mare handle it.

Imbri's speech balloon appeared over her head. "Mairzy Doats! It's me, Night Mare Imbrium!"

Mairzy froze in place. "Imbri! I didn't recognize you in human cloth-ing. I thought you retired years ago. What are you doing here?"

Now Imbri manifested in equine form. "I did retire. But something came up."

"You, too? We're having a horrible time."

"So I understand. The Stallions got switched."

"Yes! Now we day mares have to deliver bad dreams. It's awful! But what can we do? The Stallion's word is law."

"My human companions have a mission. They don't know what it is, but it just might be to switch the Stallions back. But they need a day mare. Are you interested?"

Mairzy considered. "I would do anything to get my sweet dreams back."

"You would have to take a human host."

Mairzy reared back, her hooves flashing sparks. "Anything but that!"

"They ride in a very nice boat with a fiery sail."

"I have seen it in passing. Would I get to ride in that?"

"Yes. They stock excellent oats."

Mairzy wavered. "I do like oats."

"And you just might save the Day Stallion from his horror. I suspect he would be rather pleased with you."

A smaller picture flickered within Mairzy's speech balloon, showing a handsome stallion getting wind of her. Jess realized that individual day mares probably got little direct attention from the Stallion. She was having her own little day dream, perhaps allowed because she did not have to deliver it elsewhere. "I—"

"So you'll do it," Imbri said decisively. "For the good of Xanth."

"For the good of Xanth," Mairzy agreed as the inset pictured stallion sniffed her tail. "But do you have a human host?"

"Yes. My host's friend Myst." Imbri indicated the girl.

"A child! But day dreams are not limited to the Adult Conspiracy."

"They bypass it," Imbri said. "You know that. Dreams can't be censored, not even naughty ones."

"Especially naughty ones," Mairzy said.

"This girl really likes horses. We won't tell if you don't tell."

"I suppose . . ."

"Take her hand," Imbri said, nodding to Myst.

Myst extended her hand. The day mare put a fore-hoof to it, and faded out. Her speech balloon popped out of existence.

"Are you there, Mairzy?" Imbri asked.

Myst's expression changed, becoming oddly equine. "I am here," she said without a balloon.

"And how is your host?"

Myst's features reappeared. "I'm fine! She's nice."

"She's a horse," Magnus said.

"That's what I said."

Jess saw that the merger was compatible.

"Who will run Abandon Hope in your absence?" Magnus asked, ever practical.

"My assistant, little Lamzy Divey. She's overdue for a promotion, anyway." Mairzy pursed her human lips and whistled. In a moment a pretty little lamb gamboled up. "Lamzy, I have to go with these human folk," Mairzy said, in a speech balloon that appeared over her head. "Can you handle the course?"

"Sure!" Lamzy replied in her own balloon. "It's easy. They're already in the mood for bad dreams."

Mairzy turned to Imbri. "Now let's see that boat."

They retired to Fibot, which became visible as they approached. They boarded, and Nia already had a basin of oats ready. She had also rearranged the children's room to make it look more like a stable. Ula, Squid, and Santo did not mind at all; they too liked horses, and were glad to see their siblings happy.

The children were thrilled to have another mare on board. Soon Imbri and Mairzy were on the deck, showing off their now-solid filly forms. Ula and Squid were getting rides, squealing with delight. The boat was floating well above the gulf course, which from this vantage looked like sausage links. The sail was quiescent, as they weren't traveling at the moment, and the adults were watching from the seats. There were four adults and only two seats, but somehow they all fit comfortably. It seemed to be part of the magic of the craft.

A small cloud formed beside the mast. "What have we here?" it demanded.

"What have we what?" Jess asked, perplexed by a talking cloud.

"Audio, ears, sound, perception, presence, absent from there—"

"Here?"

"Whatever," the cloud agreed, annoyed. "Something interesting may be happening."

"Metria!" Nia said.

"Who?" Jess asked.

"Who else?" the cloud demanded as a pair of eyes formed in its side.

"It's the demoness-small-d Metria," the peeve said. "A chronic nuisance. Ignore her and maybe she'll go away."

"Not if something interesting is happening, bird brain," the cloud said as it continued to expand. "What are two ephemeral mares doing on deck?"

"What kind of mares?" Squid asked from the back of Imbri.

The cloud was assuming the vague semblance of a curvaceous woman. "Brief, short-lived, transitory, evanescent, dreamy—wait! I used the word correctly. You've got a night and day mare here, in solid form. That's bound to be fascinating."

"Bleep," the peeve said. "We'll never get rid of her now."

"What I want to know is who the bleep is this demoness," Jess said. "This isn't any of her business, is it?"

"That's why she's interested," the peeve said. "Metria is interested in everything that isn't her business. She's a prime annoyance."

"I certainly am," the demoness said. She was now a fully formed naked nymph. The children would have been interested in the peek, except that they were girls and the boy was gay. Had the demoness known that? Still, it was an annoyance.

"You know how to get rid of her," Nia murmured to Jess.

Oh. Jess got up and approached Metria. "You fascinate me," she said. "I want to know everything about you. I'm sure you have a phenomenal story to tell."

The demoness looked at her. "As if I could ever take you seriously," she said, and faded out.

"That curse does have its uses," Magnus remarked.

But Jess wondered whether it had been too easy. Had the demoness really gone, or did she merely want them to think she had gone?

Regardless, they now had their mares. But where should they go from here?

Chapter 5

PRINCESSES

"Where, indeed," Magnus agreed. "Normally in a fantasy adventure, which is what this seems to be, they assemble the cast of characters, then they tackle their mission together. Maybe that's what we have to do."

"And we still have two princesses to find," Jess said.

"I understand that Ula has been known to host one."

"I'll fetch her," Myst said eagerly. "Imbri is curious, too."

In perhaps a moment and three quarters, plus an instant or two, Myst was back with Ula. "Yes, I host Princess Kadence," Ula said. "She's my age, ten, when she visits."

"She's not ten at other times?" Jess asked with a hint of irony.

"No. She's only one year old now. But she visits from nine years in the future, when she's ten."

"Isn't there a certain, well, conflict?" Magnus asked. "What about paradox?"

"I don't know. She stays away from her baby self, because it might mess up her time line, and that would affect Kadence. It's only her spirit visiting, anyway. Maybe that doesn't count."

"If she's satisfied, then I think we must be satisfied," Magnus said. "Especially since we may need her to complete our complement."

"Oh, you don't have to compliment her. She mostly keeps her royalty low key, with us. She just wants friends."

Magnus smiled. "I used a similar sounding word. Compl-E-ment, not compl-I-ment. It means being part of a, well, group."

"Oh," Myst said somewhat blankly. "Okay."

"Are Princess Kadences's visits random, or can you summon her?"

"Neither. She comes when she chooses, but she checks every so often to see if there's a reason."

"Would our mysterious mission be a reason?"

Ula's features shifted subtly. "Yes," she said in a new voice.

"Hello, Princess Kadence!" Magnus said. "I am Magnus, and this lady is Jess. She is cursed so that nobody takes her seriously, though she is a serious person. That's why I am doing the talking at the moment."

"Now that is interesting," Kadence said. "May I touch you, Jess?"

Jess shrugged. "If you wish. But the contact may repel you."

"We shall see." Kadence held out her hand.

Jess took it—and immediately felt a subtle but amazing power. "You're a Sorceress!"

"I am. All descendants of Great Grandpa Bink are. My talent is Alignment, making things align to a beat, or a cadence; in that manner organizing them."

"But you . . . what I'm feeling—"

"I am aligning you to my frame of reality. I can take you seriously, at least while I am touching you."

Jess laughed ruefully. "I wish you could hold my hand while I'm kissing Magnus!"

"I could, and he would take you seriously. But I suspect you want adult privacy, and I'm a child."

And there was the flaw: the bleeping Adult Conspiracy. "At any rate, according to the Good Magician, we need to have two princesses in our complement. That is—"

"In your group," Kadence said. She smiled, and it was a princessly smile. "No, I did not know the word. I got it from Ula."

"Are you interested, Princess?" Magnus asked.

Kadence eyed him with an expression not entirely childlike. "To work with you, handsome man? That could be interesting."

Oh, no! It seemed it was not just grown women who threw themselves at Magnus. The girl was only ten years old, like her host, but she was a princess. They might follow different rules. She was remarkably mature for her age. What would happen if the girl Sorceress physically touched Magnus? That power of alignment . . .

Then the figure shifted back to Ula. "Kadence gets crushes, as girls do. But she's smart enough to know they are largely meaningless, just passing fancies. She doesn't take them seriously. She had one on Dell last year, and that passed."

"That is good to know," Magnus said. "I like children, but not in that way."

"She understands." Now Ula eyed him. "But there is something about you. I feel it myself."

"It's my talent," he said. "To make things come together compatibly. Maybe it is related to the Princess's talent of Alignment. Women do tend to respond to it. You are a girl, but soon enough you will be a woman, and your reactions are orienting. But I have every intention of being true to Jess, even if I can't take her seriously."

Jess was relieved to hear that. Magnus was an honest man. That was one of the myriad things she liked about him. If only she could—but she couldn't.

Then the girl's aspect shifted again. "I understand," Kadence echoed. "Apart from that, I do believe your mission is important. I can sense that we are approaching a nexus that could be vitally relevant to the welfare of the Land of Xanth, and you, Jess, are in its center. I will join you, though I don't promise to remain in this host all the time."

"You'll take other hosts?" Jess asked, alarmed.

Kadence paused, then touched her hand to get serious. "No. This is my only host currently. It's that I do have a life of my own, in my own time, much of which is public, and my folks would be annoyed if I were absent too much. Princesses can have a hard time getting much privacy. As it is, my parents are not completely sanguine about my time traveling. But Ula will let me know if there is something urgent, and I will come."

"We appreciate that, Princess," Magnus said, and Jess saw the way his speech compelled the girl's attention. She might understand how crushes came and went, but there were nervous aspects. "You mentioned a nexus. It seems we do have a mission that needs to be accomplished without undue delay. But we may still need one more princess. Is this something you can help us with?"

"Yes, I believe I can," Kadence said. "My cousin Aria, Princess Melody's daughter, is my age. We play together often, and understand each other pretty well. There are times when she feels similarly stifled by the show business that is royalty. In fact she envies me my connection here. I believe she would participate, if there is a suitable host."

"Um, Ula, Win and Myst are taken as hosts," Squid said. "That leaves me. I'd love to be a princess!"

"Then let's try it," Kadence said. "I will fetch her." She faded, and Ula returned.

"Um, about you—" Ula said. "There may be a complication."

"No, I'm glad to do it," Squid said.

"What I mean is—"

Kadence returned. "Take my hand," she told Squid. "I will guide her in, this first time. After this she will know the way."

Squid extended her hand. Kadence took it.

Squid's aspect changed.

"Oops," she said in a new voice. "This isn't going to work." The aspect changed back.

Squid burst into tears. "I wanted to be a princess!"

Jess wanted to comfort her, but knew she couldn't do it because of the curse.

Then Kadence put a hand on Jess's shoulder. The power manifested.

Jess brought Squid into a comforting hug, and let her cry against her other shoulder.

After a suitable interval, Squid recovered without leaving Jess's embrace. "I didn't mean to make a scene," she said. "It was just—"

Now Kadence spoke to her, while leaving her hand on Jess's shoulder. "Squid, there is something I regret I did not think of in time. It is not that you are not a worthy person. It is that the requirements for hosting are rather stringent. The gender must match, which is why Santo wouldn't do. The age must match, which is why neither Jess nor Nia would do. You are fine in those respects. But also the species must match, and you are not human. The parameters are skewed. It's like trying to fit a square house on a triangular base. It just doesn't work."

"I understand," Squid said. "Sometimes I forget I'm not human."

"We are sorry," Kadence said. "We did not mean to tease you. I know you from my prior visits here. You're a good person. Just not suitable in this particular manner."

"I know." Squid drew herself from Jess's embrace and went off by herself.

Jess hated the situation. The girl was being good about it, but she was hurting.

"Maybe we can make it up to her, some way," Magnus said. "But right now we need another host."

A bulb flashed over Win's head. "Noe!"

"No?" Magnus asked.

"No, not no. Noe. Santo's girlfriend. She's eleven. That's close enough, isn't it?"

"Noe," Kadence repeated. "Yes, I believe she would do. She's a good girl. But we'd have to fetch her."

"Santo's girlfriend?" Magnus asked. "I thought he was gay."

"He is," Win said. "But Noe understands. She gives him cover from folk who *don't* understand."

Magnus spread his hands. "You know her. I don't. If she's what we need, we should talk to her. Where is she?"

"On another planet," Win said. "The World of Three Moons."

"Another planet!"

Win smiled. "Right next door, for us. Now you'll see Santo in action."

"The one who makes holes?"

"The same. I'll go tell him."

"She's teasing you," Ula said, reappearing. "Santo makes big holes."

Dell and Nia came on the scene. "Win says we need Noe," Nia said.

"For a host for Princess Aria," Magnus said. "But is she really on another world?"

"She really is. But we go there routinely on behalf of Queen Jenny, who has friends there. Win and Santo will handle it."

Magnus bounced a look off Jess and shut up. Jess agreed: it seemed best just to wait and see what occurred.

Not long later, it did occur. They watched on deck as Santo focused and a giant hole in the sky appeared before the boat. A hole between worlds? He was a Magician, or close to it! Jess was amazed, as he had never said anything about it. He was, it seemed, a modest boy.

Then Win blew the boat through the hole. On the other side was a completely different world, one with a plaid sky and three moons colored white, black, and red respectively. But that was not the oddest thing.

Each moon had its own orbit. The white moon circled the world around the equator, which seemed reasonable enough. The black moon orbited around the poles; Jess could see the contrails of its prior passages, at right angles to the white moon, and passing neatly over each pole. The red moon orbited slantwise, crossing the orbits of each of the others.

Apart from those details it seemed to be a fairly normal world, with seas, lands, fields, jungles, mountains and rivers.

They sailed toward a small house at the edge of a jungle. The peeve flew down to the house. In two-and-a-quarter moments the inhabitants emerged; a woman and eleven year old girl. "Santo!" the girl cried, waving vigorously. Santo leaned over the rail and waved back. He looked happy.

Win guided the craft down to land. The girl came running toward them, her hair flaring in the breeze of an approaching storm, and Santo jumped out to meet her. The two collided in a big hug. They clearly were thrilled to see each other.

Was he really gay? Jess decided that probably he was, as he had little reason to lie about that. He just liked this girl as a friend.

The two separated and faced the boat. "This is my girlfriend Noe," Santo said. Jess saw that her hair and eyes were the color of hope. "She is not the prettiest, smartest, or luckiest person, but she will do. Then, to Noe: "You know my siblings and loco parents. Here also are my other sister Myst, and her loco parents Magnus and Jess. They're on a mission for the Good Magician."

"Hello, loco and sibling," Noe said, suddenly shy.

"They need you for something very special."

"Sure. Will I get to ride on Fibot?"

"Yes. They need you to host the spirit of a princess, the way Ula does."

Noe clapped her hands in glee. "I'll do it!"

"But will your family go for it?"

Noe hesitated. "They may take some persuading."

"So we'd better ask them."

"Start with the adults," Noe said. She seemed wary of pleading her own case to her mother.

Jess and Magnus joined with Dell and Nia and walked to the house. Noe's mother came out to meet them. She was of course a generation older than her daughter, with hair and eyes the color of experience. "What elicits this visit, Dell and Nia?" she asked.

"Noleta, these are Magnus and Jess," Nia said. "They are on a mission for the Good Magician. They require another princess."

"More than Kadence?" The approaching storm was echoed in her countenance.

"Kadence's cousin Aria, the same age."

Noleta nodded. "And she'll need a host of similar age." Experience was evidently a good teacher.

"She tried Squid, but needs a human."

"Will you treat Noe as you treat Ula?"

"Yes, of course. She's Family."

"This princess—is she of good character?"

"We don't know her yet," Nia said. "But she's of a good family."

"I'd better meet her."

Nia signaled Ula, who came forward. "Tell Kadence to bring Aria." Then she signaled Noe. "Princess Aria will talk with your mother."

The girl was silent, knowing that the decision was out of her hands.

A light rain began, as if signaling Noleta's mood. They ignored it.

Ula changed. Kadence was present. "I can assure you that Cousin Aria is a responsible princess, as I am."

"As if that suffices."

Kadence laughed. "You know me too well, Mother. No. I am a typical girl when away from my station. So is Aria. So is Noe."

Noleta was plainly reluctant, but she thawed slightly, evidently liking Kadence. "What's her talent?"

"She sings."

The woman thawed a bit more. "Noe would like to sing, but we can't afford training."

"She could learn from Aria." Kadence reached out her hand to take Noe's hand. "She's here."

Noe's expression changed. "Hello, all."

"Aria," Kadence said. "This is Noe's mother Noleta." She gestured to the others. "Magnus and Jess, who have the Quest. Myst, the other sibling from the future." Then, to them: "This is Princess Aria, from my time. Her talent is singing."

Now the rain was thickening, threatening to soak them all. But they had to complete the introduction, lest they lose permission.

"Let me demonstrate," Aria said. Then she broke into song, a children's ditty. "Rain, rain, go away! Come again some other day."

Jess felt the power of her sorcery surrounding them. Not only was the simple melody beautiful, it was intense.

The rain fled.

If the princess could do that with a childish melody, what might she do with a real song? Jess saw that the others were similarly impressed. For it was Noe's body doing it; the princess was with her only in spirit.

Noleta capitulated. She could not deny her daughter this phenomenal experience. No mother could.

Noe reappeared. "Thanks, mom!" she exclaimed, hugging Noleta.

So it was that Noe joined them on the boat. Jess and Magnus chatted with Santo while the arrangements were being made.

"We were surprised when we learned you had a girlfriend," Jess said. "But Noe seems like a very nice girl."

"She is," he agreed. "Here is the thing: I don't want to have to constantly justify my orientation to strangers, and she shields me from that. She will soon enough be a young woman, a rather pretty one, and she doesn't want to have to constantly fend off too-friendly boys, so this makes sense for her, too. It isn't that I hate girls or she hates boys; they're fine as friends, for now, and I love my sisters. We just don't want to have to be romantic with them. So Noe and I hug and kiss only in public."

"But you know the princesses are other people," Jess said. "They may have ideas of their own."

"Yes. Kadence regards me as a bit of a challenge. But Magnus is more of one for her."

"More of one," Jess agreed morosely.

"And what of Aria?" Magnus asked.

"She'll be after us both," Santo said. "To rival her cousin. They know better, but they're impulsive children. They want to try things just to see if they can do them, like intriguing boys or even grown men."

Jess saw that Santo, only twelve years old himself, was a pretty sharp observer. Maybe his orientation made him more objective about romantic relations.

"I hope we can identify and complete our mission quickly," Magnus said.

"Meanwhile you will fake it with Jess, with her cooperation, just as I do with Noe."

"And if the princess comes when you're faking it with Noe?" Jess asked.

"I'm terrified," Santo admitted. "Because Aria will know I'm not responding to her, and I don't want a Sorceress mad at me. Especially one I have to kiss in public."

"You do have a case," Magnus agreed.

Nia emerged from the boat and approached them. "I believe we're ready to sail back to Xanth proper," she said. "But there's a complication."

"We don't need any more of those," Magnus said as they boarded the boat.

"A local villager saw the boat arrive, and caught on that Noe would be departing on it. They want a farewell show. She really can't turn them down; they're her friends."

Magnus sighed. "We'll do a show."

"I didn't know they cared," Noe said a trifle wistfully as they settled in the main room.

"You will have to participate," Jess said.

The girl laughed. "Yes, that would be a joke."

There it was again. "Ula, could I borrow Princess Kadence? Just the touch of her hand."

Ula came to her, her features shifting. She put her hand on Jess's arm. It was Kadence's touch; Jess felt its hidden power. "Thank you."

Santo nodded, understanding what was happening.

Jess tried again. "Noe, you have to participate, because this show is in honor of you."

Now the child took her seriously. "Sorry; I thought you were joking. But I have no idea how to do one of your shows. I would only mess it up."

"They are highly informal. Magnus tells the players what to do, and speaks their lines for them. You could be the lead character."

"Oh no!" Noe protested, appalled. "I would perish of stage fright!"

"She's right," Santo said. "She's all right person to person, but public scenes make her nervous."

Jess considered. This was a malady many folk suffered from. It resembled her curse in its way. Then a bulb flashed over her head. "But Princess Aria surely does not get stage fright. She could take over, and the audience would think it was you."

Noe's features shifted. "I am not sure of that," Aria said. "My manner differs from hers."

Bleep! Jess focused again, and a dimmer bulb flashed. "Maybe a non-speaking part. She could just be there, looking just like herself even if it was the princess."

"Looking just like a dummy," Noe said sourly.

"She needs to play a significant role," Santo said. "So the villagers can applaud her."

There was the crux of it. The princess could play a role without stage fright, but was not the one the villagers wanted to see. How could Noe play a role herself?

Then a third bulb flashed, brighter than the others. "She could sing!"

Noe brightened. "I do like to sing. Then she dimmed. "But not alone. I sing in a chorus. That gives me company so I'm not facing the audience alone."

"We don't have a chorus," Magnus said. "I speak the roles, and I'm not a singer."

Aria appeared. "I can sing solo. But I don't know the local songs. That would give it away."

Bleep again! But then Kadence spoke. "She could hum! That's Ula's idea; she gets them unexpectedly. That would not give away anything."

"She could hum to the mood of the scene," Magnus said. "Could you do that, Aria?"

"Readily," the princess agreed. "I love the emotions in music. Humming evokes them, too."

"Then I think we've got it," Magnus said. "Let me go over it with you, Aria, so you know exactly what to expect."

"Of course," the princess agreed, sending him an evocative look. "I will be happy to work closely with you."

Bleep, Jess thought. But what could she do? It was her idea to have Noe participate.

Santo glanced at her with perfect understanding. That hardly helped.

Aria glanced at Squid, who was hovering unhappily in the background. Jess knew why: she had hoped to be the host of the princess, so that she would be the center of attention, at least vicariously. This was what she was missing. "Squid, may I talk with you first?"

That caught Squid off-guard. "I guess." She came across and took a seat beside Jess, as if seeking mute support.

Aria pulled up another chair. "Squid, I am sorry about what happened before. I couldn't use you as a host, but that does not mean you are not a nice person."

"I'm an alien animal."

Aria put a hand on Squid's arm, much as Kadence did on Jess's arm. Jess knew that though her magic talent was different, the touch still had phenomenal impact. She saw Squid thaw, emotionally. "You are technically an alien animal, yes, but I touched your essence, briefly, and know that you are the kind of person I would like to have as a friend. That is feasible even if hosting is not."

Squid was amazed, as was Jess. "But you're a princess! Why would you want anything to do with me?"

Aria smiled. "Let me tell you something about being a princess. At my home, nine years in your future, I am constantly surrounded by servants, courtiers, instructors, and other royals. Everything is structured. I must play my role perfectly, all the time, or I will soon regret it. I have almost no time to myself. That is one reason this visit to your time appeals to me; I can associate with others on a more even basis. At home I think I have only one friend, Kadence, who is in a similar situation. She is friends with the siblings, and with you. But I am new to this scene. I have yet to make friends, and don't really know anyone here except Kadence. I am a stranger here even if I don't look it because of my host. I am from another time and another station." Now she took Squid's hand. "Squid, you know how it is to be different even if you look the same. You have adapted to the challenge. You can teach me so much, if you care to. When no one else understands, a friend understands. When no one else wants to help, a friend helps. When others judge, a friend does not judge. I desperately need a friend." Now there were tears in her eyes. "I know this is asking a lot of you, considering how briefly we have known each other. But you are my age and distance from the others, albeit in a different direction. Squid, please, please, be my friend."

Squid melted. A glacier would have melted! "Yes."

"Oh thank you! Thank you!" The two embraced. Jess knew that was the end of any resentment Squid might have had. Jess had no reason to doubt the princess's sincerity, but she also appreciated the art of her presentation. Aria was a mistress of persuasion.

Thereafter the two associated constantly. Anything about this time and situation Aria found confusing, Squid helped her understand. With this guidance, the princess soon melded with the group, so that it could be difficult to tell when it was Aria and when it was Noe. Santo, at first wary of Aria, gradually relaxed; she was not out to impress him or embarrass him, and she faded out when he needed to make a scene with Noe. Squid helped similarly when Aria worked with Magnus, preparing for the show. Jess, too, was relieved. It was almost as if the princess now had a chaperon.

They did the show. This time, by popular demand, Noe participated, in the manner they had crafted: Princess Aria, anonymous, provided background music. She could hum as well as she could sing, and it did lend conviction to the activities.

Magnus introduced himself, and the music made him seem twice as imposing. Jess watched and listened with mixed emotions. She loved that it was working, but feared that it was working almost too well. She had felt the power of a Sorceress herself, and Aria was another Sorceress. She was only ten or eleven, depending on whether she was the princess or her host, but—

Magnus avoided the pretty girls who tried to mob him, selected volunteers and took them aside for briefing. Then Jess took the floor with her stories of romantic disaster, and the music enhanced those, too. The princess really was good at this. The audience was pleased, thinking that Noe was doing it.

"So I am being more careful with my third boyfriend," Jess continued as the music assumed a confidential tone. "I'm not telling him, so he can't laugh his head off or puke all over my never-mind. He is my secret love. No one will ever know."

She paused to glance significantly at Magnus, who was facing away from her as he talked with the volunteers. The music broke off, as if protecting the secret.

"But maybe at night, when he is sleeping, I will come to him and sneak a kiss." Now the music turned romantically dreamy. "When he wakes he may remember it, but won't take it seriously, of course." The music dissipated, no longer serious.

When Magnus returned to the stage, he paused as if taken by an errant thought. "You know, last night I dreamed that a nymph came to my bed and kissed me. It was so real! But why would a nymph ever do that? I almost wonder if—" The music formed a tremulous question. He glanced in Jess's direction, but she happened to be facing away so was theoretically unaware of it. "No, I can't take that seriously!" The music crashed.

The audience loved it, partly because it seemed to be Noe onstage performing, as well as their own volunteers, and partly because her music was so persuasive. They really felt for this secret love.

Then when the show was finished, and Boy had recovered Girl and hummed her a wonderful aria of love, and the show was shutting down, Magnus retired behind an opaque screen to rest. But the lighting was such that his form cast a silhouette on the screen. Then came the silhouette of Jess, sneaking quietly in to join him. She bent down to kiss him, and the screen showed it plainly. The music crescendoed at the touch. Fortunately he didn't wake as the light faded.

The audience applauded as it dissipated. They liked that concluding touch.

"You do enhance the show," Magnus told Aria as they sailed into the sky so that no more villagers could petition them. "You have the touch. Great job!"

"Thank you," Aria said, eyeing him speculatively before fading out. Jess looked away.

The boat took off, and Santo made a Hole, and Win guided the craft through it. Soon they were back in Xanth. "Now I suspect you have your full complement," Nia said. "Let's relax the night, and you can figure out your mission in the morning."

They were satisfied to do that. The two princesses took a room together, having much to catch up on, joined by Squid. Win came to join Myst in the room with Magnus and Jess, so that the two mares could catch up on things similarly.

"Something Santo said," Magnus remarked. "About hugging and kissing Noe only in public. Would that work for us?"

Jess hugged and kissed him. "Yuck!" the two girls exclaimed in unison.

They laughed. If it looked real enough to evoke that reaction, they were making progress.

Jess slept. She had an awful dream. She woke screaming.

"Jess, what is it?" Magnus asked, holding her close.

"I had a bad dream! It terrified me."

"And I know you well enough to know that you are not being facetious." He turned to the two girls. "She had a bad dream."

Win and Myst were chagrined. "We must have done it," Win said. "I hold the night mare." Then her face and voice changed. "I didn't do it. I can deliver only good dreams now."

They looked at Myst. She burst into tears. "I did it!" Mairzy said. "I got this dream to deliver, I didn't know what it was but thought it was pleasant, the way they always were. I forgot how it's changed."

"But here aboard Fibot we are protected from bad dreams," Magnus said. "You have no connection to your errant stallion. Where did you get the dream?"

"Squid gave it to me." Myst paused, surprised. "We were having a snack while the others were sleeping, and she had it, so she passed it along to me. It didn't occur to me that there was anything wrong with it."

Magnus shook his head. "I think we had better find out where Squid got it. She's not a normal dream carrier."

This was indeed a mystery. Jess's horror was fading as she dressed, but she remembered the dream clearly. It might have been delivered by the day mare, but it was definitely a bad night dream.

"This is serious business," Magnus said. "It seems there has been a breech in Fibot security. Maybe it relates to our mission."

"Our unknown mission," Jess agreed. She was of course ignored.

Soon they were meeting with Dell and Nia and the others. Nia took over the questioning. "Squid, where did you get that bad dream?"

Squid was in tears, too. "I—I don't know, exactly. Princess Aria came to me in the night, really upset. She touched me—and then she faded out, and only Noe was left. I—I was holding the dream. I guess she gave it to me. I didn't know what to do with it, so I gave it to Myst, for Mairzy."

"It was for Jess," Mairzy said. "So I delivered it. Maybe I shouldn't have."

Nia focused on Noe. "We need to question Aria."

"She's gone," Noe said. "I was just getting to know her, and now she's totally absent."

"So is Kadence," Ula said. "She was upset, too. She left the same time Aria did, and there's been no sign of them since."

"This is curious," Nia said. "Those princesses are not mean spirited, no pun intended. Why would Aria do a nasty thing like that?"

"I'm sure she didn't mean to," Nia said. "I think she was caught by surprise, and had to go instantly, along with Kadence. She was talking with Squid when it happened, maybe about to explain what she had, and I guess she just had to ditch the dream somewhere and go."

"But it was marked for Jess," Mairzy said. "It was not an accident."

"Something is rotten in the marked den," Magnus said grimly. "There's a smell."

Nia looked at Jess. "The key must be in the dream itself. Can you describe it?"

"Oh, yes," Jess said. "It was a vision of the future, where the two princesses come from. Something utterly horrible was happening."

The others laughed, not taking her seriously.

"I think I need Kadence."

"And she's gone," Magnus said. "Tell me, and I will translate." This was something he had learned to do, though it was not easy for him.

"I don't know whether I should say it, because—"

Magnus relayed that.

"I think you had better," Nia said grimly. "I doubt that this mischief is coincidence. Your mission requires two princesses, and this seems to involve them."

"Yes," Jess agreed. Then she described her dream, with Magnus rephrasing her words so that the others could accept them. "I was in the princesses' time, and it was awful. Ragna Roc—"

"Who?" Nia asked sharply.

"He's a big bird who—"

"I know who he is. We had a peripheral brush with him last year. But he is safely confined."

"No he isn't," Jess said.

"Hold a moment." Nia faced the others. "For those who don't know, Ragna is a roc bird who considers himself to be a god. He tried to take over Xanth over a decade ago. His power is rendering real people into illusions; they can be seen, but no longer are able to act in the real world; they can't touch or be touched. Just about the worst thing that could happen to Xanth would be for Ragna to get loose again. And it may be he has, if we can believe Jess's bad dream." She took a deep breath. "Go on, Jess."

"In my dream, Ragna somehow got loose, and resumed his conquest of Xanth, in our near future. The three princesses, Melody, Harmony, and Rhythm, tried to stop him, before, so they were at the top of his list for revenge. They may have been abolished—that is, deleted, rendered into illusions—and now Ragna is going after their children. That is, Melody's daughter Aria and Rhythm's daughter Kadence. I thought it was just a bad dream, but—"

"It's not a dream," Nia said. "It's a vision of the future. That's why it didn't go through regular dream channels. That must also be why the two princesses vacated so abruptly; they had to flee for their lives before Ragna found them."

"And all Aria could do on such short notice was leave the story with her friend Squid," Magnus concluded. "If this is not just a dream."

"I don't think it is," Nia said grimly.

"I think now we finally know what our mission is. Not the exchange of stallions; that may be just a distraction to keep us from the real one. We have to stop Ragna Roc from escaping before it happens. We must have time, as we are in the princesses' past."

"And just how do we do that?" Jess asked.

Magnus's smile was a rictus. "Consider it a challenge."

Chapter 6

BAD DREAMS

Nia looked around. "Does anyone have any notion, however silly or far-fetched it may sound? We need a basis to start from. Even nonsense will do."

Squid raised a hand tentatively. "I—there is one other thing. I can't make sense of it, so maybe shouldn't mention it."

"Mention it," Nia said shortly.

"Aria said as she fled 'Great Uncle Dolph.' That's all."

"That's Prince Dolph," the peeve said in Jess's voice, because it was perched on her shoulder. She hadn't noticed until it spoke. "Now an old fogy of forty-five. He has nothing to do with anything. Maybe his nieces like him."

"Isn't he a shape changer?" Magnus asked. "I've heard of him."

"He can become anything," the peeve said. "He probably gives the girls dragon rides. That must be why they like him."

"I don't think so," Jess said. Then, before they could laugh her off, she looked at Magnus.

"She says she doesn't think so," Magnus said. "I appreciate why: Princess Aria is a serious and thoughtful girl. She's not given to incidental irrelevancies. This must be a hint, maybe an important one. All she had time for."

Now the others nodded. "We need to know more about Prince Dolph, then," Nia said.

Tata's screen flickered. "Delivered in the year 1074, or rather, found under a cabbage leaf; the stork evidently didn't have time to dally," the peeve translated. "King Dor and Queen Irene were satisfied, regardless, though his older sister Ivy had doubts. In 1083 at the age of nine he set off on a quest to find Good Magician Humfrey, who had disappeared. He was accompanied by the adult walking skeleton Marrow Bones. Captured by Mela Merwoman, who thought to hang on to him until he came of age, then marry him so she could be a princess. Wins free and gets betrothed to princess Nada Naga. Also gets betrothed to Electra, and marries her when she turns eighteen, letting Nada go. Their children are the twins Dawn and Eve. That's in this reality; in other timelines he marries Princess Taplin and—"

"Thank you, Tata," Nia said. "I believe we have sufficient background. I gather Prince Dolph has retired into nonentity. That leaves open the question of why his great niece saw fit to give his name as a message to us."

"Maybe she just meant that she wished she could have another dragon ride with him," Squid said. "I shouldn't have mentioned it."

Nia gave her a steely eye. "She told you for a reason. Stop doubting and find that reason."

Tata's screen flickered. "There is a codicil," the peeve said. "Prince Dolph was present at the wedding of Cheiron and Chex Winged Centaur when all the winged monsters swore to protect their coming foal Che Centaur and his ward Sim Chick, son of the Simurgh, not yet hatched, from harm. Dolph counted as being a winged monster because of his dragon form. He was the most important participant in that oath. His action would change the history of Xanth, in due course."

Nia Nodded. "Now that has a stronger smell of relevance. Have we seen Dolph change the history of Xanth yet?"

The screen flickered. "Only slightly," the peeve said.

"So perhaps the major change is yet to come?"

The screen flickered. "Data insufficient."

"I will take that as a yes: it hasn't yet happened." Nia looked around. "Does it make sense that this crisis the princesses face could be that history that needs changing?"

A look circled. In fact it looped about several times until pretty much knotted. It did seem to make sense.

"So is Prince Dolph on the case now?" Dell asked.

Tata's screen flickered. "No. He seems to have forgotten about it."

"Then we should go remind him!" Jess flared.

Everyone laughed. Then Magnus repeated it, and no one laughed.

"I think we had better set sail for the residence of Prince Dolph," Nia said grimly. "That must be at least part of our mission."

Tata, the peeve, and Win went topside to get the craft under way. Jess heard the clank as they weighed the anchor; apparently they needed to be sure it was intact before sailing.

"Oh!" Ula said. Then her features changed. "We're here," Princess Kadence said.

"Thanks to your decision," Princess Aria said from Noe's mouth.

"You're back!" Squid screamed, running to hug her. Then there was a brief medley of pleasant confusion as the children gathered in close.

"What happened?" Myst asked breathlessly.

"That's an unpleasant story," Aria said.

"Tell it, anyway," Nia said grimly.

Aria began to talk.

Princess Aria was scheduled to sing at the ceremony of the twentieth anniversary of the confinement of Ragna Roc, where her cousin Princess Kadence had been instrumental. Kadence had had to travel to a time before her own delivery, or for that matter, the marriage of her parents, so as to use her talent to make the undeleted egg that was to hold the big bird. It had worked, and Xanth had been saved, and Kadence had returned to her own time, still a child.

Ragna Roc had regarded himself as a god whose natural destiny was to conquer Xanth and anything else that might interest him. His talent was deletion: anything he focused on, he could render into illusion. The people and things he deleted remained visible, but no longer had any substance. Anyone who opposed him was instantly deleted. Only he could undelete them, which he rarely did. Why should he bother? He deleted whole villages, and the people there continued much as they always had, except that they were now real only to themselves, and could not affect the real world. A few tried, but were dismissed as ghosts, which they pretty much were. The survivors soon got the message: obey Ragna, and worship him as a god, and they would prosper.

The big bird had a castle made for him from rock candy, a beautiful edifice. He had all manner of servants, and indeed, it was not a bad life for them. His influence expanded steadily. He had spies to ferret out any likely opposition, which he deleted before it manifested.

Until the triplet princesses, Melody, Harmony, and Rhythm, then twelve years old, decided to stop him. Any one of them was a Sorceress in her own right; any two of them together squared their power, and the three of them together cubed it. Only capital D Demons had more magic power than that, so they figured they could handle the roc. Unfortunately they were mistaken; they were children, while he was adult; their power was still forming, while his was mature. They faced each other in his rock candy castle, and while neither he nor they moved physically, the castle began to melt from the invisible power of the warring magic.

And Ragna was too much for them. Princess Melody fell, then Princess Harmony. When Princess Rhythm fell, her secret boyfriend (because she was underage) Cyrus Cyborg tricked the big bird into entering the big undeleted eggshell Kadence had crafted with her talent, and sealed him in. The thing was that any substance Ragna deleted, then undeleted, could no longer be deleted; it was like ashes that could no longer be burned. So he was trapped by his own refuse and could not escape.

Kadence had saved Xanth. But since she did not yet exist, technically, she had to go, and Cyrus was banished for violating the Adult Conspiracy. But Rhythm still loved him, and when she became of age, she married him, and Kadence came to be. Aria herself came to be about the same time, the daughter of Princess Melody, and they became firm playmates and friends.

Now it was the twentieth anniversary of that great event, and Kadence was to be honored for her vital role. Aria was to sing the story for all to hear, which was why she had studied it and knew it so well. They had overstayed their visit to the past, and had to depart suddenly when they remembered.

Only to discover disaster. Somehow Ragna Roc had escaped, and come secretly to Castle Roogna, lurking. Then as the three princesses and Kadence and Aria took the stage, the big bird appeared.

SQUAWK!

"Now you will pay!" a woman cried. "I am Em Pathy, and I am Ragna Roc's minion, translator, and chief of staff. The princesses will be deleted, but others can save themselves by swearing immediate fealty to your new ruler, the Roc of Ages."

There was pandemonium as the people saw the huge bird and realized that the ultimatum was no bluff.

They had no chance to consider. "Squawk!"

"Starting with the arch-traitoress Kadence," Em translated.

The bird's huge eyes focused on Kadence.

"No!" her mother Rhythm cried, leaping to interpose herself between Kadence and the bird.

Rhythm became ghostly, her substance gone. She had been deleted.

"Get out of here, girls, both of you!" Melody called. "We'll handle this."

Aria and Kadence hesitated. This was too awful for them to assimilate instantly.

"Go!" Melody cried.

Then she turned ghostly. She, too, had been deleted.

King Ivy strode to center stage. "You can't do this!" she shouted at Ragna.

Ivy was deleted.

"Grandma!" Kadence cried, horrified anew.

"Come *on*," Aria told Kadence, grabbing her arm. "We know what to do!"

Aunt Harmony intercepted them. "I hate this, but I must go with you!" she said. "I am Queen now, by default, and must protect myself."

So she was; Harmony had long been designated the next King of Xanth. "This way," Aria said.

The three of them fled the chamber. The big bird saw them. "Squawk!"

"After them!" Em cried. "They must not escape!"

But it seemed that only Ragna Roc and Em Pathy were active. All the rest were members of the established order. They had no idea what to do, and confusion reigned.

The entire section of the castle ahead of them winked into non-existence. The stone above crashed down, no longer supported. Ragna had deleted the ground floor.

But this was an advantage of a kind. "Run through it," Aria cried. "The dust and illusion will hide us!"

So it did. They ran into the illusion of the first floor, which now concealed the reality of the fallen second floor. The two were distinguishable at close range, since they knew what to look for. They dodged around piles of real, not illusory rubble and made their way out of the castle.

And there was the moat. The moat monster lifted up its head, astonished.

"Over here!" Em called, emerging from the rubble. She had kept her eye on them, dismayingly competent.

Ragna, flying over the rubble, landed. His head turned, seeking his targets.

The moat monster recognized the bird as an enemy. It lunged, jaws gaping.

And became illusionary, only its outline remaining.

"Run around him!" Aria said. "He can't see us up close!"

They ran around and under Ragna's huge tail feathers, while the roc tried to twist in place to catch them. But of course they couldn't keep that up long.

"Hide in that rubble, where he can't see us!" Aria cried, while shaking her head no. "This way!" She ran for the rubble while the big bird was still turning in place.

But the moment they reached the cover of the rubble, Aria dodged to the side, pausing only to throw her voice to the other side. That was one of the audio tricks she had developed, at first for its novelty, then for its mischief, and finally as a means of self defense. The ability to throw her song to a far corner, so that she could seem to be coming or going while staying put.

Ragna finally oriented, his beak pointing to the rubble where Aria's voice was sounding. There was a crash as more rubble above dropped where the lower rubble had been deleted.

But Aria, Kadence, and Aunt Harmony were going in the other direction. "Under the drawbridge," Aria whispered. "Don't let him see you."

They clambered into the service ramp below the upper surface, where workmen stood to make repairs on the superstructure. Kadence and Harmony crossed while Aria sang another refrain, this time projecting it deeper into the rubble of the castle. Then she whirled and ran across herself while catching her breath.

She rejoined them at the far side. "Get into the orchard!" she said. "But stay behind trees. Make your way to the plaque for Zombie Pie."

"What?" Harmony asked. "This is no occasion for joking."

"She means it, Aunt," Kadence said. "That's where we hid the escape."

"But no one goes there except zombies," Harmony said. "It's some sort of shrine for them. Even the picture of the pie is rotting."

"Yes."

Then Harmony did a double-take. "Which would be the perfect place to hide something!"

"We'd better go there separately," Aria said. "So that we can't all be caught together."

The others nodded grimly. One might be deleted, or two, but chances were the third would make it.

They separated and flitted from trunk to trunk, hiding from the direction of the castle. In little more than a moment and a half, Aria had little idea where the other two were. Good.

Now that she was alone, she had time to catch up on the horror of what had happened. Her mother and grandmother had been deleted! Much of the castle had been destroyed. The moat monster was gone. The kingdom was in peril. Could it get any worse?

There was something else she had to do: warn the folk of the past. So that maybe they could stop this disaster before it happened. She focused on zipping back to the past, to her host there—

And found herself with Squid. In her desperate haste she had gotten the wrong one. She could stay only about a moment and a half before the wrongness cast her out, as it had before. But she didn't have time to do it again, correctly, so she did what she could. She dumped the vision of horror on Squid and labeled it for delivery to Jess, who perhaps would know what to do.

Was that enough? She feared it wasn't. So she added information about who might help them: "Great Uncle Dolph is supposed to save Xanth. This must be where he does it. Go to him." But even as she sent it, she was wrenched back to her own time. How much of that message had gotten through? She didn't know.

"They're not here," she heard Em Pathy call. "They must have escaped to the orchard. We must get them before they reach the forest beyond; we'll never find them there."

There was a blast of wind as the big bird spread his wings and flew over the moat. He looked as if he were about to crash into the trees of the orchard, but just before he landed, they dissolved into illusion, leaving him a cleared landing field.

Aria hoped that neither of her companions had happened to be in the deleted section. She also hoped that enough of her message to the past had gotten through. But she couldn't dwell on any of that at the moment. She continued flitting from trunk to trunk, now making sure to hide from the roc. Fortunately the orchard was large, surrounding the castle, so searching it all was a big chore.

Aria sent another song out behind her, and was rewarded by another blast of deletion.

"We have to be careful," Em cautioned Ragna. "If we delete indiscriminately, we won't know when we get them, and could waste a lot of energy uselessly."

That woman was entirely too smart.

Aria continued flitting, and in due course reached the plaque. Was she the only one? She went to it, looking around.

Kadence appeared. "You made it!" she said.

"But what about Aunt Harmony?"

"Present," the woman said, stepping from behind a trunk. "Now what do you girls have here that I never knew about?"

"No one knew about it, Aunt," Kadence said. "We had to keep it secret, or it might be useless."

"But what is it?"

"It's a tunnel," Aria said. She reached down to catch the edge of the rotten zombie pie, and the plaque came up in her hand, opening like a trapdoor. Which it was. Below it was a narrow stairway descending into darkness.

"It is safe?" Harmony asked.

Kadence snapped her fingers, and dim lights came on to illuminate the stairs.

"Magic is happening!" Em cried. "I sense it! Over in the other part of the orchard. They must be there!"

"Bleep that woman!" Aria swore. "Hurry!"

Kadence led the way down the stairs. Harmony followed. Aria took several steps, then turned to carefully close the trapdoor lid behind her. It wouldn't stop Ragna long, but any delay at all was valuable.

The passage leveled off. Ahead was a tunnel leading to a special destination. They hurried along it.

"But won't Ragna simply fly to its other end and nab us there?" Harmony asked.

Both girls laughed. "No," Kadence said. "It goes to another world."

"Another world!"

"It was a very special project," Aria said.

"Who made it?"

"The children of Fibot," Kadence said. "Mainly Santo and me."

"Squid helped," Aria said.

Harmony was silent, perhaps not wanting to express burgeoning confusion. She probably wasn't easy trusting her welfare to two ten-year-old nieces to begin with.

"About them," Aria said. "I sent a message back. I hope it was enough."

"You sent a message back in time?" Harmony asked. "That's dangerous, because of paradox."

"Because *this* is dangerous," Aria said. "We do need to change history."

Harmony was silent again. That seemed to be her way of agreeing.

They came to the end of the tunnel. Aria opened another zombie pie plaque, and they emerged into light.

"The sky is plaid!" Harmony exclaimed. "Whatever world is this?"

"The World of Three Moons," Aria answered.

"Three Moons! Isn't that where Princess Jenny visits?"

"Yes. We have friends here."

Harmony turned back to face the plaque. "Suppose the minions of Ragna follow us here? I realize the tunnel is too small for the big bird, but Em could use it, and other people."

"The zombies maintain it," Kadence said.

Now Harmony laughed, though it was a trifle strained. "And who is going to use a zombie tunnel?"

"Ragna can't get here," Aria said. "The royals here will welcome you to set up the Xanth government in exile, so that you can direct the resistance in safety."

"You planned this ahead? How did you know Ragna would escape?

"We hoped he wouldn't," Kadence said. "But we prepared in case he did."

Harmony looked at the plaque again. "When did you do this?"

"Nine years ago," Aria said.

"When you were babies!?"

"We had help," Kadence said. "Look, we'll tell you all about it, but let's get ourselves settled here first. You need to meet Noe's folks."

"Who?"

"Noe is my host of nine years ago," Aria said. "When she was eleven."

Harmony shut up again. They took the path through the jungle and walked the short distance to Noe's house. "Aunt Noleta!" Aria called.

Noe's mother emerged. "Do I know you?"

"I'm Princess Aria. Noe hosted me before, but now I'm here in person. We used the tunnel." She sang a fragment of an aria.

"Aria," Noleta agreed, recognizing her voice. "But why? That tunnel is only for dire emergency."

"This is that emergency," Aria said. Then she introduced her companions and quickly summarized their situation.

"Oh, my, yes," Noleta agreed. "Do come in."

"Where is Noe now?" Aria asked after they had cleaned up and been served some pie.

"She is twenty, and orienting on the dating scene. There are some nice young men, and she is attractive. Only—"

"Only she still likes Santo," Aria said.

"And he likes her," Noleta agreed. "Only not in that way."

"And if they do go their ways," Aria said, "they will have to officially break up. They don't want to do that."

"Emotions can be complicated, for the young," Noleta said. She turned to Harmony. "You will want to go to the palace and govern from there. I'm sure they will help you."

"Yes," Queen Harmony agreed. "But first I want to discover whether Bryce escaped. I can't focus on anything until I know."

"Bryce?"

"My beloved. It's another story."

"Emotions are complicated for the mature folk, too," Noleta said. She glanced at the two princesses. "And you?"

Aria exchanged a glance with Kadence. "We don't know," she said.

"You have no idea what to do, now that you have escaped deletion?"

"None," Kadence said. "It is almost as if we have been rendered illusory after all."

"Uh-oh," Harmony said. "I think I smell paradox after all. What you have to do is in the past, to prevent Ragna Roc from ever escaping. You have to act there, not here."

"Yes!" Aria said, seeing the light where a bulb hadn't quite flashed. "We'll go back now."

"Yes," Kadence agreed.

They focused on their hosts in the past. Nothing happened.

"Why isn't it working?" Aria asked.

"I think I know," Noleta said. "It is because paradox is harder to achieve than it may seem. You can't go back with the intention of changing your own present situation here. That would be paradox."

"Someone else has to make the key decisions," Harmony said, agreeing. "When you went back before, you were just entertaining yourselves, not changing history. But with the advent of Ragna Roc, that has changed. It is no longer incidental. I may be subject to the same stasis, since I am involved with you."

"But we have to do *something*!" Kadence wailed.

"Great Uncle Dolph!" Aria said. "He's the one who can do it. I did tell them that. I think. I hope."

"He would be the key," Harmony agreed. "If your friends in the past go to him, they can save Xanth. You can probably help them do it if they decide to; you just can't make decisions affecting your own timeline."

"Keep trying to return," Noleta said. "If you find an avenue, stay there. We'll take care of your bodies here."

"Keep trying," Kadence said. "It may be our only hope."

They kept trying. Then, suddenly, they made it.

"And that is why we were absent for a time," Aria concluded. "You must have decided to go to Prince Dolph, and that freed us to return."

"Your message to Squid did it," Jess said. "And the vision you sent me."

"How could she do that then, and not thereafter?" Magnus asked.

"You must have been in flux, Aria," Nia said. "Able to do just a little before paradox shut you down."

"But it was Aria's message that enabled us to make the decision that removed the paradox," he protested. "Isn't that paradox itself?"

"Maybe the fringe of it," Nia said. "As it was, it was a close call, and we still don't know the outcome. There must be decisions yet to be made, actions to be taken. Like that tunnel to the World of Three Moons you are about to make."

"I think my head is starting to swell," Jess said. But of course nobody took her seriously.

"There remains another matter," Magnus said. "The switching of the stallions. We need to know whether this is part of our quest, or irrelevant to it. It's too important simply to guess. It could mess up everything if we get it wrong."

They considered, and concluded that they did need to know. Now, while they were traveling, seemed to be the time. "In fact, I believe we should pause in our travels," Magnus said. "Because there is no point in heading for Prince Dolph if the matter of the stallion is only going to mess it up. We need to be clear before we broach him."

The others agreed. Win anchored the boat high in the air, invisible, so that it would not be disturbed while they pondered. Win, Tata, and the peeve came below.

They talked to the two mares. "Did either of you go to your stallion and ask about the switch?" Nia asked.

Win and Myst, hosting the two mares, shook their heads. "A night mare does not question her stallion," Imbri said in her speech quotes. "A mare merely does as the stallion directs."

"True for day mares, too," Mairzy said in her speech quotes. They appeared above Myst's head. "Besides, it's the wrong stallion."

"No mare questioned a stallion?" Nia asked.

Win and Myst shook their heads, speaking for the mares they hosted.

"Well, we should do it," Nia said. "There might be a simple answer."

"Oh, we couldn't," Mairzy said. "No mare would do that."

Jess saw Nia suppress a sigh of exasperation. "Well, maybe you should carry a couple of folk who will," she said. When the mares did not object, not questioning any authority, Nia looked around. "Who should ride the mares into the dream realms?"

"Only one dream realm is necessary," Magnus said. "Either stallion can answer the question, if he wants to."

Ula shrugged. "I will go," Kadence said.

Nia looked sharply at her. "Aren't you worn out if not freaked out by the horrors of your own time? This distraction would only add to your burden."

"This distraction will distract me from my burden," Kadence said. "I know that the moment I let myself relax, those horrors will crush me. I must stay busy elsewhere."

Nia nodded. "Do you feel similarly, Aria?"

Now Noe shrugged. "I think not. Maybe I am nastier than Kadence. I want revenge. If this stallion exchange relates in any way, I want to deal with it. I don't want anything to stop us from putting that ill bird away again, forever."

"Well spoken!" Magnus said.

Noe actually blushed. "Thank you," Aria said.

Jess once again suppressed her irritation. Were they deliberately flirting with each other, the princess and the showman? Of course not! Yet there was a level of her awareness that was suspicious.

"So you will be satisfied to remain on the boat and relax?" Nia asked.

"Yes. Noe is a calming influence."

Nia looked around again. "Then who else might like to tackle this spot mission?"

Jess spoke before she thought. "I would."

"Are you serious?"

Ula extended her hand. Jess took it, connecting with Kadence. "Yes."

Nia considered. "There are occasions when your curse can be advantageous. Maybe the spooks of the dream realm will be daunted. And since Kadence will be along, when you do need to be taken seriously, you can be." She looked around. No one objected.

Thus it was decided. Win and Myst became the night and day mares, respectively, in their black and white equine forms. Ula mounted Mairzy, and Jess mounted Imbri. Belatedly Jess remembered that she was not an experienced rider. "Maybe someone better at this should—" she began.

"You'll be fine," Imbri's speech balloon printed over her head. "I have had experience carrying human riders. I won't let you fall off."

"Thanks," Jess said, relieved.

"Where are we going?" Ula asked as they stepped through the hull of the boat and out into the air. "To the Day Stallion or the Night Stallion?"

Jess realized that this detail had not been discussed. "I don't want to endure another gulf course."

"Night Dream Stallion it is," Ula said, laughing. It hardly mattered whether she took Jess seriously. "Or whoever is in his place."

Imbri oriented and galloped through the sky. Mairzy followed.

"Um, is there a convenient access?" Jess asked.

"There's a portal atop Mount Neverest," Imbri's balloon printed. "That's the closest one." She seemed to have no trouble taking Jess seriously.

"You can't just, well, phase through from anywhere?"

"In my centuries as a night mare, I could, of course. But I am retired, so lack that power. But there are alternate routes, and I remember them."

They made swift progress across the sky. Jess realized that the mares could travel as fast as thought, because dreams were a form of thought. Soon the peak of a giant mountain appeared ahead.

"Wow!" Ula called. "That must be the tallest mountain in Xanth!"

Now Mairzy's speech balloon appeared, and Jess could read it, too. "Yes. It is one inch taller than Mundania's highest. Their mountain paused to rest, while ours didn't."

Jess had not realized that mountains could be competitive, not that it mattered.

They came to stand on the top. "But there's nothing here," Jess said.

"Surely you jest," Imbri's print said. She stepped forward, and a giant gourd appeared before them. The two mares walked on inside.

There was a sadly fenced yard enclosing a dismal house. Weeds grew all around the path. Not only was the scene not impressive, it was somewhat eerie. Jess felt a chill. She wished she could be well away from here.

"This is the standard opening gambit for entry to the realm of bad dreams," Imbri's print said. "The house contains all manner of spooks, ranging from ghosts to poltergeists. There are ignorant folk who find that frightening."

Jess was glad she was not one of those folk.

"We will bypass it, of course," Imbri continued. "The path we need is worse."

"Worse?" Jess asked faintly.

"It is littered with awful puns, ones hardly worth groaning at. They sicken most folk, so they avoid it. That's why it is private."

"That makes sense," Jess agreed, uncertain which was worse: a spooky house, or a pun infested path.

They followed the path. It led to a stream where big ugly fish crowded hungrily. They would have to wade through. "Carp Diem," Imbri printed. "They will seize anyone who tries to wade through by day."

"We don't want that," Jess said, shuddering. "Is there a safe way to pass?"

"Yes, for those who know it. Harvest some of those pills."

Jess dismounted and walked to the nearby pill box. She took a handful of the little pills. "Oh, they're cold!"

"They are chill pills. Toss them in the water."

Jess did. The water immediately cooled, and a thin crust of ice formed. The carp hastily swam downstream, escaping it. Jess remounted, and the two mares splashed through the icy water. One pun had driven off another. Well, that was one way to do it.

They came to a table set with dainty cups of tea. The table blocked the path. "Let me guess," Jess said, resigned. "We have to drink the tea to get by. And we won't much like it."

"That depends on which cup you choose," Imbri printed. "Once you drink it, you can lead Mairzy and me safely past the table."

Jess and Ula both dismounted and approached the tea table. Each cup was labeled. Relativi tea, bat tea, goat tea, gravi tea, uppi tea, LGB tea.

"I don't trust any of these," Ula said. "I don't want to become a relative, or a bat, or a goat."

"And I don't want to get really heavy," Jess agreed. "Or uppity, or— What's LGB?"

"I think Santo would know," Ula said. "But I'm pretty sure it's not for us."

They continued looking. "Maybe this one," Ula said. "Novel tea."

"But don't novelists get blocked?"

"I think they do. "So that's no good."

"What about this one? Naugh tea."

"Maybe."

They each took a cup and drank it. It actually tasted good.

Several young men going the other direction approached the table. "Well, now," Jess said.

One man spied them. "Girls!" he exclaimed. The others looked, too.

"Not interested," Jess said quickly. But of course he didn't take her seriously.

"My talent is metamorphosis," the man said. "Changing things to other things. I think I'll change your dresses to transparent jelly. Make you look real dreamy."

"Yeah, yeah," the other men agreed. "Dreamy."

And of course this was the realm of dreams. But the male dreams did not necessarily coincide with female dreams.

"Are you thinking what I'm thinking?" Ula asked.

"You bet," Jess agreed.

They turned around, hoisted their skirts, and flashed the boys with their panties.

The men froze, stunned.

"Oh, we shouldn't have," Ula said without regret.

"This is weird," Jess said.

"What, being naughty? That's what the tea does."

"No. It's that my panties don't fascinate men. They turn them off. I'm really not exaggerating much in my Atrocia spiel."

"And mine are too young to have much effect," Ula said. "But we're in the dream realm. Haven't you dreamed of being able to do that? I have."

"Yes, but—" Jess stopped. Maybe it did make sense. Those men weren't real, they were dream figures, reacting as they were supposed to. It wouldn't happen in real life. They really had become dreamy.

They led the mares past the table, then resumed riding. Soon they came to a flight of steps. "You don't want to take those," Imbri printed. "That's a stare way."

"Oh, the kind that looks up a girl's skirt?"

"That's a variant. To use these you must stare straight ahead, and the footing can be tricky."

"We won't take them," Jess agreed.

There was a galloping noise. "Oops!" Imbri printed. "That's a spearhead of unicorns. They'll run us down!"

"So we'll have to take the stairs, anyway?"

"No. All you need to do is distract them with interesting food."

Jess looked around. "All I see is fresh noodles and pie plants."

"They will do. Throw them on the path before the unicorns."

Jess and Ula hastily harvested a number of grass-like noodles and small pies, getting them on the path just before the spearhead arrived.

The herd screeched to a halt. The unicorns greedily ate the pasta, and stood bemused. They were suffering pasta flashbacks. Others ate the custard pies, and started making vile whinnies and snorts, turning the surrounding vegetation brown: they were cussing.

During that distraction, the two mares and their riders were able to sidle by and get beyond. They were past the worst of it.

They came to a vast landscape where several demons were scooping up handfuls of glop from the ground, and radiating scintillating energy. The path led through the center of their number.

"There's something odd about those creatures," Jess said, uneasy. "What are they eating, and why are they glowing?"

"Those are images of Demons eating Dark Matter," Imbri printed.

"Images?"

"Capital D Demons are too big to fit in any local framework, so the Night Stallion made a miniature representation to track their progress. The Stallion wanted to be sure they kept at it."

"Kept at what? That looks like mud."

"It's artificially colored. Actually Dark Matter is invisible and untouchable."

"And why are they eating it?"

"So they can radiate Dark Energy. That is what powers the universe."

"Oh." Jess let the subject fall with a thud, having no idea whether it made any sense at all.

At last they came to a standing horse, a magnificent beast. His coat was scintillating brightly. This was the Day Stallion, here in the night realm.

They trotted up, and Jess and Ula dismounted. Jess, abruptly awed, was unable to formulate a question. Neither, it seemed was Ula.

Then Princess Kadence spoke, completely unabashed. "Day Stallion," she said. "Why are you here in the Night Stallion's domain?"

The Stallion's head turned to orient on her. His ears twitched. *WHY ARE YOU HERE?* he thought powerfully. *DON'T YOU BELONG IN THE FUTURE, CHILD PRINCESS?* Obviously he knew all about her.

"Disaster is overtaking the future," Kadence said. "Ragna Roc has escaped and is deleting anyone even capable of opposing him, including especially Xanth royalty. My mother Rhythm is gone. My grandmother King Ivy is gone. Princess Aria and I are here with Queen Harmony to try to prevent his escape, so that the disaster never happens. Do you have anything to do with it?"

The stallion actually seemed to be set back. *THAT BAD? I DID NOT KNOW. WE DO NOT APPROVE.*

Jess began to breathe again.

"You are not part of it?" the princess asked. "Then why have you been switched, and how can that be undone?"

WE MEAN NO HARM TO XANTH. QUITE THE CONTRARY. THAT BIG BIRD IS MISCHIEF.

"Who has switched you? Can we help restore you to your proper places?"

NOBODY SWITCHED US, the Stallion thought. *WE GET BORED EVERY FEW CENTURIES, SO WE SWITCHED PLACES FOR A CHANGE. WE HAVE DONE IT BEFORE.*

Kadence was astonished, as were the rest of them. "This is just a joke?"

NO. MERELY A CHANGE OF PLACE. WE'LL SWITCH BACK AFTER A MONTH.

"You are causing all this mischief just from boredom?" Kadence demanded with princessly outrage.

WHAT BUSINESS IS IT OF YOURS, ROYAL CHILD?

"The future welfare of Xanth is my business," Kadence said angrily. "As it should also be yours. How can we focus on a cure for what ails the kingdom while you irresponsible horses capriciously mess up our minds? We need everyone on board if we are to save Xanth from disaster. You should be ashamed!"

Jess had to admire the spirit of the princess. She was only ten years old, but she had a sensible grasp of things, and courage to match. She would probably be the next queen after Harmony.

The stallion considered briefly. *YOU HAVE A POINT.*

The equine form quivered. Then it changed. The darkly scintillating form of the Night Stallion appeared. *SATISFIED, PRINCESS?*

The two stallions had switched back. Now the dreams would be in order. At least that distraction had been dealt with.

"Yes, thank you," Kadence said.

GOOD TO SEE YOU AGAIN, MARE IMBRIUM.

Imbri was startled, thinking herself unnoticed. Her print balloon said only "Neigh?"

AND THIS FOR YOU, PROTAGONIST. The Stallion twitched an ear and a shining token flipped toward Jess. She caught it automatically. WHEN YOU NEED ME, INVOKE IT. Then the Stallion faded out, leaving them alone.

"Protagonist?" Jess asked blankly as she stared at the token. On one side it had an image of the stallion with the word TROJAN. On the other it said HORSE OF A DIFFERENT COLOR.

"The main character of this story," Kadence said. "Every story has one. Didn't you know?"

"But I can't be! Nobody takes me seriously!"

The princess laughed. "Nobody's perfect." She glanced back the way they had come. "Time for us to go home."

Then they set out for the boat.

Chapter 7

GREAT UNCLE DOLPH

"So that's the story," Jess concluded, with Kadence's hand on her shoulder. "It was just a diversion for the Day and Night Stallions, but now they are back on track and folk can sleep and daydream in peace."

"It is good to get that out of the way," Magnus said. "But it doesn't directly address our problem with Ragna Roc."

"Indeed it doesn't," Nia agreed. "It seems we still need Prince Dolph for that." She turned to Aria. "Do you know anything else about his relevance?"

"Nothing," Aria said. "But I'm very sure he does relate, because the Simurgh said so, and she knows everything. She has seen the universe destroyed three times."

"Which is another question," Nia said. "If she knew so much, why is she sitting this crisis out, as far as we know? A more direct word from her could have saved a phenomenal amount of mischief."

"I think I know, or at least can guess," Jess said. "We have been struggling with possible paradox. The princesses could not return here until we made our decision independently to seek Prince Dolph; the threat of paradox prevented them. They could not directly interfere with their own past. Similarly there could be more paradox if the Simurgh intervenes, because she knows too much. She might know that her direct participation would strain the fabric of space-time-magic and bring about the fourth destruction of the universe. We would not like that."

Nia made a silent laugh. "We probably would not. Point made."

"There's another thing," Jess said.

"Out with it, girl," Nia said. "You seem to make an uncommon amount of sense when we are able to take you seriously. We may not always have Kadence to counter your curse."

"It's that the tunnel needs to be built," Jess said. "Otherwise Aria, Kadence, and Queen Harmony won't be able to escape Ragna and organize to abolish his escape. I suspect that could be quite a project."

"Yes," Aria said. She and Kadence had had time to rest, fight back their grief and clean up their tears, and were functioning more or less normally again. They were marvelous girls, not at all frivolous when push came to shove. "Noe needs to tell her mother Noleta about it and gain her cooperation and I think silence, to avoid paradox and to keep it secret from Ragna. That's a whole other project. We'll need Santo, of course."

"Maybe we can charm him into helping," Noe said mischievously, touching her skirt as if to pull up the hem.

"I will help because it needs to be done," Santo said, unamused.

"Just teasing."

But Jess wondered. Noe and Aria working together could probably charm the fire out of a salamander, and they just might want to try. They were naughty at heart, as all children were. "After we get in touch with Prince Dolph," Jess said firmly.

But there was one more thing that bothered her. "If we build the tunnel to the World of Three Moons, because the princesses will need it in my future, isn't that interfering with the princesses' past? Because we're doing it because of our understanding of the crisis in the future."

Both girls paused for at least a moment and a half. "This bothers me," Kadence said. "It does smell like paradox."

"Ask Tata," the peeve suggested.

They asked Tata. His screen flickered then clarified. "Okay," the peeve said. "It's not paradox, it's juxtaposed timelines. Alternate histories. The alternate histories are nestled in together so closely that you can practically see across them. Each differs from the next by maybe only half a detail. So you're not changing your own timeline, exactly, you are shifting into a new one."

Seeing their blank stares, the peeve rephrased. "Think of them as like pages in a book, each so similar to its neighbors that they look the same until you find that one tiny change. If you start on page one, and make a change, that puts you on page two. Make a change there, and you're on page three. So when the princesses found the tunnel, that was put there by the folk of the prior page. The tunnel you build here will be used for the

folk on the next page. Not paradox, but multiple timelines. You're all helping each other. But you don't want to change things too much, because
you might wind up in a completely foreign alternate history. The idea is
to change history as little as possible while still getting the job done. And
Prince Dolph is the one in a position to get the job done with hardly any
change at all."

The blank stares were hardly less vacant, but nobody argued the case
further. Jess decided to think about it at her leisure, hoping to improve her
comprehension bit by bit until she got it clear. Maybe. For now she was
happy to take Tata's word that they were not starting a paradox that would
wipe them all out. She hoped.

"Then we shall resume our journey to see the prince," Nia said.

Win, Imbri, Tata, and the peeve went topside to put the boat back
in motion. The others relaxed as much as they were able. Soon Myst,
Mairzsy, Noe, Aria, Ula, Kadence and Squid were playing a game of Nineteen Questions centering on "Does He or Doesn't He?", while Jess, Magnus, Dell and Nia talked about nothing in particular while relaxing in
chairs. It was pleasant aboard Fibot; Jess only wished it could have been
without so disturbing a mission.

In due course, which actually was not too long, they arrived at Castle
Roogna. King Ivy welcomed them, knowing that anyone aboard the fire
boat was worthwhile. Jess was startled to see her, before reminding herself
that this was the present, not the future; she had not been deleted in this
time.

But of course they couldn't tell her, because the knowledge of her own
deletion in the future would surely change her actions now, leading again
to paradox. Their own group seemed to have some immunity, but it would
not be smart to push it.

"What brings you here, Dell, Nia and children?" Ivy asked. The two
princesses were not manifesting at all, only their hosts, Ula and Noe.

"Jess and Magnus have a traveling show," Nia explained. Jess of course
could not explain it herself. "They have commissioned Fibot to take them
to different villages to put it on. The children help." Nia was actually
eleven years older than Ivy, but looked young enough to be her daughter.

"You must do a show here!" Ivy said.

Oops. Now they would have to.

"First we have private business to discuss with Prince Dolph," Magnus said. "But after that we should be able to do it."

"My little brother and his wife Electra went flying this afternoon," Ivy said. "You should be able to find them in the sky. He will be in dragon form. A smoker, I think; she likes to sky-write."

"Thank you," Nia said. "We will check the sky."

"Meanwhile I will gather an audience," Ivy said. "It's dull here since the princesses moved out. No more mischief, you know."

Nia laughed. "Our children have not yet moved out. We do get mischief."

They returned to the boat. Soon they were sailing back into the sky. Win guided the boat back and forth, canvassing the area.

Then, near a pile of what vaguely resembled entrails, they saw a flying dragon with a woman riding on his back. That had to be Dolph, in dragon form. He was emitting puffs of smoke, forming vaporous words in the sky. NEED THREE MORE PLAYERS FOR GULF QUARTET.

"Oh, no!" Magnus groaned. "He wants to play gulf!"

"But if we don't join him, we may not get to talk with him this afternoon," Jess pointed out.

"Maybe we can intercept him before he finds his gulfers," Nia said.

"Maybe," Jess agreed dubiously. The last thing she wanted was to get into another horrible game of gulf.

They sailed close, and Magnus waved. "May we talk with you?" he called.

"Sure!" the prince called back. "Have you three gulfers?"

They were not going to escape. "Tell him yes," Kadence said. "Aria and I will do it."

"Yes!" Magnus called.

"See you there!" The dragon glided down toward the intestines, which on closer inspection turned out to be gulf links.

"I guess I'm in for it," Magnus said, looking ill.

Jess couldn't stand to see him like that. "I'll do it," she said morosely, hoping he would decline.

"Oh thank you!" In his relief he actually managed to kiss her as if he meant it. She was definitely stuck for it.

"Question," Nia asked rhetorically. "Can you girls identify yourselves?"

Kadence considered. "I think in this instance we'll have to. If we are to work together to save Xanth, Uncle Dolph will have to know the score."

"But we'll have to swear him to secrecy," Aria said. "He should understand."

The dragon landed, and the boat docked beside it. The woman climbed off, and the dragon became a portly man. Jess and the two princesses walked across to them.

"Hello," Jess called as Kadence put a hand on her arm. "I am Jess, and these are—two princesses, who must remain anonymous to all others."

Prince Dolph looked at them. "You remind me oddly of my nieces Melody and Rhythm. There's a strong family resemblance."

"Yes," Kadence said. "You must keep the secret, for fear of paradox. I am Kadence, Rhythm's daughter, and this is Aria, Melody's daughter. You and I have met before. Remember Ragna Roc?"

"Kadence!" he exclaimed. "You saved Xanth by making the eggshell! You were from the future, then. Paradox indeed!"

"I'm still from the future, Uncle. A few years later. I'm ten now. In a host." She faded out for a moment so he could see Ula. Aria did the same, showing Noe.

"Hosts in the present. I understand. Yes, I will keep the secret; this must be a very private matter." He turned to his wife. "You too, Electra?"

"Of course, dear," she agreed. "I know about the oddities of time travel, having suffered a variant myself. This has to be very important."

"It is," Aria said. "Kadence and I are babies now, at this present time. We must not interact with them at all. We have to be known as our hosts, Noe and Ula, to everyone else. We can't tell King Ivy or our mothers. But you alone have to know."

"Of course." Dolph laughed; he was evidently an affable man. "And to think I took you for gulf partners."

Kadence grimaced prettily. "We must make sacrifices for our mission. Even gulf."

"There will be plenty of time to talk as we play," Dolph said. "Then you can let me know what is going on, and how I can help."

"Yes," Aria said. "But we don't mean to squeeze out your wife."

"I don't play," Electra said. "I can't stand the game. I start radiating electricity. I just cheer him on. Recently even the daydreams have turned awful."

"They will be good today," Kadence said.

Electra frowned. "I am not sure you understand, if you haven't been playing."

"We do understand," Jess said. Kadence was still touching her. "We went to the Day and Night Stallions and got them to return to their proper stations."

"You did that?" Electra asked, amazed.

"Kadence lectured them," Jess said, smiling. "They saw the error of their ways. She is good at making things align."

Electra stared at her, her amazement magnifying. She did indeed seem to be radiating electricity. It was her talent.

"I suspect this is going to be a most interesting dialogue," Dolph said.

"One other thing," Jess said. "You may have noticed Kadence touching me."

"We did," Electra said. "We assumed there is a reason."

"Yes. It's that nobody takes me seriously; it's my magic and my curse. But Kadence's magic of alignment aligns me with the rest of you so that you can take me seriously. She's a Sorceress, so her power overrides mine. However—"

Kadence removed her hand.

"When I talk alone, I come across as a jester," Jess finished. "Not to be taken seriously, even if you know better."

Both Dolph and Electra burst out laughing. "You're hilarious!" Dolph agreed.

Electra returned her hand. "But if I am to explain to you the complexities of our situation," Jess continued, "as I think I should, being the adult in our trio, this may be a problem. Kadence can't constantly touch me while playing gulf."

Both of them sobered. "Now I appreciate your problem," Dolph said.

"I may be able to help," Electra said. "Sometimes there is an electrical component to curses. If I electrify your club, and you keep touching it, it may disrupt your curse enough to enable you to speak plainly. I can recharge it as necessary."

"I don't know," Jess said. Electricity?

"We can try it," Dolph said. "My wife can do marvelous things. I get tingly just touching her."

Jess was not sure that was the same thing, but did not argue the case.

They arrived at the Fantastic Scenes Gulf Club. The two princesses withdrew into their hosts, leaving Ula and Noe to handle the details. "We hosts are just ordinary girls," Ula said as they walked as a foursome plus Electra toward the course. "My talent is being useful in unexpected ways, and Noe's is being noe the prettiest, smartest or luckiest girl, but she gets along."

"Being right for the occasion, perhaps," Electra said. "That's subtle magic."

Noe smiled, appreciating the phrasing.

"Party of four," Dolph said to the proprietor. "Three ladies and me." Ula and Noe tittered at being called ladies, while Jess was silent, now that Kadence was no longer touching her.

The proprietor was a somber troll. Jess knew that some trolls were actually civilized, performing useful roles such as managing the Trollway or baking Troll-house cookies. He issued each of them appropriately sized gulf clubs and small colored balls. Dolph got a purple one, as he was royal; Jess got a green one, Ula a red one, and Noe a yellow one. Jess understood that this way there would not be confusion about whose ball was whose.

"If I may," Electra said, taking Jess's club. She held it for two and a half moments in her hands, concentrating, then returned it.

Jess was shocked. But after the first pulse, the club settled down, and she was able to hold it comfortably. Electra had certainly charged it up.

They walked to the first link. From up close it was not at all like a sausage link, fortunately. This one was a lovely garden, with milkweeds, assorted pie plants, chocolate burrs, lollipops, sparkling soda ponds, and boot-rear and beer-barrel trees around the edges. The bunkers were filled with sugar sand. It all looked good enough to eat.

"Uncle Dolph—" Ula started, speaking for herself and Kadence.

"Yes, of course; everything here is edible," Dolph said. "We don't want hungry gulfers. But stay clear of the beer trees, at your age."

"Only boot rear," she agreed.

The two girls ran to pick burrs and pops, and get booted, while Dolph and Jess walked to the tee-off spot. Electra went to stand by an acorn tree bearing candy acorns, out of the way, as she was a spectator. "Can you take me seriously?" Jess asked cautiously, holding the club tightly.

Dolph nodded. "Yes. I am not even cracking a smile."

"That's a relief."

"There is something I should explain about this course," Dolph said. "It is competitive, but not entirely in the normal manner. Individual matches are determined in the usual manner, with the lowest scores winning. But there is a daily special prize of significant value. The winners of those are not the ones with the lowest scores, but the ones that the course itself selects. Its rules are subtle, and change day by day, as do the prizes, so it is difficult to be certain how anyone will do."

"We're really not here to win anything," Jess said. "Or even for fun. We just need to talk with you."

"I understand that. However, I do hope to win the special prize. I am playing for a friend who needs it. So please don't take it amiss if I focus intently on my game."

"As you wish, Prince," Jess said, resisting the urge to pry into that obscure matter. It wasn't her business.

Dolph teed off. His purple ball flew down between the lines of trees to stop in the middle of the fairway. He was plainly practiced in the sport.

Jess took her turn. Her ball skittered to the side and plopped into a bunker, where it stayed. "I haven't played this game much," she said apologetically.

"It hardly matters."

They stood aside as the two girls came up to take their turns. They were both well coordinated, and their balls landed in the center, though only half as far as Dolph's.

This was not nearly as bad as the other game had been. Dolph hit his ball to the green at the far end of the fairway. Jess walked to the bunker and tasted the sand. "Genuine cane sugar," she said. She finally managed to get her ball back onto the fairway, though well behind the others. She realized that while the ball was taking her efforts seriously, because of the electrified club, she still was stuck with her duffer's ability to play the game. She was clearly the least practiced of their foursome.

Dolph walked with her as she chipped out of the bunker in three tries, getting powdered sugar in her face and hair. At least her slowness enabled them to talk longer than would have been feasible had she been a good player.

"You look good enough to eat," Dolph said, brushing some of the powder from her.

"Thank you," she said, removing her hand from her club for that instant.

"Now about your business here," Dolph said as they moved on.

Jess told him of the disaster in the future, with Ragna Roc deleting Ivy, Rhythm, and Melody, and chasing Harmony and the two young princesses. How they had made it to the tunnel, which took them to the World of Three Moons and safety. "So Queen Harmony will set up a government in exile, hoping to somehow stop the big bird from completely wiping out the kingdom," she concluded.

"This is certainly serious business," he agreed. "You realize of course that paradox will prevent you from actually changing your own timelines. What you hope to accomplish is a shift to an alternate timeline where Ragna remains confined."

"I suppose," Jess agreed. "I can't say I understand it very well. I'm just trying to help the princesses do what they need to do."

"Of course. Now I need to know how I am to be involved in this effort."

"I think it dates from when you attended the wedding of Cheiron and Chex Centaur."

"Oh, yes. The Simurgh herself performed the ceremony. I was then but a child of nine." He smiled reminiscently. "I had a rather adventurous childhood, in my fashion."

"Yes. Didn't the Simurgh make you swear an oath to protect their future chick, so that Xanth's future would not be changed too much?"

Dolph clapped a hand to his head. "Why so I did, joining the winged monsters, as I was then in my dragon form. I had quite forgotten."

"We think that if the Simurgh thought it was important, it must be important. So we think we need you now."

"You surely do," Dolph agreed. "Though I am unclear how."

"You don't know?" Jess asked, alarmed.

"I never had any idea. But it has to relate to Che Centaur, the son of

Cheiron and Chex. He became tutor to Sim, the Simurgh's own chick. As you may know, it is Sim's duty to learn everything there is to know in the universe, so that if it should be destroyed again, he can restore that knowledge."

"We are hoping that destruction can be avoided."

"Of course. I may have to ask Sim Bird. He may by this time be aware of my proper role in this matter."

"I hope you know how to contact him."

"I have no idea. But I believe I know how to contact Che Centaur, if I can reach him in time, and he should know where Sim is."

Jess smiled. "As it happens, we have good transportation."

"Oh, yes, that had slipped my mind. I may have to ride with you."

Since Dolph could assume dragon or roc form and fly extremely swiftly, Jess wondered where Che Centaur could be that Dolph could not quickly reach.

Meanwhile she had plunked her ball into a tsoda pop puddle and had to take a penalty stroke. She licked off the ball to clean it somewhat. "Lemon marmalade!" she exclaimed. "My favorite flavor!"

"I think you could find some good in Hell itself," Dolph remarked wryly.

"Isn't that where Princess Eve lives? She's good."

"My daughter Eve," he agreed. "Of course. She married Demon Pluto. She lives in Hades, technically, but I believe that makes my point."

They completed the first hole. On that one the level "green" was formed of green candy grass that the girls tasted. Dolph's score was three. Jess's score was twelve. The two girls were at sixes and sevens.

They played on, because they did not want to make it evident that they had more on their minds than gulf. That would have been unforgivable here on the gulf course. They had to finish the round.

"You're right," Electra remarked. "The sweet daydreams are back. That will make the game of gulf popular again."

The next link resembled the Faun & Nymph retreat. Jess was alarmed, knowing that just about all the fauns and nymphs did all day was chase each other and "celebrate" in a manner children were forbidden by the Adult Conspiracy to witness.

"Have no fear," Dolph murmured. "This is an emulation, not reality. All they do here is hug and kiss."

Oh. She saw that it was true; the fauns were endlessly chasing the nymphs, who were not trying very hard to flee. When they caught up with each other, they hugged and kissed, then separated to try other partners. "That's a relief!"

"It's no joking matter," Dolph reproved her.

Jess paused, then looked at her club. She took it to Electra for a recharge. She returned to Dolph. "That's a relief!" she repeated.

"It is indeed," he agreed. He looked at her gulf club. "Oh—the charge was down! No wonder."

This time Jess did better, taking only eight strokes to make a par three hole. She noted that the fauns and nymphs never interfered with the actual gulf playing, but hovered around the edges. They were incidental scenery, as it were. Now that it was clear that nothing serious was being violated, Jess was almost coming to like the game of gulf. It consisted of skill in striking and aiming the ball; most else was background.

Of course she plopped her ball into another puddle. A passing nymph saw the wretched shot and tittered. Distracted, then the nymph tripped and splashed into the puddle herself just as her pursuing faun caught up.

"Oh, my," Jess said as the nymph got back to her feet caked in tsoda and chocolate mud. "Your lovely hair is a mess!" That was hardly all. The faun was eyeing her with misgiving, not wanting to get caked himself. "Maybe you should go for a swim in deeper water to get properly cleaned off." The nymph nodded and ran for a suitable pond.

Which left the faun without a partner. He was plainly distressed. "My fault," Jess said, as she fished out the ball. "I'm sorry I deprived you of your squeeze. Will I do instead?" She opened her arms to him.

The faun hugged and kissed her. He was a surprisingly manly creature, and his attention was actually quite pleasant.

"You're a wonder," Dolph said as the faun ran off.

"Well, my bad play did mess them up. I just wanted to make up for it."

"I believe it did," he agreed.

"It is curious that the Simurgh made you take the oath, then never reminded you later," Jess said as they played on. "We conjecture that she could not intervene directly herself, because that could trigger serious paradox mischief. But if you are essential to this effort to save Xanth, why would she let you forget it?"

"She's a very old bird," he said thoughtfully. "If I forget some things at my age, think of how much she could forget at her age! Probably it's such an incidental detail that it slipped beneath her notice."

"Or maybe she knew we would remind you."

"We mortals lack the mindset to fathom the mental processes of such great minds," he said amiably.

Only when they had finished the hole did Jess realize that there had been a ring of sleeping nymphs around it, that they had had to chip over. She had been distracted by her dialogue with Dolph. It was such a pleasure to discuss serious matters seriously, for a change.

The girls finished their holes. Their scores were still better than Jess's, but not by as much. They moved on to the next.

The third hole was a simulated griffin's den. That could have been dangerous territory in real life, but here the fabulous beasts merely watched the players as they passed. They had the head and wings of eagles, and the bodies of lions, and were formidable predators. There was a huge nest on a simulated crag where a mother griffin spread her wings protectively over the baby griffins within. They were the color of shoe polish, as all griffins were. But Jess noticed something.

"The father griff has a thorn in his paw!" Indeed, the creature was trying to pick at his front paw, but his eagle bill was not suitable to extract it without worse damage.

"All part of the display," Dolph agreed.

"Not a necessary part," Jess said, annoyed. She walked to the big creature. "Peace," she told him. "Will you let me try to help you?"

The griffin merely looked at her.

Jess squatted before him. "Give me your paw, please."

He let her have his sore paw. Sure enough, there was a huge thorn embedded beside a claw. The flesh was swollen around the area. Jess brought out a pin from the emergency kit all women carried, along with some salve. "This will ease the pain," she said, spreading salve on the reddened area. "Now hold still a moment." She pried at the thorn with the pin, but it wouldn't budge. Then she put her mouth down and clamped her teeth on the base of the thorn. Slowly she drew her head back, wrenching the thorn from the flesh. It was done.

"It will take a few days to heal fully," she said. "But it should be all right now." She got up and returned to her game. The griffin merely watched her go.

Dolph shook his head. "If you had existed in my day, I think I might have married you."

"No, you would never have taken me seriously."

Dolph made another par on the hole. Jess made a triple bogey, but it was nevertheless an improvement. The girls were in between again.

The fourth hole was a grove of tangle trees, which looked ordinary only from a distance. Up close their dangerous masses of tentacles showed. Only a fool ever went within grabbing range. Yet the green was surrounded by them. Jess was taken aback. "Are you sure it's safe?"

"Here, yes," Dolph said. "In the rest of Xanth, never."

"They look so—so alert."

"They are." Dolph threw his ball at the nearest tree. A tentacle whipped out and caught it, then threw it back to him. "But under strict instructions to leave the players alone." He smiled grimly. "We get very few intruders or vandals here. They are not protected."

They played, and naturally Jess sent her ball well into the rough. It came to rest by the trunk of a sadly drooping tree. Its tentacles hung loosely, and some were turning brown. "There's been a drought," Dolph explained.

"Don't they water the course when it's too dry?"

"Yes. But this is the kind of isolated section only you could find in normal play. They must have missed it."

Jess considered. This was the first and maybe the last time she would ever have sympathy for a tangle tree. But she had to do something. "I need a bucket."

"Don't tell me you're going to fetch water!"

"What else? It's not right to let the tree suffer. Here it is obeying the rule and not grabbing people, and how is it being treated in return? It's not fair."

Dolph sighed. "I will find you a bucket." He changed form to a hawk and flew away. In barely three moments he was back, now in the form of a roc, with two big buckets of water in his talons. He set them down carefully and changed back to manform, clothing and all.

"But I didn't mean you had to do it. Prince Dolph," Jess protested. "I was going to haul the buckets myself."

"Which might have taken the rest of the day. We have a game to play." He picked up a bucket, hauled it to the base of the tree, and dumped it out on the ground. Jess did the same with the other bucket, though it was so big and full she could barely manage it.

"I'm sorry," she gasped. "I guess I wasn't thinking."

"Let's get some more." He changed form again, picked up the buckets, and flew away to refill them.

Eight buckets later, they seemed to have brought enough. The tree was turning green and looking distinctly more perky.

"You watered a tangle tree?" Noe asked, amazed, as the girls discovered their activity.

"I'll probably never forgive myself," Jess confessed.

A look circled around, somehow managing to miss Jess.

The fifth hole was an underwater scene. There were fish swimming through, and seaweed growing, yet somehow the players were able to breathe normally and the balls flew through the (air) without trouble. At least there were no ailing creatures. There were patterns of stones and sand that formed a lovely underwater tapestry.

"It beautiful," Jess said. "A whole underwater landscape. The fish are so graceful! I'm glad I got to see it."

"You're welcome," Dolph said. "I have played here many times, but am finding a new appreciation of its details."

Then a mermaid swam down, her fair hair flowing out behind her head. "And its sea-tails," Dolph amended, though he did not seem to be looking at the tail.

Jess could only wish she had a shape like that, at least from the waist up.

They finished the hole and moved on to the next. The sixth hole was a moonscape with craters and seas. As with the seascape, they had no trouble breathing; it was another emulation, not the real thing.

Then Jess noticed something. The sea they were playing across was quite shallow, and the water did not interfere with the balls. It was the name: MARE IMBRIUM. It was Mare Imbri's home turf! Odd that it was a sea.

But there was a smell. Jess oriented on it and it got stronger, until the stench was almost overpowering. Finally she located it: someone or something had dumped a load of green cheese on it and left it there to spoil.

"This won't do," Jess muttered. "Imbri would have a fit if she knew."

"Are you spying something that needs fixing?" Dolph inquired warily.

"This is the base of one of my friends. I realize it's just an emulation, but she would be most annoyed if it stank like this. I need to clean it up."

"What friend?"

"Mare Imbri. She used to be a night mare, before she retired."

"I know of her. She had a whole story to herself, and shared in another."

"Imbri!" the girls said almost together. "Yes, we have to help her."

"Then we need to gather up this dumped cheese and recycle it, or whatever they do on the moon."

They got to work, and soon had several cheese barrels full of the dreadful stuff. They dumped it down the mouth of an old volcano. Then they used the water of the shallow sea to swish out the region so that it was clean again. Imbri's turf was no longer an embarrassment.

Jess made her usual bad score, but hardly cared. Cleaning up the gulf course had become more important to her. She continued to talk with Dolph, finding him pleasant and knowledgeable. She was also coming to appreciate how socially pleasant such a game could be.

The next hole was a cityscape evidently modeled after a typical Mundane metropolis. Big ugly blocky buildings stretched as far as her eyes could see in every direction. The fairway was an eight-lane highway passing through the center. They had to try to avoid veering into the spot forests that were parks, the ponds that were cesspools, and the slums that were bunkers.

Dolph, as usual, hit straight down the center of that fairway, deviating neither left nor right. The girls hit along the edges, but still out of bad trouble. Jess hit straight into a park. There she found a lost child, a little five-year-old boy alone and crying. So maybe he was part of the background scenery; she still had to try to help him.

"Where is your mother?" she asked the boy.

"She's stuck in a traffic jam," he wailed. "She sent me out to find a way clear, but now I'm lost."

"Jess's doing it again," Dolph muttered to the girls. "If we don't help, she'll never get through this hole." That was a pretty sharp assessment.

So the others helped. Dolph changed to helicopter form, which was a weird creature with a whirling propeller over his head. He picked up the boy and the others and flew over the mass of stalled vehicles that was the traffic jam. Jess, following, didn't even need to taste the jam to know it tasted horrible; it looked way too metallic and polluted with noxious gas. The boy, however, seemed used to it, and was enjoying the flight.

"There!" the boy cried, pointing to the very center of the jam.

It was a traffic light stuck on red. No cars could move until it changed to green, and it refused to do this.

"I can fix it," Kadence said. "I can align it more properly." Ula made her way through the stalled cars to the stalling light. Kadence reached up and touched it.

There was a multi-colored flicker. Then the light locked on green.

Immediately the cars started to move. In a few moments and many bleeps the jam was cleared.

Dolph flew down to the car in the center and returned the child to his mother. "Oh thank you so much!" she exclaimed, and zoomed away.

They resumed their game, with the usual spread of scores.

The eighth hole was a snowy mountain, with snow that wasn't actually cold. It was a challenge reaching the frosty green, which was in a mountain pass, and of course Jess messed it up. Her ball landed right before a white monster with monstrous feet.

"That's Bigfoot!" Dolph exclaimed, astonished. "No one has seen him in centuries."

"I'm sorry," Jess said. "I just can't seem to hit the ball straight."

"That's not bad, dear girl. That's a remarkable accomplishment."

"I don't know. He doesn't look happy."

Indeed, the monster was staggering. There seemed to be something wrong with his huge foot.

"He stubbed his toe!" Noe said. "That's why he's in sight. He couldn't get away."

"With feet his size, that must be awful uncomfortable," Ula said.

"We have to help him," Jess said. "But I don't know how."

"I do," Dolph said. "I keep some healing elixir in case of emergency."

But Bigfoot was clumsily fleeing the scene. He was so big that even badly limping he made good progress.

Then Aria manifested, and sang a lullaby. It was so compelling that the monster slowed, stopped, then fell asleep. Jess had to fight off sleepiness herself.

Dolph, with his Magician caliber talent, seemed unaffected. He walked to the creature and poured some liquid from a vial directly onto the sore foot. In barely three quarters of a moment, the foot healed.

Aria halted her song. Bigfoot revived and charged up the mountain slope and away. Soon he was gone, leaving only his giant tracks in the snow.

"He didn't even say thank you," Ula said.

"He's a monster," Dolph said. "They don't know those words."

The ninth hole was another complete change: a maze-cave. There were several routes, each walled off by waist-high board fences. It was possible to see over them, but the larger pattern was such a confusing array that dizziness soon followed. They had to hit their balls along the winding passages without getting lost.

"Each day it's a different pattern," Dolph said. "I have gotten apt at analyzing them, but can never be certain. It's always a gamble." He promptly hit his ball down the third of four passages.

The others considered. "Why don't we each take a different passage?" Noe asked. "That way one of us will be sure to get the right one."

Ula shrugged. "Why not." She hit her ball down the first passage.

Noe then hit hers down the second passage.

That left the fourth one for Jess.

Well, she couldn't go far wrong, because the ball bounced off the walls and continued down the passage. When it rolled to a stop, she hit it again, harder. She really didn't care if she hit it out of the fairway, if there was one; she just wanted to get through the course and be done with it. The passage curved around until it crossed another passage. That made her think of the challenge at the Good Magician's castle, though there was probably no parallel.

Indeed, it was different, because as she got closer she saw it was actually four passages crossing, or eight paths coming together. Still, it could be the same in that maybe the four passages crossed each other here, so it was possible to take a different route if a player changed her mind. Maybe the challenge was not to decide which course to choose, but which one to stay on. Did that make any sense?

Well, she would stay her course. She hit the ball down through the intersection so that it would sail on straight ahead. It disappeared.

She paused, staring. She had been watching her green ball, expecting it to roll rapidly past the converging passages with nary a hesitation. Instead it had vanished. Had she not been watching it, she might have assumed it had rolled on and was now out of sight in the far passage. But it had not gotten there.

Something was odd.

She walked to the intersection, carefully tapping the floor with her club. When she got there, the tapping stopped, because there was no floor to tap. The club passed though as if there were nothing there. Had she not been proceeding slowly, she might have stepped into it and dropped into who knew what.

This needed a more thorough investigation. Jess got down on her hands and knees and felt around the floor. There was a panel missing, covered over by illusion. This was dangerous!

"Bleep!" she muttered. Then she retreated a few paces, set aside her club so as to be free of its magic charge, and advanced on the intersection.

Sure enough, the illusion did not take her seriously. The missing panel was now plain by its absence. The edges of the hole were ragged; it had worn through because of frequent use, and finally dropped down.

A repairman must have spied the gap and rather than take the trouble to fashion a new tile, simply covered it over with spot illusion. Sloppy work that could have caused a bad injury. It must have happened not long before they reached this hole.

Then she froze. The missing tile—could it have been deleted? When Ragna Roc deleted something, it looked the same, at least for a while, but was no longer real. Could he be lurking?

Then she caught up with herself. No, this was the present, not the future. Ragna Roc remained confined. She looked more carefully, and saw the tile resting on the ground a few inches below the hole. No deletion.

This needed to be fixed. She glanced about, saw nothing useful, so got brutally innovative. She banged on a section of the wall, knocking out a four-panel section, and laid that carefully over the hole. That would do until there was time for a proper repair.

Then she heard something down a side hall. Another player! She hastily drew back. A purple ball came cruising down that passage, crossed the intersection, bounced on her panels, and went on.

Followed by Prince Dolph. "Oh, hello, Jess," he said, seeing her in her own passage. "I'll be out of your way in a moment." He moved on.

Then she realized that in her effort to cover over the hole, she had forgotten to recover her own ball. Well, she would let the others play through, then lift the panel and locate it, and resume play.

Soon the two girls played though, each following her own passage. Only then did Jess get down to fetch her ball. She decided not to say anything to the others. But she would notify the management, in due course.

She finished last, as usual, but was quietly satisfied with her performance.

The somber troll appeared as Jess sunk her ball. "The winner—" he said as they stood around the hole together with Electra.

"I want to speak with the management," Jess said, clutching her club tightly. She hadn't waited because she was afraid he would disappear the moment his announcement was made.

"I am the management," the troll said.

"Your maintenance here is atrocious," Jess said indignantly. "The creatures and plants are serving you loyally, but you are not treating them fairly. You ignore their hurts and needs, and your neglect of the ninth hole is dangerous. You should be ashamed!" She realized that shame was a largely foreign concept to the average troll, but it was the appropriate word.

"How so?"

He wanted to know? Jess went into it in detail, telling of the griffin with the sore paw, the tangle tree that was drying up, the mud puddle that was a hazard to nymphs, Bigfoot with the stubbed toe, the lost child from the traffic jam, and the unfixed hole in the maze. "You should shut this course down until you get these things fixed," she concluded.

"Now if I may continue my announcements," the troll said.

He was ignoring the problems? Jess was fit to be tied, but realized that would not solve anything. So she shut up, steaming.

"Winner of the round, with the lowest score, Prince Dolph."

Dolph nodded, not surprised.

"Winner of the special prize, Jess."

It took three quarters of a moment for that to sink in. Then her outrage exploded. "I don't want any prize! I want you to fix the problems!"

"The prize is Frankie, the prospective bride of Frank Monster."

Dolph sighed. "I had hoped to win her for him."

It took the final quarter of the moment for that to sink in. "I told you I don't want any prize," Jess said. "I want you to—"

Dolph put his hand on her arm. His Magician aura silenced her. "Take Frankie," he said. "You can bring her to Frank as readily as I can. I will help you."

"But—"

The troll smiled, which had to be a rare thing, because his face almost cracked. "The vote this time was unanimous, which is an extremely rare thing." He waved a hand, and a curtain that Jess had not known was there dropped. Behind it stood the creatures and plants of the gulf course, from fauns and nymphs to the suffering tangle tree. Not only were they well, they did not look as if they had ever been unwell. "It was based on alertness, expedience, and compassion. You were the one who best exhibited these qualities."

"They weren't really suffering," Dolph murmured. "I admit to wondering, because this course is normally very well cared for."

"You got us all to help, Jess," Ula/Kadence said. "That was so good of you."

"We wouldn't have noticed on our own," Noe/Aria said. "You reminded us of our better qualities."

"But all I wanted—"

"With no thought for yourself," Electra said. "You are such a fine person, Jess. No wonder you are the protagonist."

It had been a kind of set-up, and she had fallen right into it. What was she to do with her burgeoning anger? It had nothing remaining to focus on.

"Uh, thank you," she said lamely. She simply did not know how to handle being taken seriously.

Which was readily fixed. She handed the gulf club to Electra. Now no one would take her seriously. She was used to that, and could handle it.

But this had been an interesting experience.

Chapter 8

FRANKIE STEIN

The somber troll took them to the chamber where Frankie the monster girl was held. To Jess's surprise she was no grotesque patchwork thing; she was an outstandingly beautiful woman, with luxurious black hair curling around her body to her knees so that it was difficult to tell whether she was wearing anything under it.

"Well, now, Prince Dolph," she said, eyeing him suggestively.

"That's the Goddess Isis!" Electra snapped. "What is *she* doing here?"

The notorious Goddess Isis? Jess had heard of her but never expected to meet her. This was weird.

"Oh, don't get all charged up, Tingles," Isis said to Electra. "I'm not really after your man. It's just a bit of window shopping. I'm married myself, now."

"You're supposed to be in Mundania, or in your restricted Xanth zone," Electra said.

"Except when I'm doing bit parts for bad dreams, or animating spot hosts who need help. That way I get to travel in Xanth. It can be fun."

"The present bit part being Frankie, the patchwork woman," the somber troll explained. "Filling in as a prize while searching for her ideal partner."

"My host looks like this," Isis said, becoming a female creature composed of assorted poorly matching body parts. One arm was femininely delicate, but the other was brutally muscular. One leg was long and shapely, the other short and hairy. Her hands and feet were similarly mismatched, and her head was a combination of features. Patches of her hair were of different colors and lengths; her ears were large and small, and her eyes were respectively sky blue and mud brown. She was definitely no beauty. "So I enhance her slightly, not that anyone should notice."

Jess realized that a man probably wouldn't notice, being half stunned by the illusion. She did seem to have all the body parts, and presumably they functioned normally. So who would be her ideal partner? Frank Stein, the patchwork man. So why weren't they together?

That was what Prince Dolph was trying to do: win the prize for the lonely monster man. Only Jess had won instead, messing it up, of course.

Ula walked to her and touched her arm. Kadence manifested in that touch.

Now Jess could safely speak. "I will take you to Frank Stein, your ideal partner."

"Oh, thank you, kind lady," Frankie said. But her words came out slurred and misshapen. Her teeth did not match, and neither did her lips; she had a problem talking clearly.

The grotesque face transformed into the dazzling features of the Goddess. "I will speak for her, until she gets together with her ideal man."

Jess had to agree it was a worthwhile service.

They returned to the boat, where Electra kissed Dolph and bid him parting. Evidently she was not concerned about the Goddess seducing her husband. Not after seeing the actual host body she was using, however masked it might be by illusion.

The boat cast off and sailed into the sky, where they could safely relax. There was a suite for Dolph, and another for Frankie/Isis.

Naturally Jess had another question. She got Kadence to touch her so she could express it properly. "We need you, Prince Dolph, to finesse the timelines with minimal damage. You need Che Centaur to clarify your role for you. But why do we need Frank Stein, apart from doing him a favor along the way?"

"Oh, did I neglect to clarify that? My apology. It's that Frank knows how to find Che. I don't. So I need to find Frank to find Che."

Jess was not the only one perplexed by that. "How does Frank know?"

"That's an interesting little story I learned by the grapevine."

"The grapevine," the peeve said. "A magical network that spreads minor gossip around."

"Exactly," Dolph agreed. "It seems that one day Che Centaur was on business high in the sky when a button on his vest popped. Centaurs generally don't wear clothing, at least not for modesty, but do for practical reasons. It was cold aloft, so the vest kept him warm. But when he lost the button, the vest fell open and he got chilled. So he landed on Mount Rushmost, where the winged monsters hang out, and set out to mend the vest. He had a replacement button, and thread, and a needle. But his eyes were still a bit teary from the cold, and he couldn't see well enough to thread the needle. It was frustrating. Then another monster saw his problem and came to help. This was Frank Stein, who was certainly a monster, but qualified as a winged monster only because there was one small useless wing on his shoulder. He had been assembled from body parts and somehow that one got added to the mix."

"I know how that is," Frankie said. "I've got more parts than body."

"Frank's left hand was fine and feminine; he never inquired exactly where it came from, but it was good for delicate tasks. His left eye was similarly fine, and could see close detail very well. He took the needle and threaded the eye with no problem. That set it up so that Che could complete his repair. He appreciated the help, so he asked whether he could do Frank any return favor. Frank declined, but Che wasn't satisfied, so he put a mark on Frank's wrist, the one supporting the hand that had so nicely threaded the needle, that would enable Frank to find Che at any time, should he ever need a return favor. The mark was in the form of a ring with a bright spot, and that spot always pointed the direction where Che was to be found. So Frank can find Che when he wants to."

Dolph looked around. "Now I have no idea where Che Centaur is at the moment. So I made a deal with the Night Stallion, that if I delivered Frankie to Frank, he would make a path to lead me to Frank so I could do it. So I believe I can find Frank, and Frank can find Che."

"This is interesting, Uncle," Aria said. "But why did the Night Stallion want Frankie delivered to Frank?"

Dolph nodded. "It seems she was crafted in the depths of the dream realm, and served as a horror figure for bad dreams, and did such a good job that the Stallion wanted to reward her, but she didn't want anything. When he learned that Frank had entered Xanth, he knew how to do it. This is it."

"So now it all comes together," Jess said. "Things make some sense after all, in their devious fashion." But nobody paid attention.

"So how do we get to Frank?" Magnus asked.

They looked at Dolph. "It seems that he is now making bad dreams. It is an irony that he has replaced Frankie in that capacity. Had she but remained where she was, they might have gotten together by this time."

"I was getting tired of making bad dreams," Frankie said. "I wanted to make some good dreams. But I got lost on the way, and had to work at the gulf curse instead."

Gulf curse? Was that a typo? Jess wasn't sure it was.

"So now when I enter the dream realm," Dolph continued, "I will find the path to Frank."

"We will all find the path to Frank," Magnus said. "We know of an access to the dream realm. The boat is sailing there now. In the interim, we can rest."

They rested. "I hear you acquitted yourself well at the Fantastic Scenes Gulf Club," Magnus told Jess when they were alone.

"I just did what I had to do."

"I want so much to kiss you and make it count."

"Fake it." She hated that she was coming across as insufferably needy, but she couldn't help it.

He did, and she loved it.

Then she remembered something she had been meaning to ask him about. "Some folk are calling me the protagonist, the main character of this story. Can that be right?"

Magnus paused. "And this is a serious question?"

"Yes."

"Of course you are the protagonist. I knew there was something special about you the moment I first met you. Now I think I know more of what it is. You're the focus!"

"But I'm nothing special. I can't even be taken seriously. Who would ever be interested in a story about me?"

"I would." He put his hand across her mouth to stifle her protest. "I know that's not what you mean. But here's the thing: the protagonist is not necessarily the object of attention. It's not *about* her. She is the viewpoint character, one who sees what is happening. The one who happens to be there when the real story unfolds. She's the camera eye. Few folk take the camera seriously; it's just looking."

Jess was surprised as understanding wedged into her mind. "Nobody has to take *me* seriously. Because I'm not the point. I'm just the storyteller. Not even that. I'm the conduit through which the story is told. I'm just a channel, not important myself."

"Now you know. But Jess, you're important to me regardless. I wish you had a rose or a gulf club or a Sorceress's hand on your shoulder all the time. I wish I could love you."

"Instead of faking it," she agreed.

"I'm faking the close expression of it. I don't think I'm faking the emotion itself."

"Oh, Magnus! That's such a nice thing to say!"

"And my mind knows that's not sarcasm, even though my immediate feeling thinks it is. Oh, Jess, I'm tormented!"

And she saw a tear lurking in the corner of his eye. She knew he meant it. But could not act it.

"Magnus, I know this is a lot to ask. But could you just lie there a while and choke back your laughter while I love you?"

"I will try."

He lay there while she hugged him and kissed him and ran her fingers through his hair. She whispered sweet nothings in his ear. When she saw him holding his breath in an effort not to burst out laughing she gave it up; the curse really could not be circumvented this way. Bleep.

"We are approaching Mount Neverest," Dell's voice came from a spot on the wall. "Those who wish to participate should assemble topside in fifteen minutes."

"The boat has a general speaker system," Magnus said. "I didn't know that."

"Neither did I," Jess said. "I hope it doesn't have a general spy-eye system, too. Not that we were doing anything worth spying on."

"I would rather we had been doing something spy-worthy."

She got a wild notion. "Let's do it! We have fifteen minutes."

"But we just tried to, and didn't get anywhere."

"Let's try harder! Stand up."

Perplexed, he stood there. She quickly took off his clothing, then her own. Naked, she wrapped her arms around him and kissed him, flattening herself against him. "Hold me up," she said, climbing on him and spreading her legs to clamp around his waist as he held on to her bottom to prevent her from falling. She managed to catch his face and kiss him ardently.

But it was impossible to hold the position long. Slowly she slid down him, until she had to put her feet down lest she land on her bottom. Nothing significant had happened.

"Oh, bleep!" she cried tearfully.

"Bleep," he echoed. "If any other woman did that—"

"Don't I know it." Once again, the curse had prevailed.

"Not that I'd want her to."

"Of course." And that was meant not to be taken seriously. She was probably the only young woman who could have failed to seduce any young man that way.

Only as they were dressing did Jess remember Nia's talent with the floating spectacles. She could have watched the whole disaster. Had it been worth watching. Jess would have been glad to do it regardless, had she only been able to. She was sure Magnus felt the same.

Topside, they saw the giant gourd atop the mountain peak. The one that she had entered with the mares. Now it loomed ever larger.

The deck was crowded. All the personnel were there. They had all heard of the minor adventure getting the stallions switched back. This was another. Everyone wanted to participate! But of course only a few of them could.

That gave Jess an idea.

Ula forged toward her. "We saw that dim bulb flash over your head! Out with it." Her hand caught Jess's arm, and she felt the power of the Sorceress.

"We all want to go," Jess said. "So why don't we? Let's sail Fibot there."

So many glances went out that they crashed into each other and dropped helplessly to the deck, where, soiled, they faded out. All except Nia's, which caught Dell's eye and held it. "Well?"

"Prince Dolph," Dell said. "Is there any reason why not?"

Dolph shrugged. "If there is, the boat won't be able to get into the dream realm."

Then Nia's glance caught Win's eye, as she guided the boat. "What does Mare Imbri say? She knows the night dream terrain better than any of the rest of us."

"She says it's people's fears that prevent access to the worst dreams, not the size of the dream realm, which is infinite. Anyone who wants to go in can do so. But some may be sorry they did."

"You heard that?" Dell asked the group of them. "Anyone who wants to stay clear, say "Nay.""

"Neigh," Myst said, giggling. She hosted Mairzy, the day mare, who hardly feared this realm after having to deliver its bad dreams for a month.

"Then we are decided," Dell said. "Sail on."

Win revved up the wind, her blown hair pointing the way. The hexagonal firesail brightened. The boat sailed into the eye.

First they came to the dread Haunted House. The illuminated path led right to the front door. Jess was surprised. Surely Frank couldn't be working there?

The door opened as Fibot approached, and somehow the doorway was large enough to admit the boat. How could that be?

"Easy," Frankie said, or rather it was the Goddess Isis, who could evidently read Jess's thoughts, and understand her well enough when she chose. She was now standing beside Jess. "Fibot's magic enables it to pass through any channel without distorting its interior. The haunted house is not large; Fibot is now small, at least in perspective, and we along with it. It's a very nice craft."

They sailed into a hallway where empty shoes and gloves walked and waved about, and into a decrepit living room, except it was occupied by the dead: two walking male skeletons and a lady zombie. Jess wasn't certain how she knew their genders, because there was no identifiable anatomical flesh on the zombie, who was pretty far gone, and no flesh at all on the skeletons. But the two seemed to be quite interested in the one, and she returned their attention.

"She's a bleeping flirt," Isis murmured disdainfully.

Jess was curious how these dead folk proposed to make out, as they seemed to have an even worse problem than Jess did in that respect. But the boat sailed on to another room, a juvenile bedroom with dolls on the floor, where a ghost was terrorizing a sleepless child. Now Jess saw a gnome with a movie camera filming the incident: this was a dream being made, for delivery to some bad child who refused to go to sleep promptly. These were actors!

"Fascinating," Magnus murmured. "I may never be frightened by a bad dream again, knowing how they are made."

"Not so," Imbri's speech balloon printed. "We mares carry suspension of disbelief spells that make dreams seem completely real while they are occurring. You will be frightened even though you know better."

Jess was suddenly more interested. "Could one of those spells nullify a curse? Make what is happening believable?"

"Not in the waking state," Imbri printed. "That is far too cynical."

"Even a day dream dissipates when a person becomes aware of it," Mairzy printed.

Bleep, Jess thought.

"However, dear, I could make the performance real," Isis said. "It is my specialty."

She was the Goddess of Fertility, highly conversant with the mechanisms of reproduction. She surely could do it. But then it would be as if Magnus were making love to Isis rather than Jess. That was definitely not what they wanted.

Isis made a small obscure smile, not denying it.

They moved on out to the real, where shadowy wild things ranged a capacious graveyard. Skeletal hands reached out of the plots, trying to grab on to the boat as it passed.

Beyond was a moor where ghosts chased banshees, somewhat in the manner of fauns and nymphs, entertaining themselves while waiting for their next mortal customers.

Suddenly Jess caught on. "It's a tour! The Night Stallion is giving us a tour of the realm." But of course nobody took her seriously.

Next was the Slough of Despond, where sad folk sat and continually wept. But in a nook mostly out of sight a male and a female seemed to be having a tryst. It seemed the actors had their own entertainments while waiting for the next dream crafting assignment.

And a barren plain where wolf-like creatures roamed. A man was trying to sneak past, but a dire wolf winded him and charged. The man spread his arms and flapped them, birdlike, and did manage to get into the air. But not enough; his feet were low, and the wolf snapped at them. The man yanked them out of the way just in time, but it was evident that the wolf would soon catch hold of a flailing limb and drag him down for the slaughter.

"Dreams of flying," Isis commented. "And of course it's never quite high enough."

"It's a very popular dream," Imbri printed. "I delivered hundreds of them in my day."

"The inability to fully escape a horror," Isis agreed. "Fundamental insecurity. That covers a wide range."

"I'd soon be sickened, making such dreams," Jess said. Nobody paid attention.

Then they came to an ancient castle, with green slime on the stone walls and cracked steps. A young woman was trying to find a place to hide, while a patchwork assembled monster slowly searched for her. "Come to me, my dear," he called in his gravely tone. "I just want to be friendly with you."

Terrified, she fled her nook. Her nightie caught on a stone corner and ripped, exposing a fair amount of her nice torso, to her chagrin. She tried to fold the material back around to cover herself up, but it wasn't very effective. As with the flying dream, however frantic the effort, it was never quite enough. The monster, spying the exposed flesh, licked his mismatched lips.

"That would be for a bride who refuses her family's choice in husbands for her," Isis said. "Instead of gladly embracing the honor."

"But that's horrible!" Jess said.

"Exactly."

"I mean that's not the way it's supposed to be. A girl should have some choice in such an important matter. It's her body. Her life."

"In your culture, perhaps. Not in many others. A woman is fit only to serve and please a man, no matter how badly he treats her. If she fails in that, she's a failure to her gender, and deserves her shame."

"And you're a woman!" Jess flared. "Doesn't it absolutely repulse you?"

Isis considered. "I am of course no ordinary woman. I believe I prefer vengeance. A woman can endlessly torment a man, if she knows how to do it. I know how."

"I don't like that, either! Why can't men and women treat each other with mutual respect and joy?"

"But then there would be no battle of the sexes. Where is the fun in that?"

"Fun in war between men and women? I'd much rather have them at peace."

The Goddess shook her head. "No wonder nobody takes you seriously. You have delusions of decency."

Magnus touched her hand. "I wish I could love you," he repeated. "Then we might actually abolish some delusions."

Jess felt tears of appreciation and frustration. He truly was the man for her.

The boat docked beside the castle and they got out to watch the conclusion of the dream as the cameras rolled. The monster finally cornered the distressed damsel and drew her to him as she screamed in terror and revulsion. He kissed her, and ran his clumsy paw-hands all over her trembling body while she struggled ineffectively. Then finally she fainted.

"Cut!" the director gnome called.

The monster let go of the woman, who it seemed wasn't unconscious at all. "Good show," she told the monster. "But you forgot to goose me."

"Oops! I'll remember next time."

So it was all a carefully staged act. But the dreamer wouldn't know that; she would wake in a cold sweat, not aware that it had stopped short of rape.

The director turned toward the visitors. "Window shopping?" he inquired.

"No," Jess said, reaching for Kadence's hand so she would be taken seriously. "I won a prize in a gulf game, and am giving that prize to Frank."

"My job is done," Isis murmured, and faded out.

The monster scratched his head. "Do I know you?"

"No. But we need your help. I hope we can make a deal."

He scratched his head. He was not at all threatening here in real life, despite his ugliness. "What deal?"

"Take us to Che Centaur, wherever he may be. In return, here is your perfect girlfriend." Jess turned to bring forth Frankie, who was shyly hiding behind her.

Frank's eyes bugged, almost literally. "This lovely creature?"

Magnus and the others kept their faces straight. Frankie was as far from lovely as it was possible to get, now that Isis was not enhancing her. But of course to the monster she was his kind of girl.

"This lovely creature," Jess agreed. "Her name is Frankie. She was made for you."

"Hi," Frankie said.

"Beloved!" Frank exclaimed and swept her into his embrace. Misshapen little hearts flew out to circle them.

It was clear it would work out. The little hearts were a sure signal.

"We must celebrate their engagement," the director gnome said. "Why don't you put on a show in honor of it?"

"You know of our shows?" Jess asked, surprised. "Even here in the heart of the darkest dreams?"

"Especially here. Did you think we would not recognize Atrocia? We love your jesting."

Jess looked at Magnus, her glance forming a question mark.

"Certainly," he agreed. "Assemble your folk for an audience and we'll put it on."

"Great." The gnome hurried off.

Soon they were on the stage inside the old castle. There was a surprising number of creatures assembled, ranging from dwarves to giants, fairies to ghosts, zombies to skeletons, and several night mares, too. They were all actors in the bad dreams, professional folk, but it seemed they liked a show as well as anyone did. Probably they got time off to attend. The ladies of several species seemed to like Magnus personally, too.

Magnus introduced the show and made his call for volunteers. Lo, the first to volunteer were Frank and Frankie Stein. Good enough; they would certainly do for this audience. Jess took the stage while Magnus organized the players in the background.

"I am Atrocia," she began. "Nobody takes me seriously." But since for this show laughter was what was serious, she had their attention. She spoke of her several boyfriends and their problems, then went on to a string of jokes that kept them laughing. "I met a nice prospect, and asked his name. 'You're in charge' he told me. 'But I'm not in charge here,' I protested. 'I'm just looking for a date.' 'No, urine charge,' he said, pronouncing it more carefully. And he went charging through the forest to do something unmentionable to every tree stump he found, marking his territory. I barely escaped getting marked similarly."

They laughed uproariously. It seemed they liked earthy humor.

"I went to a meet market, a gathering place where folk can roam and mingle, hoping for better luck there," she continued. "But it turned out the men were looking not to meet, but for meat, and not the kind you eat. I had found the wrong market. I barely got away, and I do mean barely, with my dignity intact." They loved it.

"So I made sure to find the right spot next time. They even had refreshments. But some joker had put cough-he there, and I was too smart to fall for that, so I took a different cup. And went into a fit of coughing, anyway. I couldn't even talk to any of the men because of it. I had gotten the cough-she cup. I would have been all right with the first cup; I had outsmarted myself, which it seems is not hard to do."

The laughter continued.

"So then I tried dating a policeman, a cop. But he turned out to be made entirely of copper. So I gave up on men and tried a woman named Ana. Ana Conda. But she turned out to be a snake crossbreed with the talent of the big hug." She sighed. "So I gave up on people and got a dog. But he liked to travel. In fact he traveled by dogapult, going to visit his friend the male bovine who traveled by bullista. I couldn't keep up with them."

The laughter continued. She knew that the jokes weren't really that funny, but her curse was making her funny, and that was carrying it. She was indeed a successful jester or comedienne.

Then Magnus was ready, and the players, and they went into the familiar but strikingly original narrative of boy meets girl, loses girl, recovers girl. It held the audience spellbound. Jess had to admit that Frank and Frankie made a fine couple, here before the creatures of bad dreams where ugliness was an asset. There was prolonged applause when they finished. It was another successful show. Magnus had real talent putting it together. But Jess knew that she was contributing significantly.

Then it was time to go. Frank and Frankie Stein joined them on Fibot, and were give then bridal suite, by the art of Nia's designation.

"That was great!" Noe said. "I almost wanted to kiss Frank myself, by the end."

"I think that was me," Aria said. "I'm a sucker for a good romance."

"What did the mares think of it?" Ula asked.

Myst shrugged. "Mairzy says that it's not much for a daydream. She delivers similar ones all the time. But maybe it was more novel for a night dream, where they do more horror than romance."

They sailed on out of the dream realm, emerging into daylight above Mount Neverest. Then they parked invisibly in the sky, resting, because they didn't want to disturb the Franks, but couldn't know the right direction without them.

When Jess was alone with Magnus, she reluctantly broached something she had been thinking about. "Isis is still around somewhere, and I think not with Frankie at the moment. If I were to host her for an hour, maybe she could override the curse, and give you a phenomenal time in bed."

"No. I'm sure she could, but it's you I want, Jess, and only you, not your body without you. There has to be some other way. Eventually we'll find it."

"Eventually," she agreed, loving him all the more.

"You were fantastic in the show. They really wanted you more than me. That is, Atrocia."

"Oh, Magnus, I don't want to upstage you."

"I'm not jealous in that way. Do your best, always."

"But the same thing that makes me good with an audience makes me impossible with you. If only my real romance wasn't just as difficult as Atrocia's romances."

"I wish you could be both," he said seriously, as he was just far enough clear of her to minimize the curse. "That you could be fabulous on stage, then turn off the curse just for me, when we're alone."

She nodded, agreeing. But she doubted it could ever be. If she ever found a way to abolish the curse, she would have to choose between her career, and him. She realized that she really wanted both, not one or the other. She hated even the prospect of that choice.

In due course the Franks emerged, looking wonderfully refreshed, and Frank held forth his wrist. The compass circle pointed a direction. Win oriented the boat on it, and blew up the fire sail. They were on their way.

The compass took them to the region of the sometimes islands. They had to wait for the right one to appear. There was nothing but open water, but Frank's wrist compass pointed steadily to it.

While they waited, they relaxed. The two princesses were both a bit horse crazy, as girls of that age were, and were getting rides on the two mares. The four hosts had no objections, being girls of that age themselves. The others sat on the deck and watched.

Now they decided to have a race across the water. Kadence was on Imbri, while Aria was on Mairzy. The princesses, being girls, had already discovered how to change their hair and eyes to fit their moods. Kadence, on the black horse, had dark hair and eyes, while Aria, on the white horse, had golden hair and eyes. They were a beautiful sight as they sped over the gentle waves, the light running neck and neck with the dark, hair and tails streaming back.

"Those young girls are going to become attractive to men before you know it," Nia said wisely. "Do you agree, Dell? Dell?"

"Oh, sorry. Did you say something? I was watching the girls."

They both laughed together. Jess realized that they were teasing each other. If only she could have a relationship like that with Magnus!

Then Squid and Santo were riding, looking exactly like normal children. How deceptive appearances could be!

And finally Frank and Frankie were riding reacting just like children. Well, why not? How much actual fun had they had in their monster lives?

"Ho!" the peeve called. "Land ahoy!"

And so it was. The island was slowly fazing in. But there was something odd about it. The rocky shoreline was dark brown, and smelled of chocolate.

"Can this be right?" Jess asked.

Tata's screen flickered. He too could take her seriously when he wanted to.

"Yes, it is a chocolate island," the peeve translated. "With its traditional guardian: the Chocolate Moose."

Now they saw the statue of the great stag standing there with his widely spreading horns. He too was made of chocolate.

"This has to be it," Nia said. "Let's tag up before it fades out again."

The fire sail puffed alight in a flame-shaped configuration. Win guided the boat onto the island and to a landing beside the statue. The peeve flew up to perch on an antler. "Howdy, my deer. Mind if I poop on your feces-brown face?"

The head twitched, flicking the bird off with a squawk of surprise. It wasn't a statue!

Jess couldn't help laughing. One seldom saw the peeve caught by surprise.

"A real chocolate moose," Dell said appreciatively. "Looking good enough to eat."

"And here I thought it was spelled *mousse*," Nia said. "Shows all I know."

"I thought that was a kind of mouse," Myst said.

Tata trotted up. The moose lowered his head. They sniffed noses. The moose made a grunt.

Tata's screen flickered. The peeve flew in to read it. "Welcome to Chocolate Island, home of the Chocolate Alchemist," the bird translated. "Where is found the finest chocolate in Xanth."

"I'll say," Win said, picking up a chocolate stone and chewing on it.

"The Chocolate Alchemist?" Nia asked. "I never heard of that. We're looking for Che Centaur."

The dogfish's screen flickered. "The Chocolate Alchemist processes all kinds of chocolate. He started on a fifty-foot diameter rocky projection in the sea, but there were so many tailings as he worked that now it's an entire island, and still growing. When he melts some, it flows like lava."

"Chocolate lava?" Dell asked, licking his lips.

"Che Centaur is here, looking for chocolate truffles."

"I thought those grew underground," Nia said. "And got sniffed out by pigs."

The moose grunted. Tata's screen flickered.

"They do, and are," the peeve said. "Chocolate pigs locate them and dig them up. They're a rare delicacy."

"Growing from tailings?" Magnus asked. "Yuck!"

"Let's go find Che Centaur," Dolph said, growing impatient with these diversions.

Frank held forth his arm. "That way."

"Um, shouldn't we check with the Alchemist?" Nia asked. "Since this is his island."

The moose grunted. Tata's screen flickered. "He's too busy to socialize with visitors," the peeve said. "There would be a crisis if the chocolate ran out. Just get your business done and move on."

"There he is!" Squid cried.

Indeed, there was the winged centaur carrying a bag of truffles. "Hi. Peeve," he said as the bird flew to him. "I didn't know you had a sweet tooth. Sweet teeth don't go well with insults."

"Prince Dolph needs to talk with you," the peeve said. "Frank Stein brought him."

"Riding the three little princesses' fireboat," Che said, spotting the craft.

"They're not so little any more," Kadence said, stepping forward. "I'm Rhythm's daughter, and this is Aria, Melody's daughter."

Che stared at her. "I must have gotten sadly out of touch! I thought those two were still under one year old."

Aria laughed. "It's complicated. Come talk with us, okay? We've got serious business afoot." Both princesses smiled winsomely. They were very good at getting the attention of any male they focused on. Jess realized that Nia was right: soon they would become young ladies, and the mischief would be much worse.

Before long they had formed a group around the winged centaur, with the children chewing on chocolate tailings while the adults caught up with the mission.

"You're right," Che agreed. "This is quite serious business. I must compliment you two princesses for your poise, considering the horror you fled."

"It hasn't happened yet," Kadence said. "Our folks are fine at present."

"And we hope to see that they never get deleted in the future," Aria said. "By changing history to ensure that Ragna Roc never gets loose again. So we never will suffer that grief."

Che eyed them with a certain caution. "You do understand about paradox? You can't technically undo history. You can only change it marginally by shifting tracks."

"We do understand," Kadence said. "And we want to change it as little as possible. That's why we need Prince Dolph, and you. Because you know how."

Che shook his head. "I do not know how. That is an extremely delicate operation, fraught with mischief."

"But—" the two princesses started together.

"Peace, girls," Che said, holding up a hand in a stop gesture. "I don't know how, but I can take you to the one who surely does know how."

"And who is that?" Kadence asked.

"Sim Bird. The Simurgh's chick I tutored for years. It is his job to acquire all the knowledge of the universe so that his mother can finally retire. He has gone well beyond me now. He's a very smart bird."

That was surely an understatement, Jess thought.

Chapter 9

STENCH PLANET

Frank and Frankie decided to remain and have their honeymoon on Chocolate Island, so the others bid farewell to the happy couple and boarded the boat for the next excursion. "You do know where to find Sim Bird?" Dolph asked Che anxiously.

"Oh yes. He is now doing research in the less scure areas."

"The what?"

"Or more obscure, if you prefer that phrasing."

"This promises to be dull," Noe complained.

Che's smile became less scure. "That may depend on your perspective."

"I know about perspective," Noe said. "That's when you're zooming along on Fibot and looking at the passing scenery, and it's supposed to stay in place, but the farther away it is, the more it tries to cheat and keep up. So you have distant mountains staying right even with you, when they wouldn't dare if they were right next to you."

"Well, nobody likes to be left behind," Che said tolerantly. It was becoming clear to Jess that the centaur was no slouch at intellect, either. After all, he must have been smart enough to tutor the smartest of birds. But of course all centaurs were intelligent. "However, there are different types of perspective, and the mental type applies to the way a person views things. What is dull to one might be fascinating to another. What one likes very well another might hate."

"Okay, I dare you," Noe said. "Show me how research in obscure areas could ever be interesting to a child like me."

Che's smile played peek-a-boo with his face. He was teasing Noe, Jess saw, only she didn't realize it. Yet.

"Sim is on one of the Worlds of Ida. We'll be going there once we get clear of Chocolate Island and phase back into Xanth proper. I believe Santo has a certain talent for connecting distant worlds."

"Sure he does," Noe said. "I'm starting to get bored already."

"The world Sim is now on, where we will join him, is called Stench."

"Stench? Is that like a bad smell?"

"A very bad smell," Che agreed. "This world is where they grow stink horns, among other things."

"Stink horns! But when you accidentally step on one—"

"It makes a foul-smelling noise," Che finished. "And a filthy brown odor."

"Yes. Everyone knows that." Then Noe paused. "We're going there?"

"Indeed. Where you can step on all the stink horns you want to."

"But they're disgusting. I hate stink horns."

"They give free ones to each visitor."

"Yuck! I'm repelled."

"But not bored. No one said you had to be thrilled."

She gazed at him silently. He had skunked her, and now she knew it.

The Land of Xanth phased in ahead of them. The island was returning to reality for another brief visit. Win got her wind going and blew it at the sail, which flickered into a fiery star shape. They sailed off the island and into Xanth proper.

Che turned to Santo. "If I understand your talent correctly, it is borderline Magician caliber. You can make a hole of any size, ranging from pinhole through a sheet of paper, to fire-boat-sailing size to other planets. Am I correct?"

Obviously he was, Jess thought, and he knew it. This supremely smart centaur was just being polite.

"Correct," Santo agreed. Jess had caught on that he was no intellectual slouch himself.

"Except for one thing," Noe said. "You call his talent borderline Magician caliber. What's borderline about it?"

Che regarded her with a spark of interest. "You are his girlfriend?"

"Yes. So I defend him when he's too nice to do it himself. You didn't answer my question."

The centaur smiled. "I teased you, just now. Now you are teasing me back. You know the answer."

"Sure I do. Do you?"

Che glanced at Nia, "You are the matriarch here, young as you may appear. Noe is not the only child present. Would a straight answer in your opinion violate the Adult Conspiracy?"

Nia pursed her lips. "You don't pussyfoot around much, do you." It was not a question.

"Centaurs don't pussyfoot. We do hesitant hoof it on occasion."

They all laughed. Then Nia got serious. "These children are unusual. Four of them are from an abusive future, and have experienced serious threats to their lives after losing their original families. They are technically unrelated but regard themselves as orphan siblings. Two of them are not part of the sibling group but their association with it has matured their perspectives, as you know. Two others are spiritually visiting from a shocking future of their own; in fact we are now working to change that future if we can. Considering such backgrounds, and the importance of their participation in what may be a deadly mission, it is my judgment that the notorious Adult Conspiracy may on this occasion be bent somewhat aside without considering it an actual violation. They do need to know the straight score, and if the Conspiracy gets in the way, it should be abridged. It would be foolish to honor it to the letter if that should mean that the future of Xanth is lost."

"Well spoken, Nia. It appears that you are a significant thinker."

Nia laughed. "Hardly. I just happen to have had more social experience than the others here, and time to ponder my own mistakes and get some basics straight. I am trying to do better in my second life than I did in my first, physically, mentally, and emotionally."

"That will do," Che said. He returned his attention to Noe. "I commend you for your support of a young man who needs it."

Jess realized that he was referring to the fact that Santo was gay. But what did that have to do with the classification of his talent?

"Thank you," Noe said. "So what's the answer?"

"Santo's talent should be considered Magician caliber," Che said. "But the old order dies hard in Xanth. The senior folk who render judgments on talents have certain qualities that some might consider to be biases. They do not necessarily understand why any person should prefer romance with his or her own gender. They suspect that there is something fundamentally wrong with that, and that no person who is wrong in such a manner can be right for classification as Magician or Sorceress."

"Are you saying what I think you're saying?" Noe asked.

"I am saying that Santo's talent is Magician Caliber and some day should be recognized as such. But that classifications do not always match reality, for reasons folk are reluctant to openly express. I, however, represent only one person's opinion."

"It will do," Nia said. She put her arm around Santo's shoulders, as he looked faint. "Old timers don't know you as we do, Santo," she said.

He turned into her and sobbed into her shoulder.

Noe was bewildered. "I thought he'd be pleased."

"He is, dear," Nia said wisely.

In due course the interrupted dialogue resumed. "Santo, can you make a tunnel to a far planet you have never seen?" Che asked.

"Yes, if I have the right bearings."

"I possess those bearings. Sim Bird is currently researching on the planet Stench, as I mentioned before. We must intercept him there." Che glanced around at the others. "Though this is unlikely to be a completely pleasant excursion. The deck and interior of Fibot will be protected from the smells, but any folk who leave the boat will be subject to them. We can not be certain that we can reach Sim without at same point leaving the boat."

Nia's gaze swept across them. "Any who do not wish to take this risk may disembark here in Xanth. We can put you down in a safe place. Even the chocolate island if you wish. Who wishes to get off?"

"Oh, blip!" Noe swore. "I hate bad smells, but I'm not going to desert Santo because of them."

"Thank you," Santo said.

She made a wry smile. "You can kiss me some other time."

No one else wanted to get off. Win took her place at the stern along with Tata and the peeve, and the others settled down in the seats.

"Here are the coordinates," Che said to Santo. Then, to Win: "Please orient the craft in this direction." He pointed at an angle into the sky. Jess realized that this made sense, because a different planet was unlikely to be aligned with the local horizon.

Win's hair blew lightly forward. The sail came alive, this time in the form of a cloud of smog. The boat tilted upward, without putting its passengers off-balance. Jess kept being impressed anew by its magic.

Santo focused. A spot appeared ahead of the prow. It expanded until it was the mouth of a tunnel big enough to admit the full sailing craft.

"Weigh anchor," Win said.

Ula and Squid hauled up the anchor and weighed it on the scale. This, it seemed, was a necessary ritual. The boat was ready to travel.

Win's hair intensified. Jess knew the hair was not doing it, merely reacting to her talent of always having the wind at her back. She could vary the force of it at will. It was not Sorceress class, but it was more than good enough.

The boat sailed on into the tunnel. They were on their way.

Jess was impressed again. Santo's power surely was Magician caliber. Noe stood beside him, and she certainly looked like a girlfriend. It was hard to believe that this was a relationship of mere mutual convenience. But of course she was a friend and a girl; there was the key. It was clear that Santo did not dislike women; he just didn't see them as romantic objects.

The passage was not long; there was obviously distance contraction involved. It was not a tube between worlds, but a spot connection between them, going through hyperspace or whatever. More evidence of high-quality magic.

They emerged from the tunnel into a thick bank of evilly swirling smog. But the air on the boat was clear. Jess saw how the smog surrounded it but did not touch it; there seemed to be a translucent shield that kept the vile stuff at bay. That was a relief, because it was the stinkiest looking vapor Jess had seen. It kept writhing as if seeking some crevice to infiltrate so it could get at them.

Myst made a face at it. But Jess hoped the girl did not try to mist out herself and join it; the stink might become part of her when she reconstituted.

The hole closed behind them. Santo had done his job, and now was worn out. Noe took his arm and guided him down the hatch; he would need perhaps a day of thorough rest before he could do that again. Noe would be with him throughout, protecting him from intrusion. Jess understood that his sisters had taken turns doing it before. He simply needed someone he trusted to be there. Squid went down, too. Jess realized that it wasn't to watch Santo, but to be company for Aria, whom Noe hosted. It all made quiet sense.

"Now we orient on Sim," Che said. "He's a distance across the planet, but we'll get there."

Win revved up her wind, and it blew the sail onward. Jess noted with passing interest that the wind that brushed by them on deck was not polluted; the air inside the protective bubble remained clear. Yet it caught the sail and propelled the craft smartly forward. That did not fully accord with her notion of how a sailing ship worked. But of course this was magic.

Soon they emerged from the smog bank—and entered another. This world, it seemed, was literally covered in smog.

They encountered another break in the smog. Now the vegetation was visible, a field planted in skunk cabbage. Farther along was a lake filled with floating dead fish, the sickening odor almost tangible. Beyond that was what looked—and surely reeked—like a mountain of old vomit; with trolls with clothespins on their noses heating portions to make them ripen faster. Then a rotten egg plantation, with decaying zombie chickens laying them. And a town consisting of what looked like corpulent apes with indigestion, carefully saving their emissions in balloons. This was certainly the home of bad smells. There must be a market for them, though Jess had trouble imagining what it might be.

"Right up ahead," Che said. "Then: "Uh-oh."

Jess saw what he meant. Sim was a lovely roc-size bird, but his legs were trussed up and he was lying on his back in a cage. He was a prisoner!

"We arrived just in time," Magnus said.

"Indeed," Che agreed. "I will go out and untie him, so he can join us here on the boat."

"But will he fit? He's bigger than the boat!"

Nia laughed "You forget the qualities of Fibot. It can carry any size."

"That isn't the problem," Dolph said. "First you have to get into that cage, which looks to be woven of fine ironwood mesh which would take hours to clip through."

"And must have an alarm to summon its proprietor the moment it is breached," Magnus said. "We don't want that."

"There's also something odd about the knot holding the cord to his legs," Dell said. "I haven't seen one like that before."

"I have," Che said. "That's a Gourdian Knot."

"A Gordion Knot?" Nia asked. "The one that can be untied only by a conqueror? I thought that was lost in Mundania."

"Gourdian," Che said. "Fashioned from the vines of a peephole gourd. That can be untied only by a gourd resident with proper instruction."

"We just happen to have a night mare along," Win said brightly. "She's a creature of the gourd."

"Retired," Imbri said. "And I don't have hands to work a knot."

"But I do," Win said. "You can borrow them. With Tata to tell us how."

"And me to translate," the peeve said.

"And me and Myst to help," Ula said

"Except that the knot is on the bird, inside the cage," Nia said. "Where we can't reach."

"Perhaps we can," Magnus said. "I have had some experiences with cages. They generally have ways in and out, if you can figure them out. This one looks heavy, but is not actually anchored to the ground. It has four main supports. If a person lifted it at each support, we might get it high enough so that the children and animals could scoot under and reach the knot."

"I think we have a plan," Dolph said. "We don't want to delay, lest the proprietor of that cage return for his catch."

"Now is the time," Dell agreed.

"Except for one thing," Nia said. "It is our policy never to have all of us leave the boat at the same time, lest some intruder come to molest it. He couldn't actually use it, but he could damage it."

"We have five adult humans and a centaur," Magnus said. "We can spare one. Appoint a temporary guardian."

Nia nodded. "You, Jess," she said.

"But I don't know anything about the boat!" Jess protested.

"You don't need to, for a temporary watch." Nia drew out a large key. "Take this, Jess. It will give you control of the boat, if you need it."

"It won't take me seriously."

"Bit it will take the key seriously." Nia was already moving toward the edge of the deck.

"But why me?" Jess wailed.

"Because you're the protagonist. You can be trusted to do what's right, knowing that in due course everyone everywhere will know. Why else?"

Jess was unable to argue with that.

The others piled off the craft. Jess was left with the key, alone on the deck. "The protagonist," she muttered resentfully. But she was stuck with it. She just had to hope that nothing bad happened before they returned. It wasn't that she minded helping; it was that she strongly doubted her own competence, in case of an emergency. She had always had Magnus to be competent for them both, before.

Resigned, she stood on the deck and watched them approach the cage, gasping as they encountered the noxious smog surrounding it. They gathered around it, four adults, three children, a bird, a fish, and a centaur. If she was the Protagonist, they were her Companions. What a collection!

The four human adults took their positions at the four main cage supports. They took hold. Then, guided by Che's call, they heaved together. It was plainly heavy, but the men had the normal male muscle, and the woman was at the peak of her health. The cage slowly lifted.

The children and animal scooted under. They ran and flew to the big tied bird. Win put her hand on the Gourdian Knot. Mare Imbri manifested. "Ooops!" her speech balloon printed. "This is a sleep-gas bomb!"

Then the big tied bird dissolved into a monstrous cloud of vapor. The cloud expanded swiftly, catching them all before they knew it. All of the living folk crumpled into sleep. The cage dropped back down to the ground, imprisoning the one immune member of the company: the dogfish.

Then the whole thing sank into a slippery channel and slid again into the surrounding smog. They were gone.

Jess stood bemused. It had been a trap. The big bird had been an illusion.

And Jess was left alone on the boat, helpless.

After several fractured moments she remembered that she was not actually alone; there were three children below. Maybe one of them would have some faint notion what to do.

She hurried down, and to Santo's room. Santo was sleeping on his bed, with Noe sitting beside him, holding his hand. Squid was sitting beside

Noe, talking with Princess Aria. The three girls in two bodies looked up
as Jess entered.

"We have a problem," Jess said tersely. "I think Santo should hear it too.
Does he have to sleep now, or can he rest while listening?"

"He can listen," Noe said. "It's just making big holes that he can't do
for a while, until his magic recovers. It's a lot of work to channel between
planets for a whole boat."

Jess had to smile. "I'm sure."

"He needs emotional comfort from someone he trusts," Squid said.
"We siblings did it before Noe came on the scene."

"And did it well," Noe agreed. "He loves you."

Jess wondered again about the interplay of these children. Santo's closest friends were all girls, and they were surprisingly adult in attitude. Nia
was right: the Adult Conspiracy was not fully applicable here.

Noe lifted Santo's hand and gently squeezed it. "Dear, we need you
awake. Something has happened."

Dear? Maybe that was humorous. But maybe not.

The boy's eyes flickered. "Okay."

Jess quickly summarized the activity she had witnessed. "So they are
gone," she concluded. "Frankly, I have no idea what to do."

"Who would want to set a trap for us?" Santo asked.

"Ragna Roc," Aria said. "Who else? He wants to stop us from stopping
him."

"But he's still locked in his egg at this time," Squid protested.

Santo smiled grimly. "He should be. Otherwise we've already lost the
war."

"And we haven't lost it yet," Noe said. "If he was already loose, he'd have
come after Kadence, even as a baby, because she made the egg that locked
him in."

"And how could anyone know we were coming here, to Planet Stench?"
Santo said. "And get here before us, and lay that clever trap? Even if one of
us was a spy for Ragna, and none is, that's a tall order."

Jess was increasingly coming to appreciate the boy's intellect. He was
making sense. "Or maybe a mind reader, reading our minds from a distance," she said. "But getting here is another matter. This is not exactly a
popular tourist stop."

"Also, they couldn't read our minds from outside the boat," Noe said. "It's protected against that sort of thing."

Squid nodded. "Then who else?"

"There was mention of the Sea Hag," Jess said. "I really don't know anything about her, except that she changes bodies and is evil."

"The Sea Hag!" Aria said. "We know of her! She can't read minds, but she does take over bodies and gets their information that way. Originally her host had to die before she could move on to another, but she got better at it, and could borrow hosts for a few days and leave without hurting them much, though they hated the memory. If she intercepted someone we interacted with, then went to a host on Stench, it might be possible."

"It might be," Santo said. "That scares me."

"That scares *me*," Jess said. "If she made a deal to free Ragna, such as being made Queen of Xanth, that would explain it. How could we handle a person who could take over anyone's body without notice? I doubt we'll all be able to stay all the time on Fibot."

No one had an answer.

"Meanwhile, we'd better see about rescuing our crew," Squid said. "Maybe they'll have a better notion how to go from here."

This was the matter Jess dreaded most. "So how do we proceed?"

"We follow them," Squid said. "I can sniff them out. Maybe they haven't drifted far, yet."

That certainly wasn't the whole answer, but it would do for the interim. They went topside. "I will have to leave the boat for this," Squid said. "I'll swim below the surface and track whatever odors there are. I know the smells of every member of our party."

"But what if the Sea Hag comes?" Aria asked. "You're my friend. I don't want to lose you, apart from the importance of the mission."

"Two things: I'm a child, and the Hag isn't much for children. She prefers them nubile and sexy. And I'm not human. She definitely prefers humans."

"But if she should take you, anyway," Aria said. "What then?"

"Kill me," Squid said seriously. "No, wait; that would just release her to take the next victim. Maybe torture me instead."

"Torture you!" Noe said, horrified. "We couldn't do that!"

"Yes you could. Just grab onto a tentacle and slowly twist it off. I promise you that will hurt me awfully, even though I could grow a new one later. But here's the thing: I won't be in charge of my body; she will. She'll be the one hurting. She'll go the moment it hurts too much, and I'll be free."

A look traveled around. This did make sense. "That would apply to any of us," Santo said. "And face it: she just might have taken over one of the captives, and be hiding among us. We have to be alert. If there's any suspicion of that, we will need to grab that person and make him or her hurt."

"This is sickeningly ugly," Noe said. "Everyone aboard is our friend or sibling."

"And your friend or sibling will thank you for it, once the Hag is gone," Aria said. "We're not playing putty-cake here."

Indeed they were not. "Assuming we do rescue them," Jess said, "how can we verify that all are clean?"

"I can touch them, one by one," Aria said. "I will know."

"Even if it's Kadence?" Squid asked.

"Especially if it's Kadence."

That seemed to cover it. "Find them, sister," Santo said fervently.

"I will, brother."

"I'll track you, friend," Aria said.

Then Squid shucked her dress and dived into the muck outside the boat. Her body changed as she did, becoming the tentacular blob that was her natural form when she didn't have it squeezed into human shape. There wasn't even a splash.

Jess was impressed yet again. These children were rallying bravely and realistically, and getting the ugly job done. No wonder they had been selected to crew the magic boat.

"You have the key?" Santo asked Jess.

"Yes. Nia's key. But I don't know how to use it."

"No mystery there. You just tell Fibot what you want, and it will do it."

"Can I make it sail without wind?"

He smiled. "No. But there's almost always a little wind. Do you know how to tack?"

"Thumbtack?"

He smiled again. "I guess you don't. But I do. We'll sail if we need to."

"She's tracking them," Aria reported. "There's a trail of odors in the water." Then she paused and knocked her head with the heel of her hand. "And I can track Kadence! We're attuned to each other. Why didn't I think of that before?"

"We can't think of everything all at once," Jess said. "Is Kadence all right?"

"She's unconscious, or at least Ula is, and that limits her. But at least she's alive, and that suggests that the others are too."

"When we catch up to them," Jess said, "how will we rescue them? We don't have much magic."

"If we have to, we can sail Fibot into their midst," Santo said. "And haul them in by hand."

"Oops, Squid's losing them," Aria said. "There are too many dividing channels, with different smelly currents running through them, obliterating the traces she's tracking. She's coming back."

"Still, we're learning a lot," Jess said. "We're not helpless." She was moderately surprised to realize that.

Soon Squid returned. "I lost them," she reported sadly as she squiggled over the hull and onto the deck. The smell was awful. "Check me, Aria, to be sure I'm me."

"You are," Aria said. "Don't worry about tracking them. I realized that I can do it through Kadence, because we have a mind connection. She's all right."

"That's a relief." Squid progressed into girl form, and went to stand under the deck shower Jess had not noticed before, getting clean. The odor eased.

"There's something else," Santo said. "Jess has Nia's key."

"Yes, so she can make the boat go," Noe agreed. "If we find some wind."

"The two keys connect," Santo said. "Dell and Nia always know where the other is. Jess should be able to tell where Dell is."

"Say, that's right," Noe agreed. "You're pretty smart."

"Quit it," he snapped. "We're not in public now."

Noe turned away. "I'm sorry."

"She was just telling the truth," Squid said. "You *are* smart. You figure things out. She wasn't trying to flatter you or put on a show for outsiders. You don't need to hurt her."

Santo paused "Did I do that?"

"Yes," Jess said. Though it was minor. Still, when emotions were complicated, pinpricks could feel like stab wounds.

"She says yes," Squid said, translating.

"And you did," Aria said. "Noe does everything for you, and asks for nothing, and you treated her like dirt."

Santo turned to Noe. "I'm sorry. I didn't mean to. I'm tired from the big hole. I wasn't thinking. You're the last person I want to hurt."

"It's all right," Noe said, wiping away a tear.

Santo looked at Squid. "Is it?"

"Yes. But don't do it again."

"I'll try not to. Noe, you can call me smart if you want to."

Jess found this dialogue incidentally fascinating. Noe plainly loved Santo while understanding his nature. She had not deserved his rebuke, minor as it was. It had taken his sister to set him straight. He was mature enough to accept the correction. Were they really children?

Now Aria turned to Jess. "See if you can tune in on Dell's key."

Jess held her key up and focused on it, thinking of Dell. And there he was; she felt his presence, though he was unconscious. "Yes. I feel him, through his key. He's all right, but still asleep."

"So now we have two ways to track them," Santo said. "Princess to princess, and key to key. That helps."

"But how do we rescue them?" Jess asked.

"She says—" Squid started.

"I heard. I'm learning to take her literally. We do need to rescue them. But there's something else."

"I've got a feeling we need to hear this," Aria said. "Santo's perspective is slantwise to ours, and that can make a difference."

Slantwise, Jess thought. Santo was smart, and from the future, and had a monstrous talent, but mainly it was that he was gay. His perspective did differ. "Yes," she said.

"Somebody set a trap for us," Santo said. "We conjecture it's the Sea Hag. She must have escaped the brain coral's pool. But if it's her, and she made a deal with Ragna Roc, why is she coming after us? Why didn't she go directly to free Ragna from the egg? We need to know, so we know her motive. Maybe we can find her weakness."

They pondered that. "Ragna's locked in the undeleted egg Kadence made," Aria said. "It is hidden away where no one can find it accidentally, and guarded."

"Yes," Squid said. "His minion Em Pathy tried to corrupt Dell last year, to get the boat. So it could float through the little hole and get him out of the egg. After that they hid the egg away better."

"That's my thought," Santo said. "Maybe the Sea Hag *can't* get him out on her own. So she needs the boat. That's why she's here."

"She wants the boat!" Jess exclaimed, seeing it.

"She wants to get all of us off the boat, so she can take it over," Squid said. "And she almost did. The only reason it didn't work was because we three were below deck, and Nia left Jess in charge."

Jess was impressed yet again. Savvy Nia had routinely protected Fibot, thought not knowing of the trap.

"But now she's got most of the crew hostage," Santo said. "Seeing the way her devious mind works, I fear we'd be fools just to run in again. There's bound to be another trap, to get the rest of us."

"There is!" Jess exclaimed. "This is genius, Santo, and I'm not trying to impress you, even if you can take me seriously. What an insight."

Santo took a moment to digest that, mentally taking her words literally and accepting that she meant it. "Elementary," he said with a quarter smile.

"But we can't just leave them!" Squid said.

"We won't leave them," Santo said. "We just need to be ready for more tricks, and not fall for them. Maybe go in as if we're none the wiser, but be alert for illusions and whatever doesn't quite smell right."

They all laughed "Nothing smells right here," Squid said. "But I know what you mean."

"Whatever we do," Noe said, "We must not all of us leave the boat."

"We're expendable," Aria said. "Jess has the key. She must stay."

"But suppose something awful is happening to the rest of you, that I might stop?" Jess asked.

"If we're right," Santo said, "Something awful will. Or at least will seem to. It will be designed to make you jump off the boat without thinking. Don't do it."

He was right. "Don't do it," Jess agreed with half a shudder.

There was a slight wind; they could see it moving the sludge that passed for atmosphere here. Jess took the helm. "But the wind is going the wrong way."

"Angle the sail so you can steer correctly," Santo said. He sat down beside her and put his hands on hers, guiding them. "Instruct the firesail."

"Firesail," she said aloud, and the sail came alight, this time in a hexagonal outline. "Angle so the craft goes that way." She pointed in the direction she felt the other key.

And the sail did. Suddenly she liked it better. It took her seriously!

The boat moved forward obliquely, following the compromise between the direction of the wind and the aim of the rudder. She was sailing!

Jess felt her key. "Dell is closer," she murmured.

Then something appeared to the side. "Kadence!" Aria cried.

The figure didn't hear her. The princess was walking away from the boat, not seeing it. Ahead of her was a crack in the ground.

"Crack?" Jess asked. "But aren't we on water?"

"No," Santo said. "Fibot sails on air, remember."

Oh, that was right. "Kadence!" Aria called. "Come this way!"

But the girl kept walking.

"I'll intercept her," Noe said.

"But you can't leave the boat," Squid reminded her.

"*Jess* can't leave the boat," Santo said. "But I don't trust this. I think it's illusion. Hang tight."

So they watched. "Yes," Aria said after a moment. "I sense Kadence, but not there. I think that's a fake. An illusion, as you thought."

When it became clear that they were not going to leave the boat, something else happened. Magnus appeared. He chased after the girl, and caught her just before she fell into the crevice. He picked her up in his arms and carried her to safety.

"My hero!" Kadence said in gestures. Then she drew her face close to his and kissed him firmly on the mouth.

"What?" Jess asked, astonished and dismayed.

Santo put his hand on hers. "They're illusions," he reminded her.

Oh, yes. Still, it bothered her. The girls, including the princesses, were young, but a quarter smitten with Magnus, as so many women were.

When Magnus started responding, and kissing Kadence back, Jess was about ready to leave her seat and jump off the boat, running to intercept them.

"Kadence wouldn't do that," Aria said. "Sure she likes him, as I do, but she knows he's taken. He loves you Jess."

"And Magnus wouldn't do it, either," Santo said. "Because she's a child."

"The Sea Hag is trying to get your goat," Noe said. "So you'll run out there with the key."

That was it, of course. Jess held steady, keeping the boat moving in the right direction. "Dell is close by," she said.

The illusion couple faded, evidently giving up the provocation as a bad job.

Then Jess saw Magnus again, straight ahead. This time he was walking toward beautiful adult Nia, who was caught in entangling vines that were trying to haul her off the ground. He reached her and used a small knife to cut her free of the vines. "My hero!" she gestured, and kissed him.

"But I know better," Jess said through her teeth. "I won't react."

"How close are we to the real ones?" Santo asked.

"Almost on top of them."

"Then slow the boat. Give the key to Squid; she can steer it. You go make a histrionic scene to distract the Sea Hag while Noe and I quietly rescue the others."

"You *are* smart!" Jess said. She gave the key to Squid, and went to the edge while Squid took the tiller.

Suddenly they were up against the cage—and the boat sailed right through it as if it were illusion.

Santo and Noe slipped over the side and went to the sleeping figures within the cage.

Jess stood facing outward. "Magnus!" she screamed. "Unhand that woman. She's not nearly as young and malleable as she looks!"

The figures paid no attention to her. They were too busy kissing each other. Magnus's hands were reaching around Nia's lithe body, pulling her clothing off, and she was cooperating fully, while neither paused in their passionate kissing.

"Stop that!" Jess screamed louder. "Do I have to go out there and tear you apart from each other? He's *my* man!"

They blithely continued making out. Now Nia's bare body was showing in ever-widening places, and Magnus's hands were all over those places. They were extremely shapely places. It was starting to turn Jess on, despite the outrageousness of the scene.

"That does it!" Jess called. "I'm coming out there!" She made as if to climb off the boat. But of course she didn't.

Now the couple was lying down on the ground, getting ready for a child-forbidden performance. Illusions, it seemed, were immune to the Adult Conspiracy. Squid shielded her eyes.

"Got them!" Santo said.

Jess looked back. There were the sleeping bodies of the others, including the centaur. Tata and the sleeping peeve were there also. It had seemed like only a moment, but of course she had been distracted. "However did you haul them here? The centaur alone is many times your mass."

"This is a small planet," he explained. "It can't afford much gravity. So they were light enough for us to carry. Now sail us out of the cage."

Jess got the key back from Squid and resumed her place at the stern. She saw that the bars and mesh of the cage were enclosing them. She snapped her fingers, and the sail brightened into flame the shape of a squashed stink horn. It was right; the deck now stank from the squalor coating the rescued sleepers bodies and clothing. She steered the boat forward, and it passed through the cage wall and on into the sky.

"And I didn't even have the key!" she yelled spitefully.

Now the illusion figures reacted. They looked angry. Then they faded out.

When they were safely above the planet, Jess tossed the anchor overboard on its line, and the boat stopped moving. "At ease," she told the sail, and it died out. She was hardly a proficient navigator, but she was learning the basics.

Jess took a deep breath—and gagged on the concentrated odor. "We (choke) have to (cough) get them (retch) clean!"

"We do," Santo agreed. "Us, too." Because the rescuers were also coated. Jess was the only one still clean.

"We have a dirty job to do," Jess said grimly.

Chapter 10

SEA HAG

"I have an idea," Squid said as they gazed at the bodies strewn more or less haphazardly on the deck. "That sleep bomb that caught them—could it also have been a stink bomb?"

"Why not?" Noe asked. "It certainly stinked us up just hauling them in. All the more reason to clean them up quickly."

"Maybe not," Squid said uneasily.

"And we have to clean ourselves up promptly, too," Noe said. "Because even diluted, it could affect us similarly. I'm starting to feel sleepy myself."

"Yes, but." Squid said.

"Yes, we'll have to take off their clothes and see them naked," Noe said. "Including the adults. We can handle it, because we're like a family on the boat. We're not going to molest them. We can do what has to be done."

Still the child hesitated.

"I have seen that look on you before," Santo said. "What is on your mind, little sister?"

"I . . . I don't want to . . . maybe it's nothing."

"Come here," he said. "I promise I won't snap at you. Whisper it to me, and I'll decide whether it makes sense."

She went to him and whispered in his ear.

Santo stiffened, surprised. "And they called *me* smart!" he said. "You're right. I will tell the others."

Squid nodded, gratified.

Santo went to Noe and whispered in her ear. She looked startled, then nodded.

Why were they whispering? This wasn't a childish game they were playing.

Santo came to Jess and whispered in her ear. "The Sea Hag could be among them. They're unconscious, resistance down. Part of her ploy."

And Jess was startled, too. "Nia," she whispered back. "The one adult female."

He nodded. "They're asleep, but the Hag may not be. Don't let on. But—"

"But tie her," Jess finished. "Before washing off the stink. Just in case."

"You do it, quietly," he whispered. "We don't want her to know we're on to her. If we are. Not until we have her host bound."

"Got it," she said. The Hag might not be unconscious, but she couldn't do anything with the body while *it* was unconscious. Now Jess reflected on the manner that body in the illusion had shown remarkably realistic detail, clothed and partially clothed, as if the illusionist was working from the original body.

They got to work. First they removed the clothing. Squid took care of Ula, Win and Myst; Santo took care of Dolph, Dell and Magnus; Jess took care of Nia. She carefully bound the woman's wrists behind her, not punishingly tight, but secure. As an afterthought she also bound the ankles together.

The centaur did not wear clothing, this not being the high frigid atmosphere.

Tata came to her, his screen flickering questioningly. Jess leaned down. "The Sea Hag may have taken over Nia. We're just being careful." The dogfish nodded and went back to guard the peeve.

Once they had the bodies bare, Noe got the hose and splashed water on them all, including the dogfish and the peeve. Squid took the clothing below, to the magic washing machine.

The clinging muck reluctantly loosened and flowed across the deck, then poured down toward the ground far below in a miasmic shower.

The first to stir was the peeve. "Who pooped on the deck?" it inquired peevishly.

Tata's screen flickered. "Oh," the bird said.

Then the children stirred. "You were knocked out by a sleep gas stink bomb," Noe told them. "We had to wash you off to get you away from the gas."

The centaur stirred. Santo gave him the same message.

The men stirred. The centaur relayed the message.

Finally Nia stirred. Her eyes opened.

Jess met her gaze, and knew immediately that she was staring into the baleful eyes of the Sea Hag. The worst had happened.

The woman tried to kick, but her feet were bound. She tried to strike, but could not free her arms.

"We've got you, Hag," Jess said, her tone more even than her feeling.

The creature tried to lunge forward and bite, but could not get the teeth into play.

"Should we also gag you?" Jess asked, maintaining her supposed calm. There was nothing to be gained by letting her fear be known. "We are under no illusions about your nature."

The woman stopped struggling. "What do you want, you bleeping joker?" she demanded.

So she wasn't taking Jess seriously. Did it matter?

Jess signaled Santo, who came over. "Santo, meet the Sea Hag," Jess said.

Santo didn't flinch. "We'll torture you if we have to," he said.

There was no further need for secrecy. "Folks, the Sea Hag is among us," Jess announced loudly. "She took over Nia's body while all of you were unconscious. We have her tied up."

They laughed, then caught on and quickly clustered around, heedless of their nakedness.

"Get out of there," Dell said angrily.

The Hag turned a look of contempt on him. "Make me." She knew she possessed the body of his wife. What was he going to do to that body, torture it? She was calling his bluff.

"We have a better way," Dolph said grimly. "We'll simply take her back to the Brain Coral's Pool, where the Brain Coral will separate them and confine her."

"Over my dead body!" the Hag spat.

"If necessary," Dolph said evenly.

"But—" Dell protested, appalled.

"Nia would rather die than remain possessed by the Sea Hag," Dolph said. "You know that, don't you?"

Dell backed off. "Yes." But he looked ill.

Jess was beginning to get a hint of a glimmer why they needed Prince Dolph along. He had the nerve to do what needed to be done, if it came to that.

"We can make her hurt," Santo said. "The pain will be felt by the Hag rather than the host, because the Hag takes total possession. So if she doesn't leave, we can still take her to the Pool. One way or another, we'll get Nia back."

Che glanced at him. "You're pretty tough minded for a child."

"Thank you."

"We'll have to keep her confined," Dolph said. "While we get on with our mission to this planet." He glanced at Jess. "I think that will be your job."

"I think it will," Jess agreed.

"You will have to feed her and see to her natural functions."

"Yes."

Dolph glanced at Dell. "I think it best that you stay entirely clear of her for the duration. She has nothing but grief for you."

Dell nodded, looking faint.

Dolph looked at Ula. "You see to Dell. You know the stakes."

Ula nodded. "You need to rest, Dell," she said. She took his arm and led him away. Jess understood that she had once had a crush on him, or maybe Kadence had, and maybe still did. She wouldn't do anything untoward, but would take the best possible care of him.

There was no sign of Princess Kadence. Jess knew why: she didn't want the Hag to know she was there. She of course hated the Hag, for freeing Ragna Roc and thus wiping out her mother. Aria was similarly silent. They just might be secret weapons.

How deep were the waters they were abruptly in!

"Let all go get dressed," Che said. "Then on to find Sim Bird."

That made so much sense that no one argued.

"Meanwhile the only ones who still smell are those of you who rescued us," Dolph said with a smile. "Now we get to see *you* naked."

It was true. Seeing to the others had gotten them soiled. They stripped, and Myst took away their clothes, and Dolph hosed them down. It hardly seemed odd that a woman and three children were showering together. The important thing was that they had done what they needed to, when they needed to, to get the others back. Except, perhaps, for Nia.

Jess kept the key.

In due course everyone was clothed again. Win returned to the helm. The sail ignited, and they resumed progress toward Sim Bird.

Jess went to Noe. "I will be taking care of Nia," she said. "But I have a few things to wrap up first. Could you watch her for a while?"

Noe concentrated, digesting the words so she could take them seriously. Jess was actually asking her to stand watch over the Sea Hag. She hosted Aria, who hated the Hag, as did her cousin Kadence, for similar reason. Then she nodded. She settled down beside Nia while Jess moved on.

Dell, trailing Ula, approached Jess. "I know I haven't taken you very seriously," he said. "And I know why, because you are plainly a serious person. I just wanted to thank you for rescuing us from the Sea Hag's trap." He swallowed. "Even if you couldn't save Nia."

"Neither has she lost Nia," Dolph said. "That issue has not yet been settled."

"I wasn't blaming her," Dell said. But he sounded somewhat the way Santo had when apologizing to Noe.

"The children were great," Jess said. "Santo, Noe, and Squid. We all worked together."

"She says we children helped," Squid said. She had become Jess's principal translator.

"I said more than that," Jess said indignantly. "I couldn't have done whatever I did without you."

Squid smiled. "She says we all worked together."

"Something else," Jess said, remembering. "I've got Nia's boat key. Who should have it?"

"Who gets Nia's key?" Squid asked.

Dell considered for the better part of a moment. The two keys were vitally important for control of the boat. "Give it to Santo. He's the most sensible one among the rest of us, and he loves Nia."

In any other context that would be an odd thing for Nia's husband to say. But Santo had no romantic interest in any woman, and had turned to Nia for reassurance when the question of his likely Magician-caliber talent had been discussed. Nia was a kind of mother figure for him, at least on the boat. He had known her when she looked her age of sixty.

Ula took Dell back to his room where he could suffer privately. There were ways in which the children were governing the adults in this time of stress. Dell looked as if he could collapse at any moment. Jess knew that in their partnership, Nia was the dominant one. He was ill equipped to function long without her.

Jess went to Santo. "Nia's key," she said, giving it to him.

He accepted it, nodding. "I will give it back to her when the Hag is gone."

They all understood the importance of keeping the key away from the Sea Hag. It would be the thing she most wanted to acquire, now that she was aboard Fibot. Had Squid not thought of the chance of the Hag possessing one of them, she might have succeeded in getting it by this time. Jess's knees felt weak as she considered how close they had come to disaster. The Hag with the Boat—would spell doom to Xanth.

"Bird ahoy!" Win called from the deck.

They went topside, except for Ula and Dell, and Noe and Nia. There ahead was a golden bird the size of a roc. Jess understood that Sim had had different appearances as he slowly grew to maturity, and might change in the future. This would do; no one would confuse him with the enemy bird, Ragna Roc.

"Suppose it's another illusion?" Squid asked.

"Unlikely," Dolph said.

"Why?"

"Because obviously the Sea Hag possessed the body of an illusionist before. Now she has moved on to Nia, whose talent is seeing eyes." Then he paused. "She could be watching us!"

"Unlikely," Che said. "The Hag may control the body, but it will take her time to become proficient with its talent. She is still assimilating Nia. But it's a good point: we should be alert for traveling eyes."

The boat landed neatly beside the big bird. "Sim!" Che called.

The huge head turned. "Squawk!"

"Yes, it's really me," Che said. "I gather the illusionist has been trying to fool you with false images."

"Squawk," Sim agreed ruefully.

"We are here on Fibot, the fire boat," Che continued. "Prince Dolph is with us. He needs to know how he is supposed to help save Xanth. This is not something I know, but surely you do."

"Squawk."

"Sim will figure it out when he finishes with his present concerns," Che said. "This is not dismissive. He has a great deal to assimilate, and he needs to do it in an orderly manner, or it can get fouled up. We'll camp for a while until he is ready." Then he addressed the big bird again. "Is there a convenient local site that does not stink to high heaven?"

Something like a smile twitched at the big beak. "Squawk."

"Thank you." Che turned to Win. "Tata will guide you."

It seemed that the robot dogfish had picked up on harmonics of the final squawk. His screen flickered. "Northwest," the peeve said, indicating the direction with a pointing wing. The craft changed course.

Soon they came to what appeared to be an island flower garden. It was surrounded by oddly shaped trees whose foliage formed a kind of mesh-like wall. They sailed over the wall and down to a green glade inside. Win neatly parked the craft on the lawn.

"I will verify," Che said. He spread his wings and flew off the deck, out over the island. He landed beside a bed of brown roses.

Brown roses? Jess was electrified.

Che smiled as he returned to the deck. "No, those are not Rose of Roogna's cultivated variety, though they are related. They are a different shade. They merely suppress the magic of bad smells."

Oh. So there would no siege of Jess's curse being suppressed. She sighed internally. Eliminating the smell was certainly worthwhile.

They stepped off the craft. The air was warm and redolent of roses and new mown hay, and there was a pleasant breeze. "The ring of filter trees removes any magic-related odors," Che continued. "Since that includes the worst of the smells, that makes this an oasis. The local creatures can't stand it; the stench is natural to them. So it's a passing resort for visitors, a kind of spot paradise in hell. Sim knew of it, of course; few others do."

"Let's bring the others out," Dolph said. "They deserve some respite, too."

Soon Ula and Dell were with them, and Noe and Nia. There was still no sign of the princesses, so that the Hag would not catch on. Jess noticed that Dell did not look at Nia, though she looked at him. *The Sea Hag* was looking, Jess corrected herself. If she could tempt him into an embrace and steal his keys . . .

Jess went over. "My turn," she said, relieving Noe, who went to join

Santo. Jess loosened the rope tying the woman's feet together so that she would be able to walk but not to run, and sat her on the deck. "You know we want to be rid of you, Hag, one way or another," she said, not caring who else was listening. "Some among us would like to torture you until you depart, but we don't want to injure our esteemed colleague Nia. So we'll probably just take you back to the Brain Coral, where you belong, and make sure you never get loose again. That would be my preference."

"You can't be serious," the Hag said via Nia's mouth.

Jess smiled. "It is my curse not to be taken seriously. But if you reason it out for yourself, you will likely realize that it is not in our interest ever to let you go. We are however curious how and why you got involved in this business. Do you care to tell us?"

"No."

"As you wish. You may talk or not, as you see fit. But here is the way we see it, which you may or may not consider seriously: somehow you managed to communicate with Ragna Roc, and he promised to make you Queen of Xanth if you just got him out of his imprisonment. You, being greedy for power, of course agreed. It did not occur to your limited intellect that he would more likely simply delete you once he was free, so as to prevent you from ever getting greedy and trying to oppose him. That makes perfect sense, don't you agree? He already has a human girlfriend, if that is the appropriate term for a subservient minion. This is Em Pathy, who is pretty enough if you like that type, and who has served him loyally for many years and whom he does trust, in contrast to you."

The Hag was now watching Jess closely. Jess was speaking a language she understood. The others were also listening closely. Jess was discovering to her surprise that she was pretty good at cruel teasing when she didn't care who took her seriously. She wasn't sure she liked this capacity, but at the moment it was serving a purpose: to provoke the Hag into doing something revealing or downright foolish.

"In fact Em and Ragna have probably already determined your fate, as they have of so many others," Jess continued. "Em hardly wants a Sorceress like you competing for his attention. Sooner or later you will try to take Em over, so you're really her enemy, whatever she may say while they need your services. I doubt you will survive more than a few minutes, once he's out. And of course once you're deleted, you won't be able to take over any more host bodies. You'll be completely impotent, able only to observe, not to affect. I trust you are looking forward to that."

Now the Hag spoke. "What makes you think he'll betray me, once Em Pathy is gone? He has many minions. I would be one of them, using my talent to serve his purposes, as the others do."

There was the confirmation that the Hag meant to eliminate any competition for the bird's favor. "It's the logic of empire," Jess said. "Keep your friends close, and your enemies closer. He knows that ultimately you serve no purpose but your own. He can't afford to trust you. You can accomplish a lot independently of his favor. That's what makes you dangerous to him. His other minions will collapse in minutes without his support. He's not stupid, any more than you are. He knows you are a natural enemy."

"You lady wolf!" the Hag spat. "You've got me doubting!"

"It's not because I care half a squished stink horn about you, Hag. It's that if you release Ragna Roc, he will destroy most of what I value in Xanth. You of course don't care about that, but when you realize that you will be gone with the rest, you may reconsider doing it. Your own hide, in whatever host, is valuable to you. So you may try to free him and be doomed, or to avoid that and continue on your ugly way, ruining the lives of pretty girls and all they associate with."

"I may do that," the Hag said thoughtfully.

"And you may not," Jess returned. "We can't afford to take the chance. So it's off to the Pool with you, as soon as we finish here."

"You can't hold me. I can go any time I choose."

"And we'll have Nia back, and you can be sure she'll never let you catch her again. But we still can't trust you to stay away from Ragna. We'll have to hunt you down and put you away. You know that."

"Lots of luck there."

"I didn't say it would be easy. Just that we'll do it."

"You'll try."

There was a stir of wings. Sim glided over the trees and landed neatly in the glade. "Squawk!"

"He has wrapped up his immediate business," Che translated. "Now he can talk with us."

"All we want to know," Dolph said, "is how am I supposed to help save Xanth?"

"Squawk."

Che laughed. "He says he thought it was obvious. You are supposed to put away the Sea Hag."

"That's all?" Dolph asked, surprised.

"That's enough. Without you, this group has one chance in three to accomplish this. With you, it has two chances in three. It's that simple."

"Simple as untying an illusory Gourdian Knot," Dolph muttered.

"Squawk."

"Sim is now cataloging the assorted odors extant, as this world has a fine selection," Che said. "Once he has them complete, he will move on. He is quite busy, as there is a lot to learn, and more keeps accumulating."

"Can he spell out exactly how I am supposed to help these fine folk accomplish their mission and save Xanth?" Dolph asked.

"No."

"No?"

"Sim can acquire knowledge of everything that exists, but that is largely past history. The present is an ongoing chaos state that can't be properly defined until it becomes the past."

"Chaos?"

"A state of utter confusion. Any small influence can make a huge change in the future. It is our fate to dwell perpetually in this ongoing disorder. Knowledge of the past is only one aspect of the larger reality. We can only estimate the chances of any action accomplishing what we wish it to, never guarantee it."

"Are you saying we're on our own?" Dolph asked, frustrated.

"Yes, now that you have the odds."

Dolph glanced at Sim with understandable confusion. "And what do you feel the odds are for other matters? Are there any sure things?"

"Squawk."

Che smiled. "The odds of a parabola maintaining its form are excellent."

"A parabola?"

"A plane curve formed by the intersection of a right circular cone with a plane parallel to the generator of the cone."

"Oh come on now! Tell it in people talk."

"Think of a line," Che said. "Think of a point near that line. Like a fiery fence and a chained dragon. You don't want to get too close to either, lest you get burned, but you have to pass by them. So you try to stay just as far from the one as from the other as you walk. Your route will be a curve. That curve is a parabola."

Dolph spread his hands. "Does anybody here understand that?"

"Yes," Santo said. "It's a simple mathematical concept, useful when chained dragons have to be passed."

The others laughed.

"If this is simple, I can see why chaos is complicated," Noe said.

"It is complicated," Che agreed.

The Sea Hag cackled. "It *is* simple. You morons are just ignorant."

"And how much time have you had to learn to understand it?" Noe asked.

"A bit over three thousand years," the Hag said. "I have passed many chained dragons in my day."

"Let's relax today," Dell said. "Tomorrow we'll tunnel back to Xanth and put the Hag into the Brain Coral's Pool where she belongs, and I will have my dear wife back."

"Oh, are you lonely?" the Hag asked. "Come to my bed tonight and I will make this fine body perform splendidly, just as I demonstrated in the illusion."

"The bleep you will!" Jess snapped as Dell looked appalled. The illusion had featured Nia with Magnus, not Dell.

"Caution," Santo said. "She is trying to make us angry with each other so we'll make mistakes she can use against us. Divide and conquer."

The Hag looked at him. "Look who is talking! The one who has no idea what to do with a woman."

"No idea," Santo agreed with a smile.

"But I could show you. You just haven't encountered the right girl."

"Alas, I never will," Santo agreed pleasantly.

"See, you can't goad him," Noe said smugly.

"And the child-woman who foolishly dotes on him," the Hag said.

"Listen, you foul-minded harpy!" Noe started. But Santo put his hand on her arm, and she stifled the rest.

"Maybe it's time to take that creature to a private place," Dell said tightly. That was to say, where she could not try to sow dissent among the crew members.

"Yes." Jess got up and guided Nia's body to the boat, leaving the others outside. The Hag was managing surprisingly well, tied as she was. Maybe she had experienced similar confinement before, in her long ugly history.

They navigated the hatch and went to Jess's room. "I've got to pee," the Hag said bluntly.

"You can use the toilet. I will pull up your dress and pull down your pants." Because of course they wanted to take proper care of Nia's body, for when she got it back. Jess knew better than to give the Hag any more freedom.

They handled that, then settled in chairs. "Are you going to harangue me with more of your garbage about Ragna Roc?"

"Not if you prefer to do the talking. I think you know you are not going to persuade me to let you go."

"You've got spirit, I'll say that for you, blocked woman. It's hard to take you seriously, but you're not slipping up."

"Thank you," Jess said dryly. What was the Hag up to? Jess did not trust her at all, especially now that she seemed to be making halfway nice. But she was also quite curious about what motivated this foul creature.

"Well, I'll talk. I was part of the first human colony in Xanth, around the year minus 2200, give or take a century or two. I may have been the first full Sorceress, though that is not in the record because I had the wit to conceal it. I had a hard childhood; in fact I was married at ten."

"Ten!"

The face smiled. "So you are paying attention. Yes, it was an arranged marriage, and a bad one. It didn't matter that I was a child; I was female. The abuse I suffered at home was smoothly transferred to the abuse I suffered from that cruel man. I realized early on that being nice didn't cut it; doing what I was supposed to only made me miserable. There was far more to be gained by looking out for myself regardless of the effect on others. Do you understand?"

Jess was silent, not wanting to agree.

"Considering your curse, I think you may understand. You are clearly a decent person, and constantly paying the price thereof. If you had a way to nullify it, you surely would." She paused, but Jess did not speak; she was waiting for the punch line. "When my magic manifested—it didn't show at first—I realized that I could forever escape the degradation I had suffered. So I got me a young beautiful body, prettiest girl in the village, and made the most of it, and when that host wore out, I got another like it. I escaped my curse. And so it went for about three thousand years. I had a relatively good life. It's amazing how much a pretty girl can get away with, in contrast to the plain ones."

Jess could not remain silent longer. "And what of the poor hosts you ruined with your dissolute living? You are notorious for making pretty girls into ugly women."

"That's no concern of mine. My only real inconvenience was having to kill my hosts in order to move on to better ones. I finally learned to get around that, and now I can move on without having to die first."

"I suspect that's not because you decided to be kind to your hosts."

"Of course not. It's because death usually makes a ruckus, while I prefer to be subtle. I would rather have no one know I am among them; that saves me some grief."

She seemed to be telling the truth, but Jess didn't trust it. She was up to something.

"Then in more recent times, oh, maybe seventy years ago, I got creative. Instead of searching for the best next host body, I decided to raise it myself. I got this lovely long-haired child, Rapunzel, and raised her in a tower, instilling in her all the things to make her an ideal future host. I kept her sweet and innocent. Then, just as she was ready to be harvested, that idiot Grundy Golem came and absconded with her. All my work was wasted. You may be sure I didn't make that mistake again."

Jess knew that the lovely Rapunzel had married a golem, and they had a child named Surprise. There must have been an interesting story there.

The creature continued talking in a monotone. First Jess got bored, and then she got sleepy. It didn't really matter because she knew that she would come alert the moment the Hag tried to get close to her.

She felt a faint touching, internal rather than external. Then it turned away, not taking her seriously.

Then suddenly she was being called. "Jess Jess! Wake up! Wake up!"

It was Nia's voice. Jess snapped awake. "Don't try to fool me by imitating your host!" she said.

"Listen to me!" the Nia voice cried. "The Sea Hag is gone! She left me for another host. Aboard the boat! Don't let her do it!"

This certainly didn't sound like the Hag! But how could she be sure it wasn't a trick? "What happened?"

"She tricked you. Tricked us! She stalled for time until most of you were asleep. Then she changed. A sleeping person can't resist the way an awake one can. Jess, she's got someone else!"

Jess lurched to her feet and charged out of the room, leaving the Nia figure tied, just in case. As she ran she realized that the Hag had tried for her, as she nodded, but couldn't take her seriously as a host. Her curse had saved her!

"Dell! Dell!" she cried, bursting into his room. There he was, snoozing, while Ula snoozed in another chair. "Check on Nia, in my room! You can tell if she's real or possessed. If she's real, free her!"

Wordlessly Dell ran for the room. Ula was alarmed. "The Hag is loose?"

"I fear so." Then Jess got an ugly notion. She grabbed Ula and stared into her frightened face. But there was no sign of possession. "Not you, I think."

"Not me!" Ula agreed with a twinge of horror. "But who?"

Jess moved in, increasingly fearing that it was the truth: that the Hag had a new victim. But who, indeed?

She burst into Santo's room. He was sleeping, with Noe beside him. Jess grabbed the girl and looked into her eyes.

Noe spat into her face, then clawed her shoulder, trying to get free. This was the Hag! Jess struggled to control her, but the girl turned out to be a vicious fighter. When Jess hauled her in close, she got kneed in the belly. Somehow she hung on, turning Noe away from her. And got kicked in the shin.

Then Santo was awake. "Why are you two fighting?" he demanded.

"The Hag!" Jess screamed. "She's the Sea Hag! The Hag moved!" Would he believe her?

Santo put his hands on the girl's head and turned her face toward him. He looked into her wild eyes. "She's possessed," he agreed. "I know Noe. This is not her."

"How could you know anything, you perverted excuse for a boy?" the figure demanded. "You never touched her body!"

Together they got the girl tied hand and foot. She glared at them. "You fools will never stop me!"

Then the others arrived. There was Dell with Nia, and Nia was now disheveled but free in more than one sense. Dell looked phenomenally relieved. He had his wife back!

"The Hag tricked us," Jess gasped. "She waited for us to sleep, then changed hosts."

Santo quickly translated, to be sure they understood.

"It's true," Nia said. "I knew what she planned, but I couldn't speak at all. She had me completely clamped down."

"And now she's got Noe," Santo said. He had been effective during the fracas, but now that he had time to absorb the implications, he wilted. "Oh, Noe!"

He did love her in his fashion.

"You blubbering fool!" Noe's mouth said. "You thought you were so smart, but you lost your girlfriend. Now how do you do?"

Santo looked ready to strike her, but of course he couldn't hit Noe. He had talked of torture to get rid of the Hag, but it was clear he couldn't do it.

Nia put her arms about him, again. She understood him. She was also, it seemed, back to her old self. Either possession by the Hag was not ultimately harmful, or Nia was supremely tough in her own right. Probably the latter.

"We've got to get her out of the boat," Dolph said. "Before she changes again, maybe when we don't catch her, and gets the key. Or pretends to be gone from Noe, and grabs it from Santo."

"Yes!" Santo agreed. He gave the key to Nia, who accepted it as she held him. Then Jess grabbed Noe. Myst came up on the other side to help together they bundled the struggling girl up topside. Even tied, she was a handful. Dolph picked her up and stepped off the boat.

"Take the boat away!" Dolph shouted. "Don't let her get back on!"

Win took the till. The sail fired up. The boat sailed into the sky, leaving them below.

"You've stranded yourselves, you idiots!" the Hag spat as Dolph set her down.

"We don't matter," Dolph said. "Now you can change as often as you want, but you won't get the boat or the key. We've stopped you, Sea Hag."

"Bleep!" Even blanked out, the curse made Myst turn vaporous for a moment, and the turf under their feet turned brown.

But it was true: they had stranded themselves, along with the Sea Hag.

Chapter 11

ARIA

"I felt something," Prince Dolph said after a moment. "When I carried her."

"That was my thigh, you lecher," the Hag said. "Got a thing for under-age girls? Want me to take off my clothes?"

"Give me your hand," Dolph said.

"I'll give you more than that, if you let me go." She turned around so that her bound hands were toward him. "Grab my bouncy bottom too, while you're at it."

Jess glanced at Myst. "Remember, the creature speaking is thousands of years old. She is trying to freak him out with foul language."

"I know," Myst said. She had had the longest and closest association with Jess of all the children, and was best able to take her halfway seriously. "The Adult Conspiracy doesn't stop her."

"I think the Adult Conspiracy is in abeyance while the Sea Hag is with us. This is a special situation. But I also think it is limited to words. Brace yourself; there may be more."

"You bet there will, you backward-talking slut," the Hag said. "Bleep! Bleep! *BLEEP!!*" Even bleeped out, the words scorched more turf and left a trail of acrid smoke in the air.

"I can't even understand those bleeps, let alone the words they cover up," Myst said. "So there."

"Well, I will define them for you, brat. They mean—"

The Hag cut off in mid diatribe as Dolph grabbed Noe's hands with his own.

"Oh!" Noe's voice said. But it wasn't Noe.

"Princess Aria, my great niece," Dolph said. "I felt you before."

"Uncle Dolph," she agreed. "I felt you too, because you're a Magician."

"Are you a prisoner, too?"

"Not exactly. I can depart at any time, but I'm not doing it, because it's better to stay here and fight the Sea Hag. She can't completely dominate Noe's body despite what she says as long as I resist her."

"And you hate her," Dolph said.

"Because she loosed the thing that deleted my mother!"

Dolph turned to Jess. "Aria and I are both Magician caliber individuals, and we are related, both being of the line of Bink. So we have a certain affinity. I can drive back the Hag while I have physical contact with the host. But only while I touch her; she'll resume dominance the moment I let go. The Hag is a Sorceress, too."

"Yes she is," Aria agreed. "And she is far more experienced at occupying host bodies than I am. It's her specialty. I can't drive her out on my own."

"I know. And actually we don't want to drive her out. We want to keep her captive."

"She can't move on yet," Aria said. "It takes her a day or so to settle in completely. She controls the actions and language, but that's superficial until she penetrates to the deeper levels. Noe is fighting her too, so it's slow. But she is in control."

"I can't touch the host all the time," Dolph said. "But I will when we need to talk. Keep fighting."

"I will, Uncle," Aria promised.

Dolph let go. Immediately the girl's expression curled into a sneer. "The twit from the future is just delaying me," the Hag said. "And so are you, Prince Doofus. This body is mine."

Jess noted that Noe, the host, had never spoken. She was not a Sorceress, just a girl, so was completely suppressed. That bothered Jess on another level, but there was nothing she could do about it. "So what's next?" she asked Dolph.

"Good question, Doofus," the Hag said. "You can't get my clothes off unless you cut them off or untie me."

"We start world traveling," Dolph said. "Until we reach the Brain Coral's Pool where we can confine her."

"But the boat is gone," Jess said. "We're stuck here on Stench."

"Hardly. I know how to orient on Princess Ida, who is my sister. We'll go to her."

"I'm not sure I understand," Jess said.

"Of course you don't, slut," the Hag said. "You're just an ignorant peon."

Dolph quirked a smile. "But she is nevertheless the protagonist of this story."

"Oh for screaming at top volume!" the Hag said. "What possible reason could there ever be for that? She's nothing."

"I hear that nothings make for good pro, pro—main characters," Myst said.

"Protagonists," Jess said.

"And it means she's largely protected against complete disaster," Dolph said. "Nothing really bad happens to protagonists, and they generally conclude with happy endings."

"So why don't you make *her* end happy, Doofus? She surely needs it. Her own silly man won't touch her there."

Jess decided to ignore the filthy implication. The Hag was still trying to mess them up.

"Or maybe just spank it; she might like that," the Hag continued. "Specially if you bare it first."

Jess realized that learning of her protagonist status was really riling the Hag. Maybe that boded well for their mission.

"Why would anyone like spanking?" Myst asked.

"Oh, do you have an education coming, brat! I shall enlighten you forthwith. Little girls get spanked when they're naughty. So do big girls, but its different for them, because naughtiness means—"

"Let's move on," Jess said, interrupting her.

"I will transform to roc form," Dolph said. "You get on my back, and hold on the feathers. Can you do that and hold on to Noe's body, too?"

"We'll try," Jess said.

"If you start to fall off, I'll feel it, and will promptly land."

Then the man was gone and the monstrous bird was in his place. The bird flattened on the ground, half spreading one wing to serve as a ramp. Jess and Myst each took hold of one of Noe's arms and hauled her along, up that ramp, to the more solid back. The Hag did not try to resist, maybe knowing that they might start hurting her physically if she fought them too much.

When they were fairly centered, each of them took firm hold of the base of a giant feather with one hand, while clamping on one of Noe's arms with the other. It wasn't perfect, but it would do. "Ready!" Jess called.

The roc spread his wings, then scooted along the ground, pumped the wings, and took off. In a moment and a half they were flying above the trees.

"Whee! This is fun!" Aria said.

Jess's startle faded as it started. The host was back in contact with Dolph, so the princess was able to express herself again.

"It is!" Myst agreed. "It's not the same as when we're on the boat."

"It gets old after a century or so," the Hag said. Evidently the suppression wasn't perfect when the contact was through feathers instead of flesh.

"You don't seem to have much joy in life," Jess said.

"*Life* gets old after a century or so."

"So why do you continue?"

"What choice do I have? I'm eternal."

Jess peered down around the big bird's torso as well as she was able. The tapestry of the World of Stench was passing rapidly by. "It doesn't smell bad up here," she said, surprised.

"The air is thin," the Hag said. "No matter; you get used to it after a few years."

"I'm breathing normally."

"The air around the Magician is normal to the extent he wants. It's part of his magic."

Was she getting talkative? "What were you doing here on Stench?"

"I was exiled last time I was caught. There is not much of a tourist industry here, so they figured I'd never escape." She cackled, literally. "Until you folk came, bringing the beautiful boat."

Jess was appalled. "You mean if we hadn't come, you'd have had no chance to escape?"

"Ironic, isn't it? You sow your own destruction."

"But that's paradox!" Or was it, considering the multiple closely-set time lines? They might just be messing up the next reality.

"Not so," Aria said. "You were biding your time, Hag, waiting for the right host and the right situation. If we hadn't come, sooner or later you'd have found another way. Better for us to do it, because we know we need to confine you more safely."

"Spoilsport," the Hag muttered.

The big bird angled downward. They were approaching their destination. This turned out to be a small castle surrounded by a filthy moat, in contrast to the cultured grounds. But when they landed on a flat roof, the smell was not bad at all.

They disembarked, and Prince Dolph reappeared, complete with clothing. "The moat filters incoming air," he said. "That's why it's filthy."

So he had been able to overhear their dialog. That was surely just as well.

"This is Princess Ida's castle," Dolph said.

"I thought Princess Ida lived in Xanth Proper," Myst said.

"She does. But the Worlds of Ida, as we call them, represent an effectively infinite loop wherein reside all the folk who live on Xanth, or ever did live, or ever might have lived. It requires a number of iterations of Ida to service all those worlds. This is Stench Ida."

A woman was approaching them. A tiny staff with a swollen end orbited her head. "Well spoken, little brother!" She hugged Dolph, and he hugged her back, the orbiting object neatly avoiding them both. Jess noted that her skin was blotchy as if soiled by intrusions of stench, and her hair resembled a cloud of smog, but she seemed healthy enough.

"This is my sister Ida," Dolph said. "You can tell by her planet."

"Which is not a ball of stench, as you might expect," Ida said. "That orbits the head of the Ida of the next planet below. Mine represents the next world up, Planet Distaff. It is governed by women."

A distaff? Jess had never seen one before. But she knew what it was: a kind of staff around whose end women wound flax or yarn to facilitate spinning. It was a symbol of women's work, and thus of women.

Ida glanced at them. "And who are your companions, Dolph? Are these fair young ladies friends of Electra? One of them seems to be bound."

Myst flushed slightly at being called a fair young woman, at the age of eight. Jess hoped she herself was not reacting similarly.

"These are Jess, the Protagonist of this story," Dolph said. "Myst, a young friend. And Noe, who can't speak at the moment because she has been infested by the Sea Hag."

"The Sea Hag! We don't want her here. She's supposed to be mired in the far swamps."

"Tough feces, sis," the Hag snapped. "I got a new host."

"I will explain that in a moment," Dolph said. "Also with this host is Princess Aria."

He touched Noe's tied hand, and Aria made a little curtsy. "Hello, great Aunt Ida. It's a pleasure to meet you."

"But dear, you're only one year old!"

"In this time, yes. I am visiting from nine years in the future. It's complicated."

"Surely so," Ida agreed, briefly touching Noe's free hand herself. Jess realized that she was verifying the Sorceress quality of the visitor, and probably also the presence of the Sea Hag. "Come in all. You must catch me up on everything."

In the course of the next hour they did catch her up. "I am of course constrained to help you," Ida said. "And not merely because you are my brother and great niece; the welfare of future Xanth is clearly at issue. But there are constraints; I must maintain an essential neutrality. I must not, for example, deny the Sea Hag access to other worlds; that would violate my position of assisting all. But I may be able to assist you indirectly by proffering advice which you may or may not accept."

"We are hardly going to reject your advice, Ida!" Dolph protested.

"I phrase it in this manner to maintain my socio-political neutrality, Dolph," she said gently. "So that the choice is completely yours, not mine."

He shrugged, not really understanding the distinction. "We are listening."

"First, a mechanism to maintain your control of the Sea Hag. You can continuously touch Noe by changing form to a flea and hiding in her hair. That will give Aria ongoing control of the host without any awkward appearance of uncle handling niece."

Dolph's jaw dropped, literally. So did Jess's. Why hadn't they thought of that before? Of course he did not want to seem to be constantly handling a young girl.

"Second, with Aria in steady control, she will be constrained to honor her station. She is a princess and a Sorceress. She can't outrightly deceive others. It is not the royal way."

"But we can't just tell everyone we meet about the Sea Hag!" Aria protested. "She will twist her words to make us seem like malefactors, and soon escape our control."

"That is true, dear. But a princess must be princessly, or her reputation will suffer. Appearance can count as heavily as reality. Compromise may be necessary."

"Compromise?"

"You must always tell the truth, but not necessarily the whole truth. This is a social compromise to get along. Ugly folk do not necessarily appreciate being informed they are ugly, or dull folk that they are dull, so that truth is not always social. You may have an itchy bug bite on your bottom; you do not mention that either, because princesses are considered to have no imperfections. You may say that your full situation is complicated, but that what concerns others is that you are Princess Aria. They will assume that by omitting supplementary details you are merely being polite, and will appreciate it."

"That's not dishonest?" Aria asked.

"That is socially acceptable evasion, dear. Royalty practices it as a matter of course."

Aria nodded. She was a child, but was learning adult ways.

"We will consider your remarks," Dolph said. "And be guided or not guided as we ourselves choose."

"Exactly," Ida agreed with a smile. "Now I suspect you wish to travel to the next world. Traveling upward is generally easier than traveling downward, but eventually you will close the loop and return to Xanth proper, if that is your intention."

"It may be," Dolph said. "We need to take the Hag to the Brain Coral's Pool, so that she can't wreak further mischief."

"Then you are in luck. There is a supplementary Brain Coral complete with Pool about two worlds up, on Planet Coral."

"Excellent! We have about a day to get her there before she vacates this host and seeks another."

Myst looked troubled. Ida picked up on it. "Is there a problem, dear?"

"We don't have the boat," Myst said. "We don't have Santo to make a hole. How can we get to another world?"

"Myst, that is why my brother brought you here. I am the axis of connection of worlds. In the early days we thought that folk had to rest and let their souls do the traveling, but now we know they can do it directly. Dolph will take you to Distaff, and thence to Coral. He is familiar with the mode. It is all in the mindset."

Jess was relieved. She had wondered herself.

"I think we had better be on our way, then," Dolph said.

"Say hello to Distaff Ida for me."

"We will." Dolph let go of Noe and transformed to roc form.

Immediately the Hag tried to bolt for the woods, hopping madly. But Myst, alert for this, tackled her and both fell to the ground amid a welter of curses that blackened the nearby flowers. Jess went over and helped haul the girl back to her bound feet.

They bustled Noe onto the roc's back. "Fare well, Princess Ida!" Jess called as they took off. But where was Dolph going?

The big bird did not fly into the sky. Instead he circled Ida, going around and around her as she stood still. She seemed to be getting smaller, or rather farther away. Then Jess realized that it was actually her orbiting planet, the Distaff, that he was circling. It was growing. In fact it was becoming enormous. It was becoming a weirdly shaped planet, indeed.

Now they were gliding down towards it. Jess saw seas and continents. As they descended she saw mountains, forests, fields, and roads. Even houses. It truly was a world. The shape of it was no longer apparent; it seemed perfectly ordinary, and the air was sweet.

They landed in an isolated field. The three dismounted, and the roc became the man. "Now we need to find Distaff Ida," he said. "She is—" he paused, then pointed. "That way. I tried to land close to her. I can take us closer. But it might be better to walk, so as not to attract attention."

"Yes, untie my feet," the Hag said, sitting down on the ground. "So I can walk." She glanced at Dolph. "Unless you want me to spread my legs first."

"Your crudity is becoming tiresome," Jess said.

"All you have to do is let me go, dearie, and I'll get the bleep out of your sight and hearing."

"We may have a problem," Jess said. "We'll attract attention if we keep her hands bound, but she'll get into mischief if we don't."

"I should be able to guide Aria in the right direction," Dolph said. "As the flea."

That was right. It had slipped Jess's mind. This was workable.

Dolph untied Noe's feet. The Hag stretched her legs out as she sat, so that her skirt hiked back, exposing her thighs. "Get a good look, Doofus. See anything you want more of? My panties are almost showing."

Dolph put his arms around her upper body. What was he doing? Oh—untying her hands. Then, without separating from her, he disappeared.

"He's aboard," Aria said as she got to her feet. "I never thought I'd *want* a flea in my hair!"

"Weird," Myst said appreciatively.

"I am picking up his thought," Aria said. "I know where to go."

They started walking. Soon they came to a town. There were people doing this and that, but they ignored the visitors. Jess wondered about that; no curiosity at all?

"No men," Myst remarked.

That, too. Where were the men?

Beyond, on a hill, was a small castle. That would be the residence of Distaff Ida.

Then they came to a road block. "Halt strangers," a stern-faced woman called.

Uh-oh. It seemed that they had not been entirely ignored.

Jess was about to speak, but realized that would do no good, because they would not take her seriously.

"We are just passing through," Aria said.

"Not without kingdom bands, you aren't," the woman said. "What's your kingdom? Why are you bandless?"

Jess saw that all the villagers wore green bands on their left wrists. So did the challenging woman. She hadn't thought to notice this before. What to do?

But Aria proved to be up to the challenge. "We are interworld travelers. We wear no Kingdom Bands because we are not local. We mean to go to Princess Ida and move on to the next world."

"And who are you?" the woman demanded.

"I am Princess Aria of Xanth proper, with my associates. I am not accustomed to being challenged on the street like a common serf."

Jess was glad that Ida had advised them of the uses of partial truth. What Aria was saying was true.

"You are not where you came from, girl. Touch me." She extended her hand.

Aria strode forward and touched the hand. It was almost as if a spark jumped.

"Oh, my!" the woman said, backing off. "You're a Sorceress!" She had evidently felt the power. Jess knew what that was like.

"I am, of course," Aria agreed. "Most princesses are. Now please get out of the way and leave us to our business."

"Nuh-*uh*," the woman said. "No royals move on from here." She brought out a small mirror. "Thirza? We've got a Royal from offworld. What to do?" It was evidently a magic mirror, used for communication.

Soon they were guided into a well-appointed cell. Thirza showed up. She was a solid woman with graying hair and an air of authority. Jess took an instant dislike to her and saw that attitude reflected in her companions.

"We have verified your identity. There is a young Princess Aria. You are of course ignorant of our local policy," Thirza told Aria, completely ignoring the others. "So I will inform you. Women govern this world of Distaff, but we are short of competent rulers. Any Royal is slated to govern, because the people prefer royalty. A princess will have a kingdom. You will govern the local Kingdom of Greena, because we are the ones who found you. We are in dire need of competent government, but there are not enough royals to go around and we are at the low end of the list. So we suffer." Her mouth quirked. "We take it out on our men, sending them to the mines. That needs to change, and not just because men are useful workers and can be fun in bed."

They did seem to need better government, Jess thought. But setting Aria up as a queen was no good; she could not stay with Noe forever, and neither could Dolph. The moment they left, the Hag would take over. She would love to become a despot queen, but it would be disaster for all concerned.

"Thank you, but no thank you," Aria said politely. "We are not staying."

"You are not going. This is our planet and our law."

"I am not entirely what I seem," Aria said. "For one thing, I am using a host body, not my own. My spirit can depart at any time. You can not hold me against my will."

"And what of your servants?" Thirza demanded. "They can not escape the way you can. They will suffer in your absence. We guarantee it."

They thought that Jess was a servant woman, and Myst a servant girl, and Aria was not correcting them. She was playing it well. But this whole business made Jess distinctly nervous.

"You have the temerity to threaten me?" Aria demanded haughtily.

"No, only your servants."

Aria considered momentarily, making a show of it. "We will consider. Begone, woman."

Thirza did not argue. She backed off, literally. She had made her case, and trusted a princess to appreciate it. Soon they were alone in the chamber.

Were they being watched and listened to? Surely so! They had to be careful what they said and did.

"There is something about her," Aria said.

"She's like me," Jess said. "Cursed to be disliked."

"That's it! Yet I sense that she is not a bad person beneath that nasty exterior. She seems smart, competent, and even fair minded. A good ruler."

Jess realized that this was Dolph's opinion being relayed. He was surely a shrewd judge of upper echelon character, not unduly swayed by the superficial curse.

"We could go," Jess said, not needing to specify how. Dolph could become a fire dragon and blast a hole in the wall.

"But is that the right thing to do?" Aria asked. "They do seem to need a competent ruler."

This was curious. "What are you thinking of?"

"I could rule in absentia." This was definitely Dolph. "Using a proficient regent who might not be accepted on her own." Her mouth quirked. "She wouldn't have to be popular."

Even Myst nodded. They might be able to get out of this while doing a bit of good along the way. It did seem to be the princessly way that Aria was trying to follow.

"Could we set it up in an hour?" Jess asked, conscious of their deadline to get the Hag to the Pool.

"Perhaps. We can try."

"Then let's have a serious talk with Thirza," Jess said.

"Yes. Let her know." It had to be phrased as a directive from the princess, that the servant obeyed.

Jess went to the door. It wasn't locked, but when she opened it there was a guard outside, an alert amazon. "The princess wishes to talk with Thirza," Jess said.

The amazon turned smartly and marched away. Surprisingly soon she returned with Thirza. "You wish to speak with me, princess?"

"Yes," Aria said. "Touch my hand."

The woman put out her hand, and Aria took it. Jess saw the reaction; the Sorceress was showing her aura, her power of spirit. If Thirza had had any doubt, it was gone.

Aria released the hand. She had made her point. "As I have said, I am unable to stay on this planet long. But I believe I can solve your problem of competent governing. I will accept the Queenship of Greenia, then appoint a capable regent to rule in my absence."

"Princess, you can't leave."

"I can do what I choose to do," Aria said haughtily. "Do you question this?"

"No, of course not," Thirza said quickly. "But I am obliged to point out that you will be regarded as a captive queen, who rules but remains under guard. They will not allow you to depart."

"They?" Aria asked. "You do not agree with this policy?"

"I do not. I do not like coercion, even in a case like this. But I am not the one who sets policy. I obey and enforce what is required of me."

"And if I appoint you as regent, you will obey me."

Thirza was taken aback. "Princess, nobody likes me!"

Aria smiled. "Allow me to introduce my companion Jess."

"Hello Thirza," Jess said. "I am similarly cursed. Nobody takes me seriously."

The woman considered her, perhaps for the first time. "You are joking, of course. Yet it seems that the princess heeds you."

"Take her hand," Aria said.

Thirza extended her hand, and Jess took it. Their two similar curses met, clashed, and nullified each other. Both women were surprised.

"Now I can take you seriously!" Thirza said.

"And now I can like you," Jess said. Because she did.

"There *is* an affinity. My curse blots out friendships and romance."
Thirza smiled ruefully. "Which leaves me largely objective to deal with
problems of government. I suppose that's an advantage."

"My curse does much the same," Jess said. "I have become a jester,
making folk laugh. But a Sorceress can nullify it temporarily."

"So you can see I do have a notion of your situation, Thirza," Aria said.
"Will you accept appointment as my regent?"

"If that is your will, princess, yes, of course."

"Set up a formal gathering of the folk of Greenia. I will address them,
then appoint you, then depart, leaving the kingdom in your charge."

"As you wish, princess."

"And send me a copy of your national anthem."

Jess wondered what that was about. But Aria plainly knew the protocols of royalty.

Thirza was clearly doubtful about aspects, but did not argue. She and
Jess separated hands, but the effect lingered; Jess did not dislike her, and
knew that she could now take Jess seriously.

Thirza was certainly efficient. In a minute the amazon brought a scroll
with the music and words for the Greenia anthem, and Aria studied it.
In an hour there was a considerable gathering in the town square. Aria
mounted the central platform, looking regal; local girls had garbed her to
be queenly and done her hair. The body was that of Noe, but she did look
the part. She was a girl verging on womanhood, and now she looked like a
princess. Jess and Myst, as the loyal personal servants, stood nearby, ready
to do the queen's bidding at any moment.

"Citizens of Greena," Thirza announced, "I present to you Princess
Aria of Xanth proper, our new queen. Bow your heads."

As one, the local women bowed their heads.

Aria stepped forward. "Raise your eyes." They did, in unison. "I will
now sing the anthem." And without further adieu Aria broke into song.
Jess had never heard it before, but such was the power of the Sorceress's
talent it mesmerized her from the start. She could see that the effect was
similar on the citizens; they were in rapt wonder until it finished.

Then Aria held up her left arm. With her right hand she put the green
wrist band on. "I am Queen of Greena," she said. "My word is the law of
this kingdom."

No one questioned it.

"I am unable to remain here at this time," Aria continued. "I have essential other business elsewhere. I will appoint a regent to govern in my absence." She turned to face Thirza. "Thirza, I hereby appoint you regent of Greena, to govern until I return." The woman nodded obediently. Aria faced the audience. "She will guide you in the interim. You do not have to like her, merely obey her as you would me. If you discover problems you can't abide, stifle them until you can take them up with me." She paused a good three quarters of a moment. "And now I bid you adieu, my people. You are dismissed." She turned regally and glided off the stage.

What a performance! Jess realized that Dolph had to have been helping Aria put on the show, getting the details exactly right. It had certainly been effective.

Jess and Myst trailed Aria back to the cell. Only when they were alone did the girl relax. "Jess, please organize our escape while I recover," she said as she sank limply onto a chair.

She had had Prince Dolph's support, yes. But she had also been fighting off the Sea Hag. No wonder she was tired! Dolph was probably tired, too; the Hag was such a canine.

Jess got to it. "Myst, vaporize and check the area for guards. We need to be able to get somewhere close where Dolph can change and fly up and away."

Myst fuzzed into vapor and drifted through a wall. Jess had not realized that she could go through walls instead of around them; it had to be very thin stuff. It was also apparent that she could move about freely, when there was no wind to blow her away.

Then Jess spoke to Dolph, who remained hidden as the flea, because he could not afford to leave Noe where the Hag could take over and cry the alarm. Naturally the Hag wanted to be Queen, rather than be hauled off to the Pool. "Prince Dolph, you may be tired, too, fending off the Hag. But I hope you will be ready to transform on short notice when we find a suitable place. We may have only one chance to escape; if we muff it, they'll be twice as careful as before."

Slowly Noe's head nodded. He was ready.

Myst returned, reforming. "There are guards all over, but they're relaxing and drinking boot rear, maybe even barrels of beer. They think Aria's leaving is just talk, that maybe she'll go to a country estate. There's an open courtyard close by, and the passage there is not being watched right now."

"Lead us there," Jess said. She glanced at Noe's body. "Follow me."

"Oops," Myst said. "Mairzy says a guard just came out by chance, and is standing in our way."

Mairzy? Then Jess remembered: the day mare Myst was hosting. "I forgot about Mairzy! We haven't heard a peep from her since we left the boat."

"She's been trying to get in touch with Imbri, who is with Win, so as to send news of where we are. But she doesn't know how to jump to other worlds. She's been in a green funk."

"Well, she can help us," Jess said. "Tell her to bring a distracting daydream to that guard, so he won't notice us."

Myst smiled. "Great! She heard. She'll do it." Then: "She's there. We can go."

"Good enough," Jess said, hoping that it would work. She realized that the mare was invisible when doing her job, so as not to be seen by others.

Myst led the way. Jess followed her closely, and Noe's body followed her. Myst knew exactly where to go to avoid the guards. At one point they could hear the guards celebrating in a nearby room. It was nervous business, but they made it through to the passage where the lone guard stood. Was he distracted?

Then Jess saw that he was. The daydream was visible over his head. In it he had been transferred from dull cell duty to bright hayberry farm duty, where a golden haired damsel almost as luscious as the berries was working. "I am worried," her speech balloon said. "I am not sure this crop is good enough for the market. Here, taste one, handsome man, and tell me what you think." She picked a fresh yellow hayberry and brought it to the guard, who was bemused by her full red blouse and short green skirt.

"Uh, I don't know," his balloon said. "I'm not supposed to eat while on duty."

"But this *is* duty, silly," the damsel said. "Please, please, won't you do it for me? I'd be so grateful."

"Well—"

She leaned forward so that her low blouse gave him a deep peek into a truly evocative valley between mountains. "Only one berry. Is it good enough?" She popped it into his mouth.

He chewed on the berry. "It's delicious!" he said as he stared into her cleavage. He was of course on the verge of freaking out.

She took a deep breath that moved mountains as if they were made of jelly. "Oh, I'm so pleased. Try another, just to be sure."

But by that time Jess was past the scene and could not see its conclusion. She was almost disappointed. Would the guard get to explore those mountains before the daydream ended?

They were at the courtyard. They could not have done it safely without Myst and Mairzy.

Aria's mouth quirked. "I didn't know that soft mountain valleys appealed to fleas."

"Depends on the flea," Jess said. "And the mountains."

They laughed. Their escape was perfect so far. "Be ready to grab Noe," Jess told Myst. Then, to Dolph: "We're here. Transform."

The roc appeared beside them. The Hag opened her mouth to scream. Myst put her hand over that mouth, stifling her. The Hag bit down viciously, but the hand dissolved into vapor that filled the mouth, gagging it another way.

Jess put her arms around Noe's body and half hurled the child onto the roc's back. "Grab on!" she called to Myst. "Take off!" she told Dolph.

The huge bird spread his wings. There was just room in the courtyard. He lurched into the air.

The Hag coughed out the vapor and took a breath. But then she stalled: the host was back in contact with Dolph's body, and Aria was able to resume control.

They sailed up, up, and away. There was no outcry below; the guards had not realized that the prisoners had escaped. That was better yet! The manner of their departure would be a mystery. Thirza would probably stifle any serious investigation, as she owed her regency to Aria's absence.

The roc oriented on the castle. They glided down for a landing. Princess Ida heard the swish of air and came out to investigate. "My word!" she exclaimed as Dolph transformed back to flea form and hopped back onto Noe. She wore a swimsuit and had a piece of coral orbiting her head.

"Hello, Great Aunt Ida," Aria said. "I am Princess Aria, in a different host, and these are my friends Jess and Myst. Prince Dolph is also with us, and Mairzy day mare. And the Sea Hag."

"You must have a considerable story to tell, dear," Ida said, taking it in stride. "Come in, all."

Soon they were in her comfortable living room, which was phrased like a coral reef, explaining everything.

"You have come to the right world," Ida said as they concluded. "Our world's Brain Coral Pool is guaranteed never to let a bad prisoner escape."

If they could just get there in time.

Chapter 12

NOE

Dolph transformed again, and they circled Ida until they were able to orient on the World of Coral. This turned out to be mostly sea with scattered islands. Where was the Brain Coral? Somewhere deep in that sea. Dolph could change to whale form and reach it, if he knew where to go.

"I can vaporize and sniff it out, sensing the smart water and air near the Brain, if we get close enough," Myst said. "Within a few miles."

While the planet was a few thousand miles around. "We have a problem," Jess said.

"We can ask Aunt Ida," Aria said. And there was the answer.

Dolph flew low over the sea, orienting on Ida's castle. Soon it showed up as a vertical coral reef, with turrets reaching into the sky and foundation under the water. It was pretty in its unusual way, with pennants in the shape of fish. He landed on a reef that circled it: this world's version of a moat.

Ida heard them and came out. She had an appealing fishy aspect, and her hair resembled seaweed. Her orbiting planet was in the shape of a bird; in fact it seemed to be flying around her head.

Jess quickly explained, and Ida quickly understood. "As happens, the Brain Coral's Pool is not far from here; my brother can reach it within an hour."

The Hag tried to make a break for it, but Dolph clamped a hand on her arm and pacified her. Then Jess and Myst held her while Dolph transformed. They bundled her aboard and took off. This seemed almost too good to be true!

It was. "She's gone!" Aria said.

The roc slewed to a halt in mid air, an interesting maneuver. "Squawk?"

That needed no translation. "The Sea Hag is gone," Jess sad. "We're too late."

"Squawk!" Which also needed no translation, especially in the presence of a child. The air around them was crackling.

"Of course she vacated the moment she could," Jess said. "She knew where we were taking her."

"But we should be able to track her," Myst said.

"I am trying," Aria said. "But I don't sense her presence. She just seems to have vanished."

"We'd better go back to Princess Ida," Jess said. "Maybe she'll know what to do."

Dolph looped about and flew back to Ida's coral castle.

"But of course," Ida said. "The Sea Hag has a long and ugly history, and we know her nature. She can be detected only when she occupies a living host. Between possessions she is merely an evil spirit."

"How long can she go between hosts?" Jess asked.

"Indefinitely. Sometimes she seems to have taken time off, and has not reappeared for generations.

"So we can't hang around waiting for her to take another host," Jess said. "She can out-wait us."

"Yes," Ida said. "I'm afraid you have lost her."

"Suppose she hangs around as a ghost near us, until we go to another world?" Myst asked. "Then grabs a woman there?"

"No, she can't do that, as far as we know. Spirits can't change worlds without hosts, except in very special circumstances, such as when a person vacates her body here, and sends part of her soul to the next world. They do it that way so they can return to their world of origin; the soul remains connected. Since the Sea Hag has no body here, she can't safely travel the worlds. Her soul would dissipate, ending her existence. She must travel in a host, or not at all."

"Then we can't be sure she'll be marooned here on Coral," Jess said.

"You can be fairly sure she won't be," Ida said. "But it may take her some time to corrupt a new host and reach Xanth proper."

"Like maybe about nine years," Aria said grimly.

"Yes, dear."

"Blip!"

"But those of us who have had direct experience with her will be able to track her," Dolph said. "Especially you, Aria. And Noe."

Jess realized that Noe had been strangely silent since her release.

"About Noe," Aria said. "She is in a bad way."

Jess did not like the sound of this. "A bad way? Shouldn't she be better now, as Nia was?"

"Nia looks young, but she's a grandma," Aria said. "She's tough as fingernails. Noe isn't. She is hurting. I am stabilizing her, but that's temporary."

"How can we help her?" Jess asked, alarmed.

"I think, judging from the nuances, she needs to cry. In the arms of someone who understands. Then she needs to talk."

"I think I understand," Myst said. "But I'm too young."

"I think I understand, too," Jess said. "But I doubt she could take me seriously."

"I had two daughters," Dolph said. "Sometimes I comforted them. But I don't know Noe well enough."

"I believe I understand," Ida said. "I have seen much in my tenure as guardian of the worlds. Let her go, Aria."

Noe had been standing erect. Now she slumped into utter dejection. "I'm soiled," she said. "I think I can never be clean again."

"Come here, Noe," Ida said, opening her arms.

The girl lunged to them, sobbing as though her heart were being ripped out of her body. Ida held her close. With her eyes, Ida indicated that the others should clear out for the moment.

Jess, Dolph, and Myst exited the castle, standing beside the coral moat. "I think I was thinking too much about containing the Hag," Jess said. "And not enough about Noe."

"Me, too," Myst said. "If it had been one of the siblings, I'd have picked up on it better."

"The siblings," Dolph said. "Noe has sisters?"

"No. Noe's a girlfriend to Santo. It's a relationship of convenience. The siblings are five of us who got rescued from the future by Astrid Basilisk and Demoness Fornax. Firenze, Santo, Squid, Win, and me. We all got adopted out, but we're siblings. It's complicated."

"You were all from one family?" Dolph asked.

"No, all different families and different ages and talents. We're not at all alike. And Squid isn't even human. But that experience, and our common origin, well, it made us closer than anybody else could be. We trust each other, we'd do anything for each other, we understand each other. We'll always be brothers and sisters, no matter what. Ula isn't part of that, though we all like her, and neither is Noe, though we like her, too, and think she's good for Santo."

Jess suffered a revelation, though a bulb did not flash over her head. "Noe needs to be a sibling!"

"No, she's a girlfriend," Myst said. "That's one thing we sibling girls will never be to Santo, and not because he's gay. We're his *sisters.*"

But the idea had hold of Jess. She parked it on a mental shelf, ready to be dusted off without notice.

Ida and Noe appeared in the doorway. "Now we need to talk," Ida said.

"I'm sorry I didn't understand!" Myst said, bursting into tears. She ran to hug Noe.

"Nobody could really understand, who hasn't been taken by the Sea Hag." Noe said. "But Princess Ida has shored me up. I do have things to live for, if I can handle it."

Jess noted that Aria was now the silent one. "We will listen," she said.

They settled into Ida's comfortable living room. "When—when the Sea Hag took me, it was like drowning," Noe said. "I tried to fight her, but she overpowered me. I couldn't hold my breath long. She just pushed me down into the mud and sat on me. I could feel her fighting somebody, but it wasn't me. It was Aria. Then Aria gained strength and pushed the Hag down in the stinking mud with me, but that didn't free me; she was still on top of me. She's so awful! It was like being buried in manure. I don't think I'll ever get the filth all the way out."

Noe paused, as if expecting to be interrupted, but no one else spoke. "I clung to one thing, there in the muck: Santo. I'm just his show girlfriend; it was never real. But I always did like him; he's so smart, and talented, Magician caliber, and he treats me so well even though there's nothing womanly he wants from me. He's just a great guy."

Jess remembered how Santo had dismissed her, and how Squid had called him on it. Santo wasn't perfect, but overall Noe was right. Santo was a remarkable boy, or young man.

"I clung to him to save my sanity," Noe continued. "In my suffering mind what had been mere show became real. I came to love him, as a woman loves a man. He'll never marry me, but in my heart I'm his wife. I held on to that dream, and survived. I owe my survival to him." She paused again, but again there was no challenge. "Now the Sea Hag is gone, and she will never return to me. I'm like ashes that can't be burned again, or undeleted material, that can't be deleted again. That's the way it is with former victims, if they live; I know it now. But I don't know whether I want to live."

Now Jess had to protest. "Noe! Of course you want to live!"

"I am dirty, right through to my soul. There's a stain remaining that I can't ever wash out." She smiled briefly. "Like Atrocia's soiled panties. The only clean thing I have left is my love for Santo, and that is futile. Even if I were clean, he would not want me in the way I want him; I always knew that. And even if he were hetero, once he saw my putrid core he wouldn't want me. I have nothing for him except my foolish love. And maybe it would be kinder for him, and for me, and for everyone if I took that love to oblivion. Then he would be free, and not feel that he had to maintain any pretense about liking me."

She was a child, but she was talking like a woman. The worst of it was that she was deadly serious.

"Oh, Noe," Jess breathed with sympathetic pain.

"I think you had to hear this," Ida said to the others. "You may hate it, but at least you will understand why she does what she does. It has happened to other survivors of the Sea Hag. That's why I knew."

"She's going to kill herself!" Myst protested.

"Yes, dear. It will end her pain." Ida was plainly resigned.

Jess looked at Dolph, but he was frozen, not knowing how to handle this. He was a prince and a Magician, but also a helpless man in the face of such naked emotion. She looked at Myst, and she was neither resigned nor frozen, but had no idea what to do.

That left it up to Jess. Now she knew what she had to do, unkind as it might seem. "Noe, I listened to you. Now you listen to me. Take me seriously, if you can, because I have the answer you need. Heed me." She fixed the child with her gaze, holding it until Noe gave way and accepted her dominance.

"Yes, Jess," Noe whispered.

"You have not thought this through, or seen the larger picture; you are thinking mainly of yourself, and that is a mistake. I submit that you do not properly understand your feeling for Santo. Yes, he is a fine young man, and yes, you have been badly soiled. But that is not the end of it. What you really want is him in your life, respecting you and caring for you, as he respects and cares for his sisters. Loving you, as he loves his siblings."

"Yes," Noe whispered.

"And you want the feeling of family that the siblings have," Jess continued. "They are completely unrelated, male and female, and one is not even human, but Santo loves them all. They are as close as any people can be."

"Yes."

"You have your own family at home, but what you want now is a family with Santo, as the siblings have. What makes them siblings? Their own choice, because they share a larger background that unifies them emotionally. You do not share their origin in an alternate future, but you do share significant experience, such as hosting a Sorceress, and the need to save Xanth from a fate just about as bad as the one the siblings escaped. We need you for that continuing effort."

"But I'm unclean!"

"The bleep you are! What you suffer is the remnant of the putrid evil that is the Sea Hag. That filth can be expunged. You just need to live in a way the Hag never would, being a good person in every way that you can be. Noe, you need to become a sibling."

"But—"

"They are siblings, as I said, because they choose to be—and because they accept each other as siblings. Because of their common experience losing their original families. You have not lost yours, but you have had an experience as bad as any of theirs, that put you in doubt about whether it was worthwhile to continue your existence. That is strong medicine. You are locked into the same deadly mission they are now, trying to save Xanth from future destruction. You are one with them in spirit. They will accept you as one of them. Yes, you are not the prettiest, smartest, or luckiest girl in Xanth, but you have an underlying quality they appreciate: you are decent. You are nice. You *care*. They want you to be with them, and not just as a pretend playmate for Santo. They need you, as they need each other, as we all face the horror ahead."

"But I'm unclean!"

"Nia is as soiled as you are; she hosted the Sea Hag, too. But she's a grandmother with much experience of life; she can handle it. Consult with her, when we rejoin the community of the boat. She will help you gain perspective. So will the others. You are not alone, even in this. Do not opt out without giving them a chance. You must join them, not leave them."

"But they won't—"

Jess fixed her gaze on Myst. "Myst! You are a sibling! Would you accept Noe as another?"

"Yes!" Myst said, catching on.

"Would Santo?"

"Yes!"

Jess returned her steely gaze to Noe. "There is your course. Think of the others: what will Aria do without a host? *She saw her mother deleted*, and now she's trying desperately to stop that horror. She truly needs you, Noe. What will Squid do without her friend Aria?"

Noe's face froze. Indeed, she had not thought it through!

Jess did not relent. "And Santo. You think he won't miss you? He will think it was something *he* did that drove you to kill yourself. Everyone else will think you did it because you discovered he was gay, and he won't be sure they aren't right. You won't be there to tell them otherwise, will you, Noe? Is this how you propose to show your love for him?"

The girl was transfixed with sheer horror. "No, no—"

"Don't hurt Santo by dying. Help him by *living*. He does love you in his fashion, and wants you with him. Become his sibling. That will be for life. You can still play-act at being his girlfriend, to keep judgmental strangers at bay. Not only will you help him, you will be part of a larger family, and you will have regular access to Fibot, no minor thing in itself. Do it!"

"Yes," Noe whispered tearfully.

"And one more point. We all need you in our fight against the Sea Hag, now that you are immune to her possession. When we finally corner her, to carry her away and put her in the Pool, she will be desperately looking for a new host. That's what happened when she was in Nia, and left her to take you. You can grab her host and hold her without being at further risk, unlike other women. She will have to vacate, and maybe by then we will have the means to catch her mean spirit. It will be an ugly scene, but you can do it, and we will need you for that."

"Yes," Noe repeated, desperate determination rising.

"Yes. Do it," Jess repeated grimly, and let her attention go.

Myst went to comfort her, as a sibling, as Noe dissolved into another siege of tears, as she had with Ida. But this time they were tears of understanding and relief. She would live, and likely prosper. She had a new mission.

Jess discovered the others looking at her.

"Now we know why Jess is the protagonist," Ida said.

"I just did what I had to do, cruel as it might seem," Jess said.

"Exactly."

"True," Dolph agreed. "You were amazing."

But Jess felt the passion draining from her. She had briefly overridden her curse, but now she was reverting to normal. It might never happen again.

Noe disengaged and straightened up, wiping her face. Then Aria spoke. "Thank you, Jess."

Jess simply nodded her head, choked up for the moment.

"I think all we can do now is move on," Dolph said. "Hoping that we will be able to orient on the Sea Hag when she takes a new host, and run her down and put her away."

"We might as well rejoin the crew at Fibot," Aria agreed. "If we can find it."

"You may be able to do that," Ida said. "I believe the World of Three Moons is about four worlds up. Won't the boat be passing there in due course?"

Noe perked up. "Yes! We have a tunnel to build there."

They thanked Ida and moved on. Dolph transformed into the roc, and they oriented on the World of Bird that seemed to be orbiting Ida's head. Jess knew now that this was more apparent than literal; it was merely a way to magically connect. But it worked, and that was what counted.

They discovered a world of towering mountains and jagged valleys, with hardly a level surface anywhere. Birds of all types abounded. A purple roc intercepted Dolph as he glided toward the only landing place in view, a rounded mountain peak.

"Squawk!" the other bird demanded.

"Squawk!" Dolph replied.

The other bird spun about in mid air, then winged away. Dolph followed. Other birds gave them leeway, except for one flock of small ones. Jess was surprised. They looked just like the peeve! They even cast insulting glances at the visitors.

Soon they came to a castle clinging to a precipice. Princess Ida's residence!

Dolph glided down to land on a flat roof, while the other roc winged rapidly away. Evidently Dolph had told it where they were going, and it had guided them there.

Ida came to the roof as they dismounted and Dolph became a man. She was birdlike in outline and manner, with a cloak that resembled folded wings. Her orbiting moon resembled an ant. "Yes, they call me Ant Ida," she said before anyone asked. "You are of course worlds travelers."

They introduced themselves, relayed the greeting of the Ida of the prior world, and caught her up on their mission. She was happy to facilitate it. She also clarified that yes, the small birds were peeves; this was their home world. "They are generally not well regarded elsewhere," she said. "It seems that other folk don't really like to be continuously insulted. Can you imagine?"

Soon they were on their way to the world of Ant. This was of course governed by ants, and featured many species. They did not land, as Ida had warned that the insects could be territorial and might resent any outside intrusion. Jess was glad; she did not want to come up against a determined army of warrior ants. Only when they reached the castle did they touch ground beside it and become a regular human party.

Not close enough. An enormous ant appeared, blocking their approach. They tried to go around, but the ant intercepted them, clacking his mandibles. He seemed determined that they not reach the castle.

"I could vaporize and choke him," Myst said dubiously. Jess could see why: the ant was so big it could probably absorb her and maybe digest her. In any event, ants did not breathe the way humans did.

"I'll handle this," Dolph said. He changed form again, this time to a similar ant. He went forward and touched antennae with the balky native.

Then the other ant walked away, no longer barring their way.

"What happened?" Myst asked.

"That is Adam Ant," Dolph explained. "The very first ant to colonize this planet. From him and his queen all the rest are descended. He values Princess Ida, so protects her castle, and is very persistent about it. In fact he is adamant."

Jess groaned internally. Adamant. Adam Ant. It was a pun.

Ida's castle resembled as elaborate ant hill, and she herself looked a bit like a sultry queen ant. Her moon was perfectly formed, but blue.

They made the usual introductions and explanations, and Ida was as sharp as her other iterations. "The folk of the next world are friendly," she said. "Yet you probably do not want to socialize overmuch, lest you become depressed. They also tend to talk a blue streak."

"We will try to be polite, but move on quickly," Dolph said.

They advanced to the Blue Moon. Everything about it was in shades of blue. The seas of course, and the sky, but also the foliage, the ground, and the animals, such as blue birds. The flowers were blue bells. The insects were blue bottles. And of course the people. They looked ordinary, but were all shades of blue. The women had long blue hair under blue bonnets, and the men wore blue jeans and had blue beards. Some at a picnic were sitting on blue grass and eating blue cheese.

Unfortunately it was a rainy day where they landed, and blue fog covered the area. They could not see where Ida's castle was, though Dolph knew the general direction. "It's not far," he said. "We can walk."

But that meant taking a circuitous route, because the most direct paths had blue policemen who would surely ask what the visitors were up to. They had had enough of that sort of thing on the female planet. So they looped around, finding open paths, slowly making their way closer. But it was dusk by the time they got there. By that time they had had their fill of the sad blue music that was universally popular here; everyone was playing and singing the blues.

At least they were shielded from it once they entered Ida's castle. This version of her looked normal, albeit garbed in blue, and had a normal colored moon orbiting her head. Except for one detail. Or three.

"The World of Three Moons!" Noe exclaimed gladly. "My home!"

But would Fibot be there? Jess kept silent.

They acquainted Ida with their nature and mission, and she was helpful. Soon they were on their way.

They arrived in darkness. Jess had never quite figured out where the sunlight came from on these worlds, or how the day and night cycle worked, but it seemed standard. Noon on one world seemed to be noon on the next, and the nights matched. "I suppose you will want to get straight home?" Jess asked cautiously.

Noe paused. "I do, but I think I need a bit more time to get my mixed emotions settled. I'm not sure yet what to tell my folks. Some of it would freak them out, and I don't want that. Could we camp in the woods until morning?"

"That seems sensible," Jess agreed, relieved. "Is it safe outside at night?"

The girl's face fell. "No. there are monsters."

"I can take care of that," Dolph said. "I will transform to a house fly."

Jess started to laugh, then stifled it. He just might be serious.

He was. He became a giant fly in the shape of a house. They were able to open the front door and enter it, and it was well appointed inside. There were a living room, bedrooms, kitchen, and even bathroom. Jess, Noe, and Myst were soon making a nice dinner from materials in the ice box.

"I confess to be pleasantly surprised," Aria said. "Uncle Dolph is even more talented than I thought."

They ate, relaxed, and retired. They decided to sleep in three beds in one bedroom, because Myst preferred company at night and Jess was a mother figure to her, while Noe remained emotionally shaky, even with Aria's company.

Aria sang them all a compelling lullaby, and they slept readily enough.

In the morning they made their preparations, then exited the house. "We're out, thank you!" Jess called.

The house shifted into a giant fly, then to Dolph. "Never tried that before," he said. "I discovered that having folk running around inside my guts tickles me. Good thing I didn't laugh."

"You were perfect, Uncle," Aria said.

"Which way is your house?" Jess asked Noe.

"That way," the girl said, pointing. "Um, when I see my folk, how much should I tell them? I don't want to freak them out."

"Tell them as much as you feel comfortable telling them," Jess said. "They love you and can handle it, as long as they know you're safe now."

Dolph looked around. "This area so so thickly wooded I'm not sure there are many landing areas for a roc. Is there a sufficient clearing near your house, Noe?"

"No. It's mostly swamp, and sometimes it fogs up so I've gotten lost in it."

"There are other creatures who can carry things," Myst said. "Other birds, even. What about a pro-duck? A big one. I've seen small pro-ducks swimming near our house, carrying things."

Jess groaned inwardly. Pro-ducks, products. A pun creature.

"A pro duck," Dolph said. "A fowl with a positive attitude. That will do." He changed, and became a huge duck-like bird. He waddled to the nearby swamp inlet and plumped down, spreading out a wing so they could use it as a boarding ramp.

Soon they were on their way as the duck moved smoothly ahead, his huge webbed feet below propelling them forward. Noe directed the route.

A big slipper rose up ahead, eyeing them hungrily. "Oops, a water moccasin," Myst said. "They're poisonous."

Jess glared at it. After a moment the moccasin concluded that it couldn't take her seriously as prey, and slipped back under the surface.

They came into sight of Noe's house. "Mom? Dad!" she cried gladly, running ahead.

Her mother, Noleta, emerged. "Noe? Are you. . . ? They said the Sea Hag—"

So much for hiding that aspect.

"I'm me! I'm free!" Then she was in her mother's arms, and both were crying.

Soon they were all inside, telling the whole story. Jess was gladder than ever that she had talked the girl out of suicide. How could they have come to her parents with that awful news?

It turned out that Fibot made regular runs to the World of Three Moons, because Princess Jenny's son had married a local princess. In fact they had fitted in a run while they waited for Jess's party to rejoin them, and Santo was recovering from that effort. He was considering making a permanent tunnel connecting the palaces so that he wouldn't have to wear himself out doing it repeatedly. Jess wasn't sure how that worked, with the worlds spinning in different directions, but of course she did not understand all the nuances of magic. So the boat had passed by, and Nia had visited to tell the parents the bad news. But there was hope, Nia had said, because she herself has escaped the clutch of the Sea Hag, and Noe could, too.

"Where is Fibot now?" Myst asked.

"Docked at the palace," Noleta said. "They mean to check here every day, in the hope that there is news of the three of you."

"Four of us," Noe said. "Counting Aria."

"Of course," Noleta agreed. "That's why you went with them, to host her. How is that working out?"

That led to a capsule summary of the disaster of the future.

"They did mention building a tunnel between worlds," Noleta said. "It seems complicated, but we are happy to do our part."

"Queen Jenny is also cataloging the local worlds," Dell said. "That's how we knew that Stench was relatively close to this world, as such things go, so we had a serious hope you would be here soon."

"Assuming you were able to deal with the Sea Hag," Nia added.

Jess made a mental note to thank Queen Jenny when she had a chance. Her connection to this world had vastly simplified their return to the fire boat.

Around noon Fibot sailed in. "Halooo!" It was Santo's voice.

Noe dashed out, Jess and the others following. Santo spied her immediately. "Noe! Are you. . . ?"

"Yes! It's me! I'm free!" Noe exclaimed, then paused as if uncertain of his reaction. Jess remembered how the girl had felt terminally unclean. Jess also remembered a wild story about savage life in Mundania, where in some parts women got raped and were then rejected by their male friends as unclean. It was crazy, but that was Mundania, and Xanth was not entirely free of such attitudes.

Santo leaped to close the gap between them, sweeping Noe into his embrace. "Oh, Noe! I couldn't make it without you! I knew that when I had to recover from the last hole. Win and Squid are helping, but it's no longer the same. You—you're better, somehow. Don't ever leave me again. I'll . . . I'll even be your boyfriend for real, if that's what it takes to keep you with me."

Well, now. Jess and the others stood back, not interfering. This was something Noe had to handle herself. In the emotion of the reunion Santo was making an offer everyone knew he couldn't really honor.

"*Pretend* boyfriend, as before," Noe said. "I'll be your sibling sister for real."

And there it was, her more realistic counter-offer.

"Oh, Noe! Thank you! I love you!" They were both in tears.

So much for getting rejected for her supposed dirtiness. Noe had played it correctly, and their relationship was complete. Jess saw Myst nodding, as well as Win and Squid, whom Myst had been briefly talking to. Noe was indeed becoming one of them.

Ula came up, and Kadence manifested. So did Aria. The two princesses embraced, and there were more tears. Squid joined them, and Aria hugged her, too. The separation had been hard on everyone.

Now Magnus came forward to embrace Jess. "Funny thing," he murmured in her ear. "Touching you I can't take you seriously; it's just show. But away from you I felt much as Santo does about Noe. So I'll say it as I rehearsed it, because it was serious then and should remain serious now. I need you for the show, Jess, or rather, I need Atrocia. All the demand is for Atrocia. Without her, we really have no show. Now with you back, we can do the show that Princess Froma wants for her wedding celebration." He took a breath. "But apart from that I rehearsed this, too: there's a need apart from the show. A personal one. The show needs Atrocia; I need you, Jess."

Jess was thrilled to hear it. But there was a problem, the one they had had all along. "I don't think you can have both, Magnus."

"That's the bleep of it! I know I can have one or the other, but I need both. So even if you find a cure for your curse, it won't solve *my* problem."

"It won't," she agreed with resignation.

"Now would you like me to kiss you? It'll be fake, but I can make it look real."

"Yes, please. It's half real: my half."

He kissed her, making it look real, and she loved it as always. But of course it wasn't enough. She could feel the lack of passion in his body. The ardor was all hers. They did it in full view of the others, but the others knew their situation, as they knew Santo and Noe's situation. They were used to such shows.

Then Jess remembered something he had said in passing. "Who is Princess Froma?"

"She's the one Prince Jerry, Jenny's twenty-year-old son, will marry. They have normal ears but four fingered hands, the way Jenny does."

"But I thought that was because Jenny came from a far planet, the World of Two Moons. No one else in Xanth has four fingers."

"The royal ancestry here is originally from the World of Two moons. That's one reason they like the World of Three Moons. Princess Froma used to wear gloves all the time, to hide her hands. Until she saw Jenny and Jerry. It was pretty much love at first sight. They will marry soon."

"Of course you must give them a show," Jess said. "Atrocia will be there in her style."

The other siblings came to congratulate Noe on her recovery, and Jess for her safe return. There was bound to be some time spent catching up on the details.

Now it was time to return to the boat. Noe bid a tearful temporary farewell to her folks, then took Santo's hand to board the boat. Jess did the same with Magnus.

But where were they to go from here, in terms of the mission? They had found the Sea Hag, and lost her, and would have to find her again and somehow deal with her. But how? Jess had no idea, and doubted any of the others did, either.

But at least she would be able to relax fully, for the first time in days. In Magnus's arms, with luck. Maybe in their sleep something would happen. It was at least worth hoping for, or dreaming of.

Chapter 13

TUNNEL

They spent the night relaxing, Magnus holding Jess close, but like a big doll. She knew that he wished as much as she did that it could be otherwise. It was as if he *was* holding a doll while longing for her, and of course he couldn't take the doll seriously. "Some day, some way, I will find a way," he promised her.

"Of course you will," she agreed. But even she couldn't take that seriously.

In the morning they held a strategy meeting, all hands and feet on deck. "Reprising what we all know, we have two things to do," Magnus told the group. "We have to put on a show for the royal wedding, and we have to fashion a tunnel between here and Castle Roogna in Xanth proper. We may have to divide our party, so that the one can attract public attention while the other proceeds unsuspected by outsiders. I think we all agree that the secret must be kept as close as possible."

"Indeed," Dolph agreed. "I wondered why I was allowed to lie fallow, all these years, until this point. Now I realize that it was to keep the secret. How could I give it away if I did not know it myself?"

"And we two princesses did not know about the tunnel until we came of age to use it," Kadence said. "Only when Ragna Roc strikes in your future, our present, did we remember it, without the circumstances of it. It did save our lives, and guided us to safe harbor, so that now we can visit with you to see about making it."

"Without paradox, we think," Aria agreed. "Because of the closely nestled alternate realities. But we must do this for whatever track it helps, as another track did for us."

"First the easier one," Magnus said, exerting his talent for organization. "Now that we have Atrocia back. The show. I will MC it as usual, and Atrocia will divert the audience while I get my volunteers ready. Aria enhanced it significantly with her humming last time; she certainly belongs in this group. Others can fill in as available. Any problems?" He looked around, finding none. "Second, the critical one, the tunnel. Santo must form it, and Noe must be by his side as he recovers from the effort. What else is required, Santo?"

"Normally my tunnels are temporary," Santo said. "But this one has to be permanent, at least for nine years. That means it must be made more firmly, and shored up. You are right that I will need Noe as well as a sister or two to shore *me* up, because I will not be able to rest until it is done and it will required a sustained effort. In addition we will need Kadence to align the lining, much as she did for the undeleted egg several years ago."

"I am ready," Kadence said. "But there is a problem. When I worked on the egg, I had a supply of undeleted remnants others had gathered from all around, wherever Ragna Roc had been. We pretty well cleaned out the supply of that. This time we'll have to work with an alternate substance, and it may not be easy to obtain."

"What substance?" Magnus asked.

"Two substances, actually. The first is the poop of the giant stone-borer worm, which coats the tunnels it drills so they don't collapse behind it. Once that poop sets it's like mundane plastic, and clings tightly." She smiled. "So all we need for that is the worm."

"Readily solved," Dolph said. "I will assume the form of the worm, and poop up a storm. However, there will have to be someone to slap it on the wall of the tunnel behind me, because it coagulates in a few minutes and I can't to it myself. Real worms have helpers. Unfortunately it stinks almost as bad as the atmosphere of Planet Stench."

"I can handle that," Squid said. "Smells don't bother me much."

"Our team is forming," Santo said. "But you mentioned two substances, Kadence. What is the second?"

"There are several, used for hardening and weathering agents, all uncommon. Probably what is best is iridium, the metal of the asteroids. With that coating the wall of the tunnel would become permanent regardless of moisture and abrasion. Iridium is very rare in Xanth, because it exists mainly in the science realm. They mine it in Mundania along with platinum and lesser metals like gold. I realize it is not feasible to go to Mundania for it, or even away from the World of Three Moons. There is bound to be some here, if we can find it."

Magnus looked at Tata. "Can you find it, dogfish?"

The robot's screen flickered. "Yes," the peeve translated. "But it is thinly spread. It will be a chore to get enough, and it will take time."

"We can't afford much time," Magnus said. "We need to get this done and depart the planet expeditiously, so there is no suspicion that we did anything but enjoy the scenery."

"Then we have a problem," Kadence said.

"We have two problems," Aria said. "Mine is that I can't sing at shows at the same time as my host Noe shores up Santo."

"O, beans!" Magnus swore. "I should have thought of that."

Dolph looked at Jess. "You are a fair hand at solving difficult problems, protagonist," he said, and Noe nodded. "Do you care to tackle these? Kadence can make you intelligible to the rest of us."

Jess almost regretted becoming so forceful when dealing with Noe's threat of suicide. Almost, but not quite. Now others thought that because she was the protagonist she could handle any problem. She didn't want to disappoint them, but she had no ideas.

Ula walked across to join her. Kadence put her hand on Jess's arm. Bleep! Now the others could take her seriously and she had to perform.

Jess focused, and it came. "For the iridium, ask Tata. Not where it may be hiding in thin layers on old rocks, but where a more convenient form of it might be available. He can point the direction, if there is one."

Tata's screen flickered. "There is," the peeve said.

"That should do it," Kadence agreed. "My problem can be handled."

"And what of my problem?" Aria asked. "Do I sing, or does Noe shore up the tunnel wall?"

"For the problem of one person being in two locations at once," Jess said, "there is a simple solution. You two princesses surely return to your original bodies regularly, to eat, pee, poop, exercise and check to be sure they remain well hidden."

"We do," Aria agreed. "It is necessary upkeep."

"Then next time you do that, when it is time to return here, switch hosts. Let Kadence go to Noe, and Aria go to Ula. Then Kadence and Noe can be with Santo, while Aria and Ula join the show. You can safely do that, can't you, as long as your hosts know about it and agree?

The jaws of both girls dropped. So did several others. "Yes," Kadence said. "We can do that."

Dolph smiled. "See? I told you she's a sensible girl, when she can be taken seriously."

"Except I won't have my friend Squid with me," Aria said.

"Oh! I didn't think of that," Squid said. "I'm sorry."

"This adventure is not yet over," Jess said. "This is only an episode. Squid will be free when the tunnel is done."

"Meanwhile, let's see about the iridium," Santo said. "So that we know we have what we need before we start."

"Tata, where is it?" Nia asked.

The dogfish's screen flickered. "That way," the peeve said, pointing with a wing.

"Let's break for lunch first," Nia said. "And the princesses can swap in that period, if they wish. That will give us all a chance to get used to it."

"Yes," the princesses said, almost together.

Then Ula and Noe took over. "They're gone," Ula said. "This may be weird. I have come to know Kadence this past year. I don't know Aria."

"She's a fine singer," Jess said. "And an assertive princess. And a decent person, I believe."

Santo came to talk with Jess. "I know what you did for Noe," he said. "Aria told me."

"I did what I had to do. I couldn't let her die."

"Yes. And you were right. If she had died, a key part of me would have died with her. I don't know how to thank you enough."

Jess smiled. "If you can ever do a similar service for me, I'll ask you."

"I will remember."

By the end of the meal, the princesses were back. "I am Kadence," Noe's mouth said. It did sound like Kadence.

"I am Aria," Ula's mouth said. And that sounded like Aria.

"They're right," Squid said. "It's weird."

"Weird," Myst agreed.

Both princesses laughed. "Say the octopus and the ball of vapor," Kadence said. "We're finding it a bit odd ourselves."

"But we can handle it," Aria agreed. "As long as we don't have to kiss anyone."

"What do you mean by that?" Kadence demanded.

"Your host wants to kiss Santo. Didn't you know?"

Noe's eyes flicked to Santo. She opened her mouth for a sharp retort.

"We have other business at the moment," Nia said quickly, in effect calling them to order. They might be teasing each other, but it was skirting the edge of serious mischief.

"How far is this source?" Jess asked Tata.

"Not far," the peeve said. "Other side of the planet."

"Um—"

"I'll take you," Dolph said quickly. "I can cover a planetary distance fast enough."

"But there's something odd about that, too," the peeve said as the robot's screen flickered. "Tata's not sure what, but it may complicate things."

"One way to find out," Jess said. "Let's get moving." But she did wonder. The dogfish was not given to humor.

They exited the boat and Dolph changed to roc form.

Jess, Tata, the peeve, and Ula/Aria boarded the big bird. Tata squawked, startling Jess. The roc spread his wings and took off. "He spoke in roc language," the peeve explained.

Evidently so. They flew up into the plaid sky, lower than the orbits of the three moons, and headed what Jess judged to be west.

"Wow!" Ula said. "This is fun!"

"Yes it is," Aria agreed. "We had some nice flights on the other planets."

"I wonder," Ula said. "If I'm with the show, well, I'm not much of a singer the way Noe is. That may mess you up."

"I doubt it," Aria said. "I will do the singing."

Jess found this dialogue interesting. The two voices issued from the same mouth, but were distinctly different.

"But—"

"I will demonstrate." Then she sang the Greena national anthem.

Jess was impressed. Ula might be the host, but it was very much Aria's voice, evocative as ever.

There was also something else. Jess found herself thinking of the Sea

Hag, for no reason in particular, since they were finally quit of her. She quickly banished the ugly memories.

"Squawk!" Tata said. The roc started gliding down toward land.

Soon they landed on an outlying field of what looked to be a small farm. They slid off, and Dolph resumed man form. Then they walked toward the modest little house in the center of the farm.

Dolph knocked on the door. In a moment it opened, revealing a tall handsome man with silvery hair and beard, though he did not look at all old. "Yes?"

"I am Dolph, from Xanth proper," Dolph said, omitting his office. He indicated Jess, Ula, and the animals. "These are my associates. We are in search of iridium."

"That I can provide. I am Ira, and conjuring iridium is my talent. It suffuses me, as you can see by my hair, beard, and eyebrows. But hardly anybody wants it, and it has a negative effect on my personality. Why do you want it?"

"That is a secret we are reluctant to share," Dolph said.

"Conjuring more than a small quantity soon becomes wearing. If you want a thimbleful, you can have it and begone. If you want more, I will need to know more."

Dolph looked at Jess. "We will need more. Do we tell him?"

"Let me try to frame it fairly," Jess said. She met Ira's gaze. "My curse is that nobody takes me seriously, though a few have learned to do it in special circumstances. Will you be able to follow an evasive discussion? Are you following me now?"

"Oh, yes. Perfectly. You fascinate me, you gorgeous creature." Ira looked around. "Come in, all of you. I believe we have something to discuss."

This was curious. Jess had felt a kind of rapport when their gazes met. This was no ordinary man.

The peeve, perched on Tata's fish-shaped shoulder, glanced up at Jess. "Caution," the bird murmured.

Caution about what? Jess wished she had a chance to learn more privately. Did the complication somehow involve her?

They were ushered into his home. Soon they were seated on his worn chairs, with Tata and the peeve beside them. The others were letting Jess do the talking, if that turned out to be feasible.

"We wish to hear your case," Jess said, cautiously. "Why is conjuring iridium a challenge for you?"

"I mentioned that conjuring iridium has a negative effect on me," Ira said. "And that fetching more than a small amount makes it worse. Even tiny amounts become cumulative, so I am careful. As it is, I trade token samples that women want for jewelry, for other things I need, with the effects on my body you can see. But worse is the effect on my personality. It attracts me to the repulsive, not in appearance, like garbage, but in magic, somewhat in the manner one positively charged bit of metal repels another while being attracted to a negatively charged bit. Most women are positive, so I can't approach them. But in your case—" He paused. "I wish I could kiss you, Jess."

What? This was a complication indeed! "I don't think you understand," Jess said carefully. "A man can kiss me only as a joke."

"Will you allow a demonstration? I promise to take no undue liberties. Let me kiss you."

"I will let you try," Jess said, standing.

Ira stood and came to her. He took her in his arms. He kissed her. He seemed to mean it. She felt nothing but desire in him, not laughter. Could this be real?

He drew back his head, still holding her. "That was wonderful. I could love you, if you let me."

A complication indeed! She needed to find out. "Take a liberty," Jess said.

"Gladly." His hands slid down her back to her bottom, and squeezed. He nibbled on her ear. His passion increased.

He really was immune to her curse. He was taking her body seriously. "That's enough," she said. As far as she could tell at the moment, this did not directly relate to their mission.

He let her go and stepped back. "That's more than enough. I don't want to get carried away and offend you."

Offend her? He had been a perfect gentleman. It was the implication of his reverse magic that she would need to think about, in due course. Right now she had to focus on the mission.

They sat down again. "You have made your point," Jess said. "My curse, that effectively repels others, attracts you. Now let me make our point."

"You have my complete attention, lovely lady."

And he was serious. But what counted this moment was that he could understand her discussion. "We are on a very special mission that involves the welfare of the whole of Xanth proper, and maybe the linked world like this one, too. That secret must not be revealed to outsiders. You might be better off not knowing it. Can we make a deal with you to get a good deal of iridium without clarifying what we want it for?"

"Two things there," Ira said. "I do care about the welfare of Xanth and the worlds. But I can't be sure whether your mission means to help Xanth or harm it. You are strangers to me. So I do need to know more, because I will not betray my worlds. The second thing is that you personally are highly attractive to me, Jess. That may be more magic than social, as I hardly know you, but considering that you are the first woman to have this effect on me, I want very much to continue my association with you. You may be the one woman I could happily marry. It would break my heart to have to turn you down and therefore alienate you, but I would do that rather than risk betraying Xanth."

Jess looked at Dolph. "I can't make a decision based on personal feelings. I think someone else will have to decide."

"A vote," Dolph said. "Do we take Ira into our confidence so we can obtain his help, or do we look elsewhere for the iridium we need?" He paused. "Aria?"

"It is clear we got the iridium, in my time, and there was no betrayal," Aria said. "I vote yes, trust him."

"Ula?"

"Yes."

"One girl gets two votes? Because she has two names?" Ira asked.

"Not exactly," Dolph said. "We will explain if the vote is positive." He looked at the dogfish. "Tata?"

The screen flickered. "He says yes," the peeve said "And so do I."

"This is really curious," Ira said.

Dolph looked at Jess. "Jess?"

"I think I should recuse myself."

"Fair enough," Dolph said. "I believe he is an honorable man, and we do need his help, so I also vote yes. So the count is five yes, and one abstention. The vote carries. We will trust Ira to keep our secret."

"I am impressed already," Ira said. "Yet somehow I suspect that this is only the beginning of the remarkable things about you as a group."

"True," Dolph said. "Now a more proper introduction. I am Prince Dolph of Xanth proper. I am a Magician. My talent is to change forms." He changed to griffin and back again, demonstrating.

"You are right," Ira agreed. "I am amazed and doubly impressed. This speaks already to the importance of your mission."

"Indeed," Dolph agreed. "My associate here, Jess, is the protagonist of this story."

Ira stared. "You mean this is being recorded for a Xanth History Volume? I am triply impressed."

"It's no special virtue in me," Jess said, embarrassed. "I'm just the convenient viewpoint character."

"It remains a signal honor. They are not carelessly chosen."

Jess shrugged. This man was pleasing her, and she did not want to be pleased. It was bound to mess up her judgment.

"Ula is an ordinary girl whose talent is to be unexpectedly useful," Dolph continued. "At the moment she is hosting Princess Aria, from the future."

"Hello, both," Ira said. "It becomes wearisome to continue multiplying my impressedness. Consider it done." He focused on Aria. "I am not a great historian, but there was a notorious incident involving a roc with the power to delete people. He was finally stopped by the intercession of a child Sorceress from the future, I believe."

"That was my cousin Kadence," Aria agreed. "Now Ragna Roc has gotten loose again, and has deleted our mothers, in my time. We have to stop him again, if we can do so without paradox."

"And your time is. . . ?"

"Nine years in your future."

"I am beginning to understand. Naturally you want to prevent that disaster."

"The bird is the pet peeve," Dolph said. "Originally a universal nuisance, now a solid citizen. He translates for Tata, the computer dogfish with a formidable memory bank. He is the one who led us to you."

"Thank you, Tata," Ira said. His gaze returned to Dolph. "Of course I will help you to the best of my ability. I had not known before how serious your mission is."

"We will need you to provide enough iridium to finish lining a tunnel we will make," Dolph said. "It is the tunnel that will enable Princess Kadence and her cousin Aria to escape deletion and come here to try to change history."

"Not so fast," Jess said, surprising herself. "We came here to make a deal for iridium, and it's going to be hard on you to provide enough. How can we repay you for your service?"

"I am ready to help regardless, for the good of Xanth," Ira said. "Had the mission been less important, then I might have insisted on a deal."

"Such as what?"

"Such as my help for your favor, you enticing creature. But as I said—"

"I love another man."

"Too bad for me," Ira said. "So I will help without any such deal."

"But you should be repaid."

"There really isn't anything else I would want. So forget it."

Jess was troubled. "Am I being unreasonable?"

"You are being princessly," Aria said. "But since you aren't a princess, that is not a code you need to honor."

"I think I do need to honor it."

"Talk with Santo," Dolph said shrewdly.

"I will."

"We have matters to discuss among ourselves," Dolph told Ira. "We will return on the morrow. Will you be prepared to come with us?"

"I have commitments to complete, these next two days," Ira said. "Then I will be free to join you."

"Then it will be merely an update tomorrow," Dolph said.

They left the house, and this time let Ira see Dolph transform, and take off with them.

"Are you crazy, Jess?" Ula asked when they were aloft. "It's almost as if you're arguing against Ira's help."

"Let her be," Aria said. "She has a case. Ethics can be tricky to understand."

Jess appreciated Aria's support as they lapsed into silence. But now she found herself thinking of the Sea Hag again. Bleep! She banished the thought.

When they returned to the group, Dolph caught the others up on what had happened.

After that Jess talked with Magnus. "Ira would like to—to be with me, and he can take me seriously. But—"

"Jess, from what you tell me, Ira can give you what I can't. He can appreciate you without hindrance. I would be a heel to try to stop you from finding your happiness with him."

"But I want to find it with you!"

"And I with you. But that's highly speculative. We don't know when, if ever, we'll find a way. Jess, I would rather see you happy with him than miserable with me. He's a bird in the hand, as it were. You can still be Atrocia in the show."

"Bleep!" she swore tearfully.

"It has to be your decision. I will abide by it."

So there was no compelling imperative there. He was being too nice about it.

Then Jess went to Santo, "About that similar service . . ."

He smiled. "I suspected."

"Ira is a good man. He would like to—to have me for his girlfriend. That would be easy enough to do, if only—"

"If only you didn't love Magnus."

"If only," she agreed sourly.

"I know I need Noe in my life, even though I can never marry her. You found a way for us. Magnus needs you in his life. I know how he was when you were gone and feared lost. It's how I was with Noe. It's love; that's not in question. What is in question is the way that love is to be expressed. For me, having Noe as a sibling is perfect; she can lie with me and hold me all night if need be, and during this permanent hole project it may indeed need be. For you, giving Magnus Atrocia in the show is perfect. If you can't be together one way, try another way. If that works out, Magnus will accept it. He understands your situation, as Noe understands mine."

"What are you saying, Santo? I don't much like the smell of it."

"I am saying you should give this man Ira a fair chance. Try it with him his way for a night. If that works out, try it for a week. If that's good, then a month. If it continues good, marry him while still being Atrocia in the show. You can have both, Jess. Just as I'll have both with Noe. Romance is not the whole of love."

"A compromise trial," Jess said, seeing it. "A night, then decide on a week. Not a whole commitment at once, but a gradual one, if it works."

"Yes. It was gradual for me with Noe. At first our relationship was pure show and convenience. But slowly in the course of a year, as I got to know her better, I came to appreciate her more. It might have gone the other way. It might for you. The fairest thing you can do for either man is to give it an honest open minded try."

Jess nodded. "When you say it, it starts to make sense. A limited fair try."

"You really helped me, Jess. I hope I am helping you."

"You have shown me how I can find out, I think. That will do." She leaned toward him. "Consider this a sibling kiss." She kissed him on the cheek.

"Siblings I can handle."

That night she told Magnus. "I will stay with Ira one night. If I don't like it, it will end there. At least I will have tried."

"That's all a person can do." He took her hand and kissed it. That much he could do.

And how much could *she* do? She truly didn't know.

Next day Dolph as the roc carried Jess, Noe/Kadence, and Myst/Mairzy, so as to introduce more of their number. Ira welcomed them, and gave them token iridium trinkets. Kadence explained more of the necessary process of tunnel-shoring, and Ira understood. "That will be hard work for me, as for you and Santo, but with proper support we should be able to manage it."

"You will have to join us on the boat," Kadence said. "For the duration. Dolph won't be able to fly you back and forth all the time."

"Yes. I look forward to seeing that fabulous boat. I have heard rumors of it."

"They do not do it justice." They both laughed.

Then it was time for them to go. "I have enjoyed seeing you again," Ira told Jess politely.

"I am staying the night."

"The night! I did not demand this."

"I discussed it with my folk, and they felt I should give you a fair chance. I can't promise you love, but I can lend you my body, and see how I feel about it."

"How you feel?"

"If I don't like it, I won't do it again. You know I love another man, though my curse keeps him at bay. I might discover that it is a reasonable compromise. I might not. I don't know. But at least I will have given it and you a fair chance."

"That is more than fair," he agreed.

The others departed. Jess had a nice meal with Ira, then got serious. "We don't have to wait for night. Let's start now." What she didn't say was that she feared that if she didn't get promptly on with it, she would lose her nerve.

"As you wish. We can hold hands at first."

He was trying to be delicate. Jess did not dilly-dally. She removed all her clothing and lay down on his bed. "Come and get me."

"Are you sure? You really don't have to."

"I do have to. I need to know whether this is possible for me. Do whatever you like with me. I will try to respond appropriately." She did know what it was all about, thanks to her night with Magnus when she had the Brown Rose, though that seemed very far away now. What she didn't know was how well she could respond with another man.

He stripped and joined her on the bed. He stroked her body. She lay with her eyes closed, willing herself not to flinch. Whatever she decided in the morning, she wanted to be sure to be responsive now.

"Oh, my," he said.

Jess opened her eyes. "Is something wrong?"

"Your face is soaking wet."

"It is?" She was surprised.

"Jess, you are crying."

She felt her face. It was completely watered with her tears. "Oh, no."

"You don't really want to do this, Jess."

"But I do! I do! I need to find out."

"You already know."

"Ooh, bleep!" she swore. "I do know. I'd rather be miserable with him than happy with someone else."

"I wish I could find a woman to love me like that."

"Maybe you will," she said desperately. "Maybe I am she. Maybe we just need to try harder."

He shook his head. "I appreciate your determination, but I fear you are a lost cause for me. I need a woman who truly wants to be with me, not one who has to force herself. I'll provide the iridium your project needs. All I ask in return is that if you ever conclude that it isn't going to work with Magnus, you will come look me up. See where it goes from there."

"Yes! I can commit to that!"

"Meanwhile, let's get dressed. I hope we can enjoy each other's company on a friendship basis."

"Yes," she said, relieved. That was how Santo and Noe worked it out, really.

"Let me give you this to remember me by." He presented her with an iridium ring.

"Yes. Thank you." She set it on the fourth finger of her right hand, where it fit perfectly. "I will be glad to remember you."

"When you wish to locate me, lift the ring and sight though it. It will show you where I am at that moment. Then you should be able to locate me."

They talked, they played Nineteen Questions, they laughed together. They were compatible. In fact she liked him. It was so great to be taken seriously in a non-serious way! Soon she found herself telling him about Atrocia. "It's the one benefit my curse provides. I am quite a hit as her."

"I am curious. Will you do your monologue for me?"

"It may not be that funny to you, because you can take me seriously. It's really not much without my curse."

"Perhaps that will make me more objective."

So she did Atrocia for him, and he was not overwhelmed but was amused. "If you told me you loved me, I would not laugh my head off. Neither would I vomit on your panties."

"Those are actually exaggerations. They didn't actually happen."

"Hyperbole, of course. Humorous exaggeration."

"Yes." He understood so well. If only she *could* love him!

"You have told me how you inadvertently traveled through several worlds. Perhaps you should parody them for your act."

"Maybe I will," she agreed.

When night came, Ira tried to give her his bed while he slept on the couch. She demurred, wanting the couch. They argued pleasantly, and finally agreed to share the bed, and if she changed her mind about something along the way, she would take the initiative.

As it turned out, she didn't, and slept well through the night. At one point she woke and gazed at him in the dim light of one of the moons. He was handsome and decent and talented, and immune to her repulsion. He would be a fine man to marry, if only. Later she half woke again and realized that he was gazing at her similarly. If only, again!

Next day Ira was busy wrapping up his business so he could be away a few days. Jess explored the property, finding it pleasant. Then the roc express arrived, and they were ready to board.

"Oops," Ira said, standing beside the big bird.

"What is it?"

"I have never flown before. I think I am afraid of heights."

"Maybe I can help you. Close your eyes. Trust me."

"I do trust you."

He closed his eyes. She took his hand and guided him onto the roc's back. Then they lay down, and she put her arms around him, holding him close to her bosom, his head cushioned. "Just relax," she murmured. "I will not let you fall."

"Physically, or emotionally?" he asked into her shirt.

She laughed, rocking his head. But it wasn't really funny.

And as they traveled, thoughts of the Sea Hag intruded once again. Why couldn't she get that foul creature out of her mind? Did she have an appetite for punishment?

They arrived safely at the boat. "We could have flown to Hell, and I would have been happy in that embrace," he said.

"Thank you." She loved the fact that he was serious.

Jess showed him around the decks and introduced him to those he had not yet met. "You do travel in style," he remarked.

Then she turned him over to the Tunnel Team: Santo, Dolph, Noe, Kadence, Tata, the peeve, and Squid. They had set up a separate cabin to work from, because Fibot would have to go with Magnus's show team.

And it was time for that diversionary expedition. They needed to justify the time they spent on the World of Three Moons so that no one would suspect that their real mission was to build the secret tunnel. The royal wedding was a convenient pretext, however serious it might be to the participants. Magnus and Aria had shown a fine inability to say no to additional engagements, so there were a number scheduled around the planet.

The Show Team consisted of Magnus, Atrocia, Aria, and assorted stage hands and supportive personnel, such as Dell, Nia, and Win to transport them, with Ula, Myst and Mare Imbri to handle details. They did a private rehearsal, then sailed to the palace.

Queen Jenny was there, of course. She greeted Dell, Nia, and the children warmly, as they knew each other from prior trips. She was more formal with Magnus and Jess, who were new to her. "But where is Kadence?" she asked, immediately recognizing the change in Ula.

"It got complicated, and I had to change princesses," Ula said. "Kadence is marvelously talented, but she can't sing. So her cousin Aria is with me now." She did not have to explain about Noe, because Santo's visits to her had been largely private and she hadn't met Jenny. Jenny knew the princesses were from the future, but not the recent future crisis.

Jess was glad they did not have to try to explain, saying it was complicated.

They also met Prince Jerry and Princess Froma, regally lovely with red hair, orange eyes, and four fingers like Jenny and Jerry.

Then it was show time. The audience was studded with royalty, as the monarchs of other kingdoms attended with their retinues. In fact Jerry and Froma, the betrothed couple, were there, to Jess's surprise. She had thought they would have better things to do than watch and listen to nonsense.

Aria briefed the cast privately. "Kings and queens, princes and princesses are people too, at heart. This is their relaxation before the big event of the wedding, where they will be on show as well as the marital couple. So treat them just like ordinary folk but don't push it. Politely lower your eyes when speaking directly with them; never meet their gaze, because that implies you regard yourself as equal to them." She smiled. "I will meet their gaze; I *am* equal, and they will know it. Don't say anything negative about anyone; word travels at the speed of thought and negatives are poisonous. Otherwise, be yourselves."

"Thank you," Nia said, appreciating the warning. "But what of Jess? If she speaks deferentially, they will not believe it, and think she is insulting them."

Aria considered. "True. It may be better if Jess never appears. Only Atrocia. That's her character; they will expect it from her. Just as Ula will not appear in public, only me."

"I'm glad of that," Ula said.

"And of course it is Atrocia they have really come to see," Aria concluded.

Could that be true? Jess could not be sure it wasn't. Her curse was becoming better known than she was.

Magnus went into his spiel, marvelously effective as always, and asked for volunteers. And the volunteers were all royal—including Jerry and Froma. That was a surprise. Other royal women were eyeing Magnus speculatively. Jess had seen that look before; it meant that even grown royals were not immune to his charm.

"Stay close, Aria," he murmured as he turned the stage over to Jess. Jess had never seen him nervous before, but she knew Aria would guide him and intervene if necessary. It might indeed be necessary, judging by the way the royal women were moving in. Aria did know the royal scene, as her tenure at Planet Distaff had demonstrated.

Atrocia took over, with her standard introduction. The royals laughed just like any other audience, which was encouraging. Then she got into her new material. "So there I was, marooned on Planet Stench. I never really believed that my act stunk; now I did. But would you believe it, they were bored, because *every* act stinks there. I had to try to get serious; then they laughed." She went on to Distaff. "Know why they have that distaff symbol of a rod with a swollen end? Because they need that in lieu of their weak-spined men." The men did not laugh as hard as the women did. And on to Planet Ant. "Just call me Ant Atrocia." It worked well enough, though she suspected that without her curse it would have fallen largely flat. Which was the thing about that: she needed her curse to be Atrocia.

Then Magnus returned, with the starkly original story of prince meets princess, loses princess, regains princess, with four fingers being the key. Aria's accompaniment lent real feeling to it, concluding with the wedding march. The audience loved it all.

Yet after the successful show, Jess thought of the Sea Hag again. Bleepety bleep! she thought furiously. She had to get her masochistic mind clean of that ugliness.

They checked back in briefly with the Tunnel Team before sailing to their next engagement. They were hard at work, with a man-high tunnel between planets, Dolph as a giant stone-borer worm, Squid scraping up the droppings and smearing them on the tunnel wall, and Ira conjuring a thin but steady supply of iridium for Tata to vaporize in a small attachment that the peeve then blew against the plastered wall by clinging to the floor and strongly flapping its wings. Kadence's magic made it all integrate.

"Ira is really working hard," Santo told Jess. "I can see how this sustained conjuring depletes him as it does me, but he's not complaining. We need to find a way to repay him."

"I promised to seek him if it doesn't work out with Magnus," Jess said.

"That's not enough. Which reminds me; Ira wants to talk with Magnus. We'd better take a break; we all can use it."

They took a break, and Ira came to greet Jess. She could see the suppressed longing he had for her. "Fetch Magnus," Santo told the peeve. The peeve flew off without backtalk; it was tired, too.

Soon Magnus appeared from the boat. "Something wrong?"

"In my delirium of effort I got a crazy idea," Ira told him.

"Oh? If it is a way to improve the tunnel, I'm not the one to see. I know nothing about the mechanics or chemistry of it."

"Not exactly. Let me talk to you privately."

The two men went aside. Jess was curious as anything what they could be talking about, but knew she had to give them their privacy.

Magnus burst out laughing. "You're right! That *is* crazy! But Xanth is crazy. It just might work. Thanks!"

"You're welcome. I hope it does."

"Now my idea," Santo told Ira. "Do you know how we found you?"

"Jess said something about Tata orienting on a supply for iridium."

"Yes. Let's ask Tata about something else." Santo addressed the dogfish. "What about platinum? That's similar to iridium, as I understand it. Don't they merge well, I mean for alloys or whatever in the science realm?"

Tata's screen flickered. "Yes," the peeve translated.

"Can you orient on a similar source for platinum?"

"Yes."

"Like maybe someone who conjures platinum?"

"Yes."

"Like maybe a young woman?"

"Yes."

"On this planet?"

"Yes."

"Oh, my," Ira breathed.

"You're really helping us," Santo said. "Maybe we can help you."

"That would be phenomenal."

"We try to pay our debts." Santo glanced at Jess. "Don't we, Jess."

"Oh, my," Jess echoed. "Yes."

Days passed as work on the tunnel progressed. Each time Jess returned, it was farther along, with first the bare substance of Santo's conjuration, then the mud of the special feces, then the silvery sheen of the iridium coating, properly aligned by Kadence's sorcery. A major project, to be sure, but progressing nicely. Meanwhile the boat sailed to several other kingdoms after the wedding, doing shows that proved to be very popular. Atrocia was being taken very seriously, in her laughable way, and of course the ladies loved Magnus. One of them actually picked herself up by the scruff of her neck and threw herself at him. He caught her, but set her down gently, not using the pretext to put his hands on evocative parts of her body. She managed to conceal most of her annoyance.

"I tried to make him laugh," Jess said in the course of her monologue. "But it seemed his funny-bone was out of order and maybe his nose; he had no scents of humor, at least where I was concerned." They laughed; what was funny was her telling of it, buttressed by her talent, rather than the situation itself. "I even tried throwing puns at him, to absorb the humor so that he might take me seriously, but they went right over his head. He didn't catch one of them. He had punfusion."

At the next village show the children were in a special program, so her audience was adult. That allowed her to get more graphic. "Then there was the demon hitman. He liked to beat up men and rape women. I was not too keen on meeting him, but he came after me, anyway. He was a brute; my talent pushed him away, but he was so intent on what he wanted that he overpowered it and grabbed hold of me. He ripped off my dress. But when he focused too closely on my body, he lost focus on my repulsion, and my talent began to get back at him around the

edges. Suddenly he broke out in assorted annoyances, like itches, hic-
cups, coughs, sneezes, cold sores, asthma, acne, allergies, freckles, and
dark spots, all at the same time. Even so he remained determined, and
I feared the worst. His lips were coming down on mine, and his groin
was advancing. But then he cried "Edie!" I think that was his girlfriend,
or maybe her initials, e.d. The thought of her must have spooked him,
because he clouded up and floated away, most chagrined. If I ever meet
her, I'll thank her."

The audience laughed, though the women seemed to find it funnier
than the men did. Some jokes were like that.

Then Jess remembered something. "The zombies!"

"The zombies?" Magnus asked.

"They maintain and guard the Tunnel, at least at the ends. We need to
make a deal with them now."

"That's right. That detail slipped my mind."

"Nine years of loyal work, for no recognition. What can we realistically
offer them in return?"

"Recognition."

"But the Tunnel has to be secret."

"Recognition as legitimate citizens of the planet," he clarified. "That's
what all zombies crave and seldom get."

"But how?"

"Queen Jenny. We shall have to take her into our confidence, and ask
her to intercede with Princess Froma's mother the queen, and issue an
edict. Our two princesses will know how to set that up, I'm sure."

"You're so smart," she said lovingly.

"I dare you to repeat that at such time as I can take you seriously."

"I will."

They talked with Aria, who set it in motion. In due course the edict
was issued. The zombies were being repaid.

When the tunnel was finished and the two ends of it duly hidden from
discovery by strangers, the zombies now on guard, the whole crew collapsed into recovery. Except for Tata, who was indefatigable, and Ira, who
had a very special interest. They enlisted Win, who guided Fibot to a village in another kingdom. The fireboat anchored invisibly in air while Jess
and Ira got off.

"I can't introduce you, Ira," Jess said. "You know why. You will have to do it yourself."

"Naturally."

"If it works out, we'll leave you alone with her. We'll return tomorrow to take you back to your home, if you wish."

"That is more than fair."

Ira walked up to the house and knocked on the door.

It opened. There stood a lovely young woman with platinum colored hair. She took one look at Ira and stepped into his embrace. Little hearts flung out and orbited.

It was done. They had repaid Ira for his labor.

They flew back to the camp. Things were quiet there. Noe was holding Santo, who was asleep; Kadence was adding to her presence, her Sorceress aura helping them both. Squid was in her natural tentacular state, soaking in the swamp. Aria, still with Ula, was with Squid for emotional support. Friendship worked both ways.

That night Jess told Magnus all about Ira's evident success with the other woman. "They do seem to have been made for each other."

"It was generous of you to do that for him. It means you have no backup romance."

"I love you. I think I will always love you. There was no sense in teasing him." Which reminded her. "What was that crazy idea he told you?"

Magnus shook his head. "It's a way I just might win you. But it's so crazy I'm ashamed to tell you. You'd probably laugh your head off, or vomit on my shorts."

A fun reference to her show, which he had heard so many times. "Atrocia might. I wouldn't."

"And it is you I want, Jess, not Atrocia, in my bed at night. I have so much love corked up that I can't properly express. If I do it and it works, then I'll tell you."

She sighed to herself. If he wouldn't tell her, he wouldn't tell her.

Next day, the others mostly recovered, they sailed Fibot to go to see Ira. The boat parked invisibly again, and Jess went alone to the house. She knocked.

The door opened. The silvery haired woman stood there, prettier and more shapely than Jess was. "Ah. You must be Jess. Ira said you would come."

"Yes. I—"

"May I kiss you?"

What? Jess stood there bemused, wondering whether he had heard correctly. The woman stepped forward, embraced her, and kissed her on the cheek.

"But—"

"Come in, Jess. I am Platina. Yes, I can take you seriously. I am like Ira in that respect. I am so grateful you introduced us. That was so generous of you, considering your own interest in him."

Oh. "You're welcome."

They entered the house. Ira was sleeping on the couch. "Poor thing," Platina said. "I know he was worn out conjuring all that iridium for your project, and I hardly let him rest all night. I couldn't help myself. I just had to meld. You did me the favor of my life, bringing him. I knew the moment I saw him that he was the man of my life. I had just about resigned myself to being old maid. I'm attracted to repulsive men, except for Ira, and that's no good."

"I understand."

"You surely do. He told me about you, about your curse. But not about your project. He said that had to be secret."

"Yes."

"Here, I will wake him up. He wants to talk with you."

"No," Jess said quickly. "Let him sleep. We can talk instead." She found herself liking Platina in much the way she liked Ira, and trusting her similarly.

"Let me give you a ring, as he did," Platina said, presenting her with a platinum ring. "In case we should wish to get together again, after this."

"Thank you. I may indeed wish to use it, once our mission is done." Now she had three special tokens, including the one from the Night Stallion.

"He told me of your relationship with Magnum."

"Magnus."

"Magnus, yes, thanks. Like mine with other men, in a way. Completely frustrating."

Maybe it was that this was the second person who was taking her seriously. Maybe it was that Platina was educated and intelligent in much the way Ira was, and easy to talk to. Maybe it was her sympathetic understanding. Before she knew it, Jess found herself telling her about the Tunnel project and the reason for it, after swearing her to secrecy. "So you see, it was vitally important that we have Ira's help, and he gave it unstintingly, though I could not give him what he wanted of me. We felt we had to do him a return favor. That favor is you."

"For which I will be forever grateful. But I wonder. There is something about your mission that bothers me."

"We have to save Xanth!"

"Oh, yes, of course. It's not the need; I truly appreciate that. It's the method. What you are doing is fine for the next track of alternate Xanth history. You are saving those folk an enormous amount of misery. But what you really need to do is fix *this* track. The one the two princesses are on, visiting you. To get their people undeleted and back in charge in their own time. To restore to life their mothers. To send Ragna Roc into permanent exile along with his foul minions. To make their lives bearable again, and future Xanth safe."

"Yes, of course," Jess agreed. "But *how*?"

"Well, I have an idea about that. It may seem far fetched, but I believe it is viable."

"How?" Jess repeated dubiously.

Platina told her. Jess was amazed. "That is so far beyond the pale that it just might work. Even I have trouble taking it seriously."

"That is my thought. The idea that it is clear no prior track thought of. That's the one you need."

"No prior track," Jess repeated musingly. "We can't do the same thing they did; we know that doesn't work."

"Exactly."

Then Ira woke. "Hello, girls. Am I interrupting something?"

"Platina has an idea," Jess said. "My mind is boggling."

"She gets those," he agreed. "She kept me busy all night."

Platina smiled. "That, too."

Jess suppressed a surge of envy. If only she could be that way with Magnus! But that was not related to the present issue.

"Tell him," Jess told Platina. "We need more minds on this."

Platina did. Soon Ira was nodding agreement. "I think they should try it."

Then they went to Fibot and introduced her to the others. Platina was as amazed as Ira, and liked the boat as well as he did. "These folk travel in style."

They took the new couple to Ira's house and left them there to work out their own arrangements. Their association with these nice folk was done for now.

They also bid farewell to Noe's mother Noleta, who would be guarding the secret tunnel for the next nine years.

Then they returned to Xanth proper, via a new temporary tunnel, delivering the royal couple to Queen Jenny's home territory. Santo rested, Noe comforting him. They all rested.

The tunneling was done. Now all Jess had to do was broach the phenomenal idea Platina had presented her with. Did it really make sense? Would the others accept it? Jess almost feared to present it, but knew she had to.

Chapter 14

STRATEGY

Something had been nagging at the fringe of Jess's awareness, and she finally realized what it was. It gave her a shudder of horror, but she could neither deny it, nor tell anyone else. Yet.

It was that she knew where the Sea Hag was. Not hiding on Planet Coral, or any other world they had traversed. The Hag was here, tagging along with Jess. She had learned to smell the evil Sorceress, not with her nose, but her mind. The Hag had not taken a host, but remained in spirit form, undetectable to all but the most sensitive folk. Jess knew it only because once the Hag had tried to approach her, for a takeover, but been repelled by her curse. She had penetrated just enough to leave her psychic odor.

Not when she was aboard Fibot, which was shielded against the Hag's intrusion. But when she was outside it, relaxing, then the awareness had intruded. She had supposed it was just her errant thoughts, but now she had made the connection. The Hag was with her, not as a host, but as someone to track.

It made sense, when Jess thought about it. Why should the Hag allow herself to be marooned on some distant world, facing the daunting chore of going from host to host, traveling through the chain of worlds to reach Xanth again? Much better to stay close to her enemies—without their knowledge. That way not only would she get a free ride back to Xanth, she would be aware of whatever they planned to stop her and Ragna Roc. She knew about the Tunnel, and in due course would tell Ragna, so that he could destroy it next time around. When it was time to strike, she would take another host—possibly another child in their group.

Had the group aboard Fibot lost the war already?

"Not if I can help it!" she exclaimed subliminally. But what could she do about it? She pondered, and an ugly idea came. But she was pretty sure that no pretty idea would ever subdue the Hag.

She would try to implement it. If she failed, she would try again some other way. The Hag *had* to stopped, or all else was lost.

But first she needed to know more about the Hag, because she could not afford to make a mistake. She had to be very sure of her information.

"Peeve," she murmured when there was a lull.

The little bird came to perch on her shoulder. "What's up, joker?"

"Something about as serious as anything can be. I need to research with Tata, privately. Without involving the others. Can you arrange that?"

"What's it concern?"

"The Sea Hag."

The peeve flew away. Soon it returned with the dogfish.

"Tata, this has to be secret, for now," Jess said. "Do you agree?"

The robot's screen flickered. "We agree," the peeve said.

"The Sea Hag is here," Jess said grimly. "Not inside the boat, but she is hanging around outside, and follows me when I am out, such as when I was dealing with Ira and Platina. I believe the Hag means to strike again when there is opportunity, and I mean to stop her. But I need to know more about exactly how she takes over a person, and why that person doesn't simply expel her. I believe you have the information I need in your data banks. Doesn't hosting normally have to be voluntary on the part of the host? What is different about the Hag?"

Tata answered, via the peeve, that a normal soul was firmly attached to its original host, leaving it only upon death, or in special cases such as the two mares and two princesses, when the alternate hosts were amenable. That yes, the host had to be willing and welcoming, and that a normal person could kick out any visiting spirit at any time. That was why ghosts did not take over the bodies of living people. But the Hag was different; she was a Sorceress with extraordinary spiritual power, which she used purely selfishly. She could not be expelled unless she wanted to go.

"When Noe and I were traveling the worlds," Jess said, "Aria's visiting spirit was able to repel the Hag somewhat. How did that work?"

The Hag had locked on to Noe's soul and could not be removed. But Aria's spirit was welcomed by the host, as the Hag was not, so they were evenly matched. Had Aria not been a Sorceress herself, the Hag might have overpowered her and locked onto her similarly. It would have fared ill for a less powerful soul.

"So it is always the soul the Hag clamps onto, not the physical body," Jess said, making sure she had it straight.

"Always," the peeve agreed.

They explored the nuances, until Jess was satisfied that she had them straight. Yes it was the soul that the Hag clutched, not the body. But since the soul governed the body, it normally made little if any difference. Except, perhaps, in the special case Jess envisioned.

"One other detail," Jess concluded. "Ida of Planet Coral said that the Hag could cross to other worlds only when in a host. But then how did she follow us here, unhosted?"

Soon the peeve had the answer: "She was familiar with your soul, having once considering latching on to it, and with Noe's soul, having ridden it, and with Aria's soul, having fought it for days. And with Dolph's soul, similarly. She probably left a cookie in Noe."

"A what?"

"A Mundane term. A small cache of information she could access at will. So she had a handhold, as it were, that she could follow across the worlds. That's probably one reason Noe felt so dirty: part of the Hag was still with her."

Jess nodded. "That explains much. Thank you. Remember, we need to keep this discussion private for now."

The dogfish's screen flickered. "Tata says you have an impressive mind," the peeve translated. "That's a rare compliment, from him."

"I'm just doing what I have to, to maybe help save Xanth," Jess said.

"That, too."

Next, Jess approached Nia. "I need to address the group, seriously. Very seriously."

Nia looked at her shrewdly. "You know you can trust me."

"Can you take me seriously?"

"I believe I can, or at least enough. Speak."

"The Hag is with us. Or with me. I think she is following me about, when I'm off the boat. I think she knows everything that has happened, off the boat."

"I believe you are right," Nia said. "I have smelled her, when I'm off the boat. I thought it was just ugly memories, from the time she possessed me."

"Yes! So did I, though she never possessed me. She was distressingly close as we traveled the worlds."

"Poor Noe," Nia agreed. "She's still recovering from that horror. And you have a way to deal with the Sorceress?"

"Maybe. I have been researching with Tata. But it's ugly."

"It is bound to be."

"I think she means to take over another one of us, so she can get back aboard the boat. Therein we just might set a trap for her."

Nia nodded. "A trap. Not a nice one. But the alternative is worse."

They discussed it, and Nia agreed. "It is ugly. But we're not playing widdly tinks here. Very well. I will do my part. Meanwhile you had better talk to Santo."

"Yes," Jess agreed grimly. "He will not be pleased."

"I will talk to him after you do, if need be. When push comes to shove, he can be tough minded."

Jess talked with Santo, after getting him to focus seriously, outlining her suspicion and her proposal for dealing with it. "Damn!" he swore, so passionately that the bleep intercept didn't catch it. "I love that girl! How can I do this to her?"

"Two things," Jess said evenly. "First, it won't actually be her, but her visiting spirit, the Night Mare Imbri, who may be as old as the Hag and I think can handle it. Second, the alternative of allowing Ragna Roc to be loosed on Xanth again—"

"I know, I know! It has to be done. But I still hate it."

"We all do," Jess said. "Let's hope that none of us ever have to get into anything this ugly ever again."

Santo paused a moment in thought. "You are right. You thought of this yourself?"

"Guilty," Jess agreed. "Then I worked out details with Tata. I'd have been happier remaining relatively innocent. But I can't afford innocence at the moment."

"None of us can," he agreed. "You know, if you were available, and I could take you seriously without special effort, and I wasn't too young, and gay, you're the kind of woman I'd want. You may be as smart as I am."

It was a highly qualified statement, but Jess understood and was deeply flattered. "I'm not smart, so much as determined. If I were available, and lacked the curse, and you were not *et cetera*, I'd surely be interested." Then she kissed him carefully on the mouth, her curse colliding with his orientation in an almost electric tingle, and departed, leaving him thoughtful. She had treated him like an adult, which was a significant return compliment in itself.

Meanwhile Nia had assembled the group, and evidently alerted them to the importance of what Jess would have to say. Ula was there again, extending her hand. Jess took it, finding Kadence; the Tunnel was done, and the princesses had returned to their original hosts, where they evidently felt more comfortable. Such was Jess's distraction with her research that she hadn't noticed Ula before, though of course she had been there. Now Jess could speak to the full group and be accurately understood.

But first she addressed Kadence privately. "I need you to make others take me seriously, yes," she said. "But there is a separate thing. I need you to promise me, on your word of honor as a princess, that after our mission is done and we all go our separate ways, you will travel back at least once more in time to make sure that your prior self does interact with Ragna Roc."

"But that's history," Kadence protested. "I don't want to mess with it."

"I am thinking that your prior self, younger than you are now, may not be entirely certain of her course. You need to assure her that she is doing the right thing. If there is a conflict involving paradox, you will not be able to talk with her. But it may be that she will need your reassurance, and it is very important that she receive it."

Kadence considered. "You know, now that you mention it, I think I do remember that I did receive some encouragement from an older self. It really helped. But paradox is all over the place, so maybe I just imagined it."

"And maybe you didn't," Jess said. "And maybe there is no paradox. This may simply be part of that prior effort, with two of your future selves collaborating."

"I suppose," Kadence agreed dubiously. "But why do you want me to promise you? And why wait until after the mission is done? Is that relevant?"

"It is relevant. I propose to use paradox to help us, rather than to block us, and you are the key."

"I don't understand."

"It is a very tricky concept. Here is how it works." Jess explained carefully.

Kadence was awed. "That's the most amazing thing I ever heard! You must be a genius."

"No, just a person with a difficult job to do. You are integral to it. Do I have your promise?"

"Oh, yes!" Kadence breathed.

"Thank you." Then Jess oriented on the larger group. It was time for the big show, and not one of Magnus's.

"I have two matters to discuss," she said. "Both are necessarily secret. The first is for all of you, the second for only some of you. I have a plan to deal with Ragna Roc, not in an alternate historical track, but in this one. It was Platina who thought of it, and I believe she is correct. Stopping Ragna on another track is a necessary thing, and we hope we are doing that by going after the Sea Hag and preventing her from freeing Ragna some time in our near future. But what of our own track, the one our two princesses are from? Putting the Hag away can not stop that, by definition. They saw their mothers deleted! That has already happened, in their time. We have to go there and deal with Ragna, and make him undelete their mothers and all others, and accept permanent exile from Xanth. Only then can we consider our mission complete."

She paused, gazing at them. They were not taking her seriously, not because of her curse, but because they thought she was advocating something impossible. But there was dawning hope in the eyes of the two princesses.

"Here is how," Jess continued. "We will go to the Timeline of Xanth, which is a kind of tower, an obelisk with four sides. Tata and the peeve know where it is. The higher you go on that tower, the further forward time is. You can go into the past or the future, and return the same way. The past is no good for us, because paradox prevents us from affecting our own personal timelines. That's why the princesses stay well away from their present-day baby selves; they would not want to interfere with their own lives even if they could. But what I propose is different: climbing to our future, to the princesses' present day time, to tackle Ragna Roc directly. There is no paradox there; we are not affecting our own lives in the interim."

Jess paused. "Are you following me here? I know this is difficult."

"I do," Santo said.

"Brother, is she making sense?" Win asked.

"Yes. It's dangerous, because Ragna can delete people with only a look. But we can go there via the Timeline." He glanced at Tata. "Right, dogfish?"

The robot's screen flickered. "Right," the peeve translated. "He has done it before."

"If you buy it, brother, then so do I," Win said.

"And I," Squid agreed.

"And I," Myst said.

Jess glanced at Noe and Ula. "The princesses buy it," Noe said. "Therefore so do we."

Jess looked at Dell and Nia. "We buy it," Nia said, and Dell nodded. He did not at all mind being in her shadow.

Finally Jess looked at Magnus. "Me, too," he said.

Jess took a breath; one hurdle had been navigated. "Now a correction. Santo said it is dangerous, but gave the wrong reason. Ragna can not delete us. Any of us. Not even the princesses. We're all immune. That's what makes this feasible."

They all looked at her with surprise. "Are you sure she's serious?" Aria asked Kadence.

"Completely."

"Persuade us," Santo said.

This was the second hurdle: their belief. "Just as we can't go back in time to change our own personal timelines, because of the paradox effect, neither can Ragna change his own timeline. He could only affect a different timeline, which is not his interest. He hardly cares more about alternate versions of himself than he does about us. He's an extremely self-centered bird. So he doesn't even want to go back in time; there's nothing there for him. He wants simply to delete any current opposition, and rule

Xanth as his personal kingdom. Power is his addiction. But here is the thing: we have been interacting with Ragna all along, indirectly, because it was Kadence who made the undeleted egg that confined him so many years. He can't touch Kadence because she is part of his history." Jess took another breath. "And we are part of Kadence's history, now. Ever since she returned to her past to join the siblings, and since Magnus and I joined them, too. We are all in this together, affecting each other. We thus have become part of her immunity, in a kind of package deal. Ragna can't delete any of us without affecting her, so the paradox effect protects us all. It is a widening cone of resistance. If Ragna were here now, he might delete some of us, but nine years from now this has become part of Kadence's past and will be immutable." Jess paused again to let them assimilate it.

"Does this make sense?" Win asked Santo again.

"I believe it does."

"Except for one thing," Aria said. "If we go with you back to the future, we will be in our second loops. Our original selves will be age ten, and our hosted spirits will be age ten also, parallel to our originals. Those originals have not had anything to do with Ragna, so will not be immune. If he takes them out, we'll be gone, too."

"They will not be immune," Santo agreed. Then he reconsidered. "Wait— Kadence is immune, as Jess reminded us. Especially since she may affect her own past *after* we deal with Ragna, so her present is part of this loop; that's about as nice a device as I have seen. But not Aria. Regardless, they will not be present at the showdown. Only you two ghosts, who *are* immune. He won't know the difference, and won't have time to figure it out."

They pondered further, and concluded that he must be right. All of them, including the two princesses, could travel to the future to brace Ragna Roc.

"My head hurts," Myst said. "These thoughts are too big for it."

"Vaporize and encompass them," Squid suggested, and the others laughed.

"There is a consideration," Nia said. "Tata knows where the Timeline is, but it's not something a person can just go to. If it were easy to find, all manner of careless folk would be trying to use it, and maybe incidentally messing up Xanth history. So there is a challenge."

"Like getting into the Good Magician's Castle?" Myst asked.

"Perhaps," Nia agreed with a smile. "For a similar reason, at any rate: to prevent careless or wrongly motivated folk from reaching it." She glanced at the dogfish. "Tata, what is the nature of the challenge?"

The screen flickered. "There were multiple paths to reach it, before," the peeve translated. "Each went there, but by different routes, some of which were more devious than others. Only the correct path would actually work."

"How do we know the correct path?" Magnus asked. "In fact, how do we know where any of the paths are?"

The robot's screen flickered again. "You must devise several paths yourselves," the peeve said. "Then choose one of them for the group to use."

The others looked at Jess. She was the protagonist, so they thought the decision might be hers. That was not the way she saw it, but she didn't care to argue. "Do we have any suggestions for paths? Maybe we can animate them as dream scenes from the mares so we can all see them before we choose."

"Tata can help with that," the peeve said. "If a mare works with him, he can show us the location of the Timeline so we can see assorted paths to it."

Win laughed. "We'll know where they go, but not which one works!"

"Exactly," Jess agreed. This seemed halfway crazy, but so was the larger situation. "Does anyone have a suggestion?"

"Sure," Magnus said. "Sail Fibot up into the sky and down to the Timeline, avoiding all the pitfalls and monsters on the ground."

Myst went to stand by Tata, resting her hand on his top fin. Mairzy animated a dreamlet that was visible to them all. It showed the Timeline Obelisk in the distance, and Fibot in the foreground, with a glowing line arcing between them, avoiding the jungle below, replete with assorted glowering monsters. Jess had to admire the proficiency of the dream maker.

"That's one," Jess said. "Any others?"

"How about one that veers through a nice gulf course?" Dolph asked with a smile.

The first dream picture faded and a new one formed. This showed the boat and Obelisk as before, but now the glowing route passed though a gulf course carved out of the jungle.

"Very nice," Dolph said. "I have missed gulf recently."

"Next?" Jess said somewhat dryly.

"Maybe one with a nice traveler's inn on the way," Noe said wistfully. "With hot meals."

The scene showed the line passing through an inn with wavy lines above it suggesting the aroma of freshly baked bread.

"And nice bedrooms," Noe added. A light came on upstairs, indicating a bedroom. Santo smiled, and the others laughed, as it was a joke.

Jess looked around, but there were no other volunteers. "My turn, then. There are enchanted paths leading here and there across Xanth, safe from all molestation. I want one that passes near the Timeline, so that we'll have only a short trek that is unprotected. We can park Fibot, as I doubt the boat can navigate the Obelisk, and make that brief excursion."

A new picture appeared, showing a curving path that passed near where they were and wound around close to the Obelisk without coming into sight of it. The line showed the way.

"You are concerned with safety?" Magnus asked. "The main threat has been the Sea Hag, and she is marooned on a far planet."

"We can not be sure of that," Jess said. "The Hag is devious in the extreme, and could have found a way back here. She will want more than anything else to stop us, because of the danger we represent to Ragna Roc. We need to play it safe."

"We do," Nia agreed. She knew how real the threat was. Also that Jess fully expected the Hag to strike in that brief window of opportunity.

"I have an idea," Myst said. "Is it all right for me to suggest it?"

"Of course it is," Jess said. "The fact that you are helping Mairzy animate the pictures doesn't make you a second class citizen."

"It's a route to go pick up Astrid Basilisk and take her with us." And that circuitous route appeared, twice the length of the others.

Everyone looked at Myst, surprised. "What is on your mind, little sister?" Win asked.

"It's—it's that I know Uncle Prince Dolph can change into a fiery dragon and toast Ragna Roc where he perches," Myst said. "But Ragna's a big bird, and that's a lot of fire. It might set fire to the whole scene. But Mama Astrid could kill Ragna with only a glance. That's safer and cleaner."

"We don't really want to kill Ragna," Jess said. "We want to force him to undelete his victims."

"Yes," Myst said. "If you were Ragna, which would scare you more: a dragon or a basilisk?"

"Oh, my," Nia breathed. "She's got a point. Basilisks practically radiate menace. There's something about dying from a glance that is more scary than dying from a toast."

Several others nodded. It was a psychological thing. The siblings weren't subject to it, because they regarded this particular basilisk as their group mother, but chances were that Ragna Roc would be terrified. As a threat, it was a great one.

"Let's see that path," Jess said.

The map picture appeared. Lo, the path passed close by the Void. That was ideal!

"I like it," Win breathed.

"So do I," Squid agreed.

"And I," Santo said. "We all love Astrid, and know we can trust her."

"That is the one," Jess said, making the choice for them all. "But there is one other thing."

"Other thing?" Dell asked, surprised.

"We can sail the boat only so far. Then we'll have to get out and walk, leaving Tata and the peeve in charge. If the Hag is near, that's when she'll strike. We're her targets, because she's unlikely to have time to nab a sleeping stranger. She won't want a man or a young child. In any event Myst should be safe because she and Mairzy have brushed with the Hag before and know her smell and will be on guard. Nia and Noe have already been taken, and as far as we know, they're like undeleted folk: they can't be taken again. Ula hosts Kadence, who as an alert Sorceress can fend off the Hag. That leaves Win, who at age nine is borderline, not that far from becoming a woman. Best not to gamble; she needs protection."

"I don't want to stay behind," Win protested. "Neither does Imbri."

"Yes. We prefer to keep the group together, especially the siblings. You relate to each other in ways others do not. So we need to arrange for protection. That's why I want Imbri and Aria to switch hosts."

Win and Noe looked at each other. "I suppose we could," Aria said. "I can fight off the Hag; I've done it."

"And Noe can fight off the Hag on her own," Jess said. "So you both will have protection. After the mission is done you can switch back to your original hosts, as Aria and Kadence did."

Both girls shrugged. "I suppose it does make sense," Noe said. "Certainly we don't want to risk Win getting possessed. It's unbearably ugly."

"And I wouldn't mind meeting Princess Aria up close," Win said. "If she can stand being in a child."

"You're two years younger than Noe," Aria said. "And one year younger than I am. That's not that much. *I'm* a child."

"And I wouldn't mind being able to turn into a horse," Noe said.

"If the four of you are amenable," Jess said, "do it, and we'll get traveling."

Both girls went blank for perhaps two and a half moments. Then Win spoke. "She's here."

"I am indeed," Aria said, and sang a bar of music to prove it.

"Oooo, I love being able to do that!" Win said.

They looked at Noe. Noe neighed.

Everyone laughed. But Jess caught Santo's eye in passing, and felt a chill. He knew what could happen, and hated it. So, actually, did Jess. But as Nia had remarked privately before, they were not playing widdly tinks.

They went topside. Win, with Aria, took the tiller. The princess was surely intrigued. Jess knew that Win was letting her try steering the craft, because it was a bit wobbly. Meanwhile Noe was getting acquainted with the night mare. She did change forms briefly, verifying that she could do it.

They came near the Void. Beyond it was where Astrid Basilisk was staying at present; all four siblings were able to orient on her location. It seemed that Astrid preferred privacy, and behind the Void pretty much guaranteed that. They anchored Fibot invisibly at an enchanted rest stop, disembarked as a group except for Tata and the peeve with the keys, and walked on.

The path here was not enchanted, mainly because there were very few calls for anyone to come this way. At the closest point to the Void, Jess raised her hands in a Halt motion. She beckoned Ula, who came to her, taking her hand. That provided contact with Princess Kadence, so that the others could take Jess seriously.

"Two things to remind all of us of," Jess said. "That shiny flicker almost within touching distance is the perimeter of the Void. Do not touch it! Nothing that passes across that invisible wall can return this way. Do not play any jump across, jump back games; crossing is strictly one way." She glared around at the children.

"We won't," Myst said. "We know how it is."

"The other thing is to all of us who have not before encountered Astrid Basilisk-Cacatrice, whom we are going to see and add to our party. By all accounts she is a very nice person. But her direct glance kills any folk who meet it, which is why she normally wears a veil or dark glasses, or both. Apart from that, she is dangerous; her very nearness is poisonous. We think of it as an intoxicating perfume, but too much of it can be lethal. So we must all treat her with extreme care. We are picking her up so that she can face down Ragna Roc in the future. If he tries to delete her, he must look at her, and when he does he will die. He will know that, so we expect him to back off and yield to our demands that he un-delete all his victims and accept permanent exile from Xanth proper. However, it is important that we catch him by surprise, so that he can't act to prevent us, especially Astrid, from getting close to him. Even a cried out warning from a distance could alert him and ruin our mission. So I want no one to speak out of turn until the deed is done."

Jess paused, looking around again. "Are we all clear on that?"

Myst raised her hand. "I think I have a question, but it's embarrassing. Can I whisper it to you?"

"Whisper it," Jess agreed graciously.

Myst came up to her, and whispered in her ear. "The Sea Hag is here. I can smell her. But she can't be."

"Where?" Jess whispered back.

The girl pointed silently to Noe.

Jess looked past her to Nia, who gravely nodded. She sensed the Hag, too.

"She can't take Noe over," Jess whispered. "But she can take Mare Imbri. That's why you're confused."

"Oh."

"Do not tell anyone else. This is where we want the Hag. Soon we will be rid of her. Trust me." Jess kissed the child's ear.

"Oh." Myst still seemed confused, but she walked away. She did trust

Jess, who had been like another mother figure to her, especially during their planetary travels.

Jess turned back to the others. "Now let's all admire the fringe of the Void, which we may never see again. Do not touch it!"

They all stepped up to face the invisible boundary, within touching distance. "Noe," Jess said sternly. "Throw Imbri into the Void."

Noe's head turned to face her. "What?"

"Now," Jess said. "Hurl her spirit forward. You can do it."

"Do it," Santo said, as sternly. "Now."

"Now," Nia echoed.

Amazed and chagrined, Noe made a kind of throwing gesture with her hands. But what counted was her spiritual effort: ejecting the spirit of the visiting mare. She might have questioned Jess, or not taken her seriously, and might have hesitated for Nia, but she truly trusted Santo.

Jess held her breath. Had it worked?

Then Noe spoke. "She's gone. They're both gone."

Jess relaxed. "Thank you, Noe. You have just done Xanth a remarkable service. When Imbri entered the Void, the Hag was carried along with her, as she did not have time to disengage. That was why it had to be a surprise, to catch her off guard."

"But Imbri! I didn't want *her* to go!" Noe turned to Santo, who held her close as her tears flowed.

"She will be all right," Jess said.

"What just happened here?" Magnus asked. "Is Mare Imbri lost in the Void?"

"Let's step back from the Void, and I will explain," Jess said, still holding Win's hand.

They all stepped back. Noe was not the only one looking at Jess with borderline horror.

"We have just sprung a very nasty trap on the Sea Hag," Jess explained. "She was following us, mainly me; I could smell her presence, spiritually, as could Win and Nia. Noe too, but she was unable to speak of it. The Hag was going to come with us to the future, then zip across to Em Pathy or some other minion and give warning to Ragna Roc about our identity and mission. He couldn't delete us, but he could stop us if he had any time at all to prepare. His minions could grab us and throw us into a cell, for example. Surprise is critical, and the Hag was going to abolish it, and thus save Ragna. We could not afford that."

"We could not," Santo agreed grimly.

"So I set a trap for her," Jess continued. "First, I explained to the rest of you, knowing she was listening, about Astrid Basilisk. The Hag knew that the minions could not stop Astrid, even with some warning; she could kill them all as fast as she looked around, and then she could kill Ragna Roc himself. There's hardly anything more deadly than a basilisk with a purpose. So the Hag knew she had to act immediately. She had to take over someone in our party, so she could stop the nasty surprise. But there was no one suitable for her to take over; we had covered almost everyone. So she took the only one she could: Mare Imbri, locking on to her spirit. That gave her access to a host, Noe, even if she couldn't control the host directly. That was a lot better for her than nothing. But she didn't want the rest of us to know, so she acted only to stifle Noe's voice, hoping we would not notice that Noe was acting like a zombie. But then we told Noe to throw Imbri into the Void, and she did. Since the Hag was infusing the mare, she could not escape on such short notice. They both entered the Void, and the Hag will not emerge; we have at last eliminated her from the scene."

"But Imbri!" Noe cried. "How could we sacrifice her? She didn't deserve that."

"Ah, yes, Mare Imbri," Jess said. "She has a history. When she killed the Horseman and threw his deadly amulet into the Void, she got caught herself and lost her body. But by then she had a soul, and souls, being immaterial, are not subject to the Void. She was not trapped there before, and is not now. She has returned to her tree."

"But the Sea Hag is a soul," Major said. "So she's not trapped, either."

"Oh, but she is," Jess said. "I did a bit of spot research on this, and learned that while a soul can not be trapped, neither can it escape unless it has somewhere to go. It is like being lost in a fog; you could get out of it, but you can't see the path, so you flounder, lost. Imbri had somewhere to go, before; actually she had half a soul, and Chem Centaur had the other half. The half soul returned to Chem, who freed it to be with Imbri, who became a day mare. It's a whole separate story. The point is, that half soul was tethered to its other half, so it had a line to follow out of the Void.

Imbri was well respected and liked in Xanth. This time Imbri has her tree, and her soul knows the way back to it. She can rejoin us, if she chooses. The Hag is another matter; no one wants her in Xanth. She has no line out."

"So Imbri is all right?" Noe asked, starting to be relieved.

"Yes. I knew she would be. But I couldn't tell the rest of you, lest the Hag overhear and know about the trap."

"I'll go back and see if she wants to rejoin us," Dolph said. "After this, she might not want to."

"Explain it to her," Nia said. "She certainly has a right to be angry about being used. But we had to get rid of the Hag. Maybe she'll understand."

"I will. Back soon." Dolph become the roc bird, and took off.

Noe, now recovered from her tears, shook her head. "I hope we never have to do anything like that again, and not just because I hated the close-ness of the Hag."

"We understand," Santo said. "I knew about it, and I hated it too, but saw no feasible alternative."

"And I knew," Nia said. "Ditto."

"But we are at last rid of the Hag," Kadence said. "Which I think is something the prior alternate tracks did not accomplish."

They resumed their walk along the path. Before long the roc returned, landing on the path ahead of them. It transformed to Dolph. "I explained. She understands. She knew we had to stop the Hag."

Noe ran up. "I'm so sorry, Imbri!" she cried. "I hated doing it! Will you take me back?"

There was a pause and a half. Then a dreamlet picture formed over Noe's head, showing the mare in human lady form. IT'S ALL RIGHT, her speech balloon printed. IT HAD TO BE DONE. I KNOW OF THE SEA HAG OF OLD. SHE'S NO GOOD.

Noe clapped her hands in a flash of joy. "I'm so glad!"

"It should be safe for Aria and Imbri to switch back to their original hosts now," Jess said. "Their exchange was for a passing purpose."

Win and Noe approached each other and touched hands. Then Noe's expression changed. "Done," Aria said. "I do prefer Noe, no offense to Win; she's more familiar."

A speech balloon appeared over Win's head. DITTO.

They moved on. Soon they came to a cute little house surrounded by a very pretty flower garden. A woman was tending to the flowers, each of which had its own little bed, complete with miniature blanket and pillow. They were obviously well cared for, and were thriving.

The four siblings charged her. Myst collided with her so hard it knocked off her dark glasses. Santo, averting his gaze, picked them up and handed them back to her. "Oh, my dears," she said, her eye covers restored. "Whatever brings you here?"

"It's a whole big story," Santo said. "But the essence is, we want you to come with us." Then, belatedly: "Folks, this is Astrid."

There followed more formal introductions, and an explanation why Jess was holding Ula's hand: to be taken seriously. Meanwhile a boy emerged from the house, and was promptly mobbed by the siblings. "Firenze!" Myst cried, not succeeding in knocking him down. It turned out that he was the fifth sibling, who had been adopted by Astrid herself. He was fourteen, on the verge of manhood, ordinary except for a some-what ruddy complexion.

"And we're adding a couple more siblings" Myst said. "Noe and Ula." She gestured to them.

"Well, hello, girls," Firenze said, clearly impressed. They were ages eleven and ten respectively, the right ages for gender interest to start. Especially Noe, who was already pretty. Not the prettiest, but pretty enough.

Noe saw his glance, and understood it perfectly. "I'm Santo's girlfriend."

"But—"

"She understands," Santo said.

Firenze nodded, understanding in turn. "Siblings it is."

They settled into their necessary discussion. Astrid seemed like a per-fectly normal and caring housewife, and soon Jess was comfortable with her nature. "So that's why we need you," Santo concluded.

"Of course I'll come," Astrid agreed. "I don't like the idea of Ragna Roc taking over Xanth, either." She glanced at her son, through the dark glasses. "But I think you need to stay home, Firenze."

The boy laughed. "Because I'm a hothead," he explained to the others.

"Because someone needs to tend the flowers while your father is busy," Astrid gently corrected him. "While I am away."

"That too," he agreed.

"I'm not sure I understand," Jess said carefully. "You have a short temper?"

Myst laughed. "Show her, Firenze. Pretend someone's beating me up."

The boy glowered. His complexion intensified, becoming downright fiery. In fact his head seemed about to burst into flames.

"I get it," Jess said quickly. "A literal hothead."

Astrid looked at the sky, which was beginning to think about darkening. "We'll go tomorrow."

No one argued. It had been a tiring day.

Chapter 15

SHOWDOWN

After dinner the siblings, now including Noe and Ula, formed a group, talking animatedly with each other. Ula, buttressed by Kadence, seemed to be making an impression on Firenze. The men, Dell, Magnus, Dolph, and Astrid's husband Art, got together to chat about man things. That left the women, Nia, Jess, and Astrid, in their own group. Astrid sat a little apart, downwind, so that the breeze carried away her poisonous perfume without affecting the others.

"I see you like flowers," Jess said.

"She says—" Nia began.

"And she's not joking," Astrid said. "I think I can understand you, Jess. I have a similar problem, in a manner, being unable to look any friend in the face. I have learned to make allowances."

That made it easier. Neither woman was what she seemed. Nia was two generations older in mind, and Astrid was not even human. Which might explain the inclusion of Squid among the siblings: they knew better than to judge by species.

"Yes, I like flowers," Astrid continued. "I am hoping to get some magic roses from Rose of Roogna to add to my garden."

Jess was electrified. "Magic roses!"

The dark glasses glanced at her. "You also have an interest?"

"Not as a gardener. But when Rose gave me a brown rose, it—" She broke off. "But that's another matter."

"The brown ones nullify magic," Astrid said. "If I hold one, I don't kill others with my glance. That has its appeal, at times."

She did understand. "It enabled Magnus to take me seriously at night, in the bedroom. I was more than willing. We—we had quite a night of it, until the rose faded."

"I can imagine."

"But I think it is not the answer, for me," Jess said. "Because I need my curse for my Atrocia show, and I don't want to impress any man but Magnus. But if I had a rose for the private nights . . ."

"It's an incomplete answer," Astrid said. "As it would have been for me. In my case, I found a man who is immune to my nature. I loved being able to meet his gaze without killing him. To clasp him without poisoning him with my ambiance. To be safely passionate."

Ah, envy! "But if there were such a man for me," Jess said, "I wouldn't want him. I love only Magnus." In fact she had been there, done that, with Ira.

"I do see the problem," Astrid said.

"Magnus believes he has an answer," Nia said. "But he won't say what it is."

"He's afraid it won't work," Jess said.

"Maybe after the mission," Astrid said. "If it doesn't work, then maybe you can take up rose gardening."

Jess sighed. "Tomorrow, the Timeline. According to Tata, the Obelisk moves every so often, to maintain its privacy. Now it seems it is behind the Void."

"As good a place as any," Astrid said. "This is a private region."

"I dread it. Not because of the time travel, but because if my theory of paradox immunity is wrong, we are going into destruction."

"It makes sense to me," Astrid said. "But of course I'm not a theologian."

Jess let the matter drop, not wanting to reveal how concerned she was. She was putting not only herself at risk, but the entire party. Ragna Roc would have no mercy if that protection turned out to be false.

"When we go there," Nia said. "Have you considered Em Pathy?

"Empathy?" Jess asked blankly.

"It's a name. Em Pathy. Ragna Roc's chief minion. Without her he could not govern effectively, if at all."

"Oh, her," Jess said, orienting on it as a name instead of a quality. But she was cautious, preferring to know what the others knew of that woman. "I know he has a human servant he has promised will be Queen of Xanth. Who cares about her?"

"We do," Nia said evenly. "Em Pathy is possibly the most dangerous enemy we face. Her touch can completely transform a person's emotion, converting an enemy to a friend, or vice versa. She uses it to win fanatic followers for Ragna Roc. We had a brush with her when Ragna wanted to take over Fibot; it was an uncomfortably close call. You have been concerned about the Sea Hag, yes; now you must be similarly concerned about Em Pathy."

Jess felt a chill. "How did you escape her?"

"She's not a Sorceress. She is limited to one person at a time. She needed help, dealing with us, and had it, but the other person suffered an attack of conscience. So we escaped." Nia fixed Jess with a look worthy of a basilisk. "We must be prepared to deal with Em Pathy, lest we lose everything."

"You're not looking at me," Astrid said. "I know pointed evasion when I see it. You know I can kill that woman with a glance before she gets close enough to touch me or anyone else."

Nia nodded. "Are you prepared to do that? You do need to know how seriously we take this mission."

"I am prepared to give her fair warning," Astrid said. "If she does not heed it, then she will bring the consequence on herself."

"That's good enough," Jess said. "We prefer that Ragna and Em be reasonable in the face of the threat. It's a finesse."

"Finesse?" Astrid asked.

"We hold a very high card that we prefer not to play," Jess explained. "Once Ragna and Em know that we have that card, which is you, Astrid, they may back off, knowing that if they don't, they will die. That it is no bluff. In that manner we hope to get what we want from them without anyone dying."

Astrid nodded. "Yes. That is the way I prefer it."

"The way we all prefer it," Nia agreed. "One other thing: Kadence told me there were telepaths on Ragna's staff, before. How can we surprise him?"

"From what the princesses say, he is still in the process of conquering Xanth, this time," Astrid said. "There should not have been occasion to assemble a full cast of minions. So probably no telepaths, yet."

"Let's hope so," Nia said grimly.

Dolph came over. "We men realized something," he said. "I can't just walk into Castle Roogna, which is where I think Ragna Roc will be, without being recognized by many folk there; I am a familiar figure. Magnus suggested that I transform into a troll, that he can use in his play." He looked carefully at Astrid. "He has in mind a kind of romance between the two of us, for dramatic purpose only. Can you handle that?"

The veil frowned. "Do I have to kiss you?"

"Yes."

"Do not remain close enough to breathe my ambiance long, or jog my glasses off."

Dolph laughed. "Oh, I won't! Electra would be most displeased if I returned to her dead, and she knew I had been trading intimate glances with a basilisk."

"Let alone kissing her," Astrid said. They both laughed.

In the morning they bid farewell to Art and Firenze, and set off again, their party augmented by the addition of Astrid Basilisk. The children were plainly in awe of her, and not because of her deadly glance. They all loved her. She had saved them, and Xanth, when she was a protagonist. Just as Jess was trying to do now.

Jess was surprised as they walked by how feminine and companionable Astrid was. She was every inch a woman despite being a basilisk. Much as Squid was all girl. It was a continuing education in perspective.

Suddenly, there it was: the Timeline of Xanth, in the form of a four sided metallic obelisk that extended downward below ground level, and upward into the sky. Its surface was densely covered with words and numbers. It could have been an inert monument, and maybe was for the average person, but they knew better.

They stood around it, gazing down and up. "This is the point where anyone who has second or third thoughts about the mission should express them," Jess said, holding Ula's hand.

There was part of a pause. "How about third, fourth or fifth thoughts?" Myst asked, tittering.

The others laughed, but not entirely easily. "Lead on, protagonist," Magnus said.

But Jess wasn't quite ready yet. "Remember, we need to get into Ragna's close presence without his knowing what we are up to. We'll put on a show for him. Then we'll unveil ourselves, as it were."

"We thoroughly reviewed this," Magnus reminded her gently. He was reproving her for stalling.

"According to Tata, all a person has to do is touch the Timeline in the right place to be transported there," Jess said. "But the gradations are so fine that if two people touched it, their fingers only a fingernail apart, they would land in slightly different times. Such as an hour ahead or behind each other. We can't afford that. So we need to go to the right level without touching it, then hold on to each other, and one person touches it. Then we all will land together."

"Makes sense," Magnus agreed.

"We have to go only nine years into our future," Jess continued. "That looks to be about head height. So we can form a chain, and the lead person can touch it."

Magnus took Jess's hand. Then the others linked hands behind him, all the way back to Myst at the end, the littlest.

Could it really be this easy? "Aria, Kadence," Jess said. "You have been there before. In fact it's your home time. Can you guide me? We want to be maybe a day after when you two princesses fled."

She felt the impulse traveling up the chain, activating her free hand. She let it be taken over by the princesses. She reached forward and touched the Timeline with one finger, at 1128. Touched and withdrew within half an instant.

Nothing happened. The line remained leading up to the Obelisk.

Then Princess Kadence spoke from the middle of the line. "We are there. See, the foliage has changed."

Jess looked—and they were there, maybe. The sun was in a slightly different place, and the nearby trees looked sightly older. "You're sure?" Jess asked.

"We're sure," the two princesses said, their hosts letting go and standing independently. "This is our home-time."

"Next question, for the record," Magnus said. "Where is Ragna Roc?"

"He came to Castle Roogna to wipe us out," Aria said. "He should remain there until he builds his own new castle. That could take some time."

There was the confirmation of what they had assumed. They did need to get it right.

"I happen to know where that castle is," Dolph said with a smile. He had of course lived there in his youth. "All aboard." He changed to roc form.

They piled on. "This is a new experience, for me," Astrid remarked as she settled in between Jess and Nia, with Myst at her feet.

"We travel in style," Jess said.

Within the hour by several moments, they landed well beyond the moat at Castle Roogna. They got off, and the roc reverted to the man. Then the man became a hideously ugly green troll. Jess was glad they had all seen it happen, so that they knew they were not under attack.

They formed into a compact group and approached the drawbridge, which was down but guarded. The guard was standing, gazing with surprise at the approach of such a party. Magnus became the spokesman, his aura of verisimilitude practically radiating out. "A greeting, my good man. We are a traveling ensemble coming to entertain Ragna Roc. Kindly allow us to cross the bridge without delay."

The guard, bemused, did just that. They were gambling that most of the castle personnel would react similarly, because Ragna's conquest was still in its first hours and new protocols had not yet been organized.

They made their way across and into the castle, not only flummoxing the guards but getting them to cooperate in clearing the way for their entry. Jess had to admire the way Magnus handled it. His talent was the opposite of hers; nobody took her seriously, but everybody took him seriously.

They came to the main audience hall. There they were intercepted by a handsome woman of middling age Dolph recognized; he signaled Magnus with a glance.

"Ah, Dame Em Pathy," Magnus said grandly. "Just the person we were looking for."

"You were *what*?" she demanded sharply. She clearly had an attitude, as befitted the most dangerous woman on the premises.

"We are a traveling ensemble," he repeated. "We have come to amaze the new ruler of Xanth, Ragna Roc. Surely he is fatigued by his recent labors, and more than ready to settle down on his comfortable nest for a relaxing show."

"What, you have someone with a spot on the wall talent?" she demanded, not at all impressed. "We've seen that sort of thing before. One man even made many tiny spots, forming a moving picture. So unless you have something more original—"

"Kindly usher us in. You will not be disappointed." Magnus reached out and smartly spanked her bottom. "That's a good girl."

Em opened and closed her mouth two and a half times, unable to get a word out to protest this phenomenal impertinence. Jess was sure that no one had ever treated her this way before. The members of the cast seemed to be biting their tongues to stop from bursting out laughing.

"Thank you," Magnus said blithely, just as if she had granted permission, and marched on by her, leading the troupe into the presence of the conqueror bird. At the moment Ragna was listening to roc music, as rocs did in their off moments.

Jess had thought she was prepared for this encounter, but discovered she wasn't. It wasn't that Ragna Roc was visually impressive; he was dull brown. It wasn't his size; Dolph in roc form was the same size. It wasn't his throne; he had none, and was resting in a giant nest on the floor. It was his sheer *presence*. The power of his magic surrounded him like a scintillating cloud. She was awed despite herself. This bird was the real thing. She remembered the legend of his contest with the three princesses, Melody, Harmony, and Rhythm, three Sorceresses whose power when they merged it was cubed, so that they could do marvelous things like making Fibot. Yet Ragna had bested them. What amazing power!

"Well, hello Ragna Roc!" Magnus said grandly, as if undaunted. "I am Magnus, Master of Ceremonies, and this is my ensemble. We heard you were in town, and we just had to come to properly entertain you. We shall put on a fine short play we are sure you will like." He was coming across just like a glad-handing rogue seeking to ingratiate himself with the new order. The kind of person the big bird surely had use for: a yes-yes man.

There was no apparent response from the big bird. Was it falling flat?

Em Pathy hurried up. "Ragna, these scoundrels just barged in!" she exclaimed angrily. "And that man spanked me! The unmitigated nerve! They need to be deleted!"

"What, before we put on our wonderful play?" Magnus asked rhetorically. "Perish the thought, lass! I should spank you again for even suggesting it." Before she could react, he turned back to Ragna. "Which would be no chore. She has a fine firm bottom with just the right amount of quiver."

Jess was not apt at judging the facial expressions of birds, but she could have sworn that Ragna's beak twitched. Even he appreciated the sheer absurd insolence of this suggestion, poking naughty fun at the most powerful woman of the new order.

Em opened her mouth and actually spluttered. "This—this—pervert actually dares to brag of it!"

"See? She agrees," Magnus said smoothly, as if this were a friendly dialogue. "Her nice buttocks must still be reverberating with the sheer joy of it. But alas this is not the time for a repeat performance." He smiled conspiratorially. "Maybe tonight, when things are more settled and cumbersome clothing can be dispensed with. That should be an inordinate pleasure for us both, as I'm sure she agrees. Right now we must assemble a suitable audience to buttress your enjoyment of the show. Tell her to see to it." He had even accented the butt part of buttress, amending the pun. He was excruciatingly nervy and sharp, impressing Jess despite her familiarity with him.

Em opened her mouth once more, practically breathing fire. But Ragna twitched one wing just slightly, hardly more than a feather, and she stifled it. She departed the scene. There was no question who governed here.

"In the interim, let me explain the nature of our show," Magnus said. "Normally I solicit volunteers from the audience to play the key roles, but that seems too awkward on this complicated occasion, so we'll do it in-house, as it were. I have here a fine cast of actors, including some pretty damsels." He glanced at Nia, who smiled, even managing to force a slight blush in the manner of an ingenue, a delicate flower of dawning womanhood. Again, the cast stifled mirth.

"And appealing girls," he continued, with a glance at Noe. She curtsied appealingly, probably guided by Aria.

"And winsome children," with a glance at Squid. She tittered winsomely.

"And ugly men." Dolph, as the green troll, grimaced in ugly fashion.

"And a couple of were-mares." Win and Myst became Imbri and Mairzy, the black and white horses. Even Ragna might have been impressed; not every show featured shape-changers.

"But mainly, we have Atrocia, our resident jester who distracts the audience while the rest of us are setting up the main show." Jess nodded without further expression. It was not quite yet time for her act. Also, she was terrified.

Meanwhile the audience had assembled. They were seated on folding chairs and the floor, forming a large half circle with Ragna in the center. Em Pathy was efficient, when given her orders. Jess found herself admiring that. She might have liked to have the woman for a friend, were they not on opposite sides.

There were a number of ladies who were watching Magnus closely, with covert smiles. Familiar story!

"And I see we are ready," Magnus said. "Hello, all. I am Magnus, with a show to amaze you and thrill you. But first, to warm you up, here is our lady jester, Atrocia." He gestured to her as he backed away.

"Hello," she said, sliding into her routine. She was glad it was so familiar, as it served as a crutch to slide her past her momentary stage fright. "I am Atrocia. Nobody takes me seriously." And nobody did; she had them laughing from the start. She was really in the groove, doing her best yet, as if her fear gave her wings. She realized that even here, performing for a scourge she meant to abolish, she really felt at home making the audience react. She *liked* being the court jester, and did not want to give it up. If only she could turn it off at night, in bed.

They loved her disastrous encounters with men. No matter what embarrassments any women in the audience might have encountered, Atrocia's were worse.

"After that last failure," she continued, "I was sick to my stomach, so I went to the bushes to relieve myself. There was a roll of paper, but when I reached for it, it avoided me. It had writing on it. In fact it was a newsletter printed with ads for children's playthings for rent. I was not a child, so couldn't take it. It was toilet paper." The children laughed hardest at that one.

"I heard there was a good man in a nearby castle. It had a moat with a drawbridge. But the drawbridge was lifted clear of the moat. There was a corpulent lady garbed like a Valkyrie on the other side. 'Please lower the bridge,' I called to her.

"'I will sing,' she said.

"I opened my mouth to protest that I didn't want to be entertained, I wanted to get across the moat. But before I could do that, she opened her

mouth and sang an aria." Princess Aria, disguised as her host Noe so as
not to be recognized, sang it very nicely.

"And the drawbridge came down," Jess continued. "Only then did I
realize that it wasn't over until the fat lady sang."

There was a solid round of applause as she finished. "You're hilarious,"
a young man called. "And really not bad looking for a clown. I'd like to
have at you with your clothes off."

"Thanks, handsome," she called back. "You can puke on my panties
anytime!" There was another burst of laughter. They loved this, and so did
she. She could banter with men on stage in a way she never could when
supposedly serious.

She retreated, and the main show advanced. "This is the story of
blighted love," Magnus said. "Once upon a time, in a fantasy realm far
far away, there was this woman with an apt figure but a face so ugly she
had to wear a veil at all times, lest it curdle milk, pollute the air, and wilt
the flowers." He indicated Astrid, who wore a close fitting gown that
flattered her surprisingly evocative figure, and a heavy veil that covered
all but her eyes, which were masked by solid dark glasses. "Her mother
was at her wits' end to figure out how to get her safely married and out
of the house, when no man would look at her face without flinching and
turning away."

There was Nia, now garbed like a matron, wearing a frown-faced
mask. She was surprisingly competent emulating the nuances of an older
woman. She shook her head in frustration. Aria's voice sounded, humming background music that generated the somber mood.

"Then she got a notion," Magnus continued. "She took her daughter
to a young seer who was just making a name for himself by providing
answers to intractable problems. He would examine her and pronounce
a remedy."

Matron Nia hauled the reluctant daughter Astrid along, using the girl's
long dark hair as a leash. The audience, primed by Atrocia's monologue,
took the humor of it in stride. They came to the seer, Santo, wearing a
mysterious headband to show his profession, who patted the girl all over
in the manner of a choice doll, evoking more audience laughter. This was
the examination. Any man of the audience would have been glad to do
a similar one on any woman, particularly one as shapely as this. Astrid

acted as though this were an expected part of the process. Here too, things were possible on stage that would have caused outrage in real life. This was a significant part of the appeal of any stage production. Suppressed desires could be flaunted. Fortunately the audience did not know that this boy was in a manner this woman's son.

"And gave the answer: she must find a man who is uglier than she. Only when they kiss will her horror abate."

The matron took the girl away and started the search, trailing their servant girl, Myst. They walked around the edge of the stage area, looking at faces, but no man in the audience was ugly enough. Then at last they came to a woodsman chopping wood, with his servant girl Win picking up the pieces and stacking them neatly to the side. He was truly ugly. In fact he was a green troll. Maybe he was ugly enough.

"Mother presented the case to the troll," Magnus said. "He was doubtful. He was looking for a wife, even a plain one, but when he looked at Daughter's face, he winced and turned away, as all men did." The troll did exactly that, as the young woman lifted away her veil for a moment, only for him, and Daughter did not look exactly thrilled by his features, either.

"Kiss her!" Mother ordered him. She had a compelling presence, so finally the troll marshaled his gumption, took the girl in his arms, squinched his eyes shut, and kissed her.

"There was a flash of light," Magnus said, and Squid lit a flare that shone brightly for a moment. "They came together ugly and uglier, but they came apart as handsome and beautiful." Indeed, the troll had transformed into a princely man, and the daughter's veil fell away to reveal scintillatingly lovely features masked only by petite dark glasses. "They were indeed now a handsome couple."

And they were.

And during the flash, the two servant girls transformed into white and black horses. Now the illustrious couple could ride into the sunset in style and live happily ever after.

"Hey!" someone called. "I've seen that man before! He's a prince!"

"And I've seen that woman before," a woman said. "She's a statue!"

Uh-oh. Dolph had slipped mentally and transformed back to his regular human form, or a younger version thereof. And many people had seen Astrid when she and Demoness Fornax had been honored for saving the children, not to mention future Xanth, and a statue in their likeness probably still graced the castle. They had inadvertently blown it.

There was an angry squawk. Ragna had caught on.

"Hold!" Magnus said. "We are now at the denouement. Keep your places, all. We have serious business with Ragna Roc."

But Jess doubted that even he, with his vaunted aplomb, could salvage this situation. They were doomed.

"The bleep you do!" Em said wrathfully. "I knew there was something wrong about you, the way you barged in here uninvited with your arrogant humor and uncouth hand. Now you'll get deleted."

Magnus walked to stand almost touching Ragna's beak. "Very well, Roc. Delete me."

The big bird focused.

Nothing happened.

"Well?" Magnus demanded insolently. "Are you going to do it, bird brain, or not?"

There was an angry squawk.

"What?" Em asked, shocked. "You can't delete him?"

Jess breathed a silent sigh of relief. It was working! She had for the moment forgotten their trump card.

"Please allow me to explain, plush bottom," Magnus said to her. "I am intimately involved in Ragna Roc's past, via a devious linking of the associations of time travel. I am from his earlier life. He can't delete me without changing his past, which he can't, because of what we call the paradox effect. I am proof against his power."

"Delete the others!" Em snapped to the big bird. Ragna might be the boss, but she was the effective executive, guiding him as Magnus guided the play.

Ragna tried, orienting on one of them, then another and another. Again, nothing happened, repeatedly. They were all proof against his power.

But Em Pathy was made of stern stuff. "You forget that there are other means of dealing with a problem," she said. "Men, kill them. Kill them all!"

Several minions stood up, drawing their swords.

"Hold!" Magnus said, as before. "We are proof against that, too. Do not try to attack us."

"Do it!" Em screamed. She was not one to be bluffed again.

Four of the men charged.

Dolph converted instantly to fire dragon form, but before he could blow a blast, Astrid whipped off her dark glasses and looked at them. The four men dropped dead. Then she replaced her glasses, but stood ready to bare her deadly eyes again. Jess cringed inwardly. Astrid was such a nice woman, but this was the other side of her. Em Pathy was not the most dangerous woman present; Astrid was.

"I tried to warn you," Magnus said in the ensuing silence. "Before you stand Prince Dolph the form changer, and Astrid Basilisk, whose very glance is lethal." He faced Em. "Give another hostile order, wench, and he will toast you or she will look at you, depending on their whims." Actually Astrid had to meet a person's gaze to kill him or her, but that was a detail others seldom recognized in time.

Em was suddenly silent. Everyone saw the dragon and had seen the men drop. No bluffing here. It was the finesse.

Magnus turned to Ragna. "Make another hostile squawk, and she will look at *you*. If he doesn't toast you first."

The dragon and the basilisk faced the big bird. The silence continued.

Then Em spoke. "What do you want, showman? I'll wager it is not my bottom."

"We are here to negotiate a truce," Magnus said. "Ragna Roc will undelete a number of people at our direction, and give up all claims to ruling Xanth. In return he will be exiled to a habitable far planet that will then be isolated from the chain of worlds, so that he will be unable to return here. He will have dominion over that planet, and you with him, Em, and any minions who wish to join the two of you. We will be at peace, without further contact."

"The bleep we will!" Em swore.

"What say you, Ragna?" Magnus asked. "Your alternative, to put it bluntly, is death. We are not playing widdly tinks here. Do we need to demonstrate more of our power?" He glanced at Em. "For you too, gal, now that the humor is over."

The big bird considered. He was at heart a realist. He squawked.

Em Pathy looked crushed. "He agrees," she said brokenly. Jess was almost sorry for her. She had come so close to being Queen of Xanth.

Jess knew it wasn't over yet, because they would have to hammer out the specific details and guard against treachery. But the corner had been turned.

Once the decision had been made, the big bird cooperated, and Em got efficiently on it, working out the details with Magnus, Nia, and Jess. It was like a new play, with the pieces falling into place. Parties were sent out to contact the colonies of the deleted, the groups including both Roc minions and members of the show's cast so that it was clear that this was real. They were persuasive. The deletes started arriving at Castle Roogna, where they formed lines before Ragna's nest for undeletion. It was all very orderly.

But Dolph kept his eyes on Em and Ragna, and Astrid stood beside him, ready to act. They had a deal, but were verifying its performance stage by stage. They would not relax until it was done.

First the royals were undeleted. The two princesses, in their human hosts, ran to hug their restored mothers, Melody and Rhythm. The third of the trio, Harmony, remained absent; she was on the World of Three Moons and would receive the glad word of her demotion soon. Her absence was a safety feature, just in case things went wrong.

"We may decide to leave my daughter Harmony as Queen," King Ivy said. "She is competent, and it is past time to be rid of this foolishness of the ruler, male or female, being called the king."

"Yes, mother," Melody and Rhythm said almost together.

"And there will be honors for you girls, Aria and Kadence," Ivy continued. "You have truly saved Xanth."

"We're just glad to have you back, grandma," Aria said, and Kadence agreed.

"And the rest of you," Ivy said, glancing at Magnus, Jess, and the others who were in sight at the moment. "We do appreciate your effort."

"Thank you," Jess said. Her knees felt weak as she slowly relaxed.

"This is not facetious," Ivy said with a small royal frown.

Kadence reached with Ula's hand to take Jess's hand. "Thank you," Jess repeated.

"Oh, of course. For a moment I fear I mistook your meaning."

"Nobody takes her seriously," Kadence said. "It's her curse."

"We'll have to put on another show," Aria said. "So Grandma can see Atrocia."

One undeletion was special for Dell. This was Anna Sthesia, a lean warrior woman he quickly hugged and kissed. "Oh, Anna, I'm so glad we were able to restore you at last!" he exclaimed. Then, quickly: "Not to marry. This is my wife, Nia."

Anna's eyes widened. "More like her granddaughter, I think."

"She was youthened forty years. It's a story in itself. But you are free to make your own life now. We owed you, for not making a deal with Ragna Roc. We knew you were tempted."

"I was," Anna agreed. "But it would not have been honorable."

Then Dell introduced Anna to the others. "Anna Sthesia, whose talent is making folk sleep. She's a warrior lass who might have made a deal with Ragna to get undeleted, years ago, and passed it up out of conscience. That saved us, before."

That explained a lot. Anna was surely a good woman.

"Thank you," Anna said. "I would have married you, Dell, for the favor of restoration, but the truth is I have found another interest during my deletion. I will pursue that now. He is about to be undeleted, too." She walked away.

Nia smiled. "I always did like her."

Then at last it was done. Santo focused and made a temporary tunnel directly to Planet Stench, as he had before.

Then Magnus talked to Em. "This tunnel leads to Planet Stench. It smells foul, but folk get used to that. It is in other respects a decent planet, settled with humans and assorted creatures and interesting plants. The tunnel will remain for one hour, which is plenty of time for you, Ragna, and the few minions who remain loyal to you to cross. Do not remain in the tunnel once you are across, because it will dissipate and anyone in it will perish in deep space. We will never see each other again. Any questions?"

"One," she said. "May I embrace you?"

Magnus was taken aback. "My humor, crude as it was, was intended to arouse your ire and disrupt your efficiency. I was trying to insult you. I have no interest in you personally."

"So you did not find my posterior interesting?"

"Actually, I did, and you are quite a woman apart from the physical aspect. But that was beside the point."

"You have won my grudging respect," she said evenly. "We are on opposite sides, but you played your hand well, in more than one sense, and I respect that. At my age of forty-five I appreciate even a facetious male compliment about my body. One hug is all I ask. I promise not to mess with your emotions."

Magnus glanced uncertainly at Jess. "Do it," she said, understanding that the woman was being gracious in defeat. Also, that even she was somewhat smitten with Magnus. "It's little enough."

Magnus opened his arms to Em Pathy. She stepped into them, drew him close, kissed him, then smartly spanked his behind. "You have a fine firm bottom with just the right amount of quiver," she told him as she pinched it. "Too bad we'll never get to put our two bottoms together." Then she disengaged and stepped into the tunnel, leading the way for Ragna to hop into it, too.

Jess almost called to her to stop, that she could stay in Xanth if she agreed to serve the new order. But she knew the woman's loyalty was with the Roc, and Jess really did not have the authority to make such an exception. This was, after all, in Xanth's future.

Magnus shook his head, bemused, as they disappeared. "She does have a fine bottom," he said. "Almost as good as yours, Jess."

Atrocia answered him. "Well, thank you for that, you ass."

Then they all laughed. Oh, it was good to relax at last.

The organization of things was now in the capable hands of King Ivy, but they couldn't go yet because the king made it clear that she expected Magnus to put on a show for the returned undeletes, so that they could appreciate the device that had enabled their restoration. They would put on the show, stay the night, and return on the morrow to their proper place in time.

"You were magnificent," Jess told Magnus as they settled into their room for the afternoon. "You came across with such confidence and proficiency, not to mention insolence. No wonder Ragna and Em backed off."

"It is my talent," he said. "But if I may make a private confession?"

"Of course."

He collapsed onto the bed. "I hope I never have to do it again." Then he broke into sobs.

So his supreme confidence had been part of the act. That impressed her even more. She joined him on the bed and put her arms around him. "Please understand," she murmured. "I'm not trying to tease you or mock you. I am trying to comfort you."

"I understand," he said into her bosom.

She held him, realizing that in other rooms Noe was holding Santo similarly as he recovered from making the tunnel, and Nia was with Dell. They all had serious unwinding to do. But what about Dolph and Astrid? The basilisk had killed four men, and that had to take a toll on her, because she was not a killer at heart. Dolph would have done it if she had not, and he was not a killer type, either. They had stood guard throughout, backing off the deadly bird with assumed confidence. The fact that they truly had the power did not mean that they had truly wanted to use it.

What a show they all had put on!

Chapter 16

SERIOUSLY

The return trip was relatively routine. They bid parting to their new friends at Castle Roogna and agreed to stay well away from each other during the intervening nine years, and not to speak about it outside their own group. They did not want to trigger any possible interference to their successful mission. It was best that they become anonymous in this respect.

Back from the future, they dropped Prince Dolph off near his gulf course, then watched him fly toward home, where Electra would be glad to have him back. The mystery of his role in saving Xanth had at last been clarified, even if he would not be advertising it. As for his supposed dalliance with Astrid Basilisk—well, that wouldn't even happen for another nine years; the two agreed that they would tell their spouses but no one else. Jess couldn't help wondering how they might have comforted each other, after the awful tension of facing down Ragna Roc, but that was not her business. They dropped Astrid off at her home; she had now had a significant hand in saving future Xanth twice. The siblings gave her a tearful farewell and returned to the boat.

Princess Kadence reported that she had traveled back to see her prior self, at the time of Ragna Roc's first attack on Xanth. "She did need some guidance, here and there," she said. "I nudged her in the right directions without revealing my presence." She smiled. "Now I remember those slight nudges; I had thought I was making up my own mind at the time. So there was no paradox; it was part of the event. Thank you for making me promise, Jess. Who knows what might have happened otherwise."

"Who knows," Jess agreed. They just might have lost the protection of paradox and been delete-able.

Princess Aria reported that things were settling in, in the future, and that, impressed with her interim performance, they really were allowing Princess Harmony to become Queen Harmony. King Ivy was retiring both the office and the title.

"And," she said with a smile, "They have made a statue in honor of you, Jess, because they know you were the true catalyst in the mission to save Future Xanth. But nobody takes it seriously."

They all laughed except Magnus, who frowned, and Myst, who shed a tear. It was humor, of course, but Jess appreciated their mute support. They were her family, in a manner.

"Kadence and I will continue to visit with Ula and Noe, because we like the siblings. Also, I have to make return visits to the Kingdom of Greena to support Thirza, as I promised. I wouldn't want my kingdom to go astray." Aria faded out.

They were back to the basic boat crew, plus Magnus and Jess. There was considerable demand for more shows, including especially Atrocia, and of course Fibot would take them to the villages for that. But first, Magnus said, he had a private mission to accomplish. It would be in three parts: a paper, a mountain, and a woman.

"A private mission?" Jess asked. "Can you tell me about it?"

"I had better. It is to win you. You're part three."

"Magnus, you've already got me."

"Not the way I want you."

Uh-oh. "If there is anything I can do—"

He put his hand on hers. "Jess, I knew when I first met you that you were the one for me. A moderately pretty girl despite the curse, a nice personality, a phenomenal stage presence, and one of the smartest women of Xanth. I knew it intellectually, but your curse balked me from taking it personally."

"It does that," she agreed ruefully.

"At least I got to verify my assessment emotionally when you had the brown rose. I had to do it."

"Oh, you did it many times that night!" she agreed. "It's a wonder that storks didn't collide on their way to fetch the signals."

He smiled. "I suspect that your curse prevented them from taking the sig-nals seriously, when they thought about it after the rose faded. I mean I had to impress you emotionally. I wanted you to be as interested in me as I was in you. I knew that if I demonstrated how it could be between us without the curse, you should like it. Rose of Roogna understood, and facilitated it."

There had been collusion? She laughed. "And here I thought it was just storks!"

"That too. But mainly I wanted you to love me."

"I do, Magnus."

"Because I courted you as well as I could despite the curse. And you have been loyal and supportive throughout, a perfect partner. Jess, I want to marry you."

"I will, Magnus."

"And I want to take you seriously. Otherwise all the rest is just a show."

"Magnus, we have talked about this before. You can't take me seriously unless I abolish my curse, and then I'll be no good as Atrocia. You need Atrocia."

"Yes! And I need her in bed, too. I suspect she could be absolutely fascinating."

He had a taste for the bizarre? "Magnus—"

"That is my spot mission. To win Atrocia. And you. Together."

"I don't think I understand. I am willing to be there for you, but we know it wouldn't work. If you got Atrocia in bed, tried to get serious with her, you really might vomit on her panties."

"Not if my mission succeeds. I don't want you to change at all. Jess, I'm going on this mission, and I hope to return to you, take you in my arms, and do the most lascivious things with you."

"You have tried before. I am eager to cooperate, but unless there's a rose—"

"No rose. Very well, I will return in a day or so, I trust."

"Please, Magnus!"

"My mind is made up."

"Then take me with you."

He paused. "You feel that way?"

"Yes! Whatever it is you have to do, I want to be there for you. To do it with you, if I can. I love you."

"I suppose that does make sense. Very well, we'll go together. But there are aspects I won't explain until the denouement."

"That's all right. I just want to be with you."

"First we have to find a cilbup yraton."

"A what?"

"A person who officially authenticates documents. They spell it back-ward in Mundania, but it's the same thing."

"You have a document?"

"I'll write my own."

Jess decided not to question it further, since she was already pushing her luck getting him to take her along. "A document," she agreed.

"An important one. Maybe the key to the whole enterprise. It was Ira's idea."

"The key," she agreed.

"Tata's a yraton," the peeve said, startling Jess; she had not realized it had joined them, but it was perching on her shoulder.

"Good enough," Magnus said. "Fetch him here while I write my docu-ment." The peeve flew off, and he settled down at a table with a small parchment and quill pen. *I, Magnus, hereby*

He looked up. "Privacy, please."

"Of course," Jess said, trying not to feel hurt. What was he up to? She walked to the other side of the room.

The dogfish trotted in. Magnus put the parchment down before his screen. "Can you eziraton that, please?"

The screen blinked. Now the parchment had a little indented circle in its corner.

"Thank you," Magnus said, rolling up the parchment and putting it in a pocket. He came across to Jess. "No we have to go mountain climbing."

"Mountain climbing?" Jess asked blankly.

"Well, I have to. To verify my change in status. But maybe it would be better for you simply to watch from the boat."

"I want to be with you," Jess said firmly.

"As you wish. I will try to help you."

"I can climb a mountain. I've done it before. It's not hard, because mountains don't take me seriously as a challenge."

"This one may."

"Which mountain is it?"

"Mount Impossible."

"But no one can climb that, by definition," she protested. "It's impossible."

"Exactly."

She halted her protest. He was up to something, and she did not want to mess it up. "Mount Impossible," she agreed.

"Can I come too?" Myst asked. "I love mountains."

Magnus shrugged. "The three of us are like a family," he said. "Come along."

Fibot sailed them there. It was deep in the heart of the Xanth wilderness where travelers seldom went. What was there to go there for? A mountain that could not be climbed?

The boat stopped beside a mountain in the shape of a monstrous cone, with a ledge spiraling around it to the top. It really didn't look difficult to ascend.

"It's deceptive," Magnus said. "We'll need staffs." He paused. "There's one other thing."

"Other thing?"

"We'll have to go bare."

"Bare?" Jess was feeling distinctly stupid.

"Obviously folk could climb it if they had magic gear. So the rule is to bring nothing. Just us versus the mountain."

"Oh." Well, why not? It wasn't as if she had anything to hide from him, and if her bare body turned him on, so much the better.

Myst clapped her hands. "I love bare!"

They stripped bare, then stepped off the boat and onto the green bank of the mountain slope. The air was pleasantly warm, and there were no burrs or nettles. So where was the challenge of the climb?

"But we can forage for things from the field," Magnus said.

"Yes." She was privately disappointed that he neither stared at nor reacted to her exposed body. She knew she was no beauty, but she did have the requisite girl parts of her gender, and most men noticed that sort of thing.

Then she remembered, yet again: he wasn't taking her seriously. Why should he look? It wasn't as if anything was likely to happen in the presence of the child.

They foraged. Magnus found water moccasins, which were of course made of solid water. Cooled, it could have been ice, but it was too warm here. Jess harvested a pair of lady slippers, and Myst found child slippers.

They came across a patch of jars sitting on the ground. Myst was intrigued. "Look—this one says North."

"North Jar?" Jess asked. "I don't get it."

Magnus pondered half a moment. "They are urns. North Urn. There's the pun."

Oh.

"Here's South," Myst said. "South Urn."

At the sides of the patch there were two birds marked East and West. Jess focused and got it. "An audio pun. East Tern, West Tern. Is there a point to this foolishness?"

"There often is," Magnus said. "But what I'm looking for is a good staff."

They found a patch of poles that should make good staffs. Magnus put his hand on one—and it passed through. Jess tried another, with the same result. They were illusions.

"Illusions," Jess said thoughtfully. "If there are illusions here, some could be dangerous."

"Yes. Like the illusion of a safe path that actually masks a pitfall. That is part of what makes this mountain unclimbable."

Jess was alarmed. "Are you sure we should be doing this? You know I am already yours to take. You don't need to brave any dangers for me."

"Oh, but I do. I need to prove myself."

"Not to me."

"Certainly to you."

This was a side of him she had not seen before. She wasn't sure she liked it, but she did not dislike it.

Well, she would try to help, in her limited way. "This may be like a challenge at the Good Magician's Castle. Which means there's a way. We just have to figure it out."

Myst laughed. "I wonder which one's the north pole?"

Was there a pun there? There had been for the urns.

"Maybe that one," Magnus said, walking across to a pole set at the north side of the patch. It was a fine solid one. He grasped it, and it was solid. "North Pole," he announced, holding it aloft.

"Well, now," Jess said. She walked to the south side, where there was another fine pole. It too was solid. "South Pole," she said as she took it.

Myst zeroed in on a smaller pole in the center. It was solid too. "Tad Pole," she said as she flourished it. She was of course the tad.

They moved on, poking at the ground ahead with the tips of their staffs. Sure enough, they started discovering hidden holes in it. They had to step carefully. But in due course the invisible holes gave up, and the ground became as solid as it looked. Still, they continued tapping it with their staffs, just in case.

There was an eerie howl or wailing. "Uh-oh," Magnus said. "That sounds like a banshee. They sound off only when someone is about to die."

"It's a bluff," Jess said, hoping she was right. "Another kind of illusion, to scare us off. I'll fend her off."

"Jess—"

"My mind is made up," she said with a certain naughty relish. She took her position between the other two and the wailing spirit, lifting her staff in a fending off pose.

An old woman with wild hair floated toward them, still wailing. She was a banshee all right.

"Is that so, you old spook?" Jess demanded.

The woman paused in mid wail to look at her, surprised. Then she burst into a cackling laughter and disappeared.

Myst clapped her hands. "She couldn't take you seriously!"

"Nobody takes me seriously," Jess agreed. "Sometimes that pays off."

"Don't ever change," Magnus said.

They went on. Now they were on the base loop of the flat path that spiraled up the mountain. So far so good.

But then there came another kind of howling. "Uh-oh," Magnus repeated. "That sounds like dire wolves. They're from past history in Mundania. They won't be dissuaded by your curse because everything is dire to them. I'm not sure our staffs will be very effective either, because there'll be a pack of them."

"Maybe we should retreat?" Jess asked hopefully. She was catching on why this mountain was unclimbable. It had ways to discourage intruders. But as she looked back, she saw what appeared to be dinosaurs, another past history creature.

"No way. There has to be an answer."

"What's that?" Myst asked, pointing. She of course had no fear of wolves, as she could simply mist out and avoid them.

"That's it!" Magnus said. "The sword in the stone."

Jess looked, but was not greatly reassured. It was just an old rusty blade stuck in a crack in a rock, as if someone had wedged it there to get rid of it. She was closer to it, so she took hold of the handle and tried to pull it free, but it wouldn't budge.

"Let me," Magnus said. He put his hand on the hilt and yanked—and not only did the sword come up and out, it glowed.

Magnus strode forward, wielding the shining weapon as the pack of wolves appeared. "Have a taste of this, beasties!" he cried, swinging it as if born to the sword.

The wolves were huge and numerous, but they made skid marks in their hurry to halt. Magnus advanced on them, and they backed off, tails between their legs. In two and a half moments they fled.

Magnus whirled and faced the dinosaurs, who were just arriving. "Your turn, lizards of yesteryear!"

And the dinosaurs backed away, and soon were scrambling back down the mountain. Again, Magnus had conquered without striking a blow.

"I didn't know you were a swordsman," Jess said, awed.

"I'm not. It's a magic sword that gives me power. It pretty much wields itself, once properly animated."

"So I see," she agreed. "It was completely inert and stuck in the stone for me."

"You are surely worthy, but it couldn't take you seriously."

"That must be it," she agreed. But she remained amazed by the way the weapon had come to life in his hand. More was happening here than she properly understood.

"Take my hand," Magnus told Jess. "And Myst, you take her hand. We need to be in contact to complete the ascent."

"Like the Timeline!" Myst exclaimed.

"Different principle," Magnus said.

They linked hands and marched on up the slope. Other monsters threatened, but dared not face the bright sword. In due course they achieved the summit, which was a slightly rounded glade surrounded by red, green, yellow, and blue berry bushes. It was very nice.

"And it is done," Magnus said, walking to another rock and plunging the sword into it. The blade returned to its thin rusty state, completely unimpressive.

"But I thought nobody could climb this mountain," Jess protested belatedly.

"That's right," he agreed. "Nobody could."

"Stop teasing me! What happened here?"

"I am Nobody." He fished out the parchment he had had deziraton.

Jess read it. *I, Magnus, hereby officially change my name to Nobody.*

"You changed your name?"

"Well, Magnus was always my stage name, and will remain so. But my real name is now Nobody."

"I don't understand."

"Nobody could climb this mountain, so I climbed it. And—" He paused, waiting for her to catch up to it.

A bulb flashed over her head. "Nobody takes me seriously!" she exclaimed. "And you're Nobody!".

"Exactly." He took her in his arms and kissed her. Now she felt his whole body reacting. He was taking her most seriously.

"Oh, my," she breathed, remembering that they both were bare.

Magnus glanced at Myst.

"Oh, I know," Myst said with resignation. "The Adult Conspiracy. It follows me around."

Mairzy appeared, and sent them a daydream of two big hearts floating in the air. One looked male, the other female, though Jess wasn't quite sure how that was done. The two came together, almost merging, and little hearts flew out and formed a ring around them.

Myst reappeared. She misted out and floated away.

"I didn't know the mares remained," Jess said, surprised. "I thought they had gone home."

"They like the adventure," Magnus said. "They will probably go home when things get dull with the girls." He looked at her, still holding her suggestively tight. "Now where were we?"

"As if you didn't know. Your body is pressed against mine and your hands are on my bare butt. I think we were about to get serious."

"Ah, now I remember," he agreed. "Let's get to it."

"Let's," she agreed eagerly.

There followed a sequence that might have made even storks blush. Certainly the grass around where they lay had turned pink.

"I have questions," Jess said as they lay holding hands.

"I thought you might."

"If your name change was effective, why didn't you just take me immediately, instead of interposing the mountain?"

"Ah, there's the crux," he agreed. "Magic is magic, but curses are hard to circumvent, especially in your case, where we want to keep the curse but make one exception to it. That really is modifying your talent, your magical nature, without doing you harm. I was also changing my own nature, to become that exception. Your curse is both physical and emotional."

"Emotional, yes," she agreed. "It affects the attitude of those I encounter. But physical?"

"What we just did was emotional *and* physical."

"Oh, yes."

"So I had to abolish the physical complement without hurting you," he continued. "So I took it out on the mountain, because it has a similar resistance to being approached. Once I had proved my case, vanquishing its curse, I was free to vanquish yours. Your curse knew then that it was lost."

"It was another finesse!" she exclaimed. "You showed your power, and my curse yielded rather than be forced."

"Exactly. I always knew you were smart."

"Still, couldn't you have at least tried taking me seriously, without the mountain, just in case it did work?"

"I lacked the nerve," he admitted. "I was so afraid it wouldn't work."

Just as she had been afraid that the paradox effect wouldn't work to make them undeletable. She had thought it should, but that treacherous doubt remained. She did understand.

She bopped him lightly on the shoulder. "Shall we get physical again?"

"Why not."

This time they turned the grass completely red.

When they were pleasantly exhausted again, she posed her second question. "That sword. Nobody took it seriously before?"

"Nobody," he agreed. "They thought it was a leftover from some Mundane legend, and maybe it is. But I knew its secret. It is powered by true love, and the phantasms of hate are unable to stand against it." He kissed her again. "My love for you, Jess. It has finally been freed."

"Oh, Mag—" she started, then rephrased it. "Nobody loves me as you do."

"Seriously," he agreed. They kissed again.

Jess knew she was going to like her life from here on. She had the rings so she could visit Ira and Platina, and the Night Stallion's token. If she ever got bored.

"Is my butt really better than Em Pathy's?" she asked teasingly.

Magnus pretended doubt. "I'd better investigate." He took hold. By the time he came to a decision, the grass was purple.

In due course Myst returned. "Are you folk done with the mushy stuff?"

"For now," Jess agreed.

"Then let's return to Fibot. I'm hungry."

"So are we," Magnus agreed. "But we have a trek to get there."

"No." Myst became Mairzy, and leaped into the sky. In barely two moments she was back with the boat in tow. They boarded.

"Congratulations," Nia said. "We can see that now you take each other seriously."

"Solid mush," Myst complained. "I had to go smell the flowers."

"When we finally grow up," Squid said, "We'll abolish the blipping Adult Conspiracy. Maybe that will squish the mush."

Lotsa luck on that, Jess thought.

"Get dressed," Win told them. "The village of trolls at the base of the mountain is demanding a show. Especially Atrocia. But the lady trolls want Magnus, too."

They laughed. "Then we must oblige them," Magnus said, seriously squeezing Jess's hand.

And she was still Atrocia to the rest of Xanth. Jess couldn't remember when she had been happier.

AUTHOR'S NOTE

I wrote this novel in the Ogre Months FeBlueberry, Marsh, and Apull. You know, when the Redberries are blue with cold, the rains turn the ground to mush, and they celebrate with a big messy tug-of-war as they prepare for the Month of Mayhem. I'm getting older, eighty-two at this writing, and can't be quite sure how many more hundred thousand word novels I'll be doing. But this one was fun in its fashion. It is more sexual than is typical of Xanth, because I tried to address issues like homosexuality honestly. Gay men do not hate women, they merely don't care to romance them. Not all women are fainting flowers when it comes to men. I think it is time to recognize such things, though I know it will annoy some readers, who feel that even panty flashing is beyond the limit.

Coincidentally, in this period, there came the news that Xanth will be made into a movie and a television series. It may have happened by the time this novel is published. The way they do it is they take an option, which means they pay for the right to make, say, a movie in the next year or two. The option spells out all the details so there will be no hassle such as arguing about terms when the time comes to do it. If they don't do it, the option expires. Xanth has had several options over the decades that have not been exercised. That's why I am cautious, having been disappointed before. But this one does seem likely.

The rule for writers is to take the money and run. That is, they know that the movie may bear little relation to the original novels, but the movie folk come bearing barrels of money, so it is better to enjoy the riches while averting one's eyes from the product. Readers are welcome to read the original books, so they will know what's there, and they can also enjoy the movies or TV series. It's a fair compromise.

A note on a character that some of today's readers may not recognize: Mairzy Doats. That's the title of a popular song in 1944. Some of the words are "Mairzy doats and dozy doats/ And liddle lamzy divey." When you catch on, they sound more like "Mares eat oats and does eat oats/ And little lambs eat ivy." Now you know. And yes, I was alive in that prehistoric era.

And one on Chocolate Alchemy: they do have an office in Mundania if you know where to look. Folk who want to process their own chocolate at home go there to get the proper tools.

Meanwhile, how is my personal life at this writing? I exercise seriously, by which I mean I don't skip it unless there is illness or injury, and I'm pretty healthy for an old fogy my age. My wife and I have been married over sixty years. We married until death do us part, but now that this prospect is slouching closer, I find I'm not keen on it. But we're doing okay, considering. My main interest is my writing, but I do take breaks with computer games, and when this novel is done I will pig out on accumulated DVD videos; I can't resist a bargain sale, and I have hundreds. I am also constantly reading. I subscribe to news and science magazines, being fascinated by the present world and the prospective future. I hope I live to learn the answers to three fundamental mysteries: why is there something rather than nothing, such as our universe? How did life come about, and does it exist on other worlds? And exactly what is consciousness, and can a robot have it? In my fiction robots are thinking feeling people, especially the lovely ladies, but what about the mundane realm?

We live on our small tree farm, and our drive is three quarters of a mile long. In the past quarter century it has gradually gotten uneven as tree roots push at it and slow sink holes find it worthwhile. So our daughter Cheryl, in the period while I was writing this novel, brought a number of truckfuls of gravel and spread them where it counted, and now we have a patchwork drive that will be more even as the gravel settles into place. Wild magnolia trees grow along the drive, because we preferred to curve it around them rather than chop them out, and their first flowers are now appearing. One little patch of stinging nettles grows besides it, that I try to protect with a mini wire fence. Maybe to you a nettle is a weed, but to me it is a pretty wild flower that is blooming now. We have a rain gauge, but a wasp has made a nest in it at the one inch line, and now there may be half a dozen wasps as the family grows. I suspect there will be a problem when our monsoon season comes in JeJune with heavy rains, but all I can do is carefully empty the gauge when it fills, and the wasps seem to understand. We came here to be with nature, and we try to be good neighbors to the plants and creatures here. Every plant in our vicinity has its history, and we value them all.

Are there aggravations? Certainly. For example I like my Linux computer program, but it has this quaint habit of abruptly disappearing. I'll be typing a sentence of the novel, and suddenly I'm typing into a blank screen. All my files have softly and silently faded away without saving. I have to call everything up again and retype my last few hundred words as well as I can remember them. Maybe it's a little joke the programmers put in for laughs. Why am I not laughing? I'm about ready to replace my system. But overall, life is reasonably good.

Now the reader suggestions. Some readers send in many, but I try to give new suggestors a credit before repeating credits on the old ones, so I have a number left over, that will be duly considered for the next Xanth novel. That will probably be #44 *Skeleton Key*, the title suggested by Misty Zaebst. The skeleton twins Picka and Joy'nt Bone will be ten years old, in the same age range as the siblings, and when their folks disappear—but let's not get ahead of ourselves; I don't want to bore you unduly. These credits are in the approximate order of the first one from each contributor.

Have a jester in Xanth (which inspired this novel)—Clayton
Boos drink—Jestin Larsen
Kraken addicted to krack—Meeran
Deposi-tree—Stefano Migneco
Gulli-bull—Tom Pfarrer
Troll Farm—James Blakeney
Rampage; swim suit; hitman and his allergies—Mary Rashford
Ana Conda—Paul and Mary Rashford
Fountain of Smart, Frankenstein's Monster appears in Xanth—Naomi Blose
Atrocia—Larry Miller
42 as the Answer—John Nanci
Talents of banish things to the Void, and recovering them—Ann Marie Mohrmann

Kitchen sync; stare way; spearhead of unicorns; dogapult, bulista—
Richard van Fossan

Spitting Image—Misty Zaebst

Polly Ester—Nancy Ann Nethken

"Curses! Foiled again!"—David Seltzer

Alphabet: A-corns, B-corns, etc.—Kari Lambert

Night and Day Stallions get switched—Kay Puccio

Talent of finding related things—Samuel Lopez

Carp Diem (seize the day) fish—William Adams

Chill pills; cough-he and cough-she; copper policeman; North Urn, South Urn; East Tern, West Tern—Joshua Davenport-Herbst

Relativi-tea, bat tea, goat tea, gravi tea, uppi tea, LGB tea, Adam Ant, talking a blue streak, house fly—Tim Bruening

Naugh tea, novel tea—Kristi King-Morgan

Talent of metamorphosis—James Beardsley

Pasta flashbacks, custard—Cuman TehHuman

Demons eat Dark Matter and radiate Dark Energy—D A Pears

Urine Charge, meet market—Richard Davenport.

Pro-ducks—Steve Pfarrer

Scents of Humor; punfusion—Patricia Blaylock

many spots on the wall talent—Kenneth Adams

Toylet paper; fat lady singing—Steve Leek from Spain

And my credit to my proofreaders, Scott M Ryan and Anne White. They chase down the errors that grow on the page after I do my editing of the manuscript.

If you enjoyed this novel and want to know more of me, you can check my website at www.HiPiers.com, where I do a monthly blog-type column, have news of my new projects, and maintain an ongoing survey of electronic publishers for the benefit of aspiring writers.

ABOUT THE AUTHOR

Piers Anthony has written dozens of bestselling science fiction and fantasy novels. Perhaps best known for his long-running Magic of Xanth series, many of which are *New York Times* bestsellers, he has also had great success with the Incarnations of Immortality series and the Cluster series, as well as *Bio of a Space Tyrant* and others. Much more information about Piers Anthony can be found at www.HiPiers.com.

THE XANTH NOVELS

FROM OPEN ROAD MEDIA

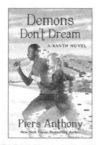

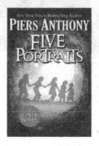

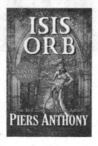

OPEN ROAD

INTEGRATED MEDIA

INTEGRATED MEDIA

Find a full list of our authors and
titles at www.openroadmedia.com

FOLLOW US
@OpenRoadMedia